THE

Nora Sakavic

ALL FOR THE GAME

-

The Foxhole Court
The Raven King
The King's Men
The Sunshine Court

CHAPTER ONE
Jean

Jean Moreau came back to himself in pieces, dragging himself together as he had a thousand mornings before. The cloud in his thoughts was as unfamiliar as the heaviness in his limbs; Josiah generally stuck to ibuprofen when patching the team up, even when it was Riko he was cleaning up behind. For him to step it up meant Jean wasn't going to like what he was waking up to.

Aside from the stinging ache along his scalp and up to his crown, his cheekbones and nose were a soupy mess of heat. Jean lifted a too-heavy hand from his side and gingerly felt out the lines of his face. Stitches and bandages were a familiar rough texture beneath his fingertips, and the blossoming ache under a bit of pressure confirmed his nose was broken again. The Ravens were going to use that to their advantage the next several weeks to keep him in his place. He'd have no choice but to protect himself against their high and brutal checks, pulling back when he should have been pushing forward.

His neck ached, but the skin there felt unbroken, and in his hazy delirium it took Jean too long to remember what had happened. The memory of Riko's hands around his throat, squeezing tighter and longer than he ever had before, sent a shiver down his spine when it finally sharpened into focus. Jean had given into fear and forgotten himself, and he'd tried pulling Riko's hands loose. Riko responded by pummeling his face with unrelenting fists. Knowing the master would beat Riko black and blue after championships for breaking the golden rule—*not where the public can see*—left Jean queasy. Riko was twice as vicious when he was hurting.

1

Jean slowly let his hand fall back to his side and struggled to open his eyes. It took a few tries, but what came into focus was an unfamiliar ceiling. Jean was sold to Castle Evermore five years ago; he knew every square inch of that stadium better than he knew his own body. This room was not in Evermore, not with such pale paint and wide windows. Someone had hooked a dark blue blanket over the curtain rod to darken the room a bit, but slivers of burnt orange sunlight still peeked through to stripe across the bed.

Hospital? A bolt of fear had him counting fingers and toes. His hands ached, but he could move them. The lack of broken fingers this time was marginally reassuring, but what had happened to his leg? His left knee screamed when he shifted, and his left ankle flared hot right after it. They were facing the Trojans in a few weeks for semifinals and championships, and this did not feel like something that would heal quickly.

Jean pushed himself up and regretted it immediately. The pain that lanced from his abdomen to his collarbone was so fierce he felt nauseous. Jean sucked in a slow breath through clenched teeth, feeling the way his entire chest twinged with the effort. The memory of Riko kicking him, over and over even as he tried to ball up and protect himself, put ice in his veins. It'd been years since Riko last fractured Jean's ribs. It'd taken Jean off the court for eleven weeks—and Riko off for one, when the master was done with him. This couldn't be that again, it *couldn't*, but the first press of his hand to his side left him ill with agony.

He nearly bit the inside of his lip to bleeding as he forced himself to look around. The lack of any medical equipment refuted his hospital guess. This was someone's bedroom, but that made no sense at all. The squat nightstand alongside the bed sported an alarm clock, lamp, and two mismatched coasters. A long dresser ran along the far wall with books and jewelry strewn across the top. Just past it was a laundry basket in dire need of emptying.

Then the only thing Jean saw, the only thing that mattered,

2

was the woman sitting in a short chair at the foot of the bed. Renee Walker sat with socked feet propped on the footboard and her arms folded across her knees. Despite the relaxed line of her shoulders and the calm look on her face, her eyes were sharp as she watched him. Jean stared back, waiting for anything about this to make sense.

"Good evening," she said at length. "How are you feeling?"

For a moment he was back in Evermore, watching the master tell Riko that Kengo had passed. The master would be taking a private jet to New York for funeral arrangements, and Riko was to keep an eye on the Ravens in his absence. Riko knew better than to argue about getting left behind, but he'd helplessly followed the master to the exit anyway. Jean had had twenty seconds of peace, and he'd wasted them texting Renee a heads-up. He'd known what was coming when Riko collected him and set off for Black Hall, but it wasn't like he could refuse Riko's orders.

His thoughts skittered past Riko's wild violence, but everything after that was a blur: muffled voices yelling from a thousand miles away, distant road noise on an unending, painful drive, and the scent of cigarette smoke and scotch as a man carried his limp and drugged body into a strange house.

No, Jean thought. *No, no, no.*

He didn't want to ask, but he had to. Getting the words out when his heart was lodged in his throat took three tries: "Where am I?"

Renee's stare was as unwavering as it was unrepentant. "South Carolina."

Jean swung his legs toward the edge of the bed, meaning to get up, but that hurt so badly he nearly threw up. He gasped for breath, heart pounding in his eyes and fingertips, and was distantly aware that Renee had moved to stand in front of him. He hadn't even heard her get up, but now she was checking the line of his ribs with careful hands.

"Let me up," he said, as if he had any control over his

body right now. He blinked black spots out of his vision, torn between the fuzzy heat of rising gorge and the dizzying sense of falling. He wasn't sure which would come first, unconsciousness or retching, but he prayed it happened in whichever order would be fatal. "Let me go."

"I won't. Lie down."

Renee moved one hand to his shoulder and kept the other on his side to steady him. Jean tried resisting for only a second; tensing up his core was a mistake he didn't want to make again anytime soon. Renee eased him onto his back and pulled the blankets back up to his collarbone. She checked his eyes one at a time, holding his chin between her thumb and forefinger when he tried to look away from her. Jean scowled at her with all the rage his exhausted, broken body could muster.

"He will not forgive you," Jean said. "Neither will I."

"Oh, Jean," Renee said, with a sweet smile that didn't reach her eyes. "I won't be forgiven for this. Try to get some sleep. It will help you more than anything else."

"No," Jean insisted, but he was already falling away.

-

It should have been a nightmare.

If there was any justice in the world, Jean would wake up in Evermore to the master's impatience and Riko's hatred. But when Jean next dragged himself out of the depths, he was still in that pale bedroom with only one bed, with Renee keeping watch from the foot of it. She was wearing something new, and the light cutting across the bed was the softer glow of morning. Jean did another mental check of his limbs before painstakingly pushing himself up again. Renee's gaze was calm, but Jean would never trust her peaceful demeanor again. She'd damned them both.

"Where am I?" he asked, praying the answer would be different this time.

"South Carolina," she said without hesitation. "More specifically, you are at the home of our team nurse, Abby Winfield. It is March 15th," she said before he thought to ask.

4

"Do you remember anything from yesterday?"

"I came here yesterday," Jean said. It wasn't quite a question, but he looked to her for an answer. He wasn't sure how badly Riko rattled his brain, and it helped a bit that Renee nodded. He'd lost an entire day past those snatches of bloody memories and the last conversation he'd had with her, but he was willing to write those gaps off as unconsciousness.

Jean carefully slid his legs toward the edge of the bed. His right leg went on its own, but he had to brace his left between his aching hands to move it. Every breath he managed and every inch he moved sent pain shuddering through him. There was deep and lingering damage in too many places. It sank through his chest and gut like acid, eating away whatever was left of him. It hurt like hell, but he'd worked through worse. He'd survive this, no matter what it cost him.

"Jean," Renee said. "I'd rather you stayed put."

"You cannot stop me," Jean said.

"I promise I can," she said. "It is for your own good. You're in no shape to be moving."

"You're the one who moved me," Jean snapped. "You should not have brought me here. Take me back to Evermore."

"I won't," Renee said. "If that doesn't satisfy you: I can't. Mr. Andritch banished you from Evermore for the time being."

Jean knew the name, but only vaguely. Renee explained when she realized his silence was more confusion than belligerence: "Your campus president."

"My—" Jean's heart hit the backs of his teeth. "What have you done?"

Renee got up and came to stand by his knee as he finally reached the edge of the bed, an unrepentant and unyielding barricade keeping him on the mattress. "I sent him into the Nest unannounced and uninvited."

"No," Jean said, staring up at her. "He does not have access. He does not have the authority."

"A rude awakening for him," Renee admitted, with a grim smile tugging at the corner of her mouth. "It took a half-dozen

5

calls to facilities and security to get the door open, and once he was in?" She spread her hands in a *there you go* gesture. "He demanded to see you, and the Ravens didn't know not to show him the way. Riko was on the court at the time," she explained before he had to ask. "He didn't make it back inside fast enough. Oh, thank you."

The last comment was directed past him. Jean couldn't turn to see who'd joined them, but soon enough an older woman came into view holding a tray. She looked distantly familiar in the way he knew meant she was associated with the sport. He'd seen her on the sidelines or at a banquet, surely, which meant she had to be the team nurse whose home he was being held in. Jean watched with hooded eyes as Renee cleared off the nightstand. Two glasses of water, a glass of pale juice, and a bowl of soup were set down within reach.

Abby made sure the tray was stable before turning a considering look on Jean. "How are you feeling?"

Jean stared stonily back at her, but a woman who had to deal with Nathaniel's and Kevin's attitudes day-in and day-out wasn't likely to be intimidated by his anger. Indeed, she just leaned in to check his injuries. Her gaze was clinical as she inspected his bandages and stitches, but her hands were light as she felt the line of his shoulders.

"He's been speaking?" Abby asked Renee.

"There's a noticeable rasp in his voice," Renee said, "but it doesn't sound like anything was damaged beyond repair."

Renee collected one of the glasses and held it out in offering. Jean hadn't even realized how thirsty he was, but he'd be damned if he took anything from them. Renee seemed content to outwait him, keeping it within easy reach without forcing it into one of his bruised hands. She watched Abby work for a minute before belatedly remembering she'd been trying to explain herself.

"I gave Andritch a choice: let me take you home with me to recover or accept that my mother would run a very thorough and graphic article on what had happened to you at his campus.

Unsurprisingly, he was very happy to buy my silence. He promised to investigate, and I promised to keep him updated on your health in return. I doubt we'll see any major changes at Edgar Allan this close to championships, but I will take my victories where I can for now."

Jean forgot his decision to remain silent. "This is not a victory, you arrogant fool."

Abby winced at the sound of his voice and pressed careful thumbs into the sides of his throat. "Breathe in for me."

He tried batting her hands away, but the attempt hurt him a lot more than it did her, and Abby simply waited for him to settle down again. He sullenly did as he was told, and Renee watched Abby carefully as the nurse felt the way his neck moved beneath her fingers. Abby shifted her grip for the second inhale, but the pressure that had been negligible before felt like a poker here, and Jean flinched beneath her touch before he could stop himself.

He tried hiding it behind irritation and waved her off. "Get away from me. How am I getting home?"

"You're not leaving," Renee reminded him. "Andritch pulled you from the lineup—or he will once his investigation is done. In no universe will he allow you back at Edgar Allan after seeing you like this."

"I am a Raven now and always," Jean said. "It does not matter what one insignificant man says."

"Perhaps," Renee said, in a light tone that said she did not believe it.

"Take me back to Evermore."

"I will say it until I'm blue in the face if I must. I will not let you leave."

"You don't have the right to keep me here."

"He didn't have the right to do this to you."

Jean laughed, short and sharp, and let the pain burn through him. Renee knew more about his relationship with Riko than she ought, thanks to Kevin's reckless indiscretion, so surely she knew what a baldfaced lie that was. The master

7

bought Jean years ago, but with so many Ravens underfoot he hadn't had the time or energy to discipline an angry child. He'd gifted him to Riko instead, trusting his nephew to handle Jean's conditioning. Riko had the right to do anything he wanted to Jean; Jean was his property from now until death.

The master would run his Ravens into the ground for their misstep and beat his displeasure into every hidden inch of Riko's skin, but Riko would forward that agony to Jean with interest as soon as the season was over. Jean hadn't let Andritch in, but it was his fault Renee had known to come looking for him. He was hundreds of miles from home because he hadn't been smart enough to keep his mouth shut.

Jean regretted ever laying eyes on Renee. He hated himself for giving in to curiosity and answering her messages in January. Hindsight was a backstabbing bitch.

"No one did this to me," he said. "I was injured in scrimmages."

"I work with the Foxes," Abby reminded Jean. "Even they can't hurt each other this badly on the court. Lord knows enough of 'em tried over the years."

"I find it unsurprising they're mediocre in everything they do."

"This," Abby said, touching very careful fingers to the side of his head, "is not from a scrimmage. Even the Ravens practice in full armor, I assume? Look me in the eye and tell me how they managed to tear out so much of your hair through a helmet."

Jean's hand went up unbidden, finding hers and then the raw aching points along his scalp. Memory skittered at the edge of his mind: one hand over his mouth and nose to hold his head down while the other hand yanked as hard as it could. For a moment the remembered sensation of ripping, peeling skin was blinding, and Jean swallowed hard against a rush of bile. He quickly dropped his hand to his lap.

"I asked you a question," Abby said.

"Take me back to Evermore," Jean said. "I won't stay

here with you."

"Abby," Renee said, returning Jean's water to its tray. She and Abby quietly took their leave without another word to him. Jean tuned out the sound of the door closing behind them in favor of figuring out how to save his own life. It all hinged on his ability to get back to West Virginia.

He couldn't change that he'd been taken or that Andritch had gotten involved, but he'd prove his loyalty by getting home as quickly as he could. He had codes for the stadium and the Nest, so he just had to slip past security and get inside. It didn't matter what Andritch told the Ravens; not a single one of them would turn him away at the door. No one walked away from Evermore.

Except Kevin. Except Nathaniel.

These thoughts were unhelpful, burning through his chest like poison, and Jean hit his thighs as hard as he could. Pain put white noise in his head, drowning out dangerous thoughts, and Jean breathed in and out as slowly as he could until his mind came back together. Jean checked his pockets for his phone and came back empty.

A moment later he realized he was wearing an unfamiliar pair of gray shorts. Gray, not black. Jean couldn't remember the last time he'd been allowed to wear color. Marseille, perhaps, but Jean couldn't be sure. He'd left France at fourteen, but too many years in the Nest had worn away everything he was before. Sixteen-hour days and Riko's heartbreaking cruelty had ripped out whatever soul he had left. Everything before was a fractured mess, dreams that dissipated before he woke enough to recall them with any clarity.

For a moment that ache felt more like grief than fear, but Jean hit himself again to sharpen the edge. It didn't matter what came before; there was no going back. All that mattered was getting through today, then tomorrow, then the next day. All that mattered was getting home.

I am Jean Moreau. My place is at Evermore. I will endure.

Jean eased himself closer to the edge of the bed and let the balls of his feet touch the coarse carpet. Getting up took five tries, as he had to push himself up off the mattress with his hands. The knifing pain each attempt caused had him sucking in shaky, desperate breaths that bit holes in his throat.

Jean tried taking a step forward, but his left leg refused to take his weight. He went down like a rock, casting about for anything to stop his fall. His hand hit the tray, catapulting its contents everywhere. The icy bite of juice and water was not nearly so bad as the scalding heat of soup. Worse than both was the shattering pain in his chest and knee when he hit the ground, and Jean bit his hand to bleeding before he could scream.

The horrifying suspicion that he was not strong enough to get back to Evermore on his own was almost his undoing. Jean bit harder, hoping to find bone, and then there were hands on him. He hadn't even heard the door open through the roaring in his ears.

"Hey," a man's voice said at his ear, and Coach Wymack tugged at his wrist until Jean loosened his death grip. A second later Wymack got both arms under him, and he lifted Jean off the floor and back into bed with startling ease. He gave Jean a quick once-over before heading for the door again.

He wasn't good enough to stay away, but at least he closed the door behind himself when he returned. He'd brought a few wet washcloths back with him. Jean tried to take one from him, but Wymack only caught hold of his forearm so he could clean the bloody bitemarks on Jean's hand. Jean wasn't concerned with the injury when his glove would hide it from view, but he couldn't pull hard enough to yank out of Wymack's grasp.

Wymack let go when he was through and set to work carefully wiping away soup and juice from Jean's bared arms and chest. Only when he was done did he turn a serious look on Jean and ask, "Did someone forget to mention you shouldn't be walking? What were you thinking?"

"I want to go home," Jean demanded.

10

The look Wymack sent him for that hurt more than anything Riko had ever done to him, and Jean had to look away.

"Get some rest," Wymack said. "We will talk this afternoon. Here."

Jean considered biting the fingers that slipped pills between his lips, but Wymack was a coach, which meant he was off-limits. He swallowed the drugs dry and stared at the ceiling as Wymack carefully got off the bed. Jean heard the clink of glass and silverware as Wymack collected scattered and broken dishes from the floor, but he was asleep before the man made it out of the room.

-

When he woke a few hours later it was Wymack once more waiting at his bedside, seemingly absorbed in a newspaper. Two mugs sat on the nightstand, and Jean smelled the enticing aroma of black coffee. It was a trigger he didn't need, reminding him how blindingly hungry and thirsty he was, and Jean sat up at a snail's pace. Despite the caution, he was barely breathing by the time he let the headboard take his weight.

He wondered if he could even manage the weight of a full mug right now. It was bad enough he was sheltering here; if they had to spoon feed him, he might as well bite his own tongue off and be done with it.

Wymack looked up. "Bathroom?"

He wished he could say no. "Where is it?"

Wymack set aside his paper and stood. "Don't put any weight on your left leg."

Jean began the too-careful process of trying to get off the bed again. Wymack took hold of his upper arms in a firm grip as Jean tried pushing himself up, and Jean understood when his legs almost gave out on him again. Wymack's grip went tight enough to bruise. It hurt, but it was enough to keep Jean from falling over, and Wymack offered his own body as a crutch. Jean chewed through the inside of his cheek so he wouldn't say anything about this miserable situation.

The bathroom was just one door down on the left, but it took an eternity to get there. Wymack propped him against the wall closest to the toilet and left him to sort out his business in peace. He was back as soon as he heard the sink running, letting himself in with just a rap of his knuckles on the door in warning. Back to the bedroom they went, moving slower than grass grew. Jean's vision was swimming by the time he reached the bed.

Maybe it was pain making him hallucinate, but now there was a steaming bowl of porridge sitting by the coffee. Jean's stomach betrayed him with a vicious growl.

"Eat," Wymack said. "We haven't been able to get anything but water down you in almost thirty hours now."

Jean looked at the bruises staining most of his hands, then dragged a reluctant gaze to the stripes of raw skin on his forearms. Riko had bound him with racquet laces, which were far too rough and ragged to be used on bare skin. Jean had rope burn in six or seven places on each arm, and his wrists were worn raw. Riko hadn't wasted time tying Jean up in years, knowing Jean would submit to any punishment Riko felt like doling out. The last time he'd had to resort to such methods was—

Jean forcibly derailed that thought, refusing to tilt sideways into memories he couldn't easily claw out of. Some boxes had to stay closed, even if he had to break every finger to hold them shut. If Riko had tied him up this time, it was because he'd deserved it. He'd proven his disloyalty the moment he tried pulling Riko's hands off his throat.

"I will eat later," Jean said.

"It's cream of wheat," Wymack said. "Do you know how awful it's going to be in about ten minutes?" He didn't wait for a response but scooped up the bowl and held it so close to Jean's face he could feel the steam licking against his chin. "I'll get this. You just worry about managing the spoon."

"I am not hungry," Jean said.

"Suit yourself, but my hands are cold, so I'm going to keep holding this bowl here."

Jean worked his jaw on words he wouldn't say, demands and questions he wouldn't trust the answers to. Surely this was an act, the carrot before the stick, a way of getting past his guard so they could use whatever they found on the other side. It had to be an act, but Wymack fell into his role like he'd done this song-and-dance routine so many times he'd forgotten to watch for the curtain to fall. He'd spent too long pretending the Foxes were a genuine investment and not a publicity stunt, perhaps.

Jean wanted to ignore the food, but he was so hungry he felt ill. In the end he decided to go with it, if only because he needed to get his strength back. Wymack had the decency to look victorious when Jean reached for the spoon; he simply pointed his gaze at the far wall so Jean could eat without Wymack's stare boring holes in his battered face. Jean's fingers throbbed as he set to work feeding himself, and he was belatedly grateful for Wymack's assistance.

Wymack traded the empty bowl for Jean's coffee. By now it was the warmer side of tepid, but Jean obediently drank through half of it. When he tilted his head away in silent refusal, Wymack put it aside and drained his own mug. Bodily functions finally tended to, Wymack leaned back in his chair and folded his arms across his chest. He treated Jean to a searching look Jean knew better than to return.

"I spoke to Coach Moriyama last night."

Jean forgot how to breathe. "How dare you speak to him while he is grieving."

"I'm sure he's real broken up," Wymack said without an ounce of sympathy. "He didn't say it in so many words, but he'd already gotten his ass chewed out by Andritch by the time I called him. I told him we'd foot your medical bills on account of us interfering before we were invited, and I agreed to send him timely updates on your convalescence. It's the same type of arrangement we had when Kevin came south. He knows I can be discreet when it suits me."

Jean wasn't sure if that curl in his stomach was regret or disgust. Wymack didn't even know how precarious his position was. The master wasn't interested in destabilizing the Class I teams by interfering with the coaches, so until Wymack forced his hand he wouldn't strike him down no matter how annoying he was.

Riko, on the other hand, had wanted to kill Wymack for over a year. His restraint could have been fear of his uncle's retribution, but Jean knew the heart of it was Riko's complicated father complex. He'd read Kayleigh's letter nearly as many times as Kevin had. Riko couldn't quite cross that line yet, and he absolutely hated that part of himself.

Jean idly wondered if Kevin had figured that out yet. "Where is Kevin?"

"Blue Ridge," Wymack said. "The Foxes rented out a cabin for spring break."

"Not Kevin," Jean insisted. "He would not go so far from a court."

"He will if he's properly motivated," Wymack said, sticking to the ridiculous lie with a carefree shrug. "They should be back in town this weekend. Sunday, I think? If you want to talk to him, I'll have him come by soon as he's unpacked. Speaking of the resident drama queen…" Wymack started, but it took him a minute to figure out how to sort out his words.

"I don't know if you're aware of this, but I know what sort of man he is. Your so-called master," he said, with a lilt in his voice that was all hatred, "and that bitch of a nephew of his. Kevin told us the truth when he transferred so we'd know what we were getting into. I know why you think you have to go back to Evermore, and I know what's waiting for you there. I will burn this house down before I let him touch you again."

If his hands ever started working again, Jean would choke the life out of Kevin next time he saw him.

Renee started texting him back in early January, but Jean

14

had waited two weeks before responding to any of her cheery questions and check-ins. It wasn't until she'd said "Kevin told me everything" that Jean was startled into breaking his silence. Finding out Renee knew about the Moriyama family was hard enough, but Jean assumed Kevin confided in her because of her past. Hearing now that all of the Foxes knew and didn't have the good sense to be terrified was ten times worse.

There was something seriously wrong with them, but Jean couldn't say that without inadvertently admitting that Kevin was right. Still, he had to wonder what could possibly cause so much irrevocable brain damage. Something in the water this far south, perhaps? Maybe carbon monoxide poisoning at the Foxhole Court.

"No one touched me," Jean said. "I was injured during scrimmages."

"Shut up. I'm not asking you for a confession," Wymack said. "I don't need one, not with you looking like this and especially not after I had to pick Neil up from the airport in December. But I need you to know that we know so that you believe me when I say we're in this fight with eyes wide open. Renee knew what she risked by going after you. She made that call knowing who she was crossing, and we will stand with her no matter what it costs us."

"It was not her call to make," Jean said. "If you will not send me to Evermore, give me back my phone. I will arrange transportation myself."

"I turned your phone off and put it in the freezer," Wymack said. "It was blowing up and I got real tired of listening to it chirp. You can have it back after we've figured out where we're going from here."

"There is no *we*," Jean insisted. "You are not my coach."

"Not your master, you mean."

Jean ignored that pointed rejoinder. "I am a Raven. My place is at Evermore."

Wymack squeezed the bridge of his nose in a silent bid for patience. Jean foolishly thought that meant he was wearing the man down and winning the argument, but then Wymack pulled a phone out of his pocket and started tapping away on it. He put it to his ear just long enough to make sure it was ringing, then switched it to speaker and held it up between them. Jean didn't have long to wonder; the call was answered on the second ring.

"Moriyama."

"Coach Moriyama, it's Coach Wymack again," Wymack said. He sent a knowing look at Jean, and Jean belatedly realized he'd gone tense. "Sorry to interrupt your day, but I need help with something. Jean here keeps trying to refuse my care and get out of bed. Abby's already said it's another three weeks before he can even think of traveling, but Jean needs a second opinion to settle his nerves. Would you tell him to sit the fuck still? I've got you on speaker with him."

The master didn't miss a beat, and his answer was exactly what Jean was expecting: "I'm sure Moreau will make his health a priority. He knows how important his recovery is to all of us at Edgar Allan."

Jean heard the hidden message loud and clear: come home as soon as possible or suffer the painful consequences. He opened his mouth, but Wymack beat him to the punch with steel in his voice.

"All due respect, I didn't call you for platitudes," Wymack said. "If I wanted that hollow bullshit, I would've picked up a get-well card at the dollar store. It's three months minimum until he's back on the court. He's no use to you right now, and it's no hardship for us to watch over him in the meantime. Tell him to stay put before he injures himself any further. Please."

The ragged bite in that last word ate through cracks Jean didn't even know existed. He refused to dwell on it but held his breath as he waited for a response.

"Your baseless antagonism is as refreshing as always," the master said. "Moreau?"

"Yes," Jean corrected himself at the last second, "Coach?"

16

"Coach Wymack has trouble enough with his own rabid lineup. Do as he tells you and stay where you are for now. We will talk again when you are well enough to be moved."

"Coach, I—" *I'm sorry, please forgive me, I promise I'm trying*, "—understand."

The line went too quiet, but it took Jean a moment to realize they'd been hung up on. Wymack snapped his phone shut with a sharp flick of his fingers, and his knuckles went white as he tried in vain to crush the small thing in his big hand.

"That man is years overdue for a high-speed, head-on collision." He picked up his mug, belatedly remembered it was empty, and drummed his blunt fingernails on the side. "That makes it easier, doesn't it? He knows we're holding you captive and he's not going to fight it."

Wymack honestly thought he'd come out on top in that conversation. Jean wanted to hate him for his naïveté, but he was so tired.

"I am safe to travel now," Jean said. "Send me home."

How Wymack could look so angry and so exhausted at the same time, Jean wasn't sure. He braced for a backlash against his ingratitude, but all Wymack said was, "No."

"You cannot keep me here."

"You're not leaving," Wymack said. "You're going to live through this even if we have to drag you kicking and screaming to the finish line. And before you even think about climbing out of bed again, remember that your own coach just ordered you to stay put. You're stuck with us for now."

Wymack waited a minute, realized Jean wasn't going to respond, and finally said, "I'll see if Abby has a bell or something we can leave in here with you in case you need us. In the meantime, rest as much as you can. Let me worry about your coach. You worry about you and nothing else, understand?"

How easily he said it, as if Jean could worry about himself separate from the rest. The man was trying to get him killed.

17

"I said, do you understand?" Wymack asked as he got to his feet.

Jean had enough self-preservation to at least point his dirty look at the far wall. "Yes."

He didn't, really, but that wasn't for Wymack to hear. The man left him to his thoughts, and Jean made himself dizzy chasing them in circles. The master had ordered him to stay put until Abby and Wymack declared him fit for travel, but did he mean it? Was it a literal order or did he expect Jean to find a way home regardless? Jean carefully felt his knee, but just the light pressure of his fingertips was enough to make his vision swim.

Abby showed up a few minutes later with a kitchen timer and a small glass half-full of water. "I couldn't find a bell, but you can force the timer to go off," she said as she set it within easy reach. The water she offered to him, and she held on until she was sure he could take it from her. "It's obnoxiously loud, so we're sure to hear it wherever we are in the house. Use it, okay? If you're bored, if you're hungry, if you're in pain, anything.

"David's out getting you some more shorts and boxers, but if you can think of anything else just let me know and I'll text him." She waited a beat to see if he came up with something before pulling a bottle of pills out of her pocket. When he didn't offer his hand, she shook two capsules onto the sheets at his side. "These'll help you sleep. The more you rest and the less you move, the better."

"What is wrong with my knee?" Jean asked her.

"You injured it in a scrimmage," she reminded him coolly before offering a real answer: "You've sprained your LCL."

Wymack hadn't been talking it up to win the master's restraint. Between his knee and his ribs, Jean was sidelined until mid-summer. The master would yank him from the starting lineup for this, and Riko would beat him black and blue for failing to live up to the number on his face. He'd heal up just in time to be taken apart again.

Jean picked up the pills. "Leave the bottle with me."

"You know I can't," she said, and left him alone with too many thoughts.

CHAPTER TWO
Jean

The week passed in a disconcerting haze. Jean tried sticking to a Raven schedule, knowing it would be hell to readjust when Wymack finally transferred him north, but without classes or practice to center him he was getting pulled out of alignment. He slept when he shouldn't, longer than he should, dragged under by Abby's medicine and the exhaustion of having to heal from so much trauma. Nightmares always woke him, leaving him gasping in breathless agony as he lashed out thoughtlessly.

Jean checked his pockets and the sheets for his phone every day in case Wymack took pity on him, but each successive demand for it back was met with calm refusal. Even promising that Wymack could watch him make his call didn't sway the older man, and Jean barely resisted the urge to throw his pillows at Wymack's face.

He looked for Zane's bed every time he sat up, but the bedroom maintained its lonely setup. They'd been roommates for three years and Raven partners for almost two: not friends, but violent allies, at least until Nathaniel destroyed everything. January was a nightmare neither of them could recover from or move past, and as unsettling as it was to be alone Jean was so desperately relieved to be free of the other man he could hardly breathe.

Riko's absence was considerably worse to tolerate. Jean had been promoted to Riko's partner after Kevin walked out on them, which meant he'd spent the last year forced to stay within a room or two of the King. It was a longer leash than Kevin had ever gotten, as it galled Riko deeply to have a

Moreau tagging along with him everywhere, but still short enough to choke Jean. His brief reassignment to Nathaniel over Christmas break had been a much-needed salve for his sanity.

Instead of Riko and Zane he had Wymack, Abby, and Renee cycling through to check on him as best they could around their schedules. They took him back and forth to the bathroom as needed, brought light meals that were easy to eat, and dropped off books he refused to read. Once a day—every other day? Jean didn't know anymore—Abby locked the door so she could wash him and check his injuries.

Jean slowly learned the full extent of what Riko had done to him. The worst of it was the three fractured ribs, with his LCL sprain and twisted ankle right behind them. The bruises that covered so much of him were in varying shades of healing, with far too many of them still uncomfortably dark. Not every cut was dire enough to need stitches, and Jean's broken nose would need a couple of weeks. It was Jean's hair that he couldn't get past when he refused to linger on everything else. He was vain enough to be deeply upset by how much Riko had managed to pull out, but not desperate enough to ask Abby how long it took hair to grow back.

His morose thoughts were interrupted by a hesitant knock at the door. None of his captors had ever sounded so leery of visiting him. Jean hadn't bothered to sit up yet, so he could turn his head that way and watch as his newest guest slipped into the room. The first sight of dark hair and green eyes had Jean sitting up faster than he ought. He hissed displeasure through clenched teeth and crumpled back against the headboard. By the time he was settled, Kevin was sitting on the bed by his knees, one long leg tucked under him and the other dangling off the side.

Jean had been so sure Wymack lied to him a few days back, but Kevin Day was tanned. "You left the court," he said, too incredulous to catch himself, "to go to the mountains? *You*? We're in the middle of championships."

"I went at knifepoint," Kevin said, lifting one shoulder in an uncomfortable shrug.

Kevin's gaze moved over Jean in a slow sweep, taking stock of his injuries. Jean knew better than to look for anger in his stare; the best Kevin could manage was bottomless guilt. Kevin had seen worse than this before. Sometimes Riko let Kevin stay with him afterward; more often Kevin had no choice but to distract the rest of the Ravens from Jean's misery by being an insufferable bitch. Luckily for them both, Kevin was a master at the latter.

"Until June," Kevin said, apropos of nothing.

"Yes," Jean said. He looked to the closed door and slipped into quiet but tense French. "Your coach called the master."

"To beg for your life?"

"Permission for me to stay for a few weeks," Jean said. He tipped his head to one side and eyed Kevin shrewdly. "Your coach claims he knows their secrets. He said you told them everything. Everything as in the Nest or everything as in…?" Even here he didn't dare say it aloud, but he trusted Kevin to fill in the blanks. When Kevin looked away rather than answer, Jean sucked in a sharp breath of disbelief. "You *imbecile*. What were you thinking?"

"I wasn't," Kevin admitted. "I was afraid he'd send me back to Evermore. I'm not sorry. I'm not," he insisted, scowling a little at Jean's skeptical look. "They deserved to know what they were getting into by sheltering me."

"They deserved to know," Jean echoed, sharp with scorn. "I've seen you lie a thousand times. You didn't have to give them the truth."

Kevin didn't waste his breath defending his idiocy but said, "I shouldn't have left you behind. I knew what he would do to you when he realized I was gone. But I—"

"—made me part of it anyway," Jean reminded him when Kevin faltered. Kevin had the good grace to flinch. Jean felt the tendrils of an old and ugly rage stir, and he knotted a bruised hand in the sheets like he could somehow hold it at bay

22

through sheer force alone.

"It was my only chance," Kevin said. "I knew you wouldn't come with me."

"My place is at Evermore," Jean agreed, "but you did not have to slit my throat on the way out."

Once upon a time he would have done anything for this stupid man and Kevin knew it. He'd used it against Jean in the end, begging Jean to distract Riko while he grieved his broken hand. Kevin left Evermore as soon as the coast was clear, and it had taken weeks to convince Riko and the master Jean was innocent and ignorant. They'd had to replace his entire set of armor before the end of January. No one could see how much blood the black padding absorbed, but all the Ravens could smell it.

It should not have taken so long to win their forgiveness after so many years of bowing his head and taking whatever punishment Riko saw fit to inflict on him, but Kevin had damned them both. Kevin had begged Riko in Japanese and English to stop hitting him and, when Riko wouldn't be swayed, panicked and turned to Jean for help in French. They'd been so discreet for so long, and Kevin had undone it all in a heartbeat. Between the ERC's assessment of Kevin's abilities and that brazen disobedience, Riko had gone right off the edge. Kevin had lost his hand, and Jean had lost years' worth of trust.

"I'm sorry," Kevin said quietly.

He held out his hand. Jean glowered at him for a moment, but Kevin was willing to outwait him. Finally Jean relaxed his grip and set his hand in Kevin's, palm-up. Kevin curled his fingers gently around it so he could turn Jean's arm this way and that. Jean didn't want to face those bruises and scabs again, so he pointed his stare past Kevin at the dark TV. Kevin tapped Jean's fingers in a silent command, and Jean made a fist in response. It hurt like hell, but he could do it. Kevin sighed, exhaustion or relief, and asked,

"What if it wasn't?"

Jean sent him a blank look. "What?"

Kevin's mouth gave a violent twitch, as if he regretted speaking. It took him a minute to find the courage to speak again, and the words had Jean snatching his hand out of Kevin's slack grip: "What if your place wasn't at Evermore?"

"Did a week away from the court damage your ball-battered brain?" Jean demanded. "I am a Raven. For you to insinuate otherwise is as insulting as it is ignorant."

"What if Edgar Allan let you go?" Kevin asked. "You belong on the court, but it doesn't have to be theirs. If it means keeping Andritch from interfering further with the Nest, the master might sign off on a transfer. It does not matter where you go; you will still end up where you belong." Kevin gestured to his own face, and Jean knew he meant the perfect Court. "That could be enough."

"Could be," Jean threw at him. "Might. You feckless child. You have forgotten yourself."

"Tell me I'm wrong," Kevin insisted.

"The master would see me dead before he let me go," Jean said, and swiped a hand through the air like he was following a headline: "'Jean Moreau kills himself after being sidelined indefinitely with injuries' would win us the sympathy of the press and an extra edge in our remaining games."

Kevin considered that before agreeing, "It would shake up the Big Three matches. Penn State wouldn't pass up a golden opportunity, but USC would hold back out of respect for a mourning lineup. It'd be better if they didn't," he said, a little grumpily. "They have a real chance this year, I think."

"Your blind loyalty to those clowns is exhausting."

"Some of them you like," Kevin reminded him.

"Don't you dare," Jean warned him, unamused. Kevin lifted one shoulder in a light shrug, unrepentant to the last. Jean resisted the urge to push him off the bed by the skin of his teeth. "The way you fawn over them is unbecoming."

"Their kindness matters," Kevin said. "If anyone were to say the Ravens only won because USC held back, Edgar

Allan's reputation holds less weight. You know the master can't allow that. That's why you're here for now and why he'll at least let you live through finals. This is your one chance to get away."

"I am a Moreau," Jean said, too sharp. "I know my place even if you've forgotten yours."

"Andritch—"

"—is not my master. He can say *go* all he likes. I will beg him to reconsider if that is what it takes."

Kevin went quiet for so long Jean assumed he'd won. It was a little unnerving that he even had to push the matter. The Kevin Day he'd spent four years living alongside would never be so deluded as to suggest Jean walk out on the Moriyamas. Just thinking it was enough to put Jean's heart in a vise, so he focused on the easier insult of leaving the first-ranked team. No other team in the nation deserved his skills.

"You are a Moreau," Kevin agreed at last. Jean had one second to think Kevin had come around and remembered himself, and then Kevin said, "He is—was—a Wesninski. He still walked away. He told us he refused to sign the transfer paperwork."

It was Jean's turn to look away. He honestly had not expected Nathaniel to survive the consequences of that ferocious defiance. If not for Jean's own weakness, maybe Riko really would have killed him that night. Holding Nathaniel down while Riko slowly waterboarded him meant he couldn't cover his ears against the noises Nathaniel made, and Jean had nearly bit through his own shoulder to keep from screaming. Once Jean started spiraling too badly to hold on, Riko had had to back off. Riko had not forgiven him for being so fainthearted, never mind his part in creating such trauma in the first place.

"Jean. *Jean.*"

Fingernails dug into the lines on his wrist, snapping him back to the moment. Jean realized too late he had a hand around his own throat. He made the mistake of looking at

25

Kevin, and the white-faced look on the striker's face said he knew exactly which memories Jean was trapped in. Jean couldn't breathe, but forcing his fingers to relax was almost impossible. Kevin had to tear scabs open and dig into the raw flesh underneath before Jean could find his center again. He sucked in a ragged, desperate gasp as he finally let Kevin pull his hand free.

"He didn't," Kevin whispered. "Jean—"

Jean almost didn't hear him through the hammering staccato of his heart. Drowning, he was drowning, he was— *please stop please stop please—*

"We did," he said, or thought he said. His mouth was heavy with the memory of wet cloth. "And then Riko had me dye his hair and send him home. He could live with us or die with them." Jean reflexively reached for his throat again, but Kevin forced his hand back down to the blankets. Jean shuddered as he tried to force his memories back into their place in the depths of his mind. The chains felt horrifyingly weak when he tried locking that box closed again. He cast about for anything to save him and stumbled over Kevin's curious phrase: "*Was* a Wesninski?"

"He refused the FBI's protection," Kevin said. "They legalized his new name."

"Just like that," Jean said, too empty to know how to react.

"Jean."

"If you tell me to follow his lead, I will cut your throat open with my teeth," Jean said. "Go away and don't come back."

He half-expected an argument, but Kevin did as he was told and saw himself out. Jean watched the door close behind him. The silence that fell in the bedroom should have been a relief after the ignorant things Kevin had said to him, but Jean's heartbeat was so loud in his ears he wanted to claw his own chest open. He put his hands over his ears instead and dug in until everything hurt, but the roaring in his ears sounded like Kevin's voice: *Walk away, walk away, walk away.*

The Foxes weren't going to let him leave in a few weeks. He knew it as surely as he knew his own name. The master would call once enough time had passed that Jean could risk traveling, and Wymack would argue against it. He'd fight to keep Jean here until summer practices started, at least, and the master would pretend to agree to throw off suspicion. Wymack had promised he'd burn the house down before he let the Ravens have Jean again, but maybe the master would beat him to the punch.

Jean had been burned before, but only with matches. Those tiny bites had hurt far more than they had any right to. He could only imagine what real fire would feel like if it caught hold of him.

"How long does it take?" he asked Wymack a few hours later, when the coach brought dinner by his room. "Getting burned alive. How long does it take to die?"

Wymack eyed him for an endless minute. "I'm happy to say I don't know the answer to that question. Do I need to check you for a lighter?"

"No," Jean said. "I just want you to remember that you did this to me."

Wymack checked the room anyway, pulling up pillowcases and sheets, emptying the pockets on Jean's borrowed clothes, and ransacking the nightstand. He sent Jean a long look when he came up empty, and Jean regarded him with a calm expression he knew wasn't at all reassuring. Wymack didn't waste his breath asking for answers they both knew he wouldn't get, and he left Jean to his meal in peace.

Wymack wasn't going to get any sleep tonight, but Jean might catch a bit of rest around his nightmares, so it still felt like a victory.

-

Victory was short-lived, because Kevin was back the next day. This time he brought Nathaniel and his pet goalkeeper with him. Nathaniel took up a perch on the edge of the mattress near Jean's knee to survey Jean's injuries with a serious look. Kevin went to the other side of the bed, arms folded so tight across his middle he looked like he was trying to squeeze himself out of existence. Jean knew how every shade of fear looked on Kevin's face, or so he'd thought. This ghastly pallor was new, and Jean was pretty sure he did not want to know what put it there.

Looking at Kevin was still easier than facing Nathaniel, because there were burns where Nathaniel's number should have been. After everything that fucking tattoo had cost Jean—he felt numb all over, then cold, and his stomach twisted so hard he was sure it ripped to pieces inside him. The urge to tear Nathaniel's face open was so fierce he could barely breathe.

"Hello, Jean," Nathaniel said.

"Go away," Jean said, in a voice he barely recognized. "I have nothing to say to you."

"But you'll listen, because I just told Ichirou where you are."

He'd misheard. He had to have misheard. In no universe would Ichirou Moriyama deign to speak to one of them. But Kevin was sagging down to sit on the mattress near his hip, and Nathaniel's expression was grim but determined as he glanced back at Andrew's impassive expression. Satisfied they were all paying attention, he turned back on Jean.

"My father got out of jail only to immediately get murdered," Nathaniel said. "I spent an entire weekend locked up with the FBI trying to piece together his crimes and contacts for them. Ichirou respects my family name enough to come to me for answers in the aftermath. He said he was calculating the value of our existence, so I paid him in the only truths worth our lives.

"I told him Riko was a risk to the stability of his new empire and how his reckless violence against everyone in this room left too many trails. An athlete should not have that kind of push and pull, and if anyone started connecting the dots between our tragedies there'd be too many dangerous

28

questions asked. It puts the Moriyama family in jeopardy, and a Wesninski of course cannot ally with such a person. I asked Ichirou to take me back into his fold."

Kevin's jaw dropped, but Nathaniel bulled on without waiting for him to argue. "I told him we are well aware we are Moriyama investments and that we are content to exist as such." Nathaniel smiled with so much ice Jean thought the room dropped a few degrees. The adrenaline rush of what he'd survived, of the trick he'd managed to play on a too-powerful man, was going to his head. It was the same arrogance that made him defy Riko over and over again despite knowing it was going to come back on him and his team.

"We talked numbers: what Kevin was worth before and after his injury, what kind of money endorsements bring in, what professional athletes make on average…" Nathaniel gave a casual wave of his hand to indicate the whole deal. "Because we fell under Coach Moriyama's thumb, the money was originally going to him to feed his pet projects. I suggested we pay it back to Ichirou instead.

"He needs it," he insisted when Kevin looked like he was going to get off the bed and flee the room. "Not even I understand my father's full reach, but everything he had is falling apart now that the FBI is picking through the wreckage. Even if Ichirou allies with my uncle for more access to Europe, he's losing money hand over fist. Money that we are happy to give back to him if he'll wait for us.

"He agreed," Nathaniel said. "It's eighty percent of our earnings from the time we make pro until… retirement? I didn't ask," he admitted. "I'd pushed my luck enough I didn't want to imply there'd be an end to the arrangement. What matters is that the deal is for all three of us. I agreed I would hash it out with you and that there'd be no problem. There isn't one, right?

"It's not a pardon and it's not really freedom, but it's protection," Nathaniel said. "We're assets for the main family now. The King's lost all his men and there's nothing he can do about it without crossing his brother. We're safe—for good."

He said it so easily, like he genuinely believed it. Jean buried his face in his hands and dug his fingernails into his temples. This was a nightmare; it had to be a nightmare. In no reality would Ichirou Moriyama have met with an insignificant brat like Nathaniel Wesninski or been swayed by the self-importance that Riko tried so hard to beat out of him. It went beyond reason to think this was real and that Ichirou fully intended to steal his brother's toys. Jean refused to believe it, because if he even stopped to consider what it meant—

The door closing sounded very final, but the weight by his side remained. Kevin touched Jean's elbow and said, "Look at me."

"No," Jean said. "I am a Moreau. I am a Raven. I know my place. I won't agree to this."

"It's done," Kevin said. "You do not have a say in it."

"You did this to us," Jean accused him as Kevin finally pried his hands away from his face. "You should have beat this wildness out of him once you learned his name."

"I couldn't," was the weary response. "Everyone who has tried to tame him has failed."

Jean cursed long and low in French and yanked out of Kevin's grip. If he'd only stayed at Evermore, he wouldn't have gotten roped into this deal. He'd damned himself back in January, knocking down the first domino the moment he responded to Renee. How appropriate, how in character, that a pretty face had fucked him over yet again. Jean ought to gouge his own eyes out so he'd never be tempted again, but without his eyes he couldn't play, and if he couldn't play—

"Riko cannot move against Ichirou," Kevin told him, low and insistent. "The master will kill him if he even suspects Riko might. Neither of them can hurt you ever again without damaging Ichirou's property. Do you understand?"

"The deal is that I play," Jean shot back. "It didn't say in what state. If Riko wants to—"

Jean's hand came up too late to snatch the words out of

the air. He froze with his fingers on his mouth, staring at Kevin and through him as he prayed Kevin would just let it slide. The intensity of Kevin's stare said he wasn't that lucky, and Jean's fist came down hard on his own side immediately. The white-hot burst of pain seared away any other reckless words he might have said, leaving him gasping for breath even as Kevin slammed him into the headboard by his shoulders.

"Don't," Kevin warned him. "You cannot lie to me, Jean. Stop trying."

He couldn't lie, but he still had to. It was the only way to stay alive. They both knew who was hurting Jean, and Kevin had been there for far too much of it, but it had been years since Jean last acknowledged it. It was easier to just bow his head and accept it. What happened to him month after month, year after year, was simply the price of being a Moreau. To assign blame was to breed resentment, and resentment would only break him. There was no getting away; there was only getting through.

"I am a Moreau," Jean said.

"Yes," Kevin agreed, "but you are not a Raven."

"My place is at Evermore," Jean said. "I've been ordered to play professionally and to give up my salary. Nowhere in there did he say I had to leave Edgar Allan. I won't. I *won't*."

"You and I both know what Riko will do to you if you go back," Kevin said. "He will kill you before he loses you to Ichirou. If he doesn't do it himself, he will force his brother to when he cripples you on the court. You know it's true even if you won't say it."

Kevin gave him a shake, but Jean stared past him and refused to acknowledge his words. Kevin dropped his free hand unerringly to Jean's injured knee and gave it a hard pinch. He didn't even wince when Jean lashed out, and Jean sullenly met his gaze at last. Kevin waited until he had Jean's attention before saying, "You are a Moreau. You belong to the Moriyamas. But not those ones, not anymore."

"Stop," Jean warned him. "Do not say such things to me."

31

Kevin ignored that. "You have a new master, and he ordered you to play for him. If you return to Edgar Allan, you do so in defiance of those orders. You do not have the right to refuse anything your master asks of you. Believe in that truth still if you believe in nothing else. It is the only thing that will keep you alive." Kevin gave him a beat to see if he'd argue before saying, "You will spend this spring healing, and then we will find you a new team to play for. You will never be a Raven again."

I am a Raven. If I am not a Raven, who am I?

Jean's chest felt like it was tearing open. All the air had gone out of the room at some point. He clawed at his shirt, wondering how something so loose could be choking him. Kevin caught hold of his face with both hands, forcing Jean to look at him when Jean tried to turn away.

"Breathe," Kevin said, from a thousand miles away.

Jean Moreau I am Jean Moreau I am Jean Moreau I am

"I'm going to throw up."

Kevin had to let go of him to lean off the side of the bed, but he had the wastebasket up and in Jean's bruised hands before Jean lost the fight with his stomach. Jean heaved so hard he felt blinded by it. Kevin said nothing about the smell or the noise but took the can back when Jean was done spitting sour mouthfuls into it. Jean's captors made sure there was always water on the nightstand, so Kevin passed that over next. Jean sipped at it, wincing at the way it only made the taste worse.

Jean knew hints of what the main family was capable of, but Ichirou had always been a ghost story: a young man destined to inherit a bloody empire that spanned the eastern half of the United States and had a half-dozen links to Europe. As far as anyone could tell, he didn't give two shits about Exy. He was a more terrifying master to follow in theory, but maybe he'd be content to sit on his throne and collect his tithes from a distance. Maybe Jean would never see a Moriyama in person again.

32

Moreau, Jean thought, a kneejerk reminder that had kept him from tipping off the side too many times over these last five years. *I am a Moreau. I belong to the Moriyamas. I will endure.*

But that was the sticking point, wasn't it? His family's debt had been to Kengo. The master stepped in and paid it off when he saw Jean's talent on the court, but Jean was all he'd wanted from them. The Moreaus still answered to the main family. Jean, like Nathaniel, was simply returning to his original place in the Moriyama hierarchy.

"You don't expect me to hinge my life on a loophole," Jean said.

"You did this to yourself," Kevin said. "Your refusal to ever name Riko as your master means you can't even fall back on your mantra to save you."

"I absolutely hate you," Jean said. Kevin shrugged that off, unmoved by such a transparent lie. "I don't trust this. The other shoe will drop sooner or later. It doesn't matter how long it takes. As soon as there's a way that won't leave a trail, I'm finished."

"Perhaps," Kevin said, "but you have no choice but to see this through to the end."

"You have a choice," Jean insisted. "Kill me and let me be done with this."

Kevin's expression was forbidding. "You made me a promise."

"Fuck you. You have no right to hold me to it."

"But I will." Kevin stared him down, and Jean hated, *hated* that he was the first to look away. Kevin at least had the good grace to not rub it in, and he slid toward the edge of the bed instead. "I have to get back to campus. If I'm late to my next class, they'll file a complaint with Coach."

He left Jean to his uneasy thoughts, and the afternoon hours dragged on at a snail's pace. Jean wasn't sure who told Abby or Wymack what Nathaniel had done, but he could tell they knew when they cycled through his room that afternoon and evening with a new energy. Wymack even brought him a laptop and a basic phone he didn't recognize. Jean looked from one to the other as Wymack set them down on the mattress within reach.

"Talked to Andritch, who talked to your teachers," Wymack said. "They're getting you set up to finish the semester long-distance. You'll have to install all the appropriate programs yourself; I can barely check my email without wanting to shoot my computer. This is a temporary line to replace yours," he said, stabbing a finger at the phone. "I figure you need to be reachable by your professors, but you don't need easy access to the bastards you walked out on. After the dust settles and you're a little more stable we'll revisit the matter."

Jean tapped the phone awake. Only five numbers were saved, and Jean didn't recognize one of them. "B Dobson," he read aloud.

"Campus psychiatrist in charge of keeping my kids in working order," Wymack said.

"Not surprised the Foxes need a shrink," Jean said.

"Don't knock it until you try it," Wymack said. "Dinner's running a bit late, but Abby should have it by in another fifteen or so. Need anything else?"

A reason to believe Nathaniel's deal wasn't going to backfire and destroy them all, Jean could have said, but he settled for an easier, "No."

Wymack nodded and left, and Jean pushed both the computer and phone off the bed.

Having classes again injected a much-needed bit of stability into his life, even if it also reminded Jean of all the pieces that were missing. Ravens always took classes with other Ravens. He'd had this class with Grayson and Jasmine, that one with Louis, Cameron, and Michael, and these two with Zane and Colleen. He knew they were all still going to the same classes, but he was so far removed it was disorienting.

34

He downloaded lesson plans and scans of his textbooks via email and felt very much alone.

He wondered what Riko was doing in his absence. Jean had been forced to sit in on his lessons after Kevin escaped, but who had taken Jean's place? Wayne Berger, likely, as Wayne was Riko's on-court partner now. Jean should email Riko to check in, but Jean was terrified of the outcome. Surely Riko had heard the news by now. If he ordered Jean to come home anyway, what was Jean supposed to say? Even with Ichirou in the mix Jean didn't have the right to tell Riko no.

Jean never wanted to speak to Zane again, but there was no one else he could reach out to. He waited until one of their shared classes began before sending a blank email to him, but the answer he got back a few minutes later turned his stomach: "Where the fuck are you, Johnny? Master fucked King up pretty good and threatened to pull him from the lineup. Everyone's jumping at shadows."

It took Jean most of the period to figure out a response, and finally he settled for: "Away, master's orders."

It wasn't technically a lie, just a careful version of the truth. There was nothing he could say about the rest of it. In no world would the master ever really sideline Riko, would he? Riko had cost the master his two most expensive players, but Riko was King. Maybe it was just a threat to keep him in line. At most it was a temporary measure to embarrass him into restraint. If the master actually went through with it, they were all dead men. Riko would not take an insult like that well.

Zane didn't respond, so Jean deleted his email and looked again for a nonexistent second bed.

Friday night both Wymack and Abby were out of the house for the Foxes' rematch against the Binghamton Bearcats. Jean finally met Dobson, who took on the role of babysitter so he wouldn't be alone in the house. Jean hated her immediately, even if she only stopped by the room long enough to introduce herself. Something about her made Jean's skin want to crawl off his bones. He told her not to come back, and she obediently kept her distance the rest of the evening.

Jean had at least sixty pages of reading left to get through, but he dug the TV remote out of the nightstand drawer. There were a dozen-odd sports channels on Abby's cable plan, and three of those tended to focus on collegiate games. Finding the Foxes' match was a matter of trial and error, and Jean settled back against the headboard to watch the pregame show.

Jean had already watched Nathaniel's interviews on Wednesday, so he knew the tiny bastard wouldn't be on the court tonight. He still looked for him where the Fox line was doing warmup laps. The evening hosts were talking a mile a minute in the foreground, spending too much time on Nathaniel's personal life and not enough on the game about to start in a few minutes. Jean knew they couldn't possibly know about the deal Nathaniel made with Ichirou, but he listened to every word with his heart pounding. When the warning buzzer sounded to signal the last five minutes before first serve, Jean nearly jumped out of his skin.

He didn't expect the match to be good by a long shot. He'd seen a few of the Foxes' games from their previous years, when the master wanted his Ravens to study each of the teams in their new district. He'd played them last fall and seen their worthlessness up close. The Bearcats the Foxes were facing tonight were not the best, but they had their moments and a massive lineup to back them up. The Foxes would fall apart before the break.

So he thought, but the scrappy team held their ground. Again and again the Bearcats fouled them. Sometimes the referees missed it; other times the Bearcats took their cards and shrugged it off as an insignificant setback. The Foxes rolled with the punches, gave ground to the violence at every turn, and put all their focus into simply playing the game as best they could. Defense fell apart more often than they should, as much to weariness as a skill difference, but Kevin's pet monster picked up the slack behind them.

Jean remembered when Kevin first presented Andrew

36

Minyard's file to Riko. How he stumbled across it, Jean still didn't know, but Kevin had looked almost ravenous as he pled his case. "We have to have him," he'd said, again and again until Riko agreed to take him south for a meeting. They'd come back the same evening with Kevin in a spectacularly bad mood. Riko had mocked him about his bad call for the better part of a year, but Kevin had tracked the Foxes' scores with a black anger that was two-thirds resentment.

Jean hadn't understood until October. Andrew had failed to keep the Ravens out of his goal, but there was something to be said for a man who pushed himself to collapse to try and hold them off. It'd be a few years yet before Andrew was truly worth Kevin's obsession with him, but watching him tonight put Jean's mind at ease. The perfect Court was in dire need of a goalkeeper. He'd be damned if he gave Kevin the satisfaction of his approval, though; Kevin was insufferable on a good day and beyond unbearable when he was right about something.

Jean almost turned the game off for the halftime break because there was only one way this match was going to end. They were a nine-man team that could only field eight, and Renee was forced out of her usual spot to play with the backliners. Second half would be a slow death for them with no relief in sight. In the end he opted to watch it, if only to judge Renee as a fellow defenseman.

Twenty minutes in, the Foxes were somehow holding their ground. With fifteen minutes remaining, Kevin scored and put the Foxes in the lead at six-five. Ten minutes later he scored again to create a two-point gap.

"This isn't happening," Jean said, but no one was around to answer him.

There was no way the Foxes could win this match, but they did, knocking Binghamton out of championships and setting themselves up to face the Big Three in two weeks. Jean watched as they dragged each other off the court to celebrate on the sidelines. The hosts were chattering away again from off-camera, commenting on plays and an unprecedented Fox success, but Jean let it go in one ear and out the other. The Foxes would get annihilated in semifinals, but they'd earned the right to face USC and Evermore.

Jean turned the TV off, then back on again. The scene unfolding before his eyes remained the same. He turned it off again, counted to twenty, and turned it on to see someone had gotten a microphone in Kevin's face.

"—to playing USC again," Kevin said. "I haven't spoken to Jeremy or Coach Rhemann since I transferred but their team is always amazing. Their season was nearly flawless this year. There's a lot we can learn from them."

"For fuck's sake," Jean said, even as the sportscaster laughed.

"Still their biggest fan," she said. "You're up against Edgar Allan again, too, in the biggest rematch of the year. Thoughts?"

"I don't want to talk about the Ravens anymore," Kevin said. "Ever since my mother died it's been Ravens this and Ravens that. I am not a Raven anymore. I never will be again. To be honest, I never should have been one in the first place. I should have gone to Coach Wymack the day I found out he was my father and asked to start my freshman year at Palmetto State."

"You would have rather died than be on this team," Jean said to the TV.

Neither of them could hear him, of course. The woman looked like she'd choked on something. "The day—did you say Coach Wymack is your father?"

"Yes, I did. I found out when I was in high school, but I didn't tell him because I thought I wanted to stay at Edgar Allan. Back then I thought the only way to be a champion was to be a Raven. I bought into their lies that they would make me the best player on the court. I shouldn't have believed it; I've been wearing this number long enough to know that wasn't what they wanted for me.

"Everyone knows the Ravens are all about being the

38

best," Kevin said. "Best pair, best lineup, best team. They drill it into you day after day, make you believe it, make you forget that in the end 'best' means 'one'."

Jean was hundreds of miles from Evermore, but listening to Kevin say these bold words without fear had him leaning hard into the headboard and checking the shadows for Ravens. When they found out Kevin was calling them out on live TV like he didn't have a care in the world, they were going to—

Jean covered his ears like he could drown out his own thoughts. He thought about Nathaniel and Kevin and Ichirou. It'd been four days since Nathaniel stopped by to tell him he'd indentured them to Ichirou, and Zane was still the only Raven Jean had spoken to. He'd expected nasty messages or interrogations from the rest once they realized he had access to his student account, but it seemed Zane hadn't told them.

Jean dropped his hands just in time to hear Kevin say, "—never been skiing? I'd like to try it one day, though."

Jean's courage broke. He turned the TV off and threw the remote across the room where he couldn't reach it.

It was over an hour before Wymack and Abby got home, and they both came together to see him. Abby took one look at his face and said, "Oh, so you saw. Are you hungry?"

She'd left him fruit and a dinner that didn't have to be heated up before she headed over to the stadium, so Jean only shook his head. Abby accepted that in silence and brought him his bottle of pills. Wymack followed her across the room and lifted his hands. In one he had an empty glass; in the other, a bottle of scotch.

"Not with his medicine," Abby chastised him.

"Maybe this would help more right now," Wymack said, unapologetic.

"Ravens aren't allowed to drink," Jean said.

"Irrelevant considering present company. But suit yourself. Just figured I'd offer before I drink the whole thing." He waited for Jean to shake his head again, accepted that refusal with an easy nod, and poured himself a drink. The ease with which he drained it was revolting, but not nearly as alarming as watching him immediately refill the glass.

Jean studied his expression, looking past the hints of tension for any sign of shock. "He finally told you," he guessed when he came back empty-handed. "You knew before tonight."

"He confessed a couple weeks ago," Wymack said. "Word is you're the one who showed Neil where the letter was hidden. He brought it back with him in December."

"He wanted to know why Kevin ran and I didn't," Jean said, swallowing his pills with some water. He should have left it there, but Jean turned his glass over and over between his fingers. "Riko's father gave him up as soon as he was born, uninterested in a second-born son. Mine didn't hesitate to sell me off if it meant his debts were squared away. Despite that, Kevin never once doubted you'd take him in. He wasn't foolish enough to say as much where Riko could hear him, but he said it to me. I laughed at him. I'd never taken him for a dreamer."

Abby sent Wymack a soft look, but Wymack pointed his gaze at the far wall and only asked, "Need anything else tonight?"

Jean motioned to where his timer was on the nightstand, and they left him to his thoughts.

-

Jean wasn't entirely surprised when Kevin stopped by in the morning, but he never would have expected the woman who came with him. Jean hadn't seen Theodora Muldani since his freshman year, as she'd been a fifth-year when he finally entered the Ravens' lineup. He'd known her for a couple years before that, on account of moving into Evermore early, but he hadn't thought he'd see her again until he entered a professional team after graduation and had to face her on the court.

"Thea," he said, startled. "Why are you here?"

"She saw my post-game interview," Kevin said, hanging

40

back so Thea could approach Jean alone. He held up his left hand and said, "She came for answers."

Thea held up a warning finger at Kevin. "Wait outside. I don't trust you not to coach him on what to say." Kevin frowned at her, but Thea stared him down until he gave an aggrieved sigh and left. Thea waited a few moments after the door closed behind him like she thought he'd come back in, then folded her arms across her chest and turned a too-heavy stare on Jean. "Good morning, Paris."

It would've been too much to hope she'd outgrown that nickname. Jean scowled at her. "For the hundredth time, *Marseille*."

"You look like hell," Thea said, neatly ignoring the correction as she had every other time. "Kev says you're sidelined for a few months. What happened to you?"

"Bad scrimmage," Jean said. "Armor was loose."

"Yesterday I might have believed that," Thea said. "But he's swearing it's something else. Try again, without lying to my face."

Without lying, she said, as if that was even possible. The Ravens were used to enduring the coaches' heavy-handed discipline, and they inflicted cruel hazing on each other without hesitation when one of them was too far out of line, but Riko was a murky mess where the team was concerned. They knew he carried violence in his heart, and they'd seen it break out on more than one occasion, but Jean and Kevin had bent over backwards to hide the true extent of his sadism from their teammates.

It wasn't for Riko's sake, surely: the Ravens could and would follow a tyrant straight into hell if that was what was asked of them. Riko was King, the beating heart around which Castle Evermore was built. Perhaps it was pride, then, or a reckless sense of self-preservation. Kevin did not want the Ravens to see him submit, and Jean was scorned enough as it was. He could not tell them *I am a Moreau, this is what I deserve* when they didn't even know who the Moreau and

41

Moriyama families really were.

"You shouldn't have come here," Jean said.

It was a waste of breath to try sending her away. Thea sat on the bed and pointed up at her face. "Look at me right now."

Try as he might, he couldn't ignore that tone. He'd spent two years watching her play from the Ravens' sidelines, enamored with how thoroughly she dominated the backline. Night after night his freshman year he'd fought to get time alone with her, escaping Riko's clutches while he was distracted with Kevin so he could ask her for advice and tips. Her little Parisian duckling, she'd joked, ignoring every plaintive demand to learn the correct city.

He'd never had good defenses against Thea, and Kevin knew that. Jean would kill him for bringing her here. For now he helplessly dragged his gaze back to hers. "Don't ask me."

"I'm not asking," she said. "Tell me what happened."

"To Kevin's hand?"

"You have twenty-one good ribs," Thea said. "For now."

There was a fifty-percent chance she was bluffing, but Jean tilted toward her anyway and said, "Do it, then. It wouldn't take much; we all know I have brittle bones."

He heard the bite in his words, but he couldn't stop it. It was as much an accusation as it was a mockery. The Ravens had said it about him for years, knowing there was more to it but opting to stay out of it. His propensity for showing up to the court with stitches was hard to ignore. The Ravens had found him at the bottom of the stadium stairs four times, and he'd brought six broken fingers to the court over three short years. It was safer to say he was ridiculously fragile than to attract unwanted attention from above by prying.

"The King is an asshole and a bully, but he would never go this far," Thea said. "Not to his Court. Not during championships."

Rejection was automatic and fierce: "He did not do this to me."

Thea considered him a few moments before guessing,

"The master, then? Jesus, Jean. Tell me you weren't up to your old tricks."

She didn't have to spell it out when her tired tone said enough. Memory had his heart crackling like breaking glass. The Ravens knew he'd fucked most of the defense line his freshman year; it was an open secret that refused to die even as most of those involved graduated from Edgar Allan. Since none of the five would betray Riko by saying he'd put them up to it, they laughed it off as the price paid for the number on Jean's face. Tolerating that ridicule and scorn was wretchedly unfair, but it was better than telling the truth. Even Kevin didn't know the full story, only the jagged half-lie Riko fed him.

Jean still remembered their names and numbers. Two had attempted to show him some patience, picking up on the distress in his unsteady hands and writing it off as nerves. The other three didn't waste their time on pretenses. The Ravens were an angry, codependent lot trapped together in the Nest for almost every hour of their day. It was inevitable they'd fuck almost as often as they fought. Jean only caused a stir because of his age and how quickly he went from one partner to the next.

Four times Jean had begged Riko not to send him to their rooms. Four times he'd begged for forgiveness and mercy, knowing Riko wasn't capable of either. The last time he'd shut up and gone where he was told, and Riko rewarded that lifeless submission by moving on to new torments the following week.

The master had not been as forgiving. As soon as he discovered his expensive investment was cultivating a reputation as a whore, he'd beaten Jean within an inch of his life.

"I made some mistakes," Jean said quietly, feeling so far from his body he couldn't even feel the sheets beneath his hands. "This was not one of them. This was just—"

It was hard to find his words; it was getting hard to breathe with Thea watching him so intently. Jean needed her

43

out of his space, out of this room, out of his life again until he could rebuild his walls. He seized on the one thing that could distract her from him and said, "Kevin's hand wasn't an accident. When he tells you what happened, believe him. You won't want to, but you must. But do not ask me—not about this, not about anything."

"Paris," she said.

"Go away, Thea."

"Marseille." A too-late peace offering.

"Go away, and don't come back," Jean said. "*Please*."

Thea hesitated a moment longer, then got to her feet and tweaked his hair. If she had a parting remark, she thought better of it, and she left him to his miserable thoughts without a backwards look.

Jean was lying down even as she made her way to the door. As soon as she was gone, he dragged his covers up over his head and willed his uncooperative body to let him sleep. He was still awake when Abby swung by to check on him a few hours later, and he didn't let her leave until she'd given him something to knock him under.

There were nightmares waiting for him at the bottom, as there always were and always would be, but at least Jean could wake up and escape from those.

CHAPTER THREE
Jeremy

Jeremy Knox was halfway through tying his laces when a breathless Bobby came skidding into the locker room. The freshman always looked ridiculously tiny next to the Trojans once they were kitted out for a game, but her size worked in her favor tonight as she had to weave around a half-dozen bodies to find USC's captain. Jeremy saw the look on her face as she hurried toward him and could guess what news she was bringing him. It made him grin as he bent to his work.

"It's time," she said as soon as she reached him. She dropped to a quick squat and gave his shin guards a hard push. Satisfied they didn't move, she settled back on one foot to look up at him. The glee in her eyes might've been at the trick the USC Trojans had planned for tonight but was just as likely excitement over being the first of the Trojans' three assistants to reach him. Jeremy put his money on the latter, since Antonio was closing in fast as well. "Security says they're heading back to inner court soon."

Tony stopped beside her and favored the top of her head with an exasperated look. "How did you even beat me in here? I was literally with Coach Rhemann when the call came in."

Bobby held up a hand, and Tony easily hauled her to her feet as she explained, "I heard the guard's radio go off. He had to let me back in because my hands were full with—oh," she said, looking stricken. "Oh no. The ice."

She took off back the way she'd come, leaving Tony to sigh dramatically. A moment later he recovered enough to send Jeremy a sidelong look. "You sure about this? For sure, sure? Because if no one else knows yet, no one can hold you to it. You have time to change your mind."

"We need this more than they do," Jeremy said. "We're sure."

Tony accepted that without further argument and looked around. "Nabil?"

"He'll be out soon," Jeremy said, and Tony accepted that with an easy nod. Nabil would be the last down to court since he couldn't gear up until after prayers. Tony had gotten into the habit of waiting for him a few months back, offering a second set of hands to make up for lost time. "Can you see if someone will get my gloves and helmet down to the bench? I'm going to go say hello to our visitors."

"Of course," Tony promised. "I'll flag Angie down soon as I see her."

Jeremy detoured past the dealers' row on his way out. Sebastian Moore and Min Cai were talking excitedly as they finished up with their gear, but since Xavier was on the outskirts of the conversation it was easy to get his attention with a light touch on his elbow. Jeremy tipped his head in the direction of the court and said, "I'm heading out. I'll meet you in inner court."

The Trojans' vice-captain gave a serious nod completely at odds with his easy, "Tell your fanboy we said hello."

"Our fanboy," Jeremy reminded him with a laugh as he got moving again.

He found the night's roster where he'd left it, taped to the wall near the locker room exit, and he peeled it down on his way into the inner court. The deafening chaos of packed stands was a familiar and exciting weight, urging him onward and forcing his gaze to the court. They were thirty minutes out from serve, but Jeremy already knew tonight was going to be a great night. Championships brought out the best and fiercest in all of their opponents, and the chance to play an unfamiliar team was a rare challenge the team craved. Tonight's experiment was the icing on the cake, an invaluable experience no matter how it ended.

Jeremy finally reached the Away side of the stadium, and

the sight of the Palmetto State Foxes gathered by their benches rattled him a bit out of his heady glee. He knew the Foxes were small, but seeing them on TV and seeing names on paper was nothing compared to seeing them in person. The Trojans had as many strikers as the Foxes had bodies on their entire line. It was jarring thinking the ERC had signed off on them. Rumor had it they were going to revisit the size rule next season, but Jeremy wasn't going to hold his breath.

Coach David Wymack was standing off to one side, between Jeremy and the Foxes, but it took no time for Kevin Day to spot Jeremy and move up alongside his coach. Jeremy's mood ticked up again immediately, and he greeted them both with a bright grin. Wymack's handshake was firm and his face kind; Jeremy liked him immediately.

"Coach Wymack, welcome to SoCal. We're excited to host you tonight. Kevin, you crazy fool," he said, and clapped Kevin's shoulder. "You never cease to amaze. You've got a thing for controversial teams, I think, but I like this one much better than the last one."

Kevin waved that off. "They're mediocre at best but they're easier to get along with."

"Same old Kevin, as unforgiving and obnoxious as always," Jeremy said without any real judgment. "Some things never change, hm? Some things do."

They'd only ever met on the court during championships, since Edgar Allan and USC played on opposite sides of the country, but before Kevin transferred off the Raven line they'd at least sent each other sporadic texts on game nights. Then Kevin disconnected his number and dropped off the face of the planet, and Jeremy had to find out weeks after the fact that Kevin had lost his playing hand in a brutal skiing accident.

He'd sent a long and heartfelt letter of condolence and support to Palmetto State, hoping for a response but not taking it personally when one never came. Kevin had lost Exy the same year he signed with the national team; of course he needed to withdraw and come to terms with his injury. Jeremy wouldn't have handled it any better.

Thinking there was more to it was enough to turn Jeremy's heart inside-out, and he couldn't not ask. "Speaking of your last team, you, uh, you created quite a stir with that thing you said two weeks ago. About your hand, I mean, and it maybe not being an accident."

Kevin was silent for so long Jeremy thought he wouldn't get a response. Maybe the friendship they had now was just a memory of what once had been and Kevin wasn't willing to confide in him? But then Kevin motioned to him to follow and said,

"I have a backliner for you. Do you have room on next year's lineup?"

Jeremy didn't miss the look Wymack sent Kevin: sharp but not alarmed. Mystified, Jeremy trailed Kevin until they were out of earshot of the rest of the team. Kevin glanced up at the crowd, studying it with a distant look. Gauging the noise level, Jeremy might have guessed, but he refused to believe it. What sort of secrets could Kevin have to share that would justify that level of precaution?

"Kevin?" Jeremy asked. "Talk to me."

"I need you to sign Jean," Kevin said, and belatedly added, "Moreau."

Jeremy opened his mouth, closed it, and tried again. "You need me to *what*?"

Kevin gave Jeremy his full attention at last, and his expression was deadly serious. "Edgar Allan cannot announce it yet, but they have cut him from the Raven lineup. The Ravens hurt him," he said, and Jeremy had the fleeting and foolish suspicion it was an understatement. Maybe not so foolish, because Kevin explained, "It was supposed to be a simple hazing to blow off steam, but it got out of hand. He's off the court for the rest of the season."

For a moment Jeremy couldn't hear the crowd. "You aren't serious. It was that bad?"

Kevin looked past him and just said, "Yes."

48

Jeremy half-expected him to elaborate and was almost glad that he didn't. He'd seen many sides of Kevin, including the scathing diva he hid from the press, but he'd never seen Kevin so rattled and quiet. Jeremy's thoughts went unbidden to the question that had started this awful conversation and he felt positively ill. If Jean Moreau was off the court due to hazing, then how much truth was in the barbed comment Kevin had made about his hand? The Ravens were famous for their violence, but could Jeremy believe they'd hurt their own star players?

"He's very good," Kevin said. "He deserves to play for a Big Three team."

Jeremy knew of Jean, even if he'd never met the man face to face. It'd be impossible not to notice the gray-eyed Frenchman with a bold number on his face. He'd been on the lineup when USC and Edgar Allan faced each other last year and the year before, but he'd started in a different half and Jeremy had never had to handle him on the court. Jeremy didn't doubt he was phenomenal if he was a Raven and one of the so-called King's perfect Court, but good wasn't enough to cut it in California.

Kevin mistook his silence for refusal and said, "But if you don't have room for him—"

"It's not that we don't," Jeremy said, though he wasn't entirely sure that was true. They had three fifth-year backliners this year, and Coach Rhemann had only signed two to replace them. "I don't know his stats but since you'll vouch for him without looking sour then I know he must be talented. It's just that he's a Raven, and we're…" He gestured helplessly up at the stands. "Could he fit in here?"

"He hasn't played a clean game in years," Kevin admitted, "but he knows how to follow orders. If you tell him to submit, he will."

"Literally the most awkward way you could've worded it," Jeremy said.

He meant to lighten the mood, but Kevin only shrugged

49

and said, "You'll understand when you meet him."

Jeremy thought it over, but what could he possibly say? Kevin was asking him for help. What kind of friend or Trojan would he be if he couldn't live up to that? "I can't promise it's a yes without talking to my coaches, but from me it's a yes," he said. "I'll hash it all out with them tonight when everyone else has gone home. Maybe you'll remember to leave me your new number so I can give you the good news."

Kevin smiled, slow and pleased. Jeremy gave his shoulder a tight squeeze in response and held up his roster. "Now that you've upended my expectations for the night, allow me to return the favor. I've got a surprise for your team."

They headed back over to the Foxes, who were trying and failing to look like they hadn't been watching the pair the whole time they'd been gone. Jeremy stopped before Coach Wymack once more and held out his paper in offering.

"Our lineup," he said as Wymack unfolded it and looked it over. "It's late to be getting it to you, I know, but we were trying to avoid as much of a backlash as possible."

"Backlash?" one of the Foxes asked.

Wymack passed the roster over so she could see it. "Your pity's a little misplaced," he told Jeremy. "Tell Coach Rhemann we don't want handouts."

"This isn't pity," Jeremy said. "We're doing this for us, not you. Your success this year has us rethinking everything about how we play. Are we second because we're talented or because we have twenty-eight people on our lineup? Are we good enough as individuals to stand against you? We have to know."

Kevin snatched the paper away from his teammate so fast he almost tore it. One of the others popped up at his shoulder to see. Jeremy couldn't see his number past Kevin, but he didn't need to. The tallest man on the Foxes' lineup was Boyd, a backliner. The chances of Boyd being his partner on the court seemed pretty high, so Jeremy sized him up as surreptitiously as possible. Most backliners he went up against

50

were stocky, trained to barrel strikers over and body them out of the way. Boyd's height was a rare challenge, and just thinking about it had Jeremy buzzing with glee all over again.

"There are only nine names on it," Boyd finally said, for the sake of those who couldn't see.

"Two goalies, three backliners, two dealers, two strikers," Jeremy agreed. "You've made it this far with those numbers. It's time to see how we'd fare in that situation. I'm excited. None of us have ever played a full game before. Hell, most of us don't even play full halves anymore. We don't have to because the numbers are always in our favor."

"And you called me a crazy fool," Kevin said. "You'll lose tonight if you play like this."

He said it like it was an accepted fact, and for Kevin to put that much faith in the Foxes had Jeremy smiling so hard his face hurt. "Maybe. Maybe not. Should be fun either way, right? I can't remember the last time I was this psyched for a game. Look at this." He held out his hands like they could somehow see how unsteady he felt with this much anticipation beating through his chest. There was more he could have said, but Bobby was at the corner of the court and waving to get his attention. He was overdue back on the Home side, so he settled for just saying, "Bring it, Foxes, and we'll bring it too."

They were bold words, and he didn't at all regret them, but when Jeremy stumbled off the court partway through second-half he dizzily thought he should have asked the Foxes for a hint of mercy. He gently beat the side of his gloved fist against his thigh, hoping to feel something other than that disorienting numbness, and let Coach White guide him over to the bench.

The majority of the Trojan lineup stood shoulder-to-shoulder down the length of the wall, far back enough they wouldn't get in the referees' way but close enough to watch the spectacle unfolding before their eyes. The bench was saved for tonight's sacrificial players, and Jeremy had never been so glad to sit down. He'd taken all of first half so Ananya could

51

get relieved by Jillian. This half, it was his turn to be saved. He fumbled with his helmet, but he didn't quite have enough coordination to undo the straps. Tony was in front of him a heartbeat later, taking over for him, and Jeremy dropped his hands to his lap with a relieved sigh.

"How are they still going?" he asked wonderingly. Jeremy didn't know if it was respect or good-natured terror pounding in his temples. Either way he couldn't look away from the court long enough to help Tony with his gloves.

The answer was obvious: the Foxes had backed themselves into this playing style years ago due to Wymack's refusal to field a large team. Losing Seth Gordon at the start of the year had been tragic, but the only difference it made to their game was where their subs were assigned. Coach Wymack had likely tailored their entire training regime toward perseverance, building his Foxes up so they could hold their own against whatever was thrown at them. Every other team focused on shorter, full-speed shifts to justify roster size.

It worked to the Foxes' advantage to meet the Trojans on their terms: they played a cleaner game than the Trojans generally saw from their opponents, checking bodies and sticks when they needed to but only with enough force to win the confrontation. Their strength and energy were better reserved for holding their ground on the court, and as the Trojans started to flag and stumble, the Foxes tapped into those reserves to get around them. Jeremy wanted to look at all of them at once, and he knew he'd be watching and rewatching this game for weeks to see every angle.

"You need to stretch out," Coach Lisinski said behind him.

"I don't know if I can stand up again," Jeremy said.

"I believe in you," was her unsympathetic response.

Jeremy groaned and let Tony haul him back up. Bobby swung by as he was stretching and pacing so she could pawn some drinks off on him. Jeremy tried swigging without taking his eyes off the game, but he still almost missed when Neil Josten scored. With that, the Foxes took the lead with twenty minutes remaining in the game. They'd started the second half three goals behind at four-seven. Now they were ten against USC's nine.

Jeremy hobbled down the length of the court behind the rest of his team. Shane Reed was at the end of the line, as expected. He'd been in goal for the first half, and now he grimly watched as Laila got the shorter end of the stick. Jeremy couldn't remember the last time anyone got more than five goals on Laila. Now she'd given up six and they still had almost half the period to go.

"They can't protect her," Shane said.

"I'll have to hear about it later, I'm sure," Jeremy said.

"So will they," Shane said, with a hint of a smile that quickly faded. "But she agreed despite knowing the most likely outcome, so she can't take it personally."

She would anyway, Jeremy knew, but she'd hoard that blame for herself despite the front-row seats to her collapsing defense line. They were too exhausted to save her, running on fumes at best. Laila was very good, but she couldn't close the goal on her own. When the Foxes scored again just five minutes later, Cat shuffled over to her to give her a short, fierce hug. Laila gently knocked their helmets together, refusing that apology, and sent her back to her starting spot alongside Neil.

The Foxes were quick to score again. Jeremy wanted to look up at the clock and see how much time was left and how much longer his Trojans had to suffer, but he couldn't tear his eyes away from the court. Xavier stumbled when he got the next serve off, and the Fox guarding him gamely hauled him back upright before running for the ball. It was a simple gesture, but it endeared Jeremy to them so deeply he almost forgot how tired and sore he was. When the Foxes scored once more in the final two minutes of the game, putting them at thirteen to USC's nine, Jeremy could only laugh.

"We have so much work ahead of us," he said. "Practices are going to hurt from here on out."

The final buzzer sounded at last, and it was like watching dominos collapse. One by one the Trojans fell across the court, too exhausted to stay on their feet now that they could finally stop moving. Boyd picked Jillian up like she weighed nothing, offering himself as a crutch, and the dealer in center court crouched down to talk to Xavier. Cody waved up at Kevin, preferring to stay where they'd fallen, but Neil got hold of Cat before she could faceplant on the hard floor. She clung to him for dear life until Laila caught up to them. Neil was free to join his team's celebration at the half-court line, and he jogged for them like he hadn't spent ninety minutes running full-tilt all over creation.

Jeremy led the rest of the Trojans onto the court for a quick handshake. Kevin had taped a bit of paper to his racquet, and he tugged it free when Jeremy caught up to him. It tried to curl up again immediately, but Jeremy unrolled it to see two phone numbers scratched out in neat font: Kevin's and Jean's.

"I'll keep in touch," Jeremy promised, and then he had to keep the line moving.

There were plenty of rested Trojans who could help their teammates back to the locker rooms, so the coaches stayed behind to compare a couple quick notes while Angie, Tony, and Bobby hurriedly gathered up the stick racks and any discarded bottles.

Jeremy was worn to the bone, but not so tired he didn't see how empty the stands were, and definitely not too tired to take quick looks around at his teammates for their reactions. A couple of them looked far away from here as they took time to process what had just happened, those who'd been on the court were too tired to be disappointed, and the rest teetered between patience and curiosity.

No one spoke until they were back in the locker room away from prying eyes, and then Xavier looked at each of the fifth-years in turn. The six of them had been the first ones approached with this idea since this was their last chance at a championships title.

Jeremy was proud of them for being the first to agree, even if their reasoning was fatalistic: whether they were eliminated in semifinals or finals, they weren't getting past Edgar Allan when it mattered most. They'd spent years trying and failing; they simply didn't have what it took to one-up the Ravens in a fair fight. If tonight's gamble meant the Trojans would be better going forward, it was worth the risk of an embarrassing loss.

"Are we good?" Xavier asked.

"Make it mean something and we will be," Renaldo said.

"It will," Jeremy said, because he had to believe it. They'd given up, but he couldn't. He had only one year left, and he refused to end his NCAA career without a single title.

The Trojans' four coaches arrived then, with head coach James Rhemann in the lead. The Trojans settled down expectantly, and he considered them all with an inscrutable gaze. "First things first: thank you all for having the fortitude and restraint to rise to tonight's challenge. That includes those of you who weren't allowed to play; if it wasn't easy for me to watch I know it wasn't any easier for you. For those on the court: not our best performance by a long shot, but circumstances being what they were, I am proud of what you pulled off.

"Take this weekend to rest and recover, because next week we can't afford to hold anything back. We'll hold off on breaking down tonight's game until Monday afternoon since some of you are already falling asleep," he sent a bemused look at Cat, who was propped against Laila and snoring quietly. "Monday morning we're at the fitness center as usual. Does anyone have anything to say tonight that absolutely cannot wait until next week?"

Jeremy put his hand up. "I have a lot I want to say," he said, and gamely ignored the way Ananya feigned shock. "For everyone's sake I'll wait, but I really, really need to talk to you and Coach Jimenez tonight if you can spare a few minutes."

Jimenez nodded when Rhemann glanced over at him, so

55

Rhemann said, "You and Shane are on press duty. After that and after you've had a chance to wash up, come find us. We'll wait."

Jeremy would've preferred to never stand up again, but as the Trojans' captain he was dutybound to face the press and defend his team's unexpected loss. He led Shane back into the inner court. Interviews were actually the easiest part of game night, since the Trojans' script was unrelenting and predictable. It was easy to be proud of his team's effort, and even easier to compliment the Foxes' inhuman resilience. It was the truth, even if it wasn't all of it.

The unavoidable parts would have to wait until the coaches could sit them down on Monday, splitting them along offense and defense to review plays. A loss was still a loss, even if none of them would have done tonight any differently. They were going to have to address that disappointment where no one could see them. Laila was going to be aching well into next season about having the worst scored-against shift in USC history.

"Neil Josten said it last fall, didn't he?" Shane said into the mic, picking up where Jeremy left off so Jeremy could catch his breath around all the smiling and praise. "It's easy to be the best when you can throw numbers at any problem you come up against. We really wanted to see who we were when we didn't have that to hold us up."

"It was the most fun I've had in months," Jeremy said, "but if you'll forgive us for fading on you, we are absolutely wiped."

"Of course," the man said, obediently withdrawing his mic from their faces. "Thanks for stopping by to talk to us, and make sure to get some rest. We're all cheering for you next week."

"Thank you!" Jeremy said and trailed Shane back to the locker room.

The shower felt so good on his aching body he would've stayed there all night if his coaches weren't waiting for him to

56

explain himself. Jeremy waved goodbye to Shane as he headed out, then went down the side hall to where the coaches' doors were. Lisinski was the Trojans' fitness coach, whereas White handled offense and Jimenez defense. That third door was open, but the room was empty, and Jeremy found Jimenez sitting at Rhemann's desk in the final office. They'd told the Trojans they'd deconstruct the game on Monday, but Jeremy wasn't surprised to see them already going over their notes.

"Coach, Coach," Jeremy said in greeting, and took a seat when Rhemann pointed to it. Rhemann pulled a notebook over on top of their work: not to hide it from Jeremy, but to ensure it didn't distract either coach from whatever potential problem Jeremy had brought to them. Jeremy folded his hands together in his lap and twirled his thumbs around each other as he tried to figure out where to start.

At the beginning, he told himself, and squared his shoulders. "I have a huge favor to ask."

-

The trick to starting Saturdays off on the right foot was to get out of the house as early as possible. He'd realized years ago that he'd never be the first one awake, but Jeremy had a quiet theory that William Hunter never slept. Maybe his parents paid their butler to stay awake twenty-four seven. Either way, he was unsurprised to slip into the kitchen at five in the morning and find a full travel mug already set aside for him. Jeremy made a face at William, who knew better than to take it personally as he sipped from his own mug.

"Early even for you," William said, without explaining how he'd known Jeremy was up and about.

"Lot to do," Jeremy said evasively. "Anything I need to know before I head out?"

"Dinner is scheduled for seven. Seeing how Bryson got into town last night for the fundraiser, you'll be expected to make an appearance."

Jeremy winced. "That was this weekend?" William's calm stare was a little too knowing to be sympathetic. Jeremy raked a nervous hand through his hair as he looked away. He'd wasted years arguing against such events, as he had absolutely no relation to his stepfather's father, but his mother refused to budge. If the Congressman needed a picture-perfect family for photo ops, the Knox family was duty-bound to dress up and smile bright for an exhausting number of cameras. "Yeah, I should've kept better track of it, I know. But I really do have some things to take care of this morning, so if they ask where I went—"

"I'll inform Mr. Wilshire you'll be back by six," William finished for him. "Try to enjoy yourself until then."

"What would I do without you?"

"What would any of you do?" William returned primly as he went back to his morning paper.

Knowing Bryson was home had Jeremy slipping out the side door. His older brother's room was directly over the foyer, and Bryson spent most of the year at Yale on eastern time. There was a pretty good chance he was already awake, and a better chance that his presence was why William was already on the clock. Jeremy would rather leave without his keys than risk a confrontation this early in the morning. He was far too tired and sore to put himself through that.

He got out of the neighborhood before calling for a taxi. He was promised a ride within ten minutes, and Jeremy stood on the curb to sip his coffee while he waited. Jeremy checked the clock on his phone, decided it was probably still early enough on the east coast he'd be considered rude if he called now, and settled in for a long conversation with his driver instead.

The coffee shop closer to Laila and Cat's place wouldn't open until six, so Jeremy picked one just east of campus that unlocked their doors at half-past four. Despite the hour and day there were already four people in there: one in the far corner who was tapping away on a laptop, a couple going over a map as they argued last-minute itinerary changes for their weekend stay in Los Angeles, and a bedraggled man at the counter

58

asking if he could please just have a cup of hot water. Jeremy politely kept his distance until the man retreated to his table at the far wall.

He'd drained his coffee on the drive over, but it didn't seem to be helping. "Enough caffeine I'll see soundwaves," he ordered, and bought breakfast and a gift card as well. The receipt went into the zippered back of his wallet so he could file it later; it was always best to have a paper trail when dealing with his mother's bookkeeper. While his espresso shots were pulling and his sandwich was being heated, Jeremy carried the gift card to the patron who'd preceded him.

"Hey, good morning," he said as he got closer. "Sorry to bother you, but I think you dropped this up there? I saw it on the floor."

"Yeah," the man said, holding out his hand immediately. "Thank you. Didn't even notice."

"No problem," Jeremy said, and went back to wait for his things.

The other man waited until Jeremy collected his food and drink from the handoff tray before shuffling over and asking the cashier to check the balance on his new card. Jeremy hid a smile in his warm croissant and stared down at his phone, silently willing the hours to move faster. He went back to the register for a newspaper and bottle of water and idly wished he'd been brave enough to get his keys. He had a key to Laila and Cat's house, so he could've sneaked in and stolen his usual place on the couch to nap until a saner hour.

At seven he risked sending Laila a simple "Awake?"

He honestly didn't expect a response, but a minute later got "Define awake" as a response.

"I left without my keys," he sent her. "Awake enough to get the door in 30?"

"It's a good thing I like you," she said, and he knew to take it as a yes.

He dropped his bottle in the recycle bin and his newspaper in a basket where anyone could comb through it after him. He swung past the register one last time to get a pound of beans. There was just enough room in the shopping bag for his empty travel mug, so Jeremy squeezed it in there and set off toward the neighborhood Cat and Laila called home.

The block had been converted into student apartments ages ago, with most houses set up to fit between seven and twelve students. Laila's was the only one untouched, as it'd originally been used by the landlord and his team as an on-site office. When her uncle bought out most of the houses in the immediate area, he'd leased it to her at a ridiculously cheap price.

Jillian, the team's only fifth-year dealer, had rented out the third bedroom for the last few years, but she was used to Jeremy camping over on the weekend. She also slept like the dead in the room furthest from the front door, so Jeremy knew he wouldn't be bothering her by arriving so early.

He found Laila in the living room, half-curled up in her papasan chair. Jeremy set the beans down where she could see the blend and eased onto the couch cushion closest to her.

"Hey," he said. "Did you even sleep?"

"A few hours," she said with a listless shrug. "You?"

"A few," he agreed. He waited to see if she brought up last night's game, but the minutes dragged by in easy silence. Jeremy checked the clock on his phone and asked, "How early is too early to call someone? On the east coast, I mean."

"Kevin?" she guessed.

"No," Jeremy said. He didn't elaborate that he'd called Kevin last night, catching him right before the Foxes boarded their flight back to South Carolina to give him the good news. Jeremy had woken up to a string of text messages this morning that did nothing to make him feel better about this. A picture was forming around all of Kevin's scattered insights, and while Jeremy couldn't quite put his finger on it yet, he was left with the unsettling conviction that the Trojans were doing the right thing by risking a Raven on their lineup.

"Hey, Laila," he said. "I need your help with something."

"Sure," she said.

Rather than answer, Jeremy scrolled to the only unused number in his Contacts and dialed out. There was a chance no one would respond, given the hour and unknown number, but someone picked up right before it could cut to voicemail. An unfamiliar and accented voice answered with a neutral, "Yes?"

"Jean Moreau?" Jeremy asked. "Jeremy Knox."

Jean immediately hung up on him. Jeremy considered the blinking timer on his phone, amused despite himself. Laila pushed herself up on one arm to stare at him, suddenly looking very awake. Jeremy grimaced an apology at her for not taking two seconds to explain and tried Jean again. This time Jean let it go to only three rings, and he answered with the same "Yes?"

"Sorry about that," Jeremy said. "I'm juggling a few things here and think I hit the wrong button. This is Jeremy Knox, from USC? I got your number from Kevin after the game last night. Do you have a minute to talk?"

The silence that followed was so profound Jeremy had to see if the call was still connected. At last Jean said, "I need a few minutes."

"Sure, of course," Jeremy agreed. "I'm free all day, just call back whenever."

Jean hung up on him again, and Jeremy could turn his full attention on Laila. "We're signing Jean to the lineup next year," he said.

"This Jean?" she asked, gesturing to her own bare cheekbone. "You aren't serious. He's the Ravens' best defenseman. They'll do whatever it takes to keep him."

"No, they won't," Jeremy said. "Rather, they can't."

He hesitated, wondering how much he was allowed to say. He'd told Rhemann and Jimenez why Jean was up for grabs, and they'd agreed they wouldn't tell anyone outside the rest of the Trojans' seven-man staff. Jeremy wouldn't volunteer anything to the Trojans Jean didn't want them to know, but Laila and Cat were different. They were his best friends, and with every one of Kevin's texts making him feel like he was getting in way over his head, he was desperate for some backup.

"They're both asleep," Laila said when she realized he was stalling. "It's just us."

Jeremy scooted a little closer all the same. "He's too injured to finish the season. Kevin called it hazing, but this morning he said Jean is off the court until late June." Laila glanced down at her hands, silently counting weeks since Jean's disappearance, and Jeremy nodded when her eyes narrowed in alarm. "Supposedly Edgar Allan is trying to hush it up by transferring him out, which means he's ours if we can convince him to come over. For now he's hiding in South Carolina with Kevin."

"Inspiration for Kevin's shade the other week?" Laila asked.

"I wonder." Jeremy flexed his own left hand with nervous energy. "I asked him what he meant by that, but he didn't answer. Laila, you ever feel like—like you're making a choice you can't come back from? But even knowing everything could go completely sideways, you'd make that choice every time?"

"Every morning I wake up and choose to be your friend," she said dryly. She eased out of the papasan chair and grabbed the beans from the coffee table. "Come on. This conversation is going to need more caffeine."

62

CHAPTER FOUR
Jean

Jean hung up on Jeremy Knox a second time and immediately called Kevin. It took two attempts before Kevin answered, and his greeting was more a grumpy yawn than anything. Jean checked the time, saw it to be half-past ten, and figured the Foxes had been up late getting back from the west coast. He didn't waste time feeling sorry for the other man but demanded, "Why is Jeremy Knox calling me?"

"If you haven't figured it out yet, I can't help you."

"You are *not* trying to send me to the sunshine court," Jean said with incredulous dismay. "The only place more inappropriate than there would be here."

"Where else would you go?" Kevin asked, losing a bit of sleepiness for impatience.

"Penn State would have made more sense."

"Absolutely not," Kevin said, and Jean could almost hear the curl of his lip in distaste. Until Edgar Allan came south this last fall, they'd shared a district with Penn State and faced them throughout the regular season. They were each other's biggest rivals, and Kevin had always let that animosity get the better of his common sense. He would admit under duress that they were a stellar team, but he'd never say it with any real warmth. "I don't trust you that close to West Virginia."

"It's not your call to make," Jean said.

"I made it anyway," Kevin said, unrepentant. "Talk to him."

"I—" Jean started, but Kevin hung up before Jean got out the, "—won't."

Jean scowled down at his phone. The temptation to call

Kevin back and argue with him was almost blinding, but common sense said to let it go. Thanks to Nathaniel's risky gamble, his very survival hinged on making a professional athlete's salary after graduation, which meant he needed to find a team. Asking someone to take him in meant accepting that he was never going back to Evermore, and Jean didn't know if he could face that yet.

I am a Raven. My place is at Evermore. They were words he'd told himself a thousand times, but the comfort was gone now that his mantra was broken clean through: *I am Jean Moreau. I belong to the Moriyamas.*

Jean's stomach churned. He teetered back and forth between the truth he'd built his sanity around to survive Evermore and the truth Kevin forced on him: Jean could not return to Edgar Allan so long as he belonged to Ichirou. Jean didn't have the right to run from Riko, but how could he possibly defy the head of the Moriyama family? From every angle he was damned.

I am not a Raven, but if I am not a Raven then I am just Jean Moreau, but—

Kevin had acted where Jean could not, but how could he be grateful for this? The Trojans were wholesome in an unsettling, unhealthy way, and Jean was an Evermore Raven. Jean weighed his dismal options before tapping through to his call history and dialing out. If he cost the Trojans their coveted spirit award it was on them; they had to know this was a disaster waiting to happen.

"Jeremy here," was the immediate and upbeat greeting.

"It's too early on the west coast for you to be calling me," Jean said.

"I'm a morning person, what can I say?"

"Of course you are," Jean muttered.

Jeremy was good enough to pretend he didn't hear that. "I had a few minutes to talk to Kevin before last night's game. Sorry for gossiping about you behind your back, but Kevin said you're a bit of a free agent right now. I discussed it with the coaches last night, and they came back with a unanimous vote. We'd love to have you on the lineup if you're interested in signing with us."

"Would you?" Jean said, more a mocking rebuttal than a genuine question. "I lack Kevin's tolerance for your ridiculous publicity stunt."

"You're going to shake things up, we know," Jeremy said. "Ideally, you'd respect the team enough to not tarnish our image right out of the gate, but we're willing to risk it to bring you onboard. We've got a lot of room left to grow, and the Gold Court could really benefit from some fresh eyes next year."

Jean stared up at the ceiling, thinking through all the ways this was going to go wrong. If they signed him and he stepped out of line, would they cut him? If two teams got rid of him, would anyone else want to touch him with a ten-foot pole? The only schools willing to risk him would be those at the bottom of the barrel. Jean's value would tank past the point of recovery, and then what would Ichirou do to him?

Jeremy was still chattering away in his ear, listing selling points of both USC and life in Los Angeles. Jean didn't wait for him to stop before cutting in with, "Is it in the contract?"

"Uhhh?" Jeremy asked. "Not tracking."

"Not ruining your precious image," Jean said. "Is it written in the contract?"

"No," Jeremy said slowly, sounding more than a little confused. "We kind of, I don't know, assume that we're all adults here?"

"You will have to pen it in," Jean said. "I won't sign it unless you do."

It was the only way this worked: if Jean signed something that said he had to behave to be allowed to stay on the lineup, he could bite his tongue and stay his fists. It'd piss him off beyond the telling, but he could follow orders if it meant surviving another day. Without that black-and-white command his nature would get the better of him sooner or later, and then there'd be no saving him. They'd yank him from the lineup to save themselves and he'd be as good as dead.

Jeremy recovered faster than Jean expected him to. "Yeah, sure, if that's what it takes, that's what it takes. Kevin said there might be a few hiccups. Disconnects between the Ravens' way of doing things and our way. We'll figure out a middle ground as we go. I'll have Coach fix up the paperwork and we'll have it emailed over to Coach Wymack first thing Monday morning. Sound like a plan?"

"I'll read it, but just so it's said: you are making a mistake."

"No, I'm pretty sure I'm not," Jeremy said, with a smile Jean could hear from two thousand miles away. Jean had seen that smile in a half-dozen broadcasts and in the endless articles about the Trojans Kevin had loved to read. He could picture it too easily, and he dug his fingernails into his own face in vicious warning. Unaware there was a problem, Jeremy continued with easy cheer: "I'll let you go, but thanks for taking my call. You've got my number now if you come up with any other questions."

It was close enough to a goodbye, so Jean hung up on him.

He was willing to think the whole thing a strange dream, but when Wymack came over for dinner Monday night he brought a folder of paperwork for Jean to review. Jean pored over it in silence, letting most of it blur away to nothing until he found the only part that mattered: *Signed player agrees to present himself in accordance with USC Trojan standards.*

Beneath it was a list of the most important talking points, to include not speaking ill of opponents to anyone who would publicize it for clout and being a good sport on the court during matches. It was exactly what he'd asked for and needed, but reading it had Jean scowling at the papers. Raven detractors could complain about attitudes and violence all they wanted, but at least the Ravens embraced the nature of the game. How the Trojans consistently ranked in the Big Three when they put muzzles on their players was beyond him. At least this fall he'd finally see how much malice simmered behind their foolish masks.

One of the final pages had the list of available jersey numbers. Seemed the Trojans stuck to a system when assigning numbers to their players: the dealers took one through five, offense six through nineteen, defense twenty through thirty-nine, and goalies had the forties. Even if his number wasn't taken, they'd never let him have it so long as he was a backliner.

Jean pressed his fingers to the tattoo on his face, stomach roiling with sudden violence. He'd had 3 since he was fifteen. As soon as Riko bestowed a number on him, the Ravens were no longer allowed to put a 3 jersey on the court. It'd waited for him until he entered the lineup. To go from that to a double-digit was unthinkable, borderline offensive.

For a dizzying moment Jean considered tearing the stack of papers in half. He ought to return to Evermore. He knew the Ravens. He knew Edgar Allan. Why was he even considering leaving? If he trusted Ichirou's word to be good and believed the master would keep Riko from interfering with his brother's business, then why shouldn't Jean go back? Jean wrung his unsteady hands together, not caring how much it hurt if it kept him from destroying his best ticket out of here. It was barely enough, so he chucked the file toward the foot of his bed.

He spent Tuesday and Wednesday with the papers scattered on the sheets in front of him, thoughts going back and forth in constant, anxious circles. Wymack and Abby couldn't miss the mess as they came through on their occasional check-ins, but neither of them asked him if he'd made up his mind. Renee was the first to broach the topic when she stopped by on her way home from practice Wednesday evening.

"Still thinking about it?" She changed out his water glasses and then set to work putting the files back in order. More than one page was bent from leaving them strewn about while he slept, but Renee smoothed the edges flat with patient hands. "Do you want to talk about it?"

"I don't belong there," Jean said.

"No?"

"You're a better fit than I am," Jean said, a touch grumpily. "Unhinged optimist."

"I am happy here, but I think you will do better than you know." She laughed at the disgruntled look he sent her. "You've endured the storm long enough. Don't you think you're overdue for some rainbows?"

"Yours was the first I saw in years," Jean said, motioning to his head to indicate her hair. "We left Evermore for classes or away games, but we didn't exist outside in the world if we could help it. We belonged to the Nest."

If she'd been thoughtless enough to look at him with pity, Jean would have been able to stop, but Renee's expression was almost serene as she studied him. Jean was the first to look away as he tried to remember where he was going with this. "Evermore was a grave, and the only color we knew was blood. I'd forgotten anything could be…" *beautiful* was too reckless to say aloud, even if it was true; just hearing it in his thoughts was enough to make him wince.

"Well," Renee said when he trailed off, "isn't that reason enough to keep living? To rediscover simple delights one moment at a time, I mean. I used to count them on my fingers, reassuring myself there was still good in the world and reminding myself to keep looking for those blessings. Butterflies, fresh-baked bread, the crunch of leaves on an autumn morning, so on and so forth.

"They don't have to be profound," she said when she saw Jean's lost expression. "I started with one: the scent of fresh-cut grass. The first time I really noticed it was a few months after I moved in with Stephanie. She came in from mowing the lawn to make us both brunch, and it was the first time I felt like I was home." Her love was so tender it looked like grief as it curled her mouth and made her eyes shine. "What you hold onto is less important than the act of holding on itself. It's so easy to get lost in ourselves and this world. Sometimes you need to find your way back one tiny miracle at a time."

"I don't believe in miracles," Jean said.

"I have enough faith for us both," Renee promised. "I know one will find you sooner or later. In the meantime, find what will keep you alive, and then find the little things hidden beneath it. This could be the fresh start you need," she said, resting her hand atop USC's paperwork. "A new school, a different team, and enough sunlight to chase away Evermore's shadows. They are willing to take a chance on you. Aren't you?"

"I don't trust them," Jean said.

Renee's smile was patient. "I mean, aren't you willing to take a chance on *you*?"

"I don't have a choice," Jean said. "He will kill me if I don't have a team."

Renee considered that for a few moments. "The way Neil explained it to me, all Ichirou wants from you is the lion's share of your earnings. It's a lot to ask for, yes, but if his interest stops and starts with your bank accounts, then everything outside of those numbers is still within your control. Whether you have fun playing, where you go between games, who you spend your time with, that's all *your* choice. You could create a new life for yourself."

Renee's phone trilled with an incoming message, saving Jean the trouble of coming up with an intelligent response. "Dan," she said by way of apology. "She's on the way back to Fox Tower with our takeout. If you were a bit more mobile, I'd invite you over to eat with us. If you're in the mood for company, I could ask them over here instead?"

"Go," he told her, and rapped his knuckles on his papers in an agitated rhythm. "I have to sort this out."

Renee slid off the bed and started for the door. Two steps later she changed her mind and returned to him. She caught his face in a careful grip and leaned in to press a soft kiss to his temple.

"Believe in yourself," she said. "It will all work out."

She left him staring after her. When the door closed, Jean reached up and dug his fingernails in the gentle heat she'd left on his skin.

If he could write Renee off as an ignorant wretch, maybe she wouldn't rattle him so much, but she'd told him a month ago what it cost her to get to this point. She'd been violated and abused, had bloodied her hands to the point she still saw shadows there sometimes, and had taken her sweet time carving a man up to repay everything he'd ever done to her. How she'd found the strength to climb out of that pit when no one else thought her worth saving, Jean didn't know, but hand over bloodied hand she'd scaled the wall. She'd chosen life; she'd chosen hope. She'd chosen second chances, and now she was watching to see if he would follow.

He could—he should—go back to Evermore. He should reject the loophole Kevin offered him, no matter how real the threat sounded. With Ichirou in the mix, surely things would be different? It felt like a lie even as he tried to feed it to himself, and Jean thought he tasted blood. Even the Ravens didn't know the extent of what happened to Jean behind closed doors, and Ichirou would be so much further away. So long as Riko didn't take Jean off the court again, he wasn't interfering with Ichirou's plans for Jean's future. He could do whatever he liked.

He might not kill me, so I should go back, Jean thought. *I am Jean Moreau. My place is at Evermore. But—*

Going back meant marching back to hell on his own strength. And maybe Jean knew all the demons there by name and had a familiar spot carved out for himself amongst the flames, but hell was still hell, and there was an open door at his back with Ichirou's name on it.

I am not a Raven.

Jean scratched through the list of available jersey numbers, striking them all off as unworthy of his consideration, and scribbled a shaky signature on all the requisite lines. He almost broke the pen after the first one, but gamely stuck to it until he was done. He dropped the pen off the side of the bed and reached for the kitchen timer on the nightstand.

Wymack and Abby had given him permission to summon them for anything he wanted these last few weeks, but he'd refused. Whether he was hungry or thirsty or had to piss, he simply waited until the next time one of them showed up for another reason and then made his needs known. He wasn't going to make them feel wanted or admit he needed help. But now he finally cranked the dial up and back again to force an obnoxious ring.

Wymack stopped by not even twenty seconds later.

"I will change my mind if you do not take it," Jean said, putting the timer away.

"I'll get it faxed over in the morning," Wymack said, and collected the papers. "Anything else while I'm underfoot?"

Jean only shook his head, so Wymack left the room with Jean's future in his hands.

Jean knew when USC received it because he got a text message from Jeremy the next day that just said "Nineteen??" Based on the Trojans' strict numbering system, it wasn't about his future jersey number, which left only one option. Just as he figured it out, Jeremy sent a clarifying text, "You're a junior."

"The master," Jean started to type, then deleted it and started over. "Coach Moriyama graduated me early so I could start with Kevin and Riko at EAU."

Jean still wasn't sure how many forged documents or dollars were involved in that fiasco, but joining the Raven lineup at sixteen had been a living nightmare. They'd all been so much bigger and stronger than he was; he'd had to rely on simply being better. Getting shown up by a child had not endeared them at all to him, especially when he'd spent a week climbing into bed with them. If not for Zane, Jean's freshman year would have been significantly uglier, he was sure.

Jeremy's text distracted him before his thoughts could tilt down dangerous corridors. All he'd sent was a thumbs-up emoji. Hoping that was the end of an unnecessary conversation but not trusting Jeremy to stop while he was ahead, Jean turned his phone off.

There were only a handful of weeks left in the semester, and only one of his teachers had figured out how to get his final exam to him. Jean wasn't worried about his classes now that he had an obscene amount of time to get his coursework done, but he had a backlog of games to watch and a new team to study. He'd only played against USC during championships his freshman and sophomore year. He knew Kevin recorded all their matches like he'd perish if he missed a single one, but Jean hadn't seen the point of obsessing over a lineup that was only relevant in passing.

He could ask Kevin to loan him the tapes, but getting Kevin started on the Trojans was always a mistake. Jean would have to do the digging himself. The perfect match was scheduled for the following night, when USC and Edgar Allan went at each other in semifinals, but Jean had plenty of hours to kill between now and then and years' worth of games to catch up on.

By the time Friday's game started, Jean had a good idea of what to expect and had managed to retain half of the current lineup. USC lost, as Jean knew they would. They were very good, but their refusal to escalate to violence held them back when it was the Ravens they were up against. Jean had seen this same restraint in the Foxes only a few weeks ago, but whereas the toll it'd taken on the Foxes to behave had been noticeable, USC never seemed to lose a beat. They played a clean and enthusiastic game like the Ravens weren't hurting them at every available opportunity.

"Unhealthy," Jean said, but of course no one in the post-match show could hear him.

Someone caught up to Jeremy as the Trojans were filing into the locker room. Jean looked for the lie in his too-bright eyes and too-wide smile. Where was the disappointment, the frustration? Where was the grief at having been so close and failing? Did the Trojans legitimately not care so long as they were pleased with their game, or had they come to terms with this loss when they set themselves up against the Foxes? Jean didn't know, and for a moment he hated it with a blinding rage. No team should be so blasé about a loss, especially one of the Big Three. They could not be this good and not be at all upset about falling short.

"—and Jean on the line," Jeremy said, and the sound of his name distracted Jean from his seething.

"Worst time of year for someone to be injured," was the easy agreement. "Rumor has it Jean won't make it back in time for finals."

"Yeah, I spoke to Jean earlier this week. He's definitely done for the year, but he'll be back in the fall. He just won't be back in black." Jeremy's smile somehow got even bigger, and he was too excited to wait for a prompt. "Yesterday he faxed us over the last of the paperwork we needed to make this thing official, so I'm allowed to tell you: he's transferring to USC for his senior year."

Jean was slowly aware of someone in the doorway. Wymack and Abby had been watching the game in the living room, and they'd decided to leave the bedroom door open tonight in case Jean needed anything from them. There was no way either of them would've been able to hear the timer's chime go off over the sound of two TVs and a closed door. Now Wymack stood propped against the doorframe with a drink in his hand. Jean didn't have to ask him why he'd come; he must have gotten up the second they started gossiping about Jean's absence.

Jean muted the TV. "He doesn't even care that he lost."

"Think so?" Wymack asked.

"Fantastic," Jean said, echoing Jeremy's word choices with a mocking edge. "Talented. Great fun."

"It's not mutually exclusive, you know," Wymack said. When Jean frowned at him, he waved his free hand around in search of the right words. "Just because he's proud of his team

73

for how they played doesn't mean he's not disappointed they lost. Maybe he simply knows that there's a time to be hurt and a time to wish the best for the person who succeeded in his stead. Getting sore about it on live TV doesn't help anyone."

"Pretending he's not bothered by it doesn't help anyone either."

"No?" Wymack asked. "If someone's watching these interviews and looking for a role model, wouldn't you rather they choose Jeremy over Riko?"

"No. Edgar Allan is undefeated."

"When we beat them in two weeks, you and I will revisit this conversation."

Jean unmuted the TV, and Wymack took the hint and left.
-

With USC out of the running, Palmetto State and Edgar Allan were given a week off to rest before they'd have to face each other at Castle Evermore for finals. Jean idly wondered how anyone was supposed to focus on schoolwork considering all the chaos on the court. If he wasn't tabbing through his assignments without seeing any of what his teachers' notes said, he was watching USC games and tracking the online backlash against his abrupt transfer.

Not all of it was negative, though any attention was enough to make Jean's skin crawl. Riko couldn't be snagged for a comment, no matter how hard people tried to get ahold of him, and the Ravens weren't allowed to speak to the press. Edgar Allan's students were called on instead, and more than one was foolish enough to say they hadn't seen Jean since before spring break. Between Jean falling off the face of the earth and Kevin hinting at a cover-up for his own injury, the conspiracy theorists were working overtime.

Despite their efforts to shape public opinion, the louder voices would always side with Exy's most spectacular NCAA team. The amount of vitriol aimed Jean's way for transferring off the lineup during championships was almost impressive.

Jean received a single email from Zane that just said

74

"What the fuck, Johnny??" that Jean deleted unanswered. Zane didn't try again, and Jean wasn't sure if it was the festering wound between them or the master's orders that stayed his hand. He didn't have long to speculate on the Ravens' opinion, because a gift arrived for him toward the end of the week. The return address on the box was Evermore, and it was addressed to him by care of Wymack at the Foxhole Court.

Jean wasn't sure which Moriyama finally told his teammates where he was hiding, but he was very sure he did not want to open this box. He couldn't not, if it was from his teammates, but Jean stared down at it in silence as he tried to steel his nerves.

"It is not for you," he said, because Abby was still hovering.

"I'm not leaving," she said.

She held out her hand, but Jean quickly looked away when he saw the box cutter sitting in her palm. He remembered too well what its edge felt like on his skin and his fleeting, foolish sense of triumph as he told Riko he'd rather die than endure another day under Riko's sadistic thumb. Riko's slow smile had given him pause, but his hungry words were what stopped Jean entirely:

"If you're going to do it, make sure you do it right. Make sure you can't be saved. If you survive, I will bury you alive."

An empty but terrifying threat, except it wasn't. The next week the coaches had new furniture brought in for the locker rooms, and Riko snagged a box to shove Jean into. He'd spent three days curled up in it as it crumpled under the weight of everything Riko piled on top of it, face pressed to the sagging wall where Riko had left him the smallest of holes for air. The fear that Riko would never let him out was only slightly overshadowed by the fear of what Riko would do if he cried out for help, so he'd fought his escalating panic with everything he'd had.

Later, while Riko and the master were distracted discussing Moriyama madness, Kevin leaned into him and said,

75

"Promise me you won't try again. Promise me, Jean. I don't want to lose you."

Promise me, except he'd walked away years later without a second thought.

"Jean?" Abby asked.

Jean forced his memories and fear away and tilted the box toward Abby in silent demand. She didn't hesitate but sliced clean lines through the tape along its edges and center flap. Jean sent her a baleful look until she took a step back, and then he pried the box open to see what the Ravens saw fit to send him.

The sight of folded cloth almost fooled him into complacency: the Ravens had emptied out his dresser drawer and sent the least worn of the clothes he'd left behind. Since Ravens spent most of their sixteen-hour days geared up at Evermore, they tended to keep only four to five outfits for attending class. Kevin and Riko had quite a bit more, since they were required to put in significantly more face time with the press and the other teams, but Jean had settled for three. The Ravens sent him a pair of jeans and two shirts, all black of course, and he assumed a freshman would inherit the rest. At least all his boxers and socks were accounted for.

Beneath the clothes were his few personal possessions: namely, postcards and magnets Kevin had bought him while on the road with Riko for press events. Jean turned one postcard over in his hand, and his stomach knotted when he saw the back. Whatever message Kevin had written him or memory he'd shared was gone forever beneath layers of ink; someone had taken a thick sharpie to the entire thing. He checked another, then another, before grabbing the whole stack and flipping them. Quick hands scattered them, looking for anything he could salvage and coming back empty.

The magnets were in only marginally better shape, their surfaces and backings scratched through in several places. Jean's favorite, a small wooden bear with a red beret, had been roughly cut in half. He tried holding the pieces together, but it was missing a chunk from the middle and wouldn't line up. Maybe the last bit had fallen to the bottom of the box? He tipped it over to look inside, but the only other contents he saw were his class notebooks.

When he realized he finally had access to the notes he'd taken all year long, he quickly dumped them onto the bed in front of him. It was late to finally have these back, seeing how finals were only a week and a half away, but Jean was eager to make use of them. They were all black, as was required, but he'd written his class names on the fronts in white-out. He spread them out until he found the one for his economics class. He flipped it open, half-afraid to find the Ravens had ripped out pages while packing them, and realized the reality was far worse.

COWARD was written diagonally across the front page in sharpie, with a scribbled border surrounding it. Jean flinched away from the accusation so hard he almost tore the page out. The backside had jagged lines only, but the next sheet yelled **WASHOUT** at him.

"Jean," Abby said, but Jean kept flipping.

Page after page had been defaced, most with repeating, angry insults, some with just angry swipes and swirls. Ten pages in, Jean found a loose piece of stationery, and he picked it up to stare down at the unfamiliar handwriting. It took two sentences to realize it was a letter from one of his teammates, and Jean's stomach churned as he slowly read through the whole thing. The amount of vitriol Phil packed into it left Jean feeling cold and clammy. He slowly returned the letter to its spot. Five pages later there was another letter, this time in a cursive he instantly recognized as Jasmine's.

Don't, he thought, but he picked it up anyway.

Jean was distantly aware that Abby was returning his clothes and gifts to the box. She was quick to pile the loose notebooks in on top of them. He should stop her, but he couldn't look away from Jasmine's note. That Jasmine hated him had never been a secret; she had been competing with him

77

for Riko's attention for years and found it unforgivable that he was the one wearing Riko's number. Phil's letter had lashed out with reactive rage over Jean thinking he could walk away from all of them, but Jasmine's letter was unmitigated venom.

"Jean," Abby said quietly. "Stop."

Jean put Jasmine's letter back and moved the notebook away from Abby when she held out a hand for it. She frowned in disapproval but didn't snatch it away from him, so he was able to turn a few more pages. Now his fingers moved to each angry epithet, tracing the letters like he could feel their curves against his skin. The third letter he found was short and to the point, messy block lettering that hit twice as hard when he saw Grayson had signed it: *Have fun whoring your way to the top of another lineup, you useless bitch. #12*

For a moment he felt teeth on his throat. Jean swallowed hard against a rush of bile that left his mouth burning and slapped the notebook closed. Abby snatched it away from him immediately and returned it to the box. It took only seconds to fold its flaps closed, and she carried the box to her closet with quick steps.

"That's mine," he said, in a voice he didn't recognize. "Give it back."

Abby put it on the shelf and came back to him without a word. She was staring down at him, waiting for him to look at her, but he kept his gaze on her closet. Jean blinked and felt hot breath on his cheeks, blinked and remembered the weight of his racquet as he broke his own fingers for Riko's amusement, blinked and *drowning I'm—*

He didn't realize he'd reached for his own throat until Abby seized his wrist hard enough to hurt. "Jean."

"You never should have brought me here. You never should have interfered. You should have just—"

"Let them kill you?" Abby asked. "No."

"They never touched me."

"Stop lying to me."

Jean pulled against her grip. "A Fox wouldn't

understand."

"Probably not," Abby said. "My Foxes chose to fight back."

Jean's arms were healed, but his skin still remembered the feel of rope digging in. He tried yanking out of her grip again, but Abby wouldn't let him go. He settled for clawing lines into his forearm instead until she grabbed hold of that hand too.

He'd been furious with his parents for sending him to Evermore, but he'd still hoped to make the best of it. He'd loved Exy then, fiercely and violently, and learning from the man who'd created the sport was the honor and opportunity of a lifetime. Reality reared its ugly face only hours after landing in West Virginia. Finding out he was little more than Riko's dog outside of practices had him lashing out with all the youthful rage he could muster.

For five months he'd spit and cursed and fought. For five months he'd dragged himself off the ground no matter what violence and cruelty Riko heaped on him, and then one day he simply didn't have the strength. It made no sense to fight. Riko was a Moriyama, and he was a Moreau. The sooner he understood his place in the world, the easier it would be for him. The pain wouldn't stop, but knowing he deserved it would make it easier to bear. He could live with that; he had no choice.

He was furious at Abby for implying he'd never tried to fight, and more furious at the Foxes for keeping it together when he'd broken. They hadn't been up against Riko, except two of them had, and both Nathaniel and Kevin had walked away.

coward washout traitor sellout reject whore

"Fuck you," Jean said quietly, then louder: "*Fuck you.*"

"Please talk to Betsy."

"Give me back my box," Jean said. "It wasn't yours to take."

Abby got up and left without another word. Jean waited until he heard the distant murmur of her voice down the hall before pushing himself to his feet. He made a careful lap around the room to the closet. He could reach the shelf easily enough, though the weight of the box sent aching pressure through his chest. Jean set his package on the mattress, breathed through the soreness in his lungs, and settled by his pillow again.

Since Abby had packed his notebooks last, they were on top now. Jean's stomach roiled as he pulled his econ notes out again. Thinking maybe he'd just been unlucky with the first one he'd opened, he thumbed through the next few notebooks. The sight of bold ink said they were all a complete loss, and he held his breath like he could keep his churning stomach under control a little longer.

He was not at all surprised when the Foxes' shrink stopped by a half-hour later. She closed the bedroom door on the way in and made herself comfortable at his side. Jean let her calm voice go in one ear and out the other as he slowly made his way through the first notebook. She was close enough she couldn't miss the bold messages scribbled on every odd page, but he didn't look to see if she was trying to read his letters over his shoulder.

"Will you talk to me?" she asked at last.

"I will bite off my tongue first," he said. "I do not need it to play."

"Do you mind if I keep talking, then?"

"It wouldn't matter if I minded," Jean said. "Prisoners have no rights."

"You're a patient, not a prisoner," Dobson reminded him gently. "But if you would rather not speak, we can stay like this a while longer."

She would get bored of sitting with him sooner or later, but for now she seemed content to gaze into the distance and think her quiet thoughts. The longer she waited, the harder it was to ignore her. Jean had been looking for Riko and Zane for weeks, and their prolonged absence had left him adrift. Some plump shrink was not a valid substitute for a Raven, especially

80

not the King, but Jean was desperate enough he couldn't help but find it comforting. It was enough to distract him from his reading, and he finally closed his notebook. He expected her to open her mouth now that he'd given up ignoring her, but she didn't even look at him.

"Take me to the court," he said.

He expected pushback, but all she said was, "Can you make it out to my car?"

"I will," he said, shifting to the edge of the bed.

His knee throbbed when he got up, but it could take his weight in short bursts. He hobbled around the bed toward the door. Dobson had a hand up in a silent offer of assistance, but she kept her hand near her side so he wouldn't feel obligated to take her up on it. When he ignored her, she went ahead of him down the hall to speak with Abby. Jean heard snatches of it as he carefully made his way down the hall and knew Dobson was borrowing Abby's key and combo for the stadium.

After so many weeks trapped inside Abby's house, the night air was invigorating enough to send a chill down Jean's spine. He'd been poisoning himself, he knew, fighting Abby every time she tried to open a window or pull the blanket down from over her curtains. He'd been trying to recreate the stifling conditions of the Nest, frantic for something familiar to hold him together when everything else spiraled out of his control. He hadn't realized just how important Edgar Allan was to the Ravens' wellbeing. Apathy toward his major and an unrelenting exhaustion made his classes such a chore he'd always looked past the blessing of fresh air.

"I started with one," Renee had said, and while Jean couldn't put stock in her faith or her lighthearted assurances, he still tapped his thumb to his index finger and thought, *a cool evening breeze.* He felt foolish as he did it, but he also felt—alive, somehow, grounded by something other than his team's vitriol.

They were halfway to the Foxhole Court before Dobson said, "I admit sports are not my forte. I've always been more into theater—plays and musicals and the like. My grasp on Exy is still a bit shaky despite all these years at Palmetto State, but from what I understand it's indoor lacrosse?"

"Using feigned ignorance as bait is transparent," Jean said.

Dobson only asked, "Are there cutouts on the walls for the goalkeepers' nets, or…?"

"There aren't *nets*," Jean said, too offended to help himself. "There are sensors in the wall to—" He cut himself off in favor of muttering rudely in French. He didn't want to have a conversation with this annoying woman, but the longer he tried to ignore her the deeper her idiotic words seemed to burrow into his brain. Finally, he gave an irritated huff and launched into the shortest explanation he could. Dobson listened to it all in obedient silence, and Jean managed to wrap it up as she parked at the stadium.

"Thank you," she said. "I wondered."

"I refuse to think none of them explained it to you," he said. "Kevin would have."

"I wondered if you cared enough to correct me," she returned easily, and gestured out her windshield toward the stadium. "I wasn't sure if we were here for comfort or contrition."

Contrition. It could have been chance that she used that word, but Jean was feeling untrusting. The look on her face had Jean reaching for his door handle, but he couldn't look away from her even when he found it. "You've been talking to Kevin."

"I am his therapist," Dobson pointed out, calm in the face of his jagged accusation. "He remembers how difficult it was to trust me when he transferred, and as such gave me open permission to share anything we've discussed if it will make you more comfortable with me. I would really like to talk to you, Jean."

"I have nothing to say to you."

"Not today, maybe," she allowed. "But if you are ever willing to talk, please know that I want to hear you. If it is easier once you've gone to California and have the safety of distance, I am willing to wait for you. At the risk of sounding immodest, I daresay I'm the most qualified person to speak to you about what you're dealing with right now."

He had his mouth open to refute that when he remembered who else was on her roster of patients: Nathaniel Wesninski and that creepy little goalkeeper Andrew Minyard. The Foxhole Court was a veritable goldmine of personal issues and abuse. Jean wanted nothing to do with her, but she'd weathered some intolerable personalities thus far. It didn't make him like her any, but he couldn't deny a smidgen of respect.

"We're going," he said, pulling the handle.

Dobson got out without further comment and let him into the stadium. They found a place up in the stands to stare at the court. Jean wasn't sure how long they sat there before Kevin, Nathaniel, and Andrew showed up. Andrew followed the weight of Jean's stare right to him. Nathaniel needed only a moment longer. Kevin saw nothing but the court, but Jean had stopped hoping for more than that years ago.

Jean wanted nothing to do with them, so as soon as the court door closed behind the last of them, he got up and went down the stairs toward the locker room. Dobson followed him down without comment and took him back to Abby's house.

"Welcome home," Abby said when they arrived.

Jean wanted to say *This is not home*, but he needed all his breath to keep moving after pushing his knee so hard. He was asleep as soon as his head hit the pillow, and this time he didn't dream.

CHAPTER FIVE
Jean

The day before Edgar Allan and Palmetto State were to face each other in finals, Abby brought Jean his dinner and an unexpected problem: "I'd rather not leave you here in the house alone tomorrow, but everyone I trust to sit with you will be in West Virginia with us."

That the Foxes were taking their shrink along was surprising, but Jean supposed she'd have her work cut out for her when the Ravens annihilated them. He didn't care why she was going so long as she wasn't here. She'd been by almost every evening since the Raven box arrived. She had nothing to say to him past a warm greeting, seemingly content to simply sit beside him on the bed, but he didn't trust her or want the comfort of her steady company.

"I considered taking the safety in numbers route and moving you to Fox Tower for it," Abby said, and remembered a moment later he wouldn't understand. "It's the athletes' dorm, which means there are plenty of bodies to be a shield. If we put some gauze over your tattoo you might fly under the radar long enough to camp out in the Foxes' empty rooms."

Aside from his one outing with Dobson, Jean had spent the last six weeks going between this bedroom and the restroom. He would prefer to return to the stadium, but he didn't think he could handle it alone. A crowded athletes' dorm sounded like the next closest thing to normal. "I will go there."

"I don't have a card to access the building, but I'll see who can come collect you in the morning," she said. "If I remember correctly, everyone's due at the court by nine-thirty so we can be on the road by ten."

Maybe he would've resisted the idea a little more if he'd realized who was going to come pick him up. Logic demanded it be Kevin, but Jean was walking careful laps around the bedroom when Nathaniel arrived at the house the following morning. Jean's bedroom door was open, so he saw his unwelcome guest heading down the hall toward him. He scowled and went back to his slow pacing. His knee still felt a bit unsteady, with a soreness that was probably his injury but just as likely disuse. He was impatient to get back to his workouts, but Abby was guessing another six weeks on his ribs to be safe.

Nathaniel stopped in the doorway to wait on him, and Jean sighed as he ended his last lap in front of the shorter man. "Of course it'd be you, you tedious malcontent."

"Good morning to you, too." Nathaniel held up an oversized bandage.

For a moment Jean was tempted to refuse it. His number was a mark of pride, proof of his importance and his ranking in Exy's future. It wasn't something to hide just so he could sneak about like a common thief. Sneaking was better than risking the press showing up, though, so Jean took the bandage and peeled the protective strips off.

He knew exactly where his number was, consequence of staring at it for so many years and tracing its lines with his fingers. He pressed the bandage into place and flicked the crumpled trash at Nathaniel. Nathaniel wasn't decent enough to take the bait but motioned for him to come along and went back down the hall.

Following was easy, and every slow step Jean took after Nathaniel eased a little of the hollow in his chest. Ravens weren't meant to be alone, and with Nathaniel here now he could feel just how worn away he was despite the Foxes' attempt to always keep another body in the house with him. Nathaniel was different; he always would be. He wasn't a Raven, but he was, same as Jean. He was Jean's misplaced

85

forever partner, an unfulfilled promise Jean had stopped believing in years ago.

There were two cars in the driveway and a third parked at the curb. It was the latter Nathaniel went for. He got the locks undone with a click of his fob and opened the passenger door for Jean. Getting in hurt, but he held tight to the top of the door and the headrest as he eased himself in. Nathaniel waited until his long limbs were out of the way before pushing the door closed and going around to the driver's side. Jean hadn't seen anyone else in the car when he got in, but he flipped down the sunshade and checked the backseat in its mirror anyway.

Jean thought maybe they'd make it to campus without a word, but of course Nathaniel had to open his mouth as soon as they were on the road: "I never thanked you for watching out for me at Evermore."

"I did no such thing," Jean said.

"Kevin knew you would. I just didn't see his message in time."

"You are only here now because you are an abominable cockroach," Jean said, because he couldn't, wouldn't dwell on that. He closed his eyes against the memory of Nathaniel's skin peeling off, thin as gauze beneath Riko's knives. Jean had been equal parts horrified and relieved bearing witness to it all: destroyed by how easy it was to fall into Kevin's bystander role but grateful to have Riko's considerable energy and imagination focused on someone else for once.

It wasn't his place to stay Riko's hand; all he could do was put Nathaniel back together afterward. Stitch by stitch, tape and gauze, Jean had done his best to keep the wayward child moving. The helpless anger—*why the fuck did he get caught*—had been mitigated by a more foolish what-if—*what if he stays*, what if Jean finally had his permanent partner and someone to suffer alongside.

Of course Nathaniel had left, but he'd still taken a number on his way out. Jean was left with the horrific fallout of shattered promises. For a blinding moment Jean felt hands in

86

his hair and rough sheets on his face; for a moment he heard Zane's bedsprings creak as he turned his back on the violence he'd invited to their room. Jean dug his nails into his arms and forced his eyes open, needing to see the morning campus instead of his shadowed room at the Nest. Zane had paid dearly for that betrayal, but Jean took no satisfaction in Riko's cruel games.

"Jean," Nathaniel said. "Andrew taught me the importance of give and take and of repaying one's debts, so I'm going to give you something in exchange for keeping me alive long enough to come home. We're going to beat Riko tonight."

"Lying helps no one," Jean said. "You have no chance."

"Promise me you'll watch the match."

"I have to watch, but I know what I'll see."

Nathaniel accepted that without argument. A few minutes later he took a curving road up a hill. Jean studied Fox Tower out of his window as Nathaniel drove around to the crowded parking lot situated out back. The only free spots were in the last rows, so Nathaniel let Jean out at the curb before parking. Jean got out the same way he got in, but getting up hurt more than getting down did, and his knee creaked as he hauled himself up. Jean kept his face turned away from the car so Nathaniel wouldn't see the face he made.

Nathaniel rejoined him as soon as he parked and got them inside with the tap of his wallet against a sensor on the door. Another set of doors let them into the dorm's main lobby. The elevator was quick to arrive and dumped a half-dozen students out as soon as the doors slid open. Most rushed past, on their way to their early morning classes, but one stopped to pump his fist at Nathaniel in enthusiastic support.

"Kick their asses!" he said.

"That's the plan," Nathaniel said, letting Jean into the elevator ahead of him.

The third floor was empty when they got out. Jean's knee was starting to fight him every step of the way, but Nathaniel didn't take him very far. He let them into a sparsely decorated dorm room. Two people were waiting for them, but Jean barely had time to register it as Andrew and Kevin before he threw himself back out of the room faster than his body wanted him to go. Nathaniel came after him immediately, grabbing hold of him before he could book it back to the elevators.

"No," Jean said. He tried to wrench free and nearly lost his footing when his ribs screamed at him. "*No*."

He dug his feet in when Nathaniel pulled, and his knee almost gave out on him. Nathaniel saw his leg start to buckle and changed tactics, pushing him at the wall instead so he had something to lean against. That hurt, too, but not as badly as falling might. As soon as Nathaniel was sure he had his balance back, he fitted himself against Jean like a crutch and forced him into the dorm room.

"What have you done?" Jean demanded in French before Nathaniel even got the door closed behind them. "You—you suicidal—"

Words failed him, because what words could possibly be strong enough for this? Kevin's tattoo was gone, hidden behind a symbol that Jean at first thought was a keyhole. Understanding was just barely out of reach, but Jean didn't need or want to know what it was supposed to be. All that mattered was that Kevin had scoured his number off his face. It was cleaner than what the Wesninski lot had done to Nathaniel, but at least Nathaniel hadn't had a choice in losing his. This was deliberate erasure from a man who knew better.

"You're going to face him tonight," Jean said, fighting for a coherent thought. "Like that? Are you mad?"

"No, I'm angry," Kevin said. Jean searched for the lie in his careless dismissal, but Kevin was too good an actor to give away the game. "I am tired of being called second when I am better than he will ever be. Tonight they'll see how wrong they were about us."

"We could get rid of yours, too." Nathaniel reached up quicker than Jean could fend him off and ripped the bandage

88

off his face.

"I will kill you and myself if you try."

"Leaving," Andrew said in English.

He stubbed a cigarette out on the windowsill and slid off of the desk he'd been using as a chair. He and Kevin collected their bags on the way to the door. Nathaniel held up the bandage in offering as Kevin approached, and Kevin applied it to his own face to hide his new marking. A surprise he didn't dare spoil too early, Jean assumed, and then Kevin and Andrew were gone.

Nathaniel closed the door behind them. He had to feel Jean's stare boring holes in his face, but he didn't acknowledge it. Instead he pointed out the most relevant and basic things about the dorm room Jean would be camping out in today.

"Bathroom around the corner with medicine above the sink. Take what you need from the fridge. Remote should be by the couch, and the TV's been set to the right channel already." He thought a moment, then pointed again. "Kevin thinks you'll spend the day watching USC games. His laptop is on his desk, and he's temporarily disabled the password for it. There should be a shortcut on his desktop to the right folder."

"What have you done?" Jean demanded.

"It wasn't my call. He didn't tell any of us what he was planning; he just came back to the dorm like that." The smile that curved Nathaniel's mouth was slow and hungry and hateful. It twitched a bit as Nathaniel tried to force it away, but he finally had to use the side of his hand to smooth it off his face. The look he turned on Jean was almost serene, but Jean still saw the madness in his eyes. "Need anything else? If not, I need to go."

"I should have let him kill you," Jean said.

"Probably," Nathaniel agreed, "but you didn't, so here we all are. Coach won't keep us there overnight, so we'll be back sometime before dawn."

He left and locked the door behind himself. Jean stayed where he was a few minutes more: in part to let the throbbing in his knee subside, in part so the pounding in his head would lessen enough he could see straight. It got to the point where standing hurt more than moving did, so Jean limped across the room. He collected Kevin's laptop before sinking onto the couch, unsure when he'd be able to stand again, but he stared down at its closed lid with dread chewing holes in his heart.

Idly he thought he should've said goodbye to Kevin, because there was no way Riko was going to let him walk away. Riko would kill Kevin, the master would kill Riko, and just like that the perfect Court was in shambles. At least Nathaniel and Andrew might survive. With Jean that made three, and three was enough to rebuild from.

Unbidden he reached for his face, and Jean traced his tattoo with a trembling fingertip.

-

Jean muted the TV at the halftime break. He didn't have it in him to turn the game off, but he didn't want to hear what anyone was saying about what was happening on the court. Jean was sickened by how easily they feigned disappointment in the Foxes' first-half performance and just as annoyed by how quick they were to remind people that the game could only end one way. Jean couldn't explain that restless rage, because of course the Foxes were going to lose. In no universe could they beat the Ravens on a fair playing field.

Rather than deconstruct that irritation, he spent the break exploring the dorm room with unabashed interest. There were four beds in the bedroom, set across from each other as two sets of bunks. Dressers packed to bursting with clothes barely fit in the remaining space, and two lumpy beanbag chairs were precariously balanced on top of them. Jean assumed Andrew's twin owned the remaining bed, but aside from his outstanding murder charge there was nothing interesting about that Fox.

The kitchen was a curious thing, and Jean took his time ransacking the cabinets. The Nest had a kitchenette, but aside from the fridge and coffee maker it required no other appliances. The Ravens' approved meals and snacks were all provided for them: in part to ensure they remained on track with their nutrition and mostly because the team had no time to prep any food for themselves. The Foxes had a two-burner stove top, a toaster, and a microwave. Jean hadn't seen a microwave in years.

Getting something made for dinner was only half the problem; the other half was in figuring out if there was anything worth eating. The freezer was a disaster, stuffed with breakfast sandwiches on croissants, some calzone-style meals with obscene amounts of fat in them, and premade pasta dishes full of processed ingredients. The fridge wasn't much better off, with milk, juice, and vodka dominating one shelf and takeout boxes haphazardly stacked on another. There was an entire drawer dedicated to cheese. How Kevin ever opened the fridge without having an aneurysm, Jean didn't know.

Before he could resign himself to going hungry, he found a plastic carton of salad mix behind the vodka and a Tupperware of cooked chicken that didn't smell like it'd gone bad yet. It took three tries to find the silverware drawer, and Jean stared down in disbelief. Half of the drawer was full of mini candy bars. He threw them all into the trash before grabbing a fork and slamming the drawer shut.

He and his chicken salad made it back to the couch with only a minute to spare. Dinner was set aside long enough for him to settle Kevin's laptop on his lap again, and Jean pulled up a fresh USC game. He couldn't not watch the Fox and Raven match, but it'd be nice to have a real match waiting as a palate cleanser.

A blur of orange had him glancing up to confirm the Foxes were at the court door. Jean looked back down at the laptop to see if the game had finished buffering, and then his brain caught up with his eyes. He shoved the laptop aside with careless urgency.

Fuck USC and all their games past and present. Kevin Day was crossing Evermore's court with his racquet in his left hand. Jean pushed off the couch and moved to the coffee table

91

for a closer view.

"No," he said to the TV. "You can't."

He couldn't, but he did.

The Ravens had watched Kevin's slow and graceless return to Exy, and they'd had ample time to study the way he was forced to play while using his less dominant hand. Somewhere along the way they'd all forgotten what he used to be like. Jean thought of Kevin's words this morning, *I am tired of being called second when I am better than he will ever be*, and his blood roared like static in his ears as Kevin made fools of the Raven defense line.

He was furious with them for falling apart, and angrier at the coaches for putting Grayson and Zane in together. They were the next-best defensemen after Jean, but they had loathed each other since Jean's freshman year. After what Riko did to them in January, they could barely stand to be in the same room together. Getting played for fools by Kevin was only throwing fuel on the fire.

It was inevitable they'd break first, and unsurprising it was Zane who started swinging. Kevin was never shy with his opinion when it came to Exy, and even now with so much on the line he was likely tearing Zane a new one for being such a fuckup. Zane went after Kevin with everything he had, and it took both teams to haul him off. He was thrown off with a red card, and Abby was let on to give Kevin a quick checkup. He waved off her concern as unnecessary and proceeded to score on the foul shot.

Kevin wasn't enough, of course. One man could not hold an entire team together. But then the Ravens made the critical mistake of fouling Andrew Minyard himself, and Nathaniel crossed the court in record time to throw Brayden off his feet. The master took advantage of the foul to call on fresh players, but Nathaniel and Boyd stayed near Andrew as the Ravens traded places. Riko's return to the court was inevitable: the King would cut his Queen's throat and be done with the whole charade at last.

In response, Andrew sent Boyd off the court. Jean saw the limp in the tall backliner's step as he made his way to the door, but his replacement didn't take his spot. The Foxes' captain instead went across the court to wait alongside Kevin. Nathaniel, in turn, moved to guard Riko.

"This is madness," Jean said. "Even you aren't that idiotic."

Kevin had sworn he recruited Nathaniel Wesninski by accident, won over by his desperate devotion and the anonymity the Foxes needed. Jean had never truly believed him, especially after seeing Nathaniel's performance on the court. October had been a rough match, but December had been awful. He'd looked much better in the USC game the other week, but he'd been playing as a striker. Nathaniel didn't have enough experience to guard Riko on the court, and with so much on the line it was ridiculous he'd even try.

The match restarted, and slowly Jean understood it wasn't his skill the Foxes were relying on. Minute by minute the match ticked away; minute after minute the fastest striker in Class I Exy forced Riko away from Andrew's goal. He was not the better player, but he didn't have to be. He simply had to put a leash around Riko's neck and pull as hard as he could. And pull he did, dogging Riko with a ferocity that made Jean's skin crawl in sympathetic irritation from all these miles away.

Kevin scored, then scored again. With Riko muzzled and Kevin free to do as he liked, the Foxes forced the game to a tie. Wayne managed to pull the Ravens ahead ten minutes later, but Kevin tied it up with five minutes to go.

They were doomed to a shootout. Jean couldn't see the Foxes' faces through their helmets, but there was a disconcerting jerk to the way they all moved that said they were barely conscious anymore between exhaustion and the compounding aches of a violent game. They'd buckle in a shootout, but that they'd forced it to this point was impressive.

With ten seconds left on the clock, Jean thought maybe he'd apologize to Nathaniel for calling the Foxes worthless trash bags. At five seconds, Jean thought he'd even admit the team had performed better than he'd thought possible.

At two seconds, Kevin scored.

The goal went red, the sportscasters came out of their seats hollering, and the final buzzer rang on a Fox win.

Nathaniel had pushed himself to the point of breaking to hold the line, and he fell like a stone to his hands and knees. Andrew stayed behind in his goal, but the rest of the Foxes ran screaming across the court toward Kevin. The Ravens were statues, all heads turned up toward the scoreboard and the unbelievable numbers there.

Jean tuned all of them out. None of them mattered save the dumbfounded King standing over Nathaniel's fallen body. The heat that ripped through Jean was so violent and hungry his vision went black for a moment.

Nathaniel pried his helmet off with obvious effort and followed Riko's gaze. The movement was enough to get Riko's attention, and Riko dragged his stare down to the Fox striker. Nathaniel's mouth was moving, because of course he'd have to run his mouth despite being worn down to the bone. Jean knew none of the players were wearing a mic, but he wanted to shush the sportscasters who were practically yelling their incredulity at the camera. He needed to know what Nathaniel was saying in this historic moment.

He changed his mind a heartbeat later, because the look that crossed Riko's face was ugly. Riko raised his racquet with lethal intent, and Jean reached for the screen like he could somehow pull Nathaniel away. There was a sharp, alarmed noise from the sportscasters as they realized too late that Nathaniel was going to get murdered on live TV. The Foxes were all the way at the Ravens' goal, and no Raven would dare stay Riko's hand. The only one who had any chance was Andrew, who threw himself out of his goal like all of hell was at his heels.

Run, Jean thought. He didn't know if he was thinking it at Andrew or Nathaniel. *Run.*

94

Riko's racquet came down, and Andrew's came up. The force of his oversized goalkeeper racquet crashing into Riko's arm threw Riko's stick one way and Riko the other.

Jean was across the room in a heartbeat to slam the TV into the wall behind it. For a perfect moment the stadium and the sportscasters were dead silent, and the only sound being broadcast was Riko's scream. It was distorted through the court walls but still loud enough to be horrifying.

Everyone was talking again. Jean heard the horror and panic in their voices as they babbled over each other, but he couldn't make out their words through the roaring in his ears. He stared at Riko where he'd fallen over, watching until the Ravens' coaches and nurses swarmed him to hide him from view. The Foxes found enough strength to do the same for Nathaniel, forming a frantic barrier around their fallen teammate.

The cameras bounced between the sidelines, first to where a referee was barely keeping Wymack and Abby from charging the court on the Away side and then to where the master stood frozen with his Ravens on the Home.

It was inevitable that it would descend to violence, but with most of the referees and Raven staff on the court, intercepting the howling Ravens was easy work. The Foxes were quick to take a hint, and they hauled each other up so they could stumble off the court together. Jean didn't watch them go. He couldn't look away from Riko where he sat defeated and broken beside Josiah. The camera cut away to the sportscasters at their table a heartbeat later, and some of their words finally made it through:

"—advised us not to show a replay," said the pale woman on the left. She was talking to the camera, but she and her partner were both watching something off-screen. Jean knew they were watching what they'd been forbidden to air, judging by the way she suddenly clapped a hand over her mouth and her partner flinched. She audibly choked as she tried to find her words again. "If you're just tuning in—"

Jean threw the TV off its stand, heedless of the white-hot pain that lanced through his chest at such a violent move. He closed his eyes and watched in his mind's eye again and again what they refused to give him. He only wished he could slow the memory down to better see it: the unnatural way Riko's forearm popped into a V, the way shattered bone tore holes in his arm under force of impact, the way he *screamed*.

Jean sank to the ground and leaned to one side to get the weight off his aching knee. He folded his arms across the entertainment center and looked to the TV where it was sideways and half-tipped away from him. He hadn't been able to send it far, and its cord was long enough that it was miraculously still plugged in. Riko was being led off the court between Josiah and Miriam, and although the Ravens' coaches tried to body the cameramen out of the way someone got a shot of the shuttered look on Riko's face and the agonized tears still streaking down his cheeks.

Jean laughed so hard he felt faint.

Unsurprisingly, the ERC chose to forego the standard championships ceremony for now. Jean watched the news for hours, sometimes flipping to other channels to see if there was any coverage. With no new news forthcoming, he kept hearing the same words and phrases repeated, and the Foxes' unimaginable victory was mostly lost behind the violent near-miss at the end. The alarm for Riko's well-being was nauseating to hear, but when the broadcast's locale finally shifted to a four-man team at the studio the conversation took a more practical turn. Before long the man at the right dragged the emphasis back to Riko's violent intentions.

"He could have died tonight," he insisted to his companions. "We all saw—"

One of his companions tried to interject, "Now, now, Joe, all of this is just hearsay right now, and—"

Joe wouldn't be deterred, even as the other kept talking: "—how close he got. If Andrew had been a half-second slower—"

"—can't just make wild accusations like this, grounded on conspiracy and not facts—"

"Where is Jean?" the lone woman on the far left asked, and that was so unexpected she startled her companions into silence. She was running her fingertips along the back of her left hand as she stared down at the desk. "Just a few weeks ago Kevin implied a cover-up regarding his own injury. No one has seen Jean in over a month, even though the official story was he was only out with a sprain. What are they doing to the perfect Court?"

"That is a very bold thing to say, Denise," the man beside her said.

There was an unspoken warning behind that reprimand: it was far too early for any of them to make such accusations no matter what they'd all seen. Jean assumed they were trying to avoid a potential lawsuit from Edgar Allan. After a tense few moments of silence, they decided either by silent vote or via a cue from their earpieces to switch the topic to the game itself.

Jean eased himself across the carpet closer to the TV. He couldn't lift it back to its stand, but with the help of some breathless swearing he was able to set it on its feet. He watched as stellar plays were rehashed and complimented. The Ravens were finally called out for their brutal playing style, two hours too late to help anyone, and Nathaniel's risky move to the defense line was lauded as genius.

"We've had pretty limited access to the Foxes since the final bell, on account of…" Joe waved his hand to indicate the obvious but didn't let himself get distracted by speaking on it again, "but what we've heard from Coach Wymack is that the idea came from Andrew. Not what any of us would have guessed, I think it's safe to say?"

He looked to his team for their emphatic nods. "For the last few years, he's made it clear that he doesn't have a horse in the race, but he's stepped it up this spring in an astounding way. That he could see exactly what his team needed in such an important match and that he trusted them to pull it off says worlds for both how far he's come and how much respect his teammates have for him. I for one am beyond excited to see how he continues to grow from here."

"He'll be Court," Jean told them, but they yammered away oblivious.

He watched and waited, sure they'd be allowed an interview with the Foxes or Ravens eventually and hoping for an update on Riko's health. Time dragged by with no real updates, and at last Jean reached for the laptop. He left the TV on in the background just in case and closed the USC game in favor of rewatching tonight's game from the top. Five minutes in, Jean's phone dinged with a text from Renee:

"Now do you believe in miracles?"

"That wasn't a miracle," Jean typed out. "That was the Foxes."

"That you admitted it is miracle enough for me," was her cheeky response. Soon after was a warning: "Sounds like we'll be staying here overnight after all so we can pick up our trophy in the morning. Coach is trying to find us a hotel, but they still won't let us leave the stadium. Will you be all right there?"

Jean looked across the room, checking the angle of the lock on the door. "Yes."

"Get some rest," she sent.

Jean sighed and set his phone aside. The TV was now displaying a scrolling list of upcoming Exy graduates who'd been signed to major or professional teams. Jean watched for the Ravens' section, took quiet note of Zane's contract with the Montana Rustics, and forcibly turned his attention back to the laptop.

Irritation had him pausing the game again, and he scrolled back to the beginning before going in search of paper and pen. Getting up sent a warning twinge through his knee, reminding him it was just barely healed, but he ignored it in favor of ransacking the desks. He found what he needed, returned to his spot on the floor, and began taking notes on every time Kevin and Nathaniel had been bullied by the Raven backliners. He went in and out of French as he wrote, depending on how agitated he was and how quickly he needed to get his thoughts out, but trusted them to be able to make sense of his scribbled tirade.

When he was done, he had almost four pages of scathing commentary and he was so tired his vision was swimming. The floor was killing his tailbone, so he hoisted himself up onto the couch. The room was warm enough he thought he could make do without a blanket, and he fell asleep with the TV humming in the background.

CHAPTER SIX
Jean

Jean was startled awake by the sound of his phone ringing. He scrubbed a tired hand across his eyes and sent a bleary look around the dorm room. Predawn sunlight was drifting through the gaps in the curtain at the far end of the room. The TV was still going, though it was currently playing commercials. Jean tried blinking the fogginess out of his thoughts and was distantly annoyed at how difficult it was. He wasn't sure how long he'd been asleep, but just a few months ago it would have been enough.

He belatedly realized what woke him, but by the time he looked for his phone the ringing had stopped. It started up again as he was reaching for it, and Jean saw Renee's number on the screen.

"Yes," he said in greeting.

"Jean," she said, with obvious relief. "Good morning, I woke you, I'm sorry."

Jean put his free hand over his ear, trying to hear past her. At least one person was yelling, but it was far too muffled for Jean to make out. She'd put a door or two between herself and the fight, he guessed. Renee wasn't waiting for him to respond, but what came out of her mouth next had him going perfectly still:

"Can you trust me one more time?"

"Your tone says I will regret it," Jean said.

"Please."

Jean looked to the dorm room door, saw it was still locked, and said, "Once more."

"I need you to keep the TV off today," Renee said. "No

news. No internet. Neil told me Kevin has a backlog of Trojan games on his computer. Watch those and nothing else. Can you do that?"

Jean's phone creaked in his clenching grip. "Are they hurt?"

"No," she said, so quickly he would have doubted her if not for the fond warmth in her voice. "No, we're all okay. I promise. It's just… I really think this is a conversation we need to have face-to-face, okay? I'll let you know as soon as we're on the road, and—" There was the sound of something heavy falling and the distinctive sound of glass breaking. The yelling had stopped, at least. "Jean, I need to go referee."

Jean looked at the TV, then slowly reached out and picked up the remote. His finger hovered over the power button as he warred between the sense that something was very wrong, and the surety Renee wouldn't lie to him about Kevin or Nathaniel. At length he pressed down to turn the TV off and said, "I won't watch."

"Thank you," she said, and was gone immediately.

It made for a wretchedly slow morning, but Jean had survived weeks of boring days trapped in Abby's house. He went from the living room to the bathroom to the kitchen as needed. That gnawing sensation in his chest never eased, but he attempted to distract himself as best he could by watching Trojan games. Partway through the second match he considered going back to bed, if only to help kill some time, and then his phone chimed on an incoming message.

It was a group text from Jeremy to Jean and Kevin: "Jesus, I'm so sorry. Are you guys okay?"

Jean's heart tripped in his chest. He looked from his phone to the remote to the darkened TV, then over at the laptop sitting on the coffee table. Whatever Renee didn't want him to know yet was starting to make the morning rounds. Renee had told him not to get his answers from the news, but she hadn't said he couldn't get it from someone else. He looked down at Jeremy's text, thumb hovering over the OK button to open a response. At the last moment he went one button over and dialed out.

Jeremy picked up immediately, and the soft care in his, "Hey, are you good?" had every hair standing on end. For a moment Jean felt the misstep and thought he really ought to wait for Renee, but he swallowed against his dread and demanded,

"What happened?"

The silence that followed was endless. Jean's mind filled it with a thousand miserable possibilities, and then Jeremy finally said: "I'm sorry. I thought you heard. I don't know if I should be the one to…" Jeremy trailed off, and Jean thought perhaps he was going to hang up rather than explain. Then he took a deep breath and said, "It's Riko, Jean. He's gone."

-

It would take weeks for Jean to patch the day back together again; for weeks it existed as fractured bursts of moments all out of alignment. He remembered Jeremy's call. He remembered the bite of wood and pop of glass as he destroyed anything he could get his hands on. Mostly he remembered the unyielding hands of campus security as they broke into the room some indeterminate time later. By the time they reached him, the shower had been cold for ages. Jean was hunched up at the far end of the tub, as far from the spray as he could get, but his legs were soaked through where he had them hugged to his chest.

He tried to fight back, but he couldn't feel any part of his body. The towels they wrapped around him felt like knives against his chilled skin, and he was half-pulled, half-carried out of the room. This time of day on a weekend Fox Tower was a bustling place, and as soon as word got out that security was breaking into the Exy dorm rooms a significant crowd had formed in the hallways.

Jean saw their faces as blurs of color as he was hauled to the elevators. His name was an echo filling in the gaps between his heartbeat as they saw the tattoo on his face. There

102

was a car, and the sickening blur of green out the window. Unfamiliar nurses pulling at sopping wet clothes, teaming up when he tried fighting them. Drugs that made his thoughts go hazy. Heat, slow then fast and far too much. White, white sheets.

A rainbow.

"Oh, Jean," Renee said at his side. "I asked you not to look."

He blinked the room into sluggish focus. She was thigh to thigh with him, perched on the edge of the bed beside him. One of his hands was clasped in two of hers. There were fresh bandages on his hands, mottled with dried blood in too many places. He closed his eyes, opened them, tried again. His head felt cottony. There'd been a bit of clarity earlier, he remembered, or thought he remembered. He'd fought back so violently they'd had to sedate him again.

"Jeremy," Jean said.

"We saw his text too late on Kevin's phone," Renee said quietly, which at least explained why someone sicced security on him. "We tried to call you, but you didn't answer."

"Where is Kevin?"

Nathaniel's voice came from somewhere across the room: "We left him and Coach Wymack in West Virginia."

He didn't say *for the funeral*. He didn't say *to mourn*. He didn't have to when Jean could put the pieces together. He couldn't say it when there was no way this was true. Jean lifted his free hand to his face and dug unsteady fingers into the tattoo on his cheekbone. Kevin had been with Riko for far longer, navigating the precarious line between beloved brother and punching bag. It didn't matter how much Riko hurt him; they'd spent too many years completely wrapped up in each other. Kevin had to say goodbye.

Not goodbye, because Riko wasn't gone. He couldn't be gone.

"It's not true," Jean said.

"There was a press conference this morning," Renee said.

103

"Coach Moriyama is accepting personal responsibility for the pressure Riko was under. He resigned effective—" She lost the rest in a grunt when Jean elbowed his way free of her. He didn't have enough balance to be upright and ended up slamming into the wall by the door. Renee's hands were on him immediately, keeping him from tipping over, and she held fast despite his attempts to pry free of her. "Jean, it's okay."

"No," Jean said, sharp and panicked. "The master would never leave. The ERC cannot make him."

"It wasn't the ERC," Nathaniel said in quiet French. Jean finally turned to try and see him. Nathaniel was the only other person in the room, standing guard in the far corner. He looked far too calm for all of this. "Ichirou was at the game, and he saw for himself what chaos Tetsuji was breeding in Evermore. When Riko took his swing at me, Ichirou picked his side."

"No," Jean said. "I won't believe it."

"After the police left, I was invited to East Tower to watch," Nathaniel said. "A show of respect, maybe, because everything I warned him came true. First, he banished Tetsuji from Exy: no more Edgar Allan, no more professional teams, no more ERC. Then he handled Riko."

"I don't believe you," Jean insisted. "Riko is King. He is the future of Exy. He is a Moriyama. They would never kill him."

"He was," Nathaniel said, with a bit of emphasis, "King. Now he's a martyr."

The last of Jean's strength left him, and he slowly sank to the ground. The shudder that wracked his chest should have been revulsion, but it fell dangerously short. This didn't feel like joy or relief; it only felt like loss. Jean hated it, hated it, *hated it*. He wanted to claw his own face open. He wanted to tear at his throat until he found the knot that was making it so hard to breathe.

Marseille was lost to trauma. Evermore's doors were closed to him. The master was exiled. Riko was dead. Everything Jean had ever known was gone. Who was he without them?

His heart twisted so violently it sent quakes over every inch of him. How wretched, how exhausting, to have one of his dearest and most desperate wishes fulfilled, and to feel nothing but this gnawing turmoil. It wasn't fair. He wanted to say it, but there was no point saying it when he didn't even believe in fairness. The best he managed was a choked sound that tore him on its way out.

"Hey," Renee said as she knelt beside him. One hand came up to cup the back of his skull, and she leaned forward to press her forehead to his temple. He could feel her heartbeat against his skin, a steady metronome he could ground his ragged breathing against. He didn't have it in him to shove her away, but he hooked a knee to his aching chest to give himself a small barrier against her comfort. "I have you. It's okay to let go."

It gave him just enough strength to say, "I won't grieve him."

"Maybe it's not about him," Renee said. "Maybe you're mourning the wreckage he made of your life. You're allowed to grieve what he took from you."

Even here, even now, denying it was instinctive: "He didn't take anything from me." He tried to pull out of her grip, but she didn't let him go. "Did you see his body?"

"No," Renee admitted.

"I did," Nathaniel said as he crossed the room. He lowered himself to a crouch in front of Jean and studied him with calm blue eyes. He waited until Jean turned a haunted stare on him before cocking his fingers like a gun and pressing them to his own temple. "*Pop*, and he was gone. It's impressive, isn't it? How easily these monsters die in the end." For a moment he looked far away from here. Jean didn't have to ask where he'd gone; the mess the Wesninskis had made of his face was hard to ignore. "He's dead, Jean."

"Promise me," Jean said, with a desperation that should have killed him.

Nathaniel didn't hesitate. "I promise."

Jean put his forehead to his knee and closed his eyes. He counted his breaths in and out, trying to calm his racing heart before it could drum a hole straight through his ribcage. The darkest thought curling around the back of his mind said to reject this, that it was an elaborate trick staged by the Moriyamas to get Riko out of the spotlight before he further embarrassed the family. He had no reason at all to trust Nathaniel, a rabid little Fox who'd had a lifetime to master his lies. If he hadn't heard it from Jeremy first, if he didn't have Renee tucked against his side, he'd be able to reject the outlandish lie outright.

But maybe it was real. Maybe Ichirou really had chosen them.

Free was a transparent lie, and *safe* was impossible to believe in, but maybe—

"I need to get back to the others," Nathaniel said.

"I have him," Renee promised. "I'll see him back to Abby's when he's ready."

Jean heard cloth rustle as Nathaniel stood, but as soon as Nathaniel stepped away Jean blindly reached out for him. He barely recognized his own voice when he said, "Neil," but it was enough the other man stopped. Jean's fingertips finally found denim, but he didn't try to get a good grip on the other man. "It was a good game."

"Yes," Neil Josten said, with a smile in his voice. "It was, wasn't it?"

The door creaked faintly as it opened and clicked even quieter when it closed again. Jean focused on the feel of Renee's heartbeat and counted his breaths until it didn't hurt so much to be alive.

-

The cruelest joke of the week wasn't Riko's death or the Foxes' unimaginable win, but that the school semester kept ticking on anyway. Monday brought with it the start of finals. Edgar Allan had agreed to let Abby administer Jean's exams so long as he took them on campus grounds; his professors would fax one over to Wymack's office once a day. Monday morning Jean got up when Abby did and rode out to the Foxhole Court in her passenger seat.

Bright orange ribbons had been wound through most of the links on the chain fence around the stadium, and students had stopped by to tape up handwritten signs of triumph and support. Socks and shirts added to the chaos, and Jean spotted at least one bra hooked around a fence hinge. It was bewildering that they'd deface their own stadium like this. Edgar Allan would have come down hard on its students for the discourtesy.

Maybe this was the one scenario they'd allow it, if the students had left tributes for Riko outside of Evermore. Jean felt his thoughts tip and his center start to give and he shoved Riko from his mind so hard his heart ached.

Abby got Jean set up in the main room, handing over the exam before reading the brief instructions aloud to him. Jean poked his fingertips with his pencil as he waited for Abby to start the timer and leave. He hadn't studied at all this weekend, but the endless hours he'd had to focus on his classes this last month and a half paid off. The one place Ravens weren't required to excel was in class; so long as they made the minimum GPA to keep their spot on the lineup the coaches expected nothing else of them. Despite that permission to half-ass his test, Jean was fairly confident in most of his answers.

He finished with a few minutes to spare. Instead of checking over his responses he got up and went to the far wall. Someone had covered it with pictures of the Foxes. Some were from game nights or clipped out of newspapers, but most were the Foxes at rest and very few of those were taken at the stadium. Jean saw movie theaters and cozy bedrooms and restaurants. There were cockeyed selfies of the women dressed for a night out, shots from Exy banquets, and more than a few of the Foxes pulling unflattering faces for the camera as they sprawled across picnic blankets or misshapen couches.

They looked ridiculous and mismatched. They looked bright and alive and carefree, like they'd somehow forgotten everything that made them qualify for the Fox lineup.

A timer sounded down the hall. Jean considered retreating back to his spot before he was caught nosing about, but in the end he stayed as he was. Near the edge of the collage was a photo of Renee. She had the back of her head to a window and was pointing up and over her shoulders with both hands. It took Jean a moment to see the rainbow in the distant sky. Someone had taped a small sticky note to the corner of the picture that read "Who wore it better??"

Abby came out to check on him and collect his test. "Let me get a look at your knee."

Jean peeled Renee's picture off the wall. Abby said nothing about the theft, though she had to have seen it, but led him back to her office in silence.

After a thorough check of that and the new injuries he'd sustained when he'd apparently demolished Neil's dorm room, she gave him permission to walk laps in the stadium. He still wasn't allowed access to weights or a legitimate fitness routine, but he would take whatever he could get.

That didn't mean it wasn't disconcerting to be completely alone in the inner court, and Jean had to force himself to start moving when everything in him ordered him back to the locker room where Abby was. He walked laps for hours, testing the easy way his knee and ankle held his weight, and added stairs in that afternoon. Now and then he felt a tired twinge from his knee, so he walked rows of seats until it faded before trying again.

Tuesday and Wednesday followed the same pattern, but Wednesday night changed things. Wednesday night was Riko's funeral. Jean stared at his dark TV all evening and imagined Wymack and Kevin sitting side by side in the church pews.

The funeral was a turning point. Edgar Allan, the Ravens, and the Ravens' most strident and fanatical followers had been

108

mired in grief and denial until now. Once the service was over and Riko was nothing but ash and bone, the conversation started to shift.

For days there'd been articles and essays about the insane pressure heaped upon star athletes and celebrities. Now the tone grew darker and angrier, as it always seemed to do when the Ravens were in the mix. The blame slowly started to slide from public consumption to the tiny team who'd destroyed Riko's reputation and to the perfect Court who'd abandoned the King who handpicked them for glory. Neil's name popped up with alarming frequency, but Kevin and Jean weren't far behind him. Jean could only tolerate a day of ugly rumors and accusations before he resolved to stop watching the news entirely.

The last days of the school year were the only thing keeping people in check, or so Abby seemed to think, and Jean heard her on the phone with her Foxes urging them to get out of town as soon as possible after they finished their exams. Jean had forgotten that some—most? all?—schools actually allowed their athletes time off in the summer. Only three Foxes were staying in town, Abby told Jean at dinner Thursday night, and Jean didn't have to ask which three. The rest would scatter to the winds before retribution found them.

On Friday Renee found him at the court, bringing with her a letter Abby must have passed her to deliver to him. It had USC lettering on it, so Jean opened it when Renee sat beside him. Inside was a plane ticket and a handwritten letter from Jeremy. They'd found a place for Jean to stay, it seemed, but they needed a week so someone named Jillian could move out first. He'd be rooming with Catalina Alvarez and Laila Dermott: a starting backliner and USC's best goalkeeper to date. Jeremy promised he'd be there to pick Jean up from the airport when he arrived.

Beneath his signature was an almost illegible scribble in someone else's handwriting, and Jean had to tilt the letter a few times before he made out an enthusiastic "Let's fucking

109

goooo!!". Jean slowly folded the letter again and looked at the ticket. Jean assumed Jeremy had hashed out the date with Kevin. He didn't know Wymack well enough to be completely sure, but he was fairly certain the man would've asked him before setting something like this in stone. Having his life decided for him was a familiar feeling, so Jean didn't waste his breath complaining.

He passed his ticket to Renee so she could see it. "That's sooner than I thought," she admitted. "I assume he wants you on the ground where their nurses can get a good look at you. Kevin never told them the extent of your injuries; all they know is you're sidelined for three months."

Renee handed it back and watched as Jean slipped both the letter and ticket into the envelope. She said, with more surety than he felt, "That will be nice. It gives you time to get used to the city before jumping into practice with a new team. I've heard only good things about your new captain."

"From Kevin," Jean guessed. "His bias cannot be trusted."

She laughed. "Perhaps, but it is a little endearing, isn't it? He is not normally so forward with his admiration."

"It is refreshing only to you. I have had to put up with it for as long as I have known him. He is a fool. 'Exy as it is meant to be played'," he said, sharp with mockery. "He would wither away if he was on their lineup; he is too ill-tempered to survive a day on their court."

Renee bumped her shoulder against his. "Whereas you will fit right in."

She was teasing, but Jean said, "I will hate them, but I will do what I must to survive."

Renee said nothing for a minute, then turned a serious look on him. "They will ask you about your injuries. Do you know what you will tell them?"

"I was injured in a scrimmage," Jean said.

Renee answered with a wry smile. "I do not think your nurses will be impressed by that answer. And Jean? It will not explain these." She rested her fingertips on his chest and studied his shirt like she could see through it to the scars beneath. "I do not remember the Gold Court being set up to facilitate privacy the way we are here. They will want to know what happened."

"The Ravens never asked," Jean said. "They knew it was not their business."

"Presumably they could also guess where they were coming from," Renee said, and Jean didn't answer that easy accusation. Renee thought for a few moments longer before letting her hand fall away. "If you will not—cannot—tell them the truth, you could settle for making them uncomfortable enough not to pry," she suggested. When Jean only looked at her, she lifted one shoulder in a slight shrug. "Imply they are older than Evermore, for example. Family inflicted."

It would be bold from anyone else, but Renee had told him stories of her parents back in February, and Jean had been honest enough to admit he hated his parents in return. He hadn't gone into details, and she hadn't pressed, but if she knew how he ended up in Riko's care she could likely guess what line of work his parents were in.

"Will that be enough?" Jean asked.

"I'm fairly sure," Renee promised. "People tend to get unsettled when the abuse comes from inside the house."

Jean considered that. "I will trust you."

They sat in comfortable silence for a few minutes before Renee asked, "Would you like me to stay with you until you fly out?"

Jean thought it over for a full minute before saying, "I don't think so."

Renee nodded as if she'd expected that. There was a sweetness to her that was both sad and beautiful, and for a moment Jean ached with the cruelty of it all. He thought about her driving all night to reach Edgar Allan after he texted her and of her turning Andritch against his own star team with an unflinching threat of retribution. He thought of her stopping by Abby's place week after week to sit with him so he wasn't

111

alone, of her unwavering faith in him to do better and be better, of her calling him from West Virginia desperate to protect him in the wake of Riko's execution.

He thought of Evermore, of years wandering windowless black halls. Heavy checks and hungry hands and too-sharp knives and *again again again* at practices that dominated most of his day. He thought of Kevin whispering French in dark corners and of drowning. A promise made on his behalf without his consent, a death that broke and changed everything, and a ticket to a fresh start he didn't deserve but which he needed if he was supposed to stay alive long enough to be worth something.

I am Jean Moreau, he thought, and then: *Who is Jean Moreau when he is not a Raven?*

It was a question that needed answering and a problem she couldn't help him with. It left a bitter ache in him not unlike a bruise, but Jean knew better than to think it could work out any other way. Maybe it was unkind to reach out for her after that rejection, but Jean gave in to temptation and tucked her hair behind her ear. She took hold of his hand so she could press a kiss into his palm, and he watched the easy way her fingers slipped between his.

"We are the right people, I think," she said as she studied him. "This is just… the wrong time. If you stayed, perhaps it would be different, but I know you won't. I know you can't," she corrected herself. "It would be unfair to ask you to and cruel of me to complicate your journey."

"I'm sorry," he said, and meant it.

"Don't be," Renee said, so calm and earnest he had to believe her. An alarm chimed in her pocket, but Renee pulled her phone out and silenced it without looking. "I only want what is best for you, and right now that isn't us. If you need a clean slate when you move so you can leave all of this behind you, I will understand, but I am always here if you need me."

Thank you felt appropriate, but all Jean managed was, "I know."

When he motioned to her phone in a question, she got to her feet. "A reminder for my last exam," she said. She stood in front of him a moment, gazing down at his upturned face with a distant look on her own, and then reached up to undo the clasp of her cross necklace. Jean put his hand up for it and watched light glint off the silver chain as it settled in a pile in his hand. Too many years in the Nest had left his childhood faith in shreds, but he closed his fingers over it anyway. Maybe it was his imagination that he felt her warmth clinging to the metal; somehow it was still comforting.

She smiled, slow and sure and brilliant, and said, "I'm so proud of you for making it this far. I'm excited to see how far you can go from here when you can finally spread your wings without fear. Fly safe, Jean. We will see you on the court in finals."

"Perhaps you will," he agreed, and she left him to his thoughts.

On his fingertips he counted to two: *A cool evening breeze. Rainbows.*

-

By Friday night, Wymack and Kevin were back in South Carolina, and by Saturday afternoon, only three Foxes were left. Jean knew far too much about the others' summer plans, courtesy of overhearing conversations between Wymack and Abby. He steadfastly tried to delete the knowledge from his brain as unimportant, because what did he care if this one was heading to Germany or that one was spending a few weeks with a cheerleader's family? All that really mattered was that he still had most of a week to waste until he flew out.

On Monday the on-campus dorms closed for summer, and the remaining Foxes moved in with Abby. The sudden arrival of extra bodies added overdue life to the house, filling in the silence and space in a way Jean's infrequent visitors never could. He woke to Kevin and Neil bickering about teams and drills and fell asleep listening to Abby harangue Andrew about his sugar intake. Now and then Andrew and Neil got going in a language he didn't recognize.

"German," Kevin said when he saw Jean watching them. It was the first thing he'd said to Jean since coming back to South Carolina. One day they'd talk about the Foxes' victory; one day they'd talk about the Ravens. Today Riko's death was a jagged chasm between them neither was ready to bridge.

"An ugly language," Jean said, and Kevin retreated into his own thoughts.

Wymack was over less frequently now that Jean was mobile, but he still stopped by every other night to take advantage of Abby's cooking and give his team grief. In the hours they were all in one place, Jean studied them, wondering how last year's mess of a team had come so far. He watched how Abby and Wymack fit together, grumbling and fussing but always with an affectionate, easy undercurrent. When Andrew's teammates were being particularly pedantic Andrew always looked to Wymack first. The cautious false-starts between Wymack and Kevin were the hardest to watch as they tested the unfamiliar lines between coach and father.

Jean noticed how Andrew and Neil moved like they were caught in each other's gravity, in each other's space more than they were out of it, cigarette smoke and matching armbands and lingering looks when one fell out of orbit for too long. He'd always assumed it was Neil's arrogance that brought him to Evermore over Christmas. Now he thought it was something else, but it wasn't his place to comment on it. Nathaniel was his broken promise; Neil's life was none of his business.

He didn't have long to dwell on it, anyway, because each day of the week brought more retribution from the fans the Foxes wronged by winning. Wymack sounded more tired than angry as he relayed each day's newest disasters: the black ink that dyed the campus pond, the **MURDERERS** and **CHEATERS** graffiti across the stadium walls, and the bomb threats and arson that meant security had to escort the Foxes back and forth to their court for their unscheduled practices.

Wednesday morning a new rumor started to circulate

among the coaches: Edgar Allan had closed the Nest. The Ravens had been scattered back to their homes for family time and mandatory counseling. Jean was out of the room before Wymack finished speaking, and he locked himself in his borrowed room with his notebooks the rest of the day. A gnawing panic almost had him ripping every page out of the books, but he managed to push them to safety just in time.

When Jean finally had to leave the room again for water late that night, Wymack was still wide awake and waiting for him. Wymack didn't ask about the Nest or the Ravens but said, "You'll be safer in Los Angeles. We're out here on our own with no one on our side and maybe twenty people on our campus security team. LA is a different beast, and USC is nestled in its heart. No one's stupid enough to start a fight with them because they know the city will always win."

It wasn't a question, so Jean didn't respond. Wymack allowed him only a few moments to digest it before saying, "I've been talking to Coach Rhemann this week, just so you know. We've been getting a bit of pressure to put you and Kevin in front of a camera. We're pushing back as hard as we can," he said at the sharp look Jean sent him, "because we know it's too soon to subject either of you to those vultures. But sooner or later our school boards are going to take the choice out of our hands."

"It is not my place to speak to the press," Jean said. "I won't do it."

"They have a lot to say about you," Wymack pointed out, not unkindly. "It wouldn't be the worst thing to respond and sort a few things out." When Jean only stared him down in stubborn silence, Wymack sighed and collected his pack of cigarettes from the counter. He tipped it to one side, checking for the weight of his lighter, and said, "Get some sleep. Tomorrow is going to be a long day."

Later Jean would understand why Wymack was so worried about him, but later was too late to do anything about it.

By the time Jeremy was able to escape the dinner table Wednesday night, he'd missed almost twenty text messages. His phone had been going off almost nonstop for over a week, starting with the news of Riko's death and continuing through Tetsuji's press conference. Most of it was spearheaded by Cat, who couldn't resist tracking online gossip and opinions, but as finals week drew to a close and the first week of summer vacation started, the group chat got going in earnest.

It was exhausting that the Palmetto State Foxes could be champions and still exist as the scapegoats of the NCAA. It seemed every time Jeremy opened his phone there was a fresh wave of rumors or word of more assaults against their campus. He'd seen this backlash last spring when Kevin Day first announced his transfer to the Foxes' Exy team, so while he was disappointed in the escalating vandalism, he wasn't entirely surprised. Kevin seemed more irritated than concerned when Jeremy checked in on him, since it meant extra precautions during his private practices, so Jeremy tried not to worry overmuch.

USC so far seemed immune to the heat, but Jeremy couldn't say the same for their newest player. The rumor mill was working overtime to decry Jean Moreau. Some of it was see-through propaganda, such as the slights against his talents when his stats were easy to look up. A lot of it was a he-said she-said mess, the "a friend of a friend who knows a friend who heard" type of nastiness better suited for high school hallways.

Jean had been on the Raven line for three years, but he'd never once spoken to the press. It wasn't unusual, since Edgar Allan made Riko and Kevin handle all interviews and statements for the team, but it meant there was nothing to hint at Jean's personality. With nothing concrete to go on, he was fair game for the anonymous haters online, and they were having a field day building a bogeyman out of absolutely nothing.

This person said he beat the Ravens' freshmen half to death on a regular basis, another said Jean was jealous of Riko's rank and bullied him relentlessly, and the loudest rumor of all claimed Jean had slept his way onto the Ravens' lineup. Jean was blamed as the reason Kevin had left Edgar Allan. One side of the story was he talked Kevin into it so as to undermine Riko's authority while the other side said he chased Kevin off with his cruelty. On and on it went, in exhausting circles.

In direct opposition to this supposed hateful side of him was the single muddled rumor from Palmetto State: apparently Jean tried to kill himself in solidarity the morning Riko died. This came straight from the athletes who'd seen security drag a bloodied and delirious Jean out of the Exy dorms. Jeremy didn't know how much stock to put in that last one, except Coach Wymack had called him from Kevin's phone that same day and asked Jeremy to keep his distance for a bit. Guilt was a gnawing, uncomfortable mouse eating away at his heart.

It was inevitable that the rumors would start getting to the Trojans, but Jeremy clung to two simple truths as he tried allaying their fears: Kevin would never have sent Jean to them if he was as much a wretch as everyone claimed, and Jean himself had requested edits to his contract to ensure he'd be bound to their good-natured presentation. There was no guarantee he would be easy to get along with, but would he have even thought to introduce those rules if he didn't intend to make this work?

Most of the time this was enough to calm their louder doubts, but Xavier messaged him privately to point out that Kevin and Jean hadn't played together in over a year. There was no telling who Jean had become in Kevin's absence once he took his place at the so-called King's side. The Trojans were worried, and they'd remain as such until they could take Jean's measure for themselves. Bringing Jean out to California

117

tomorrow, a full month and change before summer practices started, was the only peace offering Jeremy had for them.

"More drama," Annalise guessed, and Jeremy jerked his gaze up from his phone. His younger sister had her purse slung over her shoulder and her keys in her hand. Unlike Bryson, who always came home for the summer, she insisted on keeping her own place on the other side of the city year-round. Her expression was cool, not concerned, but Jeremy immediately tucked his phone into his pocket and went to meet her at the front door.

"People picking fights with our new star," he admitted as he held the door for her. "Rumor mill is working overtime."

"Overdue for a new scandal, hm?" she asked. "End the way you started."

He didn't flinch, but it was a near thing. Once upon a time she'd gone to all his high school games, but once upon a time was before the fall banquet that broke their family in half. She'd gone out of her way to forget everything she knew about Exy since then, and she'd never forgiven him for sticking with it. He'd walked through a hundred hypothetical arguments with his therapist in preparation for the day he finally fought back, but every time the chance came, he watched it slip past in miserable silence.

He followed her out to her car, but Annalise made him wait as she dug lip balm out of her purse. She applied it liberally, smacked her lips together a few times, and then sent him an arch look. "What's Grandpa think of this investment of yours?"

It was obvious bait, but that couldn't keep the edge out of Jeremy's fierce, "He is not our grandfather."

"Careful," Annalise warned him as she rummaged for her keys. "You already destroyed the family. Don't destroy my future, too. Door."

He got her car door open, jaw working on arguments that would always ring too hollow. Annalise got into the driver's seat and motioned an okay to him as soon as her legs were out

118

of the way. Jeremy pushed her door closed and took a step back. She needed a few moments to buckle and get settled, and then her car came to life with a quiet rumble. She pulled away without a backwards glance. Jeremy watched her taillights disappear as she turned out of the driveway, then turned to survey his house.

The temptation to head straight to Cat and Laila's place was almost overwhelming, but tonight was not the night. Today was their anniversary, and he wasn't going to crash that with his family drama.

He sat on the short wall of the fountain instead and went through his messages. Since Cat was distracted, most of tonight's updates were from the other gossips of the Trojan line. Jeremy wasn't sure he had the energy for more bad news tonight, but then a new text popped up from a number he hadn't had to use in months. It was from Lucas, who he didn't spend a lot of time with outside of the court. The rising junior was a solid backliner, even if he was mostly relegated to playing sub against the Trojans' weaker opponents.

"Can we talk?" was all the message said.

Jeremy called him immediately. "Hey, Lucas. You all right?"

"Grayson got home last night," Lucas said, sounding dull and distant.

Jeremy turned on his perch to put his house at his back, as if by having fewer lights in his eyes he could hear Lucas better. Lucas' older brother Grayson played for the Ravens, but Lucas went out of his way not to talk about him. Not disinterest, but grief, Cody told Jeremy once. Supposedly Ravens were forbidden to contact their own families once they signed with Edgar Allan. It sounded like hogwash, but Grayson refused to acknowledge Lucas even after Lucas signed with the Trojans.

"How is he?" Jeremy asked. "How are you?"

Lucas was quiet for an age before saying, "He's not right. I don't—I shouldn't say it, I know I shouldn't, but I…" He faltered, fighting for self-censure before he said too much. "I don't even recognize him. He's not eating, and he's not sleeping, and he's just—wait," he said, and went very quiet. Jeremy strained to hear whatever distracted Lucas, but nothing came through. An uncomfortable minute passed, then another, and when Jeremy was really starting to worry Lucas came back. "He's very angry."

"At you?" Jeremy asked, alarmed.

"At everything," Lucas said evasively. "At us. At Jean most of all."

Jeremy asked, "Do you feel safe with him there?"

"He's my brother," Lucas said.

"That's not what I asked, Lucas."

Lucas was quiet for far too long. Neither the silence nor what followed made Jeremy feel any better: "I think so."

"If that changes, do you have somewhere you can go?"

"I could stay with Cody, maybe," Lucas said uncertainly. "If they don't go back to Tennessee to see Cameron, I mean."

Not in a million years, Jeremy thought, but if Lucas didn't know how much the cousins hated each other he wasn't going to get into it. All he said was, "Yeah, that's a good idea. You know they get bored without someone to boss around."

It earned him a quiet chuckle. "Yeah, that's true." The humor was quick to bleed out as he continued. "I just… wanted to get that off my chest, I think. I'm worried about him, but I'm also worried about us now that you've brought one of them onto our lineup. If you could see what Grayson's like right now, if you knew what he used to be like, you'd understand."

"I'll look out for us," Jeremy said. "You look out for you and your brother, okay? He's had a rough end of year." It was such a simplification it felt callous, and Jeremy couldn't help but wince. "He needs you now more than ever, but if you need us, make sure you call us. I don't care what time it is."

"Yeah, cap," Lucas said. "Thank you."

Lucas bid him farewell soon enough, but Jeremy stayed where he was long after the call was over. He pressed his phone into his cheek as his thoughts ran away from him: Lucas's defeated fear, the Ravens' unkind rumors, and Kevin's earnest entreaty to make room for Jean. He thought about Kevin's broken hand, Jean hazed off the lineup mid-championships, and Riko killing himself at Castle Evermore after the Ravens' first ever loss. He thought about people saying Jean was dragged out of the athletes' dorm in bloodied towels the morning Riko died, and Jeremy put his phone away.

"This is the right move," he told himself.

He had to believe it, but Jeremy didn't think his nerves would settle until Jean was in California and Jeremy could meet him face-to-face.

CHAPTER SEVEN
Jean

If Jean had his way, he would never set foot in an airport again.

With the Ravens, it had been a non-issue: the staff had handled everything for them, and the Ravens simply had to shut up and go where they were told in a long line of pairs. The only time he'd been to an airport alone was when he'd had to collect Neil from Arrivals for Christmas break, as Riko had been busy with the master. Riko had driven them back on New Year's Eve, as Neil had been violently dissociating from Riko's cruel farewell party. Jean couldn't have gotten him across the parking lot, but he could at least manhandle him from the curb to check-in and the TSA line.

This trip was entirely different. He'd never realized how complicated the process was or just how many people could fill an airport. Jean had put up a token fight when Wymack invited himself along on the westbound flight, but by the time they hit their layover in Charlotte he was desperately glad Wymack had ignored his heated protests. The speakers were going off nonstop in alternating languages, calling out unfamiliar names and final boarding calls and gate updates. Every time Jean saw black clothes in his peripheral vision, he automatically tried to change directions and fall in line. Only Wymack's firm hand on his elbow could pull him back on track.

Los Angeles International was packed when Jean followed Wymack off the plane. He stuck as close to the coach as he could without stepping on the backs of Wymack's shoes, sure that if they got separated he'd never get out of here again.

There was a set of escalators halfway down the terminal, and Wymack stepped off to one side as soon as they reached the bottom. Tunnels stretched out to either side of them, and Wymack jerked a thumb at the signs. One way led to the next terminal while the other went to baggage claim.

"Straight down you go," Wymack said. "Are you good from here?"

Wymack had come with him with no intention of sticking around; he'd gotten himself a same-day ticket back to the east coast and would supposedly waste the middle of his day at one of the airport bars. Jean could have asked him why he bothered, but he'd bitten it back a hundred or a thousand times today already. He knew why, even if he refused to trust it. Men like Wymack didn't exist. They couldn't; they shouldn't.

"Yes, Coach," Jean said.

Wymack looked like he might say something else, but at length he clapped a brief hand to Jean's shoulder and silently turned back the way they'd come. Jean watched him go for a few moments before forcibly turning his attention toward the exit. He tightened his grip on the handle of his carry-on and grimly set off in that direction. Soon enough he was through, and Jean immediately cut left along the wall to survey the waiting crowd.

Spotting Jeremy Knox was easy enough. The Trojans' captain had come in a university shirt: not the only one in the crowd to have some USC lettering on him, but the only one in that much cardinal red. Jean slowed to a stop, taking advantage of Jeremy's distraction to study his new captain. It was a little disorienting seeing him dressed down. In all of the games he'd watched this past month and all of the articles Kevin had shown him back at Evermore, Jeremy had been in uniform. Jean had played USC a few times, but it hadn't been his job to check Jeremy. This would have been his year if he hadn't gotten kicked off the line.

Jean felt his focus start to tilt, but this was not the time or place to think about Riko. He dug half-moon indents into his palm until all he saw was Jeremy. The other man was a bit scrawnier than he'd expected, built more for nimble footwork and speedy breakaways than the violent bullying and domination Jean relied on as defense. Tousled caramel brown hair somehow managed to not look messy, and the blinding gold shorts Jeremy wore made his legs look longer than Jean knew them to be. Jean had four inches on the other man, if he remembered correctly.

Jeremy had brought a yoyo with him, of all things, and was attempting and failing to do tricks with it while he waited. He only gave up on his game after he got the string tangled in the cords for his headphones, and Jean watched him sigh exaggerated defeat as he set to work sorting the mess out.

Jeremy glanced up then, either realizing the swelling crowd around him meant a plane had landed or sensing someone watching him. Finding the one person who was standing still on this side of the room took Jeremy only a moment. He immediately switched his yoyo and headphones to one hand so he could lift the other in a wave. Jean quietly reminded himself it was too late to change his mind about this and set off to meet Jeremy halfway.

"Hello, hello," Jeremy greeted him cheerily. "How was the flight?"

The worst, Jean thought, but settled for, "Small talk is a pointless indulgence."

"I like to indulge," Jeremy said with a dimpled smile.

Kevin's words mocked him in the back of his thoughts: *"Some of them you like."* Jean cut off that line of thinking so fast he felt dizzy. It didn't matter that Jeremy Knox was annoyingly easy to look at; Jean knew better than to look at another man too long. He'd learned that lesson the hard way and would not survive a revisit.

"Baggage claim is this way," Jeremy said when Jean didn't waste his breath with a response. He started to turn away, watching for Jean to follow, and hesitated when Jean shook his head in silent refusal. "No bags?"

124

"I have a bag," Jean said.

Jeremy looked at him, then the carry-on resting by his right leg, then past him like there was another suitcase he was missing. "Mailing the rest?"

"No," Jean said. "I have everything I need."

"If you say so," Jeremy said, in a tone that said he wasn't convinced. Jean half-expected him to press the matter, but instead Jeremy motioned for him to follow. "All right, then, let's get out of here and get you to your new place. Traffic wasn't that bad on the way in, but we're getting close enough to lunch that it's probably going to be mayhem out there."

Jeremy's car was three floors up and halfway back in the parking garage. Jean knew next to nothing about cars, despite technically owning one, but he knew money when he saw it. He expected it to smell like warm leather and polish when he got in on the passenger side, but the scent of greasy food was so heavy and fresh he assumed Jeremy stopped to eat on the way to the airport. Maybe Jeremy was feeling reckless now that summer vacation was underway, but a captain ought to be the one most resistant to temptation.

"Are you hungry?" Jeremy asked. "We can stop and grab you something on the way home if so. If not it's… Thursday?" He considered it, checking his mental calendar, and nodded. Jean almost missed half of what he said when he leaned out to slip his ticket stub into the turnstile at the exit, but he could piece enough together via context as Jeremy settled again: "Thursdays are sandwich night, and I think tonight's supposed to be French dip or something. A little joke to welcome our first Frenchman to the line."

"A comedy for the ages," Jean said. "I am laughing on the inside."

"Hungry?" Jeremy asked again.

"No," Jean said. "The smell in here killed my appetite."

It bought him only a few seconds of peace. "What are you studying?"

It sounded like small talk when he said it like that, but

since academics were the necessary evil of college sports Jean couldn't justify ignoring it. "Business."

"Braver man than me," Jeremy said. "Sorry for saying it, but it sounds uninspiring."

The hint of an unexpected problem had Jean tensing. "What did they give you?"

Jeremy waited so long to answer Jean thought he was trying to build up suspense, but then Jeremy asked, "When you say 'give me', you mean like…?"

"What do the Trojans study?" Jean asked, impatient over having to clarify.

It should have been the easiest question to answer, but Jeremy prefaced his explanation with a bewildered, "Uhhh?" He thought a few more moments. "I'm in English, Cat studies computer science, Laila's in real estate development, Nabil's architecture…" He drummed his fingers on the steering wheel as he thought.

"Derek is economics. Thompson, not Allen," Jeremy said, and Jean belatedly remembered the Trojans had both a Derek and a Derrick on their offense line. "Xavier's in communication, and I think Shawn is too. Do you really want the whole lineup or is that good enough for now?"

Jean stared at him. "That's impossible."

"That I know them all? I'll probably be guessing at least half."

"That they're all different," Jean said. "Who signed off on that?"

"I'm lost," Jeremy admitted. "Help me out a bit here, because it sounds like you're implying the Ravens all study the same thing?"

"We do," Jean said, and Jeremy's knuckles went white on the steering wheel. "Ravens are required to take our classes together."

"Their," Jeremy interjected quietly. "Their classes."

Jean scowled a little at his slip. "The easiest way to ensure someone is available is to give all Ravens the same major.

Exceptions can be made at a freshman level if two students agree to pursue the same degree, but they'd have to have it approved by the—Coach Moriyama. No one is ever bold enough to ask him.

"Except Kevin," Jean corrected himself. "He wanted to study history, so he begged Riko to do it with him." Riko had agreed on the condition that Kevin do all of Riko's homework for him. It was why Jean had ended up sitting in on Riko's classes in Kevin's absence: no one else on the lineup was taking the same courses. Jean didn't have to keep up, just show up and sit in a back corner. Last fall he'd slept through them, but for a few months this spring he'd spent them texting Renee. "They're the only two I've ever known to stray."

"A little honesty?" Jeremy asked him. "That's just a mite bit hecked up. You're telling me you didn't even get a choice in what to study?"

"What I study is irrelevant," Jean said. "My only purpose is to play."

"Yes, but... You didn't even have a choice?" Jeremy asked. When Jean didn't answer, Jeremy raked a hand through his hair in an agitated gesture. "That's kind of sad. Unless you like business, of course, but I think you should've been able to choose. Probably too late to change now, being a rising senior and all, but you could pick up a minor or audit some classes, I guess. That's what I do: I pick a fun class once a semester to balance out the rest."

"School is a means to an end," Jean said. "It doesn't matter whether or not I enjoy it."

"So you don't," Jeremy concluded. "Enjoy it, I mean."

It wasn't the relevant takeaway, so Jean didn't waste his breath. Jeremy was quiet for the next few miles as he chewed on this insight. Jean assumed he'd move on to the next topic when he got his wits back, but Jeremy said, "Kevin warned me you wouldn't want to take your classes alone and that I'd have to find someone to go with you. He could have at least explained it a bit better."

"He isn't used to explaining himself," Jean said. "He's used to simply getting his way."

That made Jeremy laugh. "I get that impression of him, yeah. Oh, to be the pampered elite."

Jean blinked and saw the white scars on Kevin's hand. He remembered Kevin calling him a year ago and begging him to refute the rumors Edgar Allan was transferring districts. His stomach churned in rebellion.

"He's earned the right to be arrogant," Jean said, as evenly as he could.

Jeremy didn't notice Jean's teetering mood but said, "We'll work it out, one way or another. With twenty-nine of us surely there's got to be some overlap. Coach Rhemann is probably on vacation already, but Coach Lisinski lives in the city and she's got his credentials memorized. I can ask her to pull the full list of majors if you want to see it, but your registration window isn't open until the end of June, so I'm not sure you can do much about it yet."

"Jackie Lisinski," Jean said, testing his memory. "Fitness coach."

"Oui!" Jeremy said, looking insufferably pleased with himself for all of two seconds. "That's actually the only French I know, I think. Want to teach me any?"

"No," Jean said, so fiercely Jeremy shot him a startled look.

Jean barely saw it. He was years away, watching a different beautiful boy lean in close to say, *Will you teach me when he's not watching? It could be our secret.*

The unexpected weight of a hand on his shoulder had Jean lashing out, and the car swerved to the sound of too many horns as Jeremy briefly lost control of the wheel. Jean came back to himself with a sickening lurch as Jeremy tried to find his lane again. He folded his arms tight across his chest and squeezed like he could somehow crush his pounding heart into dust. In his peripheral vision Jeremy was waving hurried apologies out his window at the car he'd nearly sideswiped. It

128

was another mile or two before Jeremy finally risked looking at him again, but Jean kept his stare out the window.

"Sorry," Jeremy said at last. "I guess I shouldn't have asked."

Jean could have said it had nothing to do with him. "Never ask me again."

The rest of the ride downtown passed in dead silence.

Jean had incorrectly assumed Jeremy was taking him to his dorm room. He saw the USC signs start to pop up along the side of the road, along with more detailed signs with directions and distances. Instead, Jeremy turned off and entered a neighborhood of close, squat buildings and too many cars. The pale yellow house he was looking for was halfway down a narrow street. One car was already parked in a driveway barely big enough for it with a motorcycle parked lengthways in front of it, so Jeremy double-parked at the curb.

When Jean got out of the car empty-handed Jeremy prompted him, "Bag?"

Jean doubted anyone in this neighborhood would break into the car just for a small suitcase, but he didn't know the area well enough to be sure of it. He obediently pulled the carry-on out, and Jeremy locked the car from his fob as soon as the passenger door was closed.

Three uneven steps led them up to a porch barely big enough for both their bodies. Jeremy flipped through his cluttered keyring until he found the one he needed, and he let them inside with a cheery, "We're here!" that Jean didn't think anyone could hear over the music blaring at the far end of the hall. Jeremy toed out of his shoes just inside the door, so Jean did the same as he tugged the door closed behind them. The door had a chain as well as a deadbolt, but since the former hadn't been up to keep him and Jeremy out, he let it dangle free for now.

They passed a small den without slowing, intent on making it to the kitchen. Jean hesitated in the doorway to take in the chaos. The island was absolutely cluttered with

Tupperware. A rice cooker was open and billowing steam, a blender full of something very purple was leaking in two places, and three different cutting boards were covered in rejected pieces of what Jean assumed used to be actual food.

The music was from a boombox on the counter, and the room's lone occupant—Catalina Alvarez, number 37, starting backliner—was using a head of cauliflower as a microphone so she could sing along. She caught sight of them on a ridiculous whirl around and immediately cast the cauliflower to one side. Instead of cranking the boombox's volume down to a tolerable level, she simply yanked its plug out of the outlet.

"The boys!" she said, triumphant, like she'd had anything to do with their arrival. "You just missed Laila. She had to pop out for more rice."

"You just bought rice," Jeremy said. "I was there."

"Yes," Catalina said, "but I might have forgotten the bag was already open when I tossed it at the island." Jean and Jeremy both glanced down and saw the floor was littered with little brown grains. Catalina waved off Jeremy's exasperated look and leaned past him to peer at Jean. "So this is the wonder boy? You're taller in person. Nice. We need more height on the backline."

"Jean, Cat, Cat, Jean," Jeremy said, waving between them. "If you want to give him the grand tour I can try and salvage… this." He sent a meaningful look around at the chaos.

"No, no, it can sit," Cat said. "I've got a couple lids still in the dishwasher, anyway. Since you're here, we'll start here. Good? Good!" She glanced at Jean for only a second before opening and closing cabinets and drawers in rapid succession. "With Jillian we kind of just mixed all our food together, but if you want your own space for things we left you these shelves here. Don't bother doubling up on the basic stuff, okay? Space is too limited for that. Seasonings, breading, whatever, just take it from our side first.

"Fridge," she said, as if he couldn't see it, and she swung it open to indicate a clear corner. "Same goes here. Laila and I

130

do meal prep for the week's breakfasts and lunches, so we use a lot of space. Sorry in advance and good luck making anything fit. We keep stickers on the side here," she pointed to a little wire basket held in place by magnets, "and a marker so you can track expiration dates as needed. Put the marker back when you're done. *Please* put the marker back. Laila never remembers and I can never find it again. I have bought so many markers. So many.

"Pots and pans," Cat said, moving on to the cabinets built into the island. "User beware: the big pot doesn't have a lid. I don't remember breaking it, but I haven't been able to find it in like two months. Over here—"

She had to take a breath to reach her next destination, and Jean cut in with a disbelieving, "You live here."

Cat stared at him, then at Jeremy, then at Jean. "Yes?"

"I thought I told you," Jeremy said. "You're going to be rooming with Laila and Cat."

Jean was waiting for this to make sense, but each second left him feeling a little more ill at ease. Cat only gave him a few seconds to sort it out before saying, "That's not going to be a problem, I assume? Because if it is, it would've been easier to know before we forged your signature on the lease in Jillian's place."

Jean turned on Jeremy. "There has to be something else. I won't live off-campus."

"You don't want to, but you will," Jeremy said. "You're on the lease."

"Jeremy," Cat pressed.

"It's fine," Jeremy said to her.

"It's *not* fine," Jean insisted. "I can't be this far from the court. I'm not—" *allowed*. He hadn't had a say in it while he was in Abby's care, but now he had a team back. There was no legitimate reason to be so far out from the stadium. By the time summer practices started he'd be three months behind. He needed his gear. He needed easy access. He needed to prove he belonged on the lineup, that the number on his face meant

131

something even without the Ravens. His life depended on it. "Time wasted in transit is time I could be doing drills."

"We're a mile out from the stadium," Jeremy said, one hand out like he was trying to soothe a riled animal. Jean wanted to break his fingers. "I can show you the way there and back as soon as you get your stuff settled. On this side of campus it's almost a straight shot to the fitness center, and the way down to the Gold Court takes only a couple turns. Easiest route in the world, I've walked it a hundred times."

"How close is beside the point," Jean said, waving that off with an impatient jerk of his hand. "Why aren't the Trojans required to live on campus?"

Cat finally clued in that she was not at the heart of the problem. "We are our freshman year, but after that it's up to us where we go. So long as we get to class and practice on time, what's it matter? Dorms are so noisy, and they always smell like bodies. This place is much better."

Jean ignored her. "Knox."

"I'd really appreciate it if you wouldn't call me by my last name, just so it's said," Jeremy said. For once he wasn't smiling, though his expression wasn't entirely unkind as he considered his newest player. "I told you we were going to have to deal with some hiccups, a bit of compromise between your way and ours. Even if I wanted to put you in campus housing—which I *don't*—I can't. We aren't like the Ravens or the Foxes, you know? We don't room with each other exclusively."

Jean stared. "You're lying."

"The only other Trojans who share a room don't have room for you. Everyone else is mixed in with the general populace or athletes from other teams. I went back and forth with Kevin on this for days trying to figure out what the lesser evil was going to be with you, and he voted in favor of the team. That means Cat and Laila are your only option." Jeremy jerked a thumb toward Cat, but Jean couldn't look away from Jeremy.

132

"Why don't the Trojans room together?" he demanded.

"Because as much as we love each other we do like meeting other people, maybe?"

"An unnecessary distraction," Jean said. "You have to see that."

"This'll be great," Cat insisted. "I'm loud, yeah, and sometimes Laila leaves her brain lying around, but we're good roommates if I do say so myself."

Jeremy counted off on his fingers. "You're getting your buddy system, Trojans in your classes, and Trojans for your roommates. It's three out of four; I'd call that a win."

"It isn't a win," Jean said, but Jeremy only shrugged at him. Jean folded his arms tight across his chest. He clenched his jaw so hard his throat ached and finally asked, "Who is my partner going to be?"

Jeremy answered one question with two: "Do they have to share your major and do they need to be in the same position on court?" He caught himself and put a hand up. "Forget the first; we're kind of winging it on that one. I'll reword. Can you take classes with someone who isn't your partner?"

Jean didn't miss the curious look Cat sent Jeremy, but he ignored it in favor of considering the questions. "Classes are flexible so long as there are at least two enrolled. Partners are almost always on the same line, but it's not required. If one has a weakness the other shores up, then they are put together until they can even each other out. The coaches evaluate it each semester."

Jeremy put his hands on his hips, tapping his thumbs as he thought it through. When he glanced at Cat, Jean assumed she was going to be the sacrificial Trojan, but then Jeremy smiled at Jean and said, "Then it should be fine if it's me, right? I'm captain, after all. I'm not a backliner, but I bet we can learn a lot from each other on the court. You teach me some fancy Raven tricks, and I'll teach you the Trojan way of having fun on the court."

"Teach me something more relevant if you even know

how," Jean said, and sent him a shrewd look. "You don't live on campus?"

"I'm here from June until the start of the school year, and then I'm usually only over on the weekends," Jeremy said. Jean didn't miss the way Jeremy's gaze slid past him to peer into the distance, or the tight tug at the corner of Cat's mouth. Jeremy was still smiling, but the light had gone out in it. It was an easy, practiced expression, but Jean had spent too many years trying to track Riko's moods to not realize how empty it was. "I'll be living at home the rest of the time."

Either Cat was nosey beyond belief or she also noticed Jeremy's mood dip, because she turned to Jean and asked, "You have siblings? You strike me as an only child." When Jeremy pulled a face at her she said, "What? Laila's an only child. It's so obvious. I'm right, though, right?"

For a moment Jean felt a small hand tugging at his, but he slammed that memory back into place so hard his vision swam. His first year at Evermore he'd tried holding onto Marseille, wanting to believe there was something outside of the suffocating Nest and Riko's practiced cruelty. In time he'd let it all go and watched it rupture without regret. His father had sold him to the Moriyamas knowing the sort of people they were and knowing what would happen to him. Why would Jean want to hold onto any of that?

It was a touch unfair, perhaps, that he expected his parents to defy the Moriyamas when he himself could not, but did they have to agree so quickly? His father hadn't even asked for a moment to consider the master's offer or to confer with his wife, and his mother had only shrugged and changed the subject when she heard the news later.

"My personal life is not your business," Jean said, because Cat was still waiting for an answer. "Now or ever. Remember that."

"Your personal issues are if you're on my lineup," Cat said, but there was no heat in it. She was studying him with unabashed fascination. "Anyway! We never got to finish the

134

tour. Onward."

She sailed out of the room, and Jeremy motioned for Jean to follow her.

Rather than backtracking to the front door and starting from there, Cat took them down a short hall where the bedrooms were. She opened each door as she passed so Jean could see inside and rattled off a quick explanation as she went. "This one's ours. If the door's open, come on in and say hello. If it's closed, enter at your own peril. This one we converted into a study room. Rooms are too small to fit desks and beds, and no way are we getting studying done if our computers are in with the TV, right? That desk there is yours now.

"And here's your room," she said. When she pushed this last door open, she moved with it so she could lean against it where it stopped against the wall. It was bigger than the one he'd had at Evermore and smaller than the one at Abby's. It came with some basic furnishings, though the mattress and curtain rods were bare. Jean knew there wouldn't be a second bed, but he still looked for it.

"Where are your suitcases?" Cat asked. "Still in Jeremy's car?"

"He only brought a carry-on," Jeremy said.

"Oh? I'll write down our address so you can have the rest shipped, then."

Jean set his small suitcase off to the other side of the door. "What else would there be? You've made my gear irrelevant by signing me to your line."

The way Cat looked at him made him wonder how he'd possibly misspoken this time. He didn't have long to wonder because Cat started counting off options on her fingers. "Toiletries? Clothes? Shoes? If you tell me that you somehow fit everything in that little bag, I'm going to call you a liar right now." When Jean just dismissively looked away from her, she straightened with indignation. He expected her promised insult, but what came out was a strident, "You are not telling me that is everything you own. What the fuck?"

Jeremy caught hold of her to drag her out of the room. He answered Jean's cool look with an easy smile and only said, "We'll leave you to get settled. Cat, let's go fix up the kitchen before Laila comes back and sees what you've done to the place."

Jean knew they were going to be talking about him, but there was no point trying to listen in. He closed the door behind them and slowly made his way across the room to the window. There wasn't much of a view, as the houses were all packed in around here, but a low wooden fence separated this one from the next and someone had spray painted stick figures and daffodils on this side of the posts.

This was a mistake, he thought, but it was far too late to do anything about it.

Unpacking took only a few minutes. The picture of Renee he'd stolen from the Foxhole Court was set face-down on the top of his dresser beside the laptop Wymack hadn't let him return. His notebooks from the Ravens were hidden in the top drawer alongside his destroyed postcards and magnets, and his clothes fit into the second drawer with room to spare. As he was checking the pockets of the carry-on to ensure he hadn't missed anything, he found an envelope in the outer pouch. Inside was a stack of bills and an index card that just said "I'm not dealing with this again. Buy some fucking clothes. –W"

The presumption of the other man was annoying beyond belief, but Jean put the cash and note in with his postcards. The carry-on was tucked into the closet, and just like that Jean was done. There was no reason to linger here with his few things. After two months of quasi-isolation at Abby's house, he finally had a place again. He wasn't sure what to make of these Trojans yet, but his opinion came second. They were his teammates, Jeremy was his partner, and Jean had too much at stake to not make this work.

CHAPTER EIGHT
Jeremy

Cat made a beeline for the kitchen. When Jeremy realized she was going for her boombox, he caught hold of her sleeve to haul her to a stop. She pinched her fingers together rapidly, miming the flapping of a mouth, and he gestured to his ear and in the direction of Jean's room. The music would keep Jean from hearing whatever she wanted to say to Jeremy, but it also meant they wouldn't hear when Jean left his room in search of them. Whether Cat understood what he was getting at or not, she gave up on her music and whirled on him instead. She opened her mouth, put up a finger in a bid for him to wait, and then just stared into the distance.

"Yes?" Jeremy prompted her.

"He's a little off," she said.

"We knew he would be," Jeremy said.

Cat drummed her fingernails on the counter for a few moments, then put her restless energy to work at the island. She scooped rice into open Tupperware with an almost angry pace, and Jeremy went in search of the broom. "Are you sure it's the right thing to do, playing into whatever's going on in there?" She gestured to her head with her rice spoon. "You could probably split babysitting duties among a couple of us so you don't get overwhelmed."

"Buddy system," Jeremy corrected her patiently. "Kevin seems to think it's important; he said it was our only chance to acclimate Jean here." More specifically, he'd confessed his own lingering reliance on it: Kevin had gone from Riko's side to Andrew's, and in his first year he had never put more than a campus between him and the short goalkeeper. Jeremy wasn't

137

sure he was completely comfortable with the idea, but until he figured out something better it felt best to play along.

"I can help," Cat said.

"I know," Jeremy said, smiling down at his work, "but you and Laila are already helping. You're letting him stay here and watching over him when I have to go home during the week. The rest of it will be easy. I don't exactly have a lot of classes left, you know? Keeping an eye on him at campus will give me something to do this year."

"Easy," Cat echoed, with skepticism. She worked for a minute in silence, then flicked him a sly look. "Easy on the eyes, maybe."

There was no point denying it when they'd known each other this long. Jean was exactly the kind of guy Jeremy was prone to trip himself up over: raven-haired, gray-eyed, and tall without being gangly. His nose had obviously been broken more than once over the years, and his mouth was always halfway to a disapproving frown, but neither of these detracted from the overall picture. There was no point dwelling on it, though; between the unrelenting rumors and Kevin's cryptic messages, Jeremy knew a bad idea when he saw one.

"Doesn't matter," Jeremy said with a theatrical sigh. "Like you said, he's a bit off. It's not fair to either of us if I look."

Cat gave a knowing nod. "Make sure all the screws are tightened before getting on the ride, right? Safety first."

"Jesus, Cat," Jeremy said, and was saved by the sound of a door opening down the hall.

Cat turned back to her work with frenzied enthusiasm. Jeremy had half-expected Jean to ignore them as long as he possibly could, but the former Raven looked to Jeremy as he took up post in the doorway. Jeremy looked at Cat and pretended they'd been in the middle of a very different conversation: "So you said yeah? You're still good to go with me tomorrow?"

"Sure, sure," Cat agreed. "Maybe we'll all go, and Laila

can take Jean next door. Fox Hills, right?" She waited for him to nod before looking at Jean. "Jeremy's getting his hair prettied up for his last year. You know, we could probably call and see if they can squeeze you in, if you want? You're noticeably uneven. You cut it yourself, or…?"

Jean scowled. "No one asked you."

"On that note, I'm going to finish giving Jean the tour," Jeremy said, emptying his dustpan into the trash. "Yell if you break anything else."

Jean stepped back out of the doorway at Jeremy's approach. Jeremy slipped past and took Jean back down the hall, showing him the places they'd missed upon arrival: the three-quarter bathroom, the door that hid the stacked washer and dryer, and the closet stuffed to bursting with cleaners and toilet paper. The last stop was the living room that served as Jeremy's home away from home. It was one of his favorite places in the world, almost too crowded to be comfortable.

"Pretty cool, right?" he asked as he led Jean further into the room. He surveyed it all as if seeing it for the first time. Laila had brought home her papasan chair from an estate sale, and Cat had reupholstered the couch to match it. Quilts Cat's grandmother had made sat in layers across the back of it, adding pops of color. Three different end tables were set around the room with mismatching lamps, including one that looked like a pile of mushrooms. Jillian had mounted a kid's basketball hoop to the wall over the trash can, though the crumpled napkins and papers sitting around the bin said they all needed a little work on their aim.

A tabletop air hockey board was hanging from a hook between some potted plants. White Christmas lights hung back and forth in wide loops on the far wall, whereas pink hanging lights rested against the blackout curtains over the bay window. On the side of the room closest to them were two free-standing off-brand arcade machines they'd bought on sale two years back: one a retro space shooting game and the other a basic puzzle game that tended to glitch out after the eighth level.

Between them hung an evil eye Laila bought when visiting her family in Beirut.

Near the far wall was a set of matching bikes, their chains and helmets hanging off the handles. Propped up against Laila's back tire was a standee of a golden retriever that had been relegated to the kitchen for the last few weeks. Jeremy went over to it immediately.

"This is Barkbark von Barkenstein. You can call him Barkbark or Mister B for short. It's a bit of a mouthful on its own."

Jean looked from him to the cardboard dog and back again. "What?"

"I really want a dog, but my mother's allergic. Cat and Laila were willing to hide one here for me, but the lease says no pets allowed and her uncle won't budge on it. This is the best we can do for now," Jeremy said, moving Barkbark closer to the papasan chair. "Cat's brother works at a pet store, and he let us have the display when they took it down. Who's a good boy?" he asked, giving the dog's head a quick pat that nearly knocked the standee over. "And that's pretty much the tour. Questions?"

Jean was still side-eyeing the cutout dog. "What purpose does it serve?"

"It makes us happy," Jeremy said. He got the sense Jean was waiting for something a little more substantial, but it was all he had to offer. "Isn't that enough?"

The curl of Jean's lip was answer enough. "You don't have a bed."

"Nope," Jeremy said. "During the school year I'm only here on the weekends, so I usually just crash out here." He gave the side of the couch a light kick. "Technically there's a stowaway bed in here, but since I'd have to rearrange everything to use it, I tend to just sprawl out on top."

"What about in June?" Jean asked.

Jeremy shrugged. "Before I'd just move into Jillian's room after she went home for the summer. Now that you've

140

moved in, I'm good to stay out here. I don't mind, really. It's a surprisingly comfy couch." Jean didn't seem impressed with that explanation, but he kept his opinion to himself. Jeremy looked around to make sure he'd covered everything, then asked, "Ready to see the stadium?"

That got Jean's attention immediately. "Yes."

"Fair warning, though: Davis knows you're getting in today, and I promised I'd tell him if we were stopping by. He wants to get a look at you. One of our nurses," he said belatedly.

Jean was undeterred. "Take me to the court."

Jeremy stopped by the kitchen to let Cat know they were heading out, but he was only halfway back to Jean when the lock on the front door clacked undone and Laila arrived. She made it two steps inside when she realized there was a stranger in her living room doorway. She didn't have to ask, seeing how Jean had a number on his face, but she didn't take her eyes off him as she slowly closed the door behind her with her heel. She'd come back with just a bag of rice in her hands, and she chucked it down the hall in Jeremy's general direction.

"Jean Moreau," she said, stepping closer to Jean to study him. "I'm Laila Dermott."

"Goalkeeper," Jean said with a nod. "You're very good."

He didn't say it with any warmth, but there was nothing grudging or hesitant to it either. It was simple fact, recognition from one talented athlete to another. Laila was too startled to smile immediately, but when she got her wits about her, she answered with a wry, "I've had better seasons."

"You were sabotaged," Jean said. "Next year the Trojans will be champions."

He said it with such easy surety that Jeremy's heart kicked up a notch. "You think so?"

"Going to make that much of a difference on our backline?" Cat asked, following the sound of Laila's voice to the hall. She sounded more amused by Jean's arrogance than offended. "I notice you didn't say *I* was any good."

141

She was teasing, but Jean answered: "You are, but you're weaker on your left side and you don't know where your own waist is. You miss every single ball that passes between your hip and your rib cage. Your coaches should have corrected that issue years ago."

Cat laughed, delighted. "Oh, he's good. A bit rude, but I like him. I think we're going to be good friends." If she noticed the cool look Jean sent her for that, her smile didn't dim. "Any other trade secrets that'll give us an edge over the Ravens in the end?"

"You won't have to worry about them next year," Jean said. "The Court is gone, as is the—head coach. Losing the Nest will be the last strike. They will implode before long, no matter how desperately Edgar Allan tries to save them."

The edge in his voice wasn't regret, but Jeremy couldn't narrow it down. He was too distracted thinking about Grayson and Lucas. He wondered if Jean knew that one of his former teammates was in the state. Judging by Jean's tone and the nastiness circulating online, Jeremy wasn't sure this was the best time to bring it up.

Laila peered up at Jean and asked, "Are you going to be okay with that?"

Jean was silent so long Jeremy wondered if he'd already backed out of this conversation to wait for the next, but finally Jean turned a steady look on Laila. "Yes," he said, and if he didn't sound sure, he at least sounded angry. "Let them all burn. I hope none of them survive."

"I appreciate your conviction, but you're definitely off press duty," Laila said dryly.

"You mean the Nest is real?" Cat asked, eyes alight. "I've looked at Edgar Allan's campus map, you know? The Ravens have two houses earmarked for their dorms. I figured the Nest was a rumor to sell the whole 'we're a creepy cult' image. What?" she asked when Jeremy sent her a pained look. "It's been bugging me for years! I want to know all about it."

"I'm showing Jean the route to campus," Jeremy said.

142

"Laila, good luck in the kitchen. Cat destroyed it."

Laila looked to the ceiling for patience. "Babe, I left you alone for twenty minutes."

"It's not that bad anymore," Cat protested. When Jeremy laughed, she aimed a light kick at his calf. "At least pull the knife out of my back before you go, Jeremy. Damn."

"We'll be back before dinner," Jeremy told Laila when he caught up to her.

Rather than move out of the way, she got the door open for them, and Jeremy led Jean down the narrow porch steps back to street level. He stopped at his car, waited for Jean to move up alongside him, and pulled his key ring out of his pocket.

Jillian's key was hanging alongside his copy, and it took him just a little bit of wiggling to get it off its hook. He held it out to Jean, who took it after only a moment's hesitation and slipped it into his pocket. Jeremy traded his keys for his phone so he could tap out a heads-up to Jeffrey Davis that they were on the way. The response was almost immediate, and Jeremy put his phone away in favor of his newest teammate.

"Okay, so this is the starting point, right?" he asked, and pointed in the direction they'd be going. "We'll be walking back and forth with you as promised, but just in case, this is where you go. Hang a right at the corner."

Jean kept pace with him easily enough, so Jeremy filled the silence with talk of the local area: which houses tended to have the loudest parties, where the nearest grocery store was if Jean needed just a couple things, and where the closest bubble tea place was if that was something Jean was into. Jeremy wasn't entirely sure he was listening, but then Jean frowned and asked,

"Carbonated tea?"

"What? No, boba tea," Jeremy said. It didn't seem to clear anything up, so he said, "Flavored teas with tapioca balls? Really? If I tell Laila you've never had it, she'll lose her mind. Every cafe in a two-mile radius knows her name and face.

Next time you're in the kitchen just take a look at the fridge. Half of her magnets are from tea shops."

"Does Coach Lisinski know?" Jean asked.

"That she likes bubble tea?" Jeremy asked, lost. "I... assume so?"

"And she lets her drink it?"

"What?"

"It shouldn't have made it onto a nutrition plan," Jean said, not at all aware he was saying something strange. He was still studying the nearby houses with their tiny yards and decorated porches. Jeremy almost forgot what they were talking about, distracted by the blatant curiosity in Jean's wandering stare. "Either they've given her an unreasonable number of allowances because she is trapped in goal, or they do not care enough about her wellbeing. It's unforgivable either way."

"I take it the Ravens were very keen on their diets," Jeremy said, because how else was he supposed to respond to that? "Can you tell me about it?"

Jean considered that, then began counting off on his fingertips. He listed each of the Ravens' regimented meals down to the exact proportions they were expected to ingest. Jeremy felt cold all over listening to him. He could see the reasoning behind the decisions made by the Ravens' staff, but that didn't make any of this okay. That the Ravens couldn't choose their majors or what they put in their own bodies spoke to a level of control he didn't want to consider. Surely they had some autonomy?

"Okay," he said, because Jean was looking expectantly at him. He was waiting for a summary of the Trojans' diet, Jeremy realized, so he'd know how to adjust his meals accordingly. "First off, we don't do that here. We get a lecture once a semester about good nutrition, but the coaches trust us to make the right decision most of the time. If we go a little wild and have some bubble tea or some fast food, then who really cares? We're going to burn it off at practice anyway."

"Who cares?" Jean echoed. "You should care."

"You can't tell me you've never had something fun just for the sake of it. Pizza? Pie? A cheeseburger?" Jeremy waited for a confession that didn't come; Jean only looked annoyed. "I don't know whether to be impressed by your self-control or depressed. Just… keep in mind that now you can have those things. If you want, I mean. No one's going to say anything if you indulge now and again, and the coaches won't care or ask. Okay?"

Jean looked at the intersection they'd stopped at. "Across?"

Jeremy gave up the argument for now and sighed. "Yeah, we're crossing." He tapped the button for the pedestrian light and pointed across the street. "If you keep going straight, you'll pass the fitness center eventually. I'll take us home that way so you can get a good look at it. For now we're crossing and going right. Three rights so far, got it? Right out of the apartment, right at the first corner, right on Vermont."

Jean didn't answer, but he followed Jeremy across the street and south down Vermont. "This is the western edge of campus," Jeremy told him. "Once we've got you registered for your classes I'll bring you back through here and show you campus proper, okay? We'll make a grand tour of it. Check it out," he said, and gestured to the open gates they were passing. "You can technically cut through here and still make it to the court, but I figure the most straightforward route is the easiest to remember."

At Vermont and Exposition, Jeremy had Jean cross the street and cut left. He had half a mind to cut through the park, but the sight of cops lounging at the nearer entrance had him sticking to the sidewalk along Exposition. There was little to no chance he'd know them, and no reason they'd recognize him, but Jeremy kept his gaze forward and his mouth shut until they were past.

The road they needed wasn't far, and Jeremy pointed as they reached it. "Dinosaurs," he said, as if Jean could somehow look past the statues on the corner. "When you see

145

them, you turn right. Following me so far?"

Jean thought about it for just a moment. "No."

"First time is the most disorienting," Jeremy said, and pointed again as soon as Memorial Coliseum came into view. "Our football stadium. Games are hecka fun and worth checking out. Come on, we're down this way.

"You might've noticed we don't have a lot of room to expand around here between the city and student housing," Jeremy said. "USC is laid out as smart as can be, but it means when they wanted to add a new stadium they had to steal room from somewhere else. Out here was the best place they could find and still keep it near campus. It used to be a multiuse parking lot for the local museums and science centers, but USC basically paid a fortune to move the parking underground and repurpose the land.

"And there she is," he said warmly. "Welcome to the Gold Court."

USC's Exy stadium didn't have the same dramatic architecture as the football stadium, but they'd attempted to at least make it complementary with arched gates along the main entryway. Halfway down the northern wall was a narrow parking lot. Half of it was for vendors on game nights, though several of the Trojans made use of it during summer practices. The other half was reserved for the team's staff and, since there was a door to the locker room there, was fenced in. Jeremy had a key to get in the lot and the keycode for the stadium door, and he ushered Jean in ahead of him.

A short tunnel led them straight to the Home locker rooms. On game nights it was a deafening place to linger since it cut through the outer court where the vendors were. Rather than force the Trojans underground for that part, they simply built steps up and over it inside the stadium, which meant a near-constant stampede overhead until everyone got settled for first serve. Luckily the door at the far end to let them into the locker room helped keep out most of the noise. Jeremy tapped in the code and listened for the resulting beep.

146

"I could give you the codes, but we're about to lose access until mid-June," Jeremy said. "They're going to deep clean the place and refurbish it. But here we are!"

He took Jean on a meandering tour of the Trojans' headquarters. The team had separate showers, but the locker room with their gear was co-ed and arranged by line. Jeremy went straight to the backliners' section and to the locker halfway down. It was empty for now, since Jean's equipment was still on order, but Jeremy tapped his knuckles to the number freshly pasted to the front.

"Twenty-nine," he said. "That's you!"

Jean put his fingers to the number on his face. "It could have been thirty, at least."

"No," Jeremy said. "Thirty looks too much like three at an angle. This is a fresh start, right?" He gestured around at the rest of the lockers. "With you we'll have eleven backliners this fall, but two of 'em will be redshirts."

At the sharp look Jean gave him, he shrugged and said, "Exy being an exception to the NCAA rule only worked while we were still trying to get established. Now there's no legitimate reason the ERC can argue for five seasons, so sooner or later it's going to get repealed. It works in our favor to implement it preemptively, and it's good for our freshmen to spend a year just getting used to the reality of college life.

"Same for size, right?" Jeremy asked. "We've got all these big teams because we were trying to fill the major leagues and pros, and now we've got more athletes than we have places for them. Wonder how long it'll be until we're all down in the fifteen to twenty range." Jeremy cast a look around the locker room, trying to imagine it without the rowdy chaos of his massive team. "Come on."

There were only a few rooms left: huddle rooms for each line, each outfitted with whiteboards and TVs; a weights room that was more for physical therapy and warmups than daily fitness; the hall the four coaches' offices were on; and the medical ward, with a communal office for the three nurses and two separate rooms for injured players. One was intended for quick fixes and checkups, whereas the other had the Trojans' radiography equipment.

That was where they found Jeffrey Davis. The balding nurse was sitting on his backless stool, a file open in his hands. He looked up at their entrance and squinted at Jean above half-moon glasses.

"Jean Moreau, I presume. Thanks for stopping by today. I hear we've got a couple fractures to check up on."

"A couple *what*?" Jeremy asked.

Davis turned his frown on Jeremy. "You were the one who told the coaches he was sidelined with injuries. I assumed you knew the extent? My mistake." It wasn't quite an apology, but Jean seemed unruffled to have his business spilled. Davis motioned for Jean to enter. "I'll have him back to you as soon as I can. Close the door on your way out. Now, if you please," he said when Jeremy hesitated.

Jeremy swallowed every question he wanted to ask and saw himself out. He knew better than to linger and instead went back to the locker room. He had his phone out as soon as he sat down on the nearest bench. He tried calling, but Kevin didn't pick up. Jeremy checked the time, added three hours, and settled for texting: "You didn't tell me they broke bones?? That's not hazing!"

He knew he wouldn't get an immediate answer if Kevin wasn't available to take his call, but he stared down at his phone and willed Kevin to take a break from whatever he was in the middle of. It was all for naught; Jean hunted him down before Jeremy got a peep from the east coast.

"Hey," Jeremy said. "Do you want to talk about it?"

"I'm on track with Winfield's estimate," Jean said, as if that was the question Jeremy was asking. "Davis approved me for easy stretching, but he won't let me near weights until I'm a bit further along."

"I—That's good, but that's not what I meant. I knew you were injured, and Kevin said it was bad, but I didn't think…"

148

Jeremy trailed off before trying again. "I shouldn't have made you walk here, sorry. We could have brought my car."

"My legs are healed," Jean pointed out. "I should be ready by the time practices start, but he insists on assessing me again before he will sign off on me." For a moment his expression slipped; the frustration that pulled hard at his mouth was all self-directed irritation. "I haven't been taken off the court this long in years. I've fallen unforgivably behind."

"I'm literally begging you," Jeremy said, holding up a hand. "For five seconds just forget that Exy is a thing and focus on the fact that your own teammates really hurt you."

"Accidents happen in scrimmages," Jean said.

Jeremy wondered what Jean would say if he knew Kevin had already called it hazing. There was, of course, the slightest chance Kevin had exaggerated to appeal to Jeremy's better nature, but Jeremy refused to believe it. Laila had already said it: Edgar Allan would not let one of the best backliners in the country go if they had any means to keep him. Something had gone horribly wrong at Evermore.

Jeremy teetered between his options: call Jean out on his lie and force him to come clean, or let Jean hide behind his story a little longer. In the end he leaned toward discretion because he didn't want Jean to go after Kevin. He still needed Kevin's help if he was going to navigate this year and Jean's increasing number of issues.

"We don't check like that around here," Jeremy said, hating himself a little for letting it slide. "We can't not hit each other, but we don't hit to hurt, only to control the flow of the game. So long as you don't do anything reckless to set yourself back between now and then, I can't imagine they'll keep you out of practices."

It wasn't what he wanted to say, but it was the right thing to say, judging by Jean's quiet but firm, "I am not reckless."

Not a correction, but a promise: Jean would not do anything that would further delay his return to the court.

"Come on," Jeremy said, getting off the bench. "I'll show

149

you the way to the fitness center. We've actually got a couple on campus, but our team uses Lyon. We could go back the way we came, but I want to see if the bookstore's open."

He led Jean out of the stadium and locked the gate behind them. It was an easy walk north to campus, and Jeremy smiled as they headed down tree-lined sidewalks. Most of his siblings dreamed of leaving the city, but Jeremy had known all his life he wanted to attend USC. He loved everything about it, from the architecture to the well-claimed space to the way it managed to feel private and safe despite the major city hugging its borders.

He'd said the campus tour would wait until he could show Jean the more relevant buildings, but it was hard not to point out landmarks as they passed. Jean even tolerated a brief detour into Alumni Park to see the fountain and obediently studied the Tommy Trojan and Traveler statues when Jeremy stopped them there a minute later. He didn't look as interested as Jeremy had hoped, but he didn't tell Jeremy to stop talking either. It would have to be enough for now.

Turned out the bookstore was indeed still open, so Jeremy made a beeline for the corner with campus apparel. Jean had, unsurprisingly, come to California dressed in black from head to toe. Jeremy was determined to get a bit of color on him, and he started digging through the t-shirt racks for something appropriate. He wanted the loudest thing he could find, but he also wasn't sure how well Jean's sun-starved skin could handle cardinal red. There were plenty of shirts with black bases and bold lettering, but Jeremy would be damned if he put Jean in something black and red his first day in California. That left something gray or white, he supposed.

"What size are you?" he asked as he found a couple options. Jean just looked askance at him, so Jeremy said, "Housewarming gift from us to you."

"I have shirts," Jean pointed out, gesturing to the one he had on.

"Sure," Jeremy said, thinking of Jean's tiny bag. He

wanted to ask how many Jean had managed to cram in there. Instead, he chose a less intrusive approach: "How many of them are black?"

His self-censure was wasted, because Jean simply said, "Both."

The plastic hanger in Jeremy's hand gave a warning creak. Jeremy fought to relax his grip. Keeping his tone light was the easier battle after years as the Trojans' mouthpiece. "You're going to need something more in line with dress code. We're supposed to turn out in school colors on game days. We're a ways away from the first match, sure, but if we get it now we don't have to worry about it later when the campus is more crowded. Size?"

The curl of Jean's lip said he didn't buy Jeremy's story, but he tugged at his shirt collar. Jeremy saw light glint off a silver chain but tucked it aside for another day; he'd just realized what Jean was trying to do and moved to help. Jean's shirt was loose enough Jeremy could pull the tag around where they both could see it. He hoped to take the conversation on a lighter turn with a teasing, "Don't even know your own size?" but it backfired almost immediately.

"Why would I? We don't shop for ourselves," Jean asked, and Jeremy went still with his hand on the collar of Jean's shirt. He stared up at Jean, too startled to speak. It took Jean only a moment to realize he'd said something strange, and a frown tugged at his mouth as he sent a sideways look at Jeremy. "You do," he said, not quite a question.

"What do you mean, you don't shop for yourselves?" Jeremy asked in a low voice. "Obviously the school has to provide your uniforms and gear, but—your own clothes? What would they have done if you picked up a cool shirt while you were out on errands? Made you return it?"

"What errands? We didn't leave Evermore or campus unless we were going to a game."

Jeremy needed to back out of Jean's personal space, but he couldn't make himself let go of Jean's shirt. Less than two hours ago Cat had gleefully accused the Ravens of being a cult. It was true the Ravens took their image and reputation far too seriously, but Jeremy had never put much weight into that rude rumor. Maybe Cat was right for once, and Jeremy felt ill.

"Socks," Jeremy said. "Notebooks, pencils, bookbags. You had to need new ones sometime. Then what?"

"The coaches gave us what we needed if they were legitimate requests," Jean said. "We just had to fill out a form and submit it before the weekend if we wanted it back by Monday. We didn't have time to deal with distractions like that. That the Trojans somehow do speaks to an alarming amount of free time in your daily schedules. How are you a Big Three team if you spend so much time away from the court?"

"If I ask you how much the Ravens practice, will I regret it?" Jeremy asked.

"Yes," Jean said. "I asked first."

Jeremy had assumed it was a rude dismissal of the Trojans' commitment, not a genuine inquiry, but there was an edge in Jean's voice and ice in his eyes. Jean really wanted to know.

He wants to know what it was for.

The thought came out of nowhere, nearly turning his stomach inside-out. Jeremy forced himself to let go and step back at last. Jean had just finished his junior year, which meant he'd had the last three years of his life dictated to him. Everything had been outside of his control from what he'd studied to what he'd eaten to the very clothes on his back.

The Ravens had given up everything to be the undefeated champions, only to be destroyed last month by a tiny team from South Carolina. Now Edgar Allan was overhauling the program, and Jeremy understood why Jean predicted they'd implode. Everything they'd tolerated had been for nothing in the end, and maybe by now some of them had forgotten how to be their own person. Jean was in a position to finally see just how much he'd sacrificed when no one should have ever demanded it of him.

152

Jeremy scrubbed goosebumps from his arms as he debated how to answer. He could say "We're recruited from the best of what high schools have to offer nationwide," but that went for every Class I team. He could say "We were chosen to play here, so we want to give it everything we've got," but presumably those who made the cut at Edgar Allan were driven by the same need to be great. In the end the only answer he could think of was one he knew Jean wouldn't accept.

"Because we don't let ourselves get too lost in this," he said. "If we don't get bogged down in the numbers, we're free to have fun, and what's fun for us is pushing ourselves as far as we can go. We still love what we're doing, wholeheartedly and enthusiastically."

"Loving something is not enough," Jean told him, right on cue.

"When is the last time you enjoyed playing?" Jeremy asked.

"Irrelevant," Jean said. "I am Jean Moreau; I am perfect Court. I do not need to enjoy it to be the best backliner in the NCAA."

"That's really sad," Jeremy said. "You know that, right?"

"You're naïve," Jean returned. "Your team is an unforgivable anomaly."

Jeremy's phone buzzed in his pocket. Grateful for the diversion, Jeremy pulled it out to check. The text was from Kevin, but Jeremy wasn't sure he wanted to open it with Jean right there. Jeremy glanced at the shirts he'd been pawing through just moments ago, but this wretched conversation had put an ugly slant on his intentions. Jeremy turned his phone over and over between his fingers and looked at Jean.

"I've got to deal with this," he said, waggling his phone and hoping Jean wouldn't ask him about it. "Pick something out while I do, won't you?" Jean obediently turned to the rack Jeremy had just been considering, and Jeremy took careful hold of his elbow. "It doesn't have to be from this rack specifically. It can be from anywhere in this store as long as it's got some red or gold on it. Take a lap and see what all they have to offer."

It was inevitable, perhaps, that Jean would gravitate to the black and red shirts. Ten minutes ago it might have felt like defeat, but Jeremy would forgive the color scheme for now. If that was what Jean felt safest in, Jeremy would back his decision wholeheartedly. The brighter designs could wait until the season started.

He was not in the right mood to read Kevin's text, he knew, but with Jean temporarily distracted he had to know. He regretted opening it almost immediately, because Kevin had sent him a far-too-late rundown of Jean's injuries:

"Three fractured ribs. Sprained LCL. Twisted ankle. Broken nose. That's most of it."

That's most of it.

Jeremy's chest ached with tender grief. It was a heat normally reserved for game nights against their most violent opponents, a niggling sense of helplessness as people repeatedly tried to hurt a team that just wanted to have a good time. Jeremy powered his phone off before he could ask Kevin "Why?" A reason wouldn't take back what they'd done.

The why was already answered in Jean's unintended confessions and the layers behind Kevin's vague, scattered advice. The Ravens had no control over anything except how they performed and were perceived on the court. When they finally snapped, of course it'd be against their best performers: first Kevin, now Jean. Even Riko hadn't been immune, choosing to take his own life rather than live without Exy.

Jeremy was going to have to bring that up with him sooner or later, he knew—both Riko and the rumors that had the Trojans thinking twice about their unexpected recruit. But after how badly every other conversation had gone today, Jeremy didn't trust himself to get through it.

He was distracted from dismal thoughts by Jean's approach. Jean was holding his chosen shirt with just his fingertips, keeping it away from his body like it offended him.

Ready to drop it at a moment's notice if Jeremy disapproved, Jeremy thought, but he refused to look that deep into it. He forced his shadowed thoughts away, focusing instead on the tiny victory right in front him. Jeremy would have to warn Laila what she was up against tomorrow when she took Jean shopping for the rest of his things, but for now he smiled and took the shirt from Jean.

"Looks great," he said. "Anything else?"

"No," Jean said, and followed Jeremy up to the register.

Jeremy paid for it, and Jean refused a bag when the cashier offered. Jeremy kept the receipt but passed the shirt back to Jean to carry, and he didn't miss the tight grip Jean kept on it as he followed Jeremy out.

CHAPTER NINE
Jeremy

The house still smelled like food when they got back, but this time it was the headier scent of beef and not the spicy chaos that had preceded it. The sound of a TV drifted down the hall, and by the time Jeremy made it to the living room doorway he'd figured out which gameshow they were watching. Laila was sitting cross-legged on her papasan chair, brushing Cat's hair absentmindedly as she stared at the TV.

"This remote village in the Netherlands was the setting of 1991's To Death We Dance," the host said.

"Giethoorn," Laila said immediately.

One of the contestants slapped her buzzer. "What is Giethoorn?"

"Got 'em," Cat said with drowsy pride.

Jeremy had a few precious seconds during points assignment to squeeze between the TV and coffee table; although the host read off every question, Laila wanted to see it written out on the screen. There was one last question before commercials, or so the host said, so Jeremy got comfortable on the couch cushion nearest his friends while it was presented to the team. Laila only needed to hear half of it before saying,

"Hobgoblin's Thunder."

"Who are Hobgoblin's Thunder?" a man said right after her.

Laila twisted in circles, searching the cushion around her hips and thighs. With a frown she leaned forward, pushing Cat with her body so she could check the coffee table. She still came back empty-handed, and asked, "Babe?"

Cat reached back without looking and pulled the remote

control out from under the papasan chair. Laila took it, muted the TV for commercials, and put it down where she would likely lose it again. She glanced at Jeremy, then over at Jean where he'd predictably stopped in the living room doorway. Jeremy watched her gaze settle on the black cloth in Jean's hand, but Laila was good enough not to comment on the color.

"What'd you think of campus?" Cat asked.

"Green," Jean said, and didn't elaborate. He turned his shirt over in his hands, glanced Jeremy's way as if making sure he was staying put, and then vanished down the hall.

As soon as he was out of sight Laila and Cat turned expectant looks on Jeremy. He grimaced and pulled out his phone long enough to tap out, "It is way too much to write. Later, OK?" into the group chat he had with just the two of them. Laila couldn't find her phone even with the lingering chime it gave off, but Cat saw that coming and held hers up where Laila could see. Laila looked pensive but nodded. Cat was harder to deter.

"At least give us something," she sent back.

Jeremy jostled his phone between his hands. He wondered what would tide her over until later. Which insight would earn the most discretion on Jean's first night in California? If Jeremy admitted she might be right about them being a cult, she'd be too curious to bite her tongue. In the end the best he could do was borrow someone else's words, and he forwarded Kevin's last text message to them. Cat skimmed it first before starting to lift it for Laila, but her hand never made it that far. She went still as stone as she stared, and Laila had to pry her phone out of her hand to read it.

Cat got to her feet faster than Jeremy had ever seen her move outside of the court, and Jeremy grabbed at her to stop her. She sent him an impatient look that screamed *I know*, and Jeremy typed out but didn't send "He insists it happened in scrimmages." He held his phone up long enough for her to read it before deleting it. Cat balled her hands into fists, relaxed them, and did it again.

157

On the third attempt her expression cleared, and she sailed out of the room with a loud, "Jean, I'm stealing you. Come help me with dinner."

"I don't know if he'll eat it," Jeremy admitted in her absence.

Laila slid off her papasan chair and onto the cushion at his side. Jeremy propped himself against her automatically, waited for Cat's music to start up in the kitchen, and quietly recounted as much of the day as he could. Laila listened to it all without interruption, knowing they were working on whatever time Cat could borrow for them. When he finally went silent, Laila reached over and gave his hand a short, tight squeeze.

"No wonder they're so nasty all the time," she said. "They're not allowed to be human." She thought that over for a few moments, then said, "We're going to have to keep him very busy until practices start. If Ravens are only allowed to exist as players, then there's no telling what's going on up here when he can't even gear up for another five or six weeks." She gestured toward her temple.

Jeremy considered that. "Maybe being numbered helps balance it out, even if it subjects him to even greater expectations? Guaranteed spot on the lineup, kind of thing. He can take the time he needs to heal because he knows his rank is secure."

Or maybe he was used to it, but that thought was too insidious and impossible. *"I haven't been taken off the court this long in years,"* Jean had said after meeting with Davis. Jeremy wondered how literal that "taken off" was supposed to be. Had it been another accidental confession, or had he been including normal injuries as well? The Ravens weren't exactly clean players; it wasn't hard to imagine that they would sideline each other for a day or two on a regular basis.

"If they'd go so far with one of their key players, I can't imagine the rest of the lineup got off very easy," Laila said. She was speaking slowly and carefully, like she wasn't sure either of them wanted to hear what she had to say. "We are

158

learning what they did to him; we have no way of knowing yet what he did to them in exchange."

"I've heard the rumors."

Jeremy tried to reconcile that exaggerated vitriol with what he'd seen of Jean today. Jean was prickly and combative and quick with an unforgiving opinion, but also... pliant? It wasn't the right word, Jeremy knew, but he wasn't sure how to explain it to Laila.

He thought of Kevin's words at the semifinals game: *"He knows how to follow orders. If you tell him to submit, he will."* Even in his memory the wording felt a little embarrassing, but Jeremy thought he understood. Jean fussed but gave ground. There was no guarantee he hadn't participated in Raven violence, but Jeremy wanted to believe he wasn't an instigator. Until he knew for sure, though, Jeremy was determined to keep Jean and Lucas far away from each other.

At last he said, "I know it's early to say it, but I don't think he's capable of everything they say. I won't say he's innocent, but he just... doesn't seem the type. Do you feel safe with him here?"

Laila sent him a wry look. "If he starts anything, you know we'll finish it."

He'd seen how much they could bench, so Jeremy only smiled. "I know you will."

They didn't hear Cat's footsteps over the music, but suddenly she was in the living room doorway looking positively stricken. Jeremy's heart dropped, the brief return of his good humor dying immediately, but all Cat said was,

"Congratulations! I found someone more useless than you are in the kitchen. I didn't think it was possible."

"Ouch," Jeremy said. "In my defense—"

"Best not to say it," Laila advised him, but she patted his knee as she stood up. "Having a personal chef won't earn you any pity points."

They followed Cat down the hall to the kitchen, where Jeremy expected to see a mess similar to the one they'd just cleaned up a few hours ago. Instead, it looked like Cat had dumped her entire collection of utensils on the island. Jean treated her to a withering look as she arrived with an audience in tow, but rather than make him relive whatever lesson she'd just inflicted on him she picked up a vegetable peeler and put it in his face.

"This one," she said, and began clearing everything else away as soon as he took it from her. "Fair warning! I let Jeremy be dead weight in the kitchen because he doesn't live with us full time. If you're going to stick around, I'm going to make a proper cook out of you. Survival Skills 101, or something."

Jean tested the edge of the peeler with his finger. Cat set a cutting board and bag of carrots in front of him, then stole the peeler back so she could show him in a few quick swipes what to do. Jean obediently set to work while she went back to her broccoli. Jeremy knew better than to offer to help but made himself useful collecting plates and silverware. Laila checked the meat in the crockpot and went looking for the au jus.

"Anyway, you were saying?" Cat asked.

It only took a moment to realize they were talking about the Ravens' eating habits. Jean didn't seem annoyed to be hashing it over again, but Jeremy was content to let it go in one ear and out the other. He didn't miss the sidelong look Jean sent the thick rolls Laila set out or the way Jean glanced toward the fridge as if remembering his conversation with Jeremy earlier. He didn't miss a beat in his recitation, but his gaze drifted over the crowded magnets.

"I assume Jeremy already told you we don't do that here," Cat said, and glanced at Jeremy for a nod. "Good news is, sounds like Ravens basically did macronutrients, which means we can adapt. Laila and I have it down to an art form. Getting you to adjust from that to something similar but without the boring this-and-only-this should be pretty easy. We'll go grocery shopping when we get back from the mall tomorrow and I'll walk you through it. Deal?"

160

Laila hummed as she thought. "Maybe it's because I missed the first half of the conversation, but the numbers don't add up the way they ought. It's oddly weighted."

"To accommodate more practices?" Jeremy guessed with a glance Jean's way. "We never did get around to that story, past you implying I wouldn't like whatever your answer was."

"You won't," Jean agreed.

He didn't elaborate, even with all three of them staring patiently at him, until Jeremy finally said, "Is it still considered a trade secret if they're overhauling the program?"

"The—head coach gave us a special schedule," Jean said.

Laila propped her hip against the island by his side to stare him down. "I don't know if you've noticed this, but you've got this funny little hitch every time you talk about Coach Moriyama. It's always 'the—'" She put her hands up and went perfectly still, exaggerating the brief catch. "Kind of curious what it is you keep biting off. You've noticed it, haven't you?" she asked Jeremy.

"Yes," Jeremy admitted. "I thought it a conversation for another day."

"I think now's a great time," Laila said, turning on Jean again.

Unsurprisingly, Jean picked the lesser evil: "Ravens use sixteen-hour days."

Cat almost took her fingers off when she slammed her knife down. "Excuse me?"

Jean kept his attention on his carrots as he went back to work with new energy. "We took two classes a day in back-to-back periods with dedicated professors to minimize time away from Evermore. Four and a half hours for sleep, three and a half for classes and transit to campus. Odd days were eight hours on the court; evens were six with two hours for school-related necessities and personal upkeep.

"It was never perfectly static. Game nights pulled it out of alignment, as did classes. We were scattered across too many years to line our lessons up exactly. Because of it we rarely had all of the Ravens at Evermore outside of games. Holidays were a different story," he said, as if that made any of this easier to listen to. "When classes weren't in session, we ran ten-sixes: four hours to sleep, six hours to practice, two hours to rest, four hours to practice. An ideal schedule that ensured we were all in sync."

There was a fierce tug at the corner of his mouth, irritation or frustration quickly held in check, and he said, "The perfect Court had a different schedule out of necessity, as we had... extracurricular studies to tend to. Still sixteen hours, but a different breakdown. After Kevin left, I had the least amount of time to practice. It was not viewed favorably by the rest, but I will make up for it here. I will not fall behind."

Laila plucked the vegetable peeler out of his hands and cast it aside. He reached for it automatically, but Laila caught his shoulder to turn him to face her. She took hold of his face in both hands. Jeremy couldn't see her face from here, but Jean went perfectly still at whatever he saw in her expression.

"I need you to listen to me for one moment," Laila said, "and I need you to believe me when I say it. Fuck Coach Moriyama."

"So the wholesome front is an act," Jean noted. "It makes you marginally more tolerable, though it doesn't explain why you would willfully shoot yourselves in the foot."

"Do not deflect," Laila warned him quietly. "He kept you isolated and exhausted for years, and for what? None of you deserved what he put you through. Do you understand me?"

"I am Jean Moreau," he told her. "I have always gotten exactly what I deserve."

"And what did you do to deserve broken ribs?" Laila demanded.

"You would not understand, and I will not try to explain it to you."

Cat piped up, "What we don't understand is how a grown-ass man took a bunch of kids and turned them into monsters for sport. With so much money and prestige at play I know

162

why they let him get away with it, but damn. The gap between first and second place cannot be worth all that cruelty."

"Being first is all that matters," Jean said, prying Laila's hands off his face. "The Ravens understood that."

"But they're not first anymore," Laila said. "You said they would implode when everything they knew got taken away from you, and earlier I might've thought you were exaggerating. But they're all ticking bombs, aren't they? And if losing to Palmetto State didn't light the fuse, then Riko dying did."

Jean flinched, and Jeremy stepped in with a short, "Enough." It earned him a hooded look from Laila, but Jeremy only shook his head and said, "That's enough for tonight. He spent his whole morning traveling and is three hours ahead in his head still. A bit unfair to pick a fight when he's probably exhausted and half-asleep." He wasn't entirely sure Laila and Cat would back down, so instead he turned on Jean and changed the subject:

"Sure, there's a bit of an act involved in being a Trojan, but that doesn't mean it's a complete lie. Some of us are here for a good education and prestige, so it's worth toeing the line and playing along. Some of us want to be good role models for those coming after us. And some of us just really want to have fun.

"I wasn't born a Trojan, right? My high school team was just like every other school out there. So competitive, so much bad-mouthing, so many put-downs. And it was just… exhausting, playing like that. All that pressure on one side and all that antagonism on the other." He clapped his hands together as if crushing his past self between the two. "We go out of our way to be good sports for the people we play against and the people watching, but mostly it's for us. To show that we can still have fun and excel without resorting to poison."

"I like shooters," Cat piped up. "The games, I mean. Absolutely love them. I like being the better player and faster on the draw. But it's so toxic all the time, especially if you're a girl who's reckless enough to unmute her mic. It starts eating away at you, starts making you toxic as well. Act up to fit in, right? Didn't even notice how far I was sliding until my kid sis asked me why I was so angry all the time. This is much better. Also, it drives our opponents absolutely batty when they can't get a rise out of us. Case in point," she said, with a sly grin at Jean.

"We have a signal for when we have to get pulled," Jeremy said, "and I showed you the locker room earlier. That punching bag in the weights room is for working off stress and irritation until we can find our calm again. The rule isn't 'don't let them get to you', remember? It's to maintain an even keel on the court and in front of the press. You can say whatever you like to the rest of us. We've heard it all before."

Cat glanced at Laila to see if she had anything to add. Whatever she saw made her sigh, and she waggled a hand at Jean. "Tell you what, we'll start fresh with the cooking lessons tomorrow. For now go help Jeremy pick out a movie. Something fun, preferably. I think we could all use a pick-me-up right now."

Jeremy wasn't surprised that Cat cranked the volume up a bit as soon as he and Jean left. Subtlety was not exactly her strong suit, but if Jean noticed he gave no sign he cared. Jeremy dug through the movies and rattled off suggestions, trying very hard not to notice how many times Cat gave away her growing agitation by hitting her knife a little too hard against her cutting board. Laila was likely conveying all of Jeremy's insights, while Cat rehashed her side of the conversation from the kitchen.

"She means well," Jeremy felt obligated to say as he held out a few movies to Jean in offering. The man turned them over in his hands with barely a glance. "But since we've started this conversation a day or two ahead of when I meant to have it, I might as well confess: we've been hearing a lot of unpleasant rumors since we signed you. We're trying to figure you out so we know where to go from here. I'm not sure if she

164

was pushing for answers or pushing to see if you pushed back, but I promise she wants this to work."

"I know what they're saying about me out there," Jean said. "I do not care."

His tone said maybe he did care, but Jeremy wasn't going to call him out on it. "For the record, I don't believe them. I won't unless you give me a reason otherwise. I refuse to think Kevin would have come to me for help if you were the problem they make you out to be."

"I am going to be a problem," Jean said, but he said it like a tired fact and not a threat. "It is unavoidable."

Jeremy took the movies back but stared through them. "Can you at least tell me why you think you deserved to get beaten within an inch of your life?"

"I cannot tell you in a way you'll understand," Jean said again. "Leave it."

"For now," Jeremy said.

Since Jean didn't seem to have an opinion on the matter, Jeremy settled on a movie he thought they might all enjoy. By the time he had it set up, Cat was ready for them to come collect their sandwiches. She was also ready to talk Jean through his meal, spouting off numbers and facts at the speed of light. Jeremy wasn't sure if Jean was following any of it or if it just sounded legitimate enough not to push it. When he looked like he was going to peel part of his roll off, though, Jeremy chimed in with,

"Did you even eat lunch today? You can afford the carbs."

Cat looked to the ceiling and rattled off something in exasperated Spanish. A prayer for patience, most likely. "If you don't eat every last bite, I won't teach you how to cook. You can live off canned chicken for the rest of your life." She batted at his hand when that wasn't a convincing enough threat and dropped a small pile of sautéed vegetables onto his plate. "Right! Everyone out. Cleaning comes later."

Cat and Laila accepted Jeremy's choice of movie without argument. Jeremy wasn't surprised that Jean left as soon as his

165

plate was empty or that he didn't come back. What none of them expected was to carry their plates into the kitchen an hour and a half later and see he'd gone behind them to put the leftovers away. He'd even used the stickers Cat showed him to date the containers before putting them in the fridge. Cat touched the marker in its wire basket with a curious look on her face.

Jeremy went down the hall on quiet feet. Jean's door was cracked, but the bedroom light was off. He offered a quiet "Hey" in warning before easing the door open a few inches. Jean was asleep on his bare mattress, still dressed in what he'd worn all day. It was disorienting that a man so tall could look so small at rest, but Jean slept curled in on himself in the middle of his bed. Jeremy lingered a moment, then went down the hall and collected Barkbark.

Laila was coming out of the kitchen on his way by, but she said nothing until Jeremy slipped the dog inside Jean's room and eased the door closed.

"A roommate in my absence," Jeremy said as he made his way back to her. "Thank you for dinner and…" He waved a hand in Jean's general direction. "Do you want me to meet you at the mall or am I hitching a ride with you?"

"We'll come get you around nine," Laila said. "Drive safe."

"Be safe," he returned.

Laila sent a pensive look in the direction of Jean's bedroom. "Somehow, I think we are."

They saw him out, and Jeremy took the long drive back to his home in Pacific Palisades. His parents had use of the garage, so he pulled into the semicircle driveway that wrapped around the fountain in the front yard. A glance at the front of the house showed a comforting number of darkened windows, but Jeremy checked the clock on his dash before killing the engine. If Jean was already asleep, Bryson might be too.

His phone chimed, and Jeremy looked down to see William's name on the message. "Bryson is in the sitting room

166

with Mr. Wilshire."

Jeremy couldn't help but laugh. He glanced out the windshield, looking for the butler's form in one of the windows and coming back empty. With a quick, "You're the best!" he pulled his keys from the ignition and got out. He closed his door as quietly as he could, crossed the front yard on quick steps, and wasn't entirely surprised when William opened the front door for him. He could hear voices echoing down the corridor where his stepfather and older brother were having an animated discussion, so he settled for a grateful smile in William's direction before hurrying up the stairs.

He got to his room with none the wiser, changed out for bed, and collapsed into his blankets with a content sigh. Sleep was easy after a long day and a good dinner, but when he dreamed it was of bloodied ravens locked in an iron cage.

-

Judging by the number of times Jeremy's phone went off during his hair appointment the following morning, no amount of warnings could have prepared Laila for today's shopping trip with Jean. Jeremy was in no position to check his messages, but now and then Cat wandered up to him from the waiting area to let him know how many bubble teas might buy his way back into Laila's good graces. Each visit added another eight or nine to the final count.

When he was finally done and escorted up front to pay, he pulled his phone out alongside his wallet. His unread messages were standing at fifty-seven. While Jeremy hoped most were from the gossipy group chat, since Laila wasn't big on texting, the number was more than enough to make him sigh.

"Thank you," he said, taking his card and receipt and passing back a cash tip.

Cat preceded him out of the salon but waited to one side so he could note the tip on the top corner of the receipt. He tucked the receipt into his wallet before passing his remaining cash to Cat for help with groceries and rent. Cat looked weary as she pocketed it, though she had given up protesting his so-called charity a year ago. It wasn't about the money, so he didn't take it personally. Cat was more concerned with how many hoops it took him to pull it together when he was permanently on his stepfather's bad side.

Since she'd been keeping up with Laila in his stead, she knew where to lead him to meet up with the others. They were at a table on the outskirts of the food court, where Laila was vigorously stirring the last few bites of frozen custard into a sloppy mess. Ice cream was her go-to high stress food, so Jeremy attempted his best apologetic smile as he slid onto the seat across from Jean.

Laila's spoon stilled as she stared at him. "What happened to frosted tips?"

Cat threw Jeremy under the bus immediately: "He chickened out at the last possible second and made 'em bleach the whole thing. Something about how going beachboy mode was more acceptable than looking like a one-hit wonder dropout? Pussy," she said with emphasis when Jeremy grimaced at her. "You look like a Ken doll."

"That's a good thing, right?" Jeremy asked.

"If your goal in life is to be a side piece, sure," Cat said. When she saw the look Laila was giving her, she gave a world-weary sigh and clapped a hand on Jeremy's shoulder. "Yeah, man. It looks really good, honestly." And because she'd never learned to stop while she was ahead, she said, "I just think tips would've been cooler. Easier on the upkeep, too. Do you have any idea how often you're going to have to touch this up?"

"Tips next year, maybe," Jeremy said. "After I've graduated and don't have to deal with the fallout, yeah?" He looked from Laila to Jean. Jean's hands were clasped white-knuckled on the table in front of him, and his expression was carved from stone as he steadily stared into the distance. Jeremy leaned to one side to count the number of bags at his feet. Knowing neither of them was in the mood for it, he still asked, "Productive trip?"

Jean muttered something in French that sounded

168

positively rude.

"Fine," Laila said as she stabbed at her custard. "Perfectly normal day out."

"This isn't—" Jean said, turning on her with a dismissive jerk of his hand. His hand went still midair when he got a good look at Jeremy. Jeremy assumed he meant to finish with "normal", but what came out was a startled, "Blond."

Jeremy had no time at all to study the micro expression that flicked across Jean's face, because a couple of strangers invited themselves over to the Trojans' table and into Jean's space. It was a group of older men, mid-thirties maybe, and one of them was dressed in a well-worn Seattle Sasquatch shirt. The Sasquatches were a summer major league team and were set to start their season this weekend.

The Seattle fan pointed right at Jean. "Gene Moore," he said, triumphant despite butchering Jean's name six ways from Sunday. "Right? I told you it was him. Saw that tattoo all the way at our table. Heard you were coming to Los Angeles, but never on my life did I think I'd trip over you here." He looked around the table, gaze lingering briefly on Cat's USC t-shirt, and did the math. "Trojans."

"That's us," Jeremy said brightly.

"Hey, man," the stranger said, turning on Jean again. "Sorry to hear about Riko, and all. Guy deserved a lot better than what he got, amirite?"

"Deserved not to be sabotaged," the guy at his right muttered. He pushed away the unsubtle elbow jabbed into his side and kept his eyes on Jean. "Could've used you on the backline that night, don't you think? Someone who could've made a difference against Kevin."

"He's an unrepentant Raven fan," the first guy said, not at all apologetic.

Jean considered them in unnerving silence for a few moments, then slid his gaze away and stared into the distance once more. As the quiet stretched long enough to get uncomfortable, Cat leaned forward with a too-wide smile and

169

said, "Sorry, sorry! His English is a little hit and miss still. That's why you never see him talking to the press, you know?" She waggled her fingers at Jean to get his attention and said in as serious a tone as she could muster, "Voulez-vous coucher avec moi?"

Across the table from her, Laila choked on her custard. It was all Jeremy could do to keep his composure. He wasn't entirely sure Jean was going to let her get away with this, but then the Frenchman gave a lengthy response that went over everyone's head. Jeremy had never considered studying French before but hearing it from Jean was giving him ill-advised thoughts. At his side Cat was nodding along with a focused expression, never mind that she had no clue what Jean was saying to her.

After Jean quieted down, she looked back at the men and reported, "Thank you for your concern. It's a little soon for him to want to talk about it, but we hope you have a winning day!"

It was clear they weren't ready to go yet, but it'd be more awkward to stick around after that cheery dismissal, so the men shuffled defeated back to their table. Jean waited until they were out of earshot before turning on Cat.

"Your pronunciation is atrocious," he said. "Who the fuck taught you that phrase?"

"It's from a song," she said, unrepentant. "You're welcome, by the way."

"I didn't thank you."

"You could," Cat said. "You were making things awkward."

"I am not allowed to speak to the public," Jean said. "The—head coach wanted us to focus on our game and let Riko and Kevin handle all outside interactions."

At Riko's name the corner of his mouth turned down, but Jean looked off into the distance before Jeremy could catch his eye. Across from Cat, Laila said, "The—" and froze her spoon midair, very pointedly. "It's not yesterday anymore. What

170

could you possibly be trying to call him that you keep choking on?" When Jean didn't answer her, she sent him a sidelong look and said, "You really aren't used to talking to other people if you're so bad at self-censorship. You're as socialized as a stray dog."

"Are we finished here?" Jean asked.

"I'm still eating," Laila said, pushing her last spoonful of custard in circles.

"The madman," Cat guessed, counting off on her fingers. "The big cheese. The don Corleone. The big man in charge. The boss. The ass—"

"Enough," Jean tried.

"—hole who ruined your life. The master." And it was clear she intended to keep going, except Jean flinched. He was quick to try and hide it, getting up from the table to put space between them, but Cat stared at him, aghast. "You aren't serious. *I* wasn't being serious. What kind of 80s B-film horror shtick—"

"Keys?" Jeremy asked. "I'll help him get his bags to the car."

"You can't keep covering for him," Cat protested.

Jeremy gave her his best and brightest smile and said, "We are not having this conversation in the middle of the food court at the mall, Catalina."

Laila used her free hand to dig her keys out of her purse. Jean and Jeremy split the bags between them. Later Jeremy would be dismayed at how few there were. Today his thoughts were a churning mess. He led Jean around crowded tables, neatly cutting through the lines leading out from each restaurant. They'd parked down near the salon, but the exit at the food court would still get them where they needed to be. Jeremy couldn't remember which row they'd parked on, but he clicked her fob and followed the honking to Laila's car.

Jean's bags fit in the trunk easily enough. Jeremy slammed it closed and turned back toward Jean, but he forgot whatever he was going to say when Jean caught his chin in a

171

bruising grip.

"You can ask about the Ravens," Jean said, in a low and awful voice. "You can ask about Edgar Allan if you have nothing better to do with your time or curiosity. But do not ask me about Riko or the master. I will not talk about them, not with you or them or anyone. Do you understand?"

Hearing him say *the master* so easily now that Cat had figured it out sent a chill down Jeremy's spine, but he kept his expression calm as he said, "For the record, he sounds like a megalomaniac. You do know that, right?"

"Don't," Jean warned him. "Just don't."

Jeremy calculated his odds of getting anything else out of Jean today to be dismally low, so he said, "Okay. No questions about Riko or your—head coach." Jean reacted to that pointed barb with a fierce scowl, but he let go of Jeremy and stepped back out of reach. Jeremy let him retreat to a safe distance before adding, "For now."

Jean muttered rudely under his breath as he went to get in the back seat, and Jeremy sat on the trunk as he waited for Cat and Laila to catch up to them.

CHAPTER TEN
Jean

It turned out life was excessively complicated when there wasn't a staff to handle the minutiae of day-to-day existence.

Jean's first week in California fell into a loose pattern. Monday afternoons Laila and Cat gave the apartment a deep clean, prefaced by a lecture to Jean about which chemicals he was not to mix under any circumstance. Thursdays were meal prep days, supposedly to better accommodate game nights and weekend trips during the school year. Jean learned how to sort and wash laundry from Laila and got to know the local grocery store forwards and backwards from going with Cat.

Every morning they walked to the fitness center on campus. Jean couldn't be trusted to catch the weights should the need arise, so Laila and Cat spotted each other while he did stretches and walked on one of the treadmills.

Afternoons were filled with whatever the women were in the mood for that day, be it wandering downtown, shopping, or combing through estate sales. Laila dragged them to the library once, where Jean was fairly sure she scanned every single title on the shelf, and Cat took them sightseeing around the city and neighboring areas. On one sunny day Cat went out for a long ride on her motorcycle, leaving Laila and Jean behind for a blessedly quiet afternoon at the house.

Jean went where they took him because it was better than being left in the house alone, answered their least intrusive questions, and tried—failed—to not be completely overwhelmed by just how big Los Angeles was. It was as fascinating as it was horrible, and by the time they finally made it back to the safety of the house each evening his nerves felt worn raw. Helping Cat cook started to become a quiet source of comfort, a way of slowing down and letting the day's stresses slip away.

Jeremy made it over for dinner every night that week, apparently uninvited from the family table over the state of his hair. He laughed it off when he explained it, but Jean saw the shadows in his eyes and the dark look Cat and Laila exchanged as soon as Jeremy turned his back. It wasn't Jean's place to ask, at least until it interfered with their performance on the court, so he quietly tucked the knowledge aside for later.

On Friday, Jeremy made it to the house right as they were starting dinner. Laila and Jeremy made themselves comfortable on two of the three stools to chat while the other two set to work, Jean clumsily dicing peppers and Cat searing meat at the stove. Jean was halfway through his pile when Jeremy's phone quacked.

Jean had heard his phone go off enough times to know it was a backliner messaging him. Jeremy, for reasons he could not sufficiently explain, had assigned each lineup a different animal as an alert noise. His group chats had chimes in varying pitches, and his family always stood out as a jarring chord. It was a regular cacophony whenever Jeremy was over, and as annoying as it was it made Jean think of Renee, who he'd yet to reach out to since arriving in California.

Jeremy leaned to one side to dig his phone out. "Cody," he said, sounding surprised.

"Probably wondering why they haven't been invited to meet Jean yet," Laila said.

Cat brought her pan of meat over and forked the cubes out onto some paper towel. She nudged Jean with her elbow as she said, "Cody's technically got no rank on the team, but they consider themselves the de facto leader of the defense line. This summer they're down the coast in Carlsbad with Ananya and Pat, so you'll have to have a meet and greet at some point. Jeremy, ask them if they've worked up the nerve to—"

"It's Lucas," Jeremy said, in a tight tone of voice that shut

174

Cat up immediately. Rather than explain, he dialed out and put a hand over his free ear. It took almost no time at all for Cody to pick up, judging by how quickly Jeremy asked, "How is he?"

"Ah, shit," Cat said quietly.

"No, I haven't been keeping up with it. I was—" In one heartbeat, Jeremy's entire demeanor changed. Jean watched the blood drain from his face even as Jeremy hopped off his stool and turned away from them. The line of his shoulders was rigid as he listened to whatever Cody had to say. After an age he said, in a voice that didn't sound at all like his, "Thank you for taking him in. If you guys need anything, just let us know. Yeah, I—I'll handle it here."

He hung up, dropped his phone on the edge of the island, and tipped his head back to stare at and through the ceiling. Laila and Cat exchanged a long look as Cat took her pan to the sink, but Jean went back to dicing. Jeremy needed a minute or two to sort out his thoughts before he moved up alongside Jean. Jean looked from his outstretched, open hand to the only thing he was holding before finally turning over the knife. Jeremy in turn put it down as far away from both of them as he could reach.

"Lucas all right?" Laila asked.

Jeremy put a hand up in a bid for patience and kept his eyes on Jean. "There's been an accident," he said, and grimaced like it wasn't at all the word he wanted to use. He worried his lower lip between his teeth before getting right to the point: "I'm sorry. Wayne Berger is dead."

Jean stared at him as he waited for the words to make sense. "How?"

Jeremy took his time figuring out how to say it, but the truth he had to give could only be softened so much: "Word is he knocked out his therapist and stole her letter opener. She found his body when she came to. I'm sorry."

None of the Raven strikers could fill the void Kevin left, but Wayne had been the best of a second-best lot. He'd fought

175

like hell to be Riko's primary on-court partner, and his efforts and backstabbing had paid off for his senior year. Now Riko was gone, the Nest was closed, and the glorious future the master promised them was in ruins. Jean wanted to be surprised that he'd broken, but he was just tired. Ravens graduated; they didn't leave.

"Were the two of you close?" Laila asked Jean.

"He was a Raven," Jean said, as if any of them could understand the complicated emotions behind such a thing. They were an angry world unto themselves, interlocking links on a chain where compassion and consideration were outlawed. They needed each other. They were stronger together. They hated each other. They hated everyone else more. "But he was not my partner, and I will not grieve him."

He reached for the knife so he could get back to work, but Jeremy slid it further away. Jean flicked him a disapproving look. Jeremy wasn't cowed but said, "It's okay to be upset, even if he wasn't your friend or your partner. He was still your teammate for a few years. It's normal to be shocked by loss.

"I just want to make sure you're safe, okay? There were rumors the day Riko—" He remembered belatedly he wasn't supposed to discuss the fallen King and winced as he tried again. "They said you were in rough shape when security dragged you out of Fox Tower."

Jean lifted his hand and studied it, remembering the bloodied bandages he'd woken up to at Reddin Medical Center. He still wasn't entirely sure what he'd done to Neil's room; all he had to go on was Wymack's blasé and unhelpful, *"You wrecked the place."* He'd never been back to the dorm to see what chaos he'd wrought.

"Your worry is misplaced," Jean said. "I promised I would not kill myself."

"For the record, that's not a thing well-adjusted people say," Cat said.

Laila searched Jean's face, perhaps looking for a reason to distrust his calm reaction, and finally said, "We're going to

176

circle back to that in a minute. What happened to Lucas?" She looked at Jeremy at that, expression tight with concern.

"He turned up on their doorstep beat to hell," Jeremy said, gesturing to the left side of his face. "Bruised from temple to jaw with two missing teeth. Lucas Johnson," he said, turning a long look on Jean again. Jean recognized the name from the Trojans' lineup, but he wasn't sure why it was supposed to matter to him. The other man was a year behind him and only played against the Trojans' weaker teams. Jeremy connected the dots for him a second later: "Grayson Johnson's younger brother."

Jean stopped breathing.

Johnson was such a common last name he hadn't even thought to put two and two together. Ravens were Ravens; they belonged to each other and to Evermore. Entering the Nest meant leaving everyone and everything else behind. He knew Grayson hated USC, but every Raven did. Not once had he or the coaches indicated there was a personal vendetta in the mix.

"He doesn't live here," Jean said, refusing to word it like a question.

Jeremy's stare was searching. "The Johnsons live a couple hours south of here in San Diego. Lucas warned me that Grayson came home angry last week, but that was the last I heard from him. Unfortunately he was there when Grayson got the news about Wayne, and Grayson didn't handle it nearly so well as you're pretending to. Lucas's parents got him locked up for the night to cool down, and Lucas hit the ground running."

"They were friends, I'm guessing?" Cat asked. "Maybe the two of you could touch base and talk each other through this. It sounds a bit rude to suggest it, seeing how he tried to bash Lucas's face open, but Lucas wasn't a Raven. You at least know where Grayson is coming from, and you—"

"No," Jean said, so fierce Cat leaned away from him.

Jeremy propped himself against the island and stared Jean

177

down, arms folded loosely over his chest. Jean looked away, working his jaw against the remembered taste of blood and cotton. He checked the side of his neck for injuries and was dimly surprised to find the skin unbroken. The clammy feeling down his back warned him he was on the verge of getting sick.

He thought about the first time he'd really noticed Grayson: the day Riko called all the male backliners in for a meeting and asked for volunteers to break Jean in. *"Five or six should do,"* he'd said, claiming Jean wanted to get to know his new teammates better. Five hands went up, hoping to earn favor with their young King, and Grayson's had been one of them.

Having to go to them was a nightmare, but surviving the aftermath was hell. They were all Ravens, after all, and Evermore was their cage. Every morning thereafter he'd woken up alongside them. He'd gone to classes with them, taken his meals with them, and had practices and games with them. Four of them had never tried again, content to pepper Jean with cruel jokes and sly remarks when they realized the wounds were ever fresh. Grayson, on the other hand, made it inescapably clear that he would not hesitate to shove Jean down again if he could only catch Jean alone.

"Hey," Jeremy said, and louder, *"Hey.* Jean, look at me."

Jean dragged his stare to Jeremy's face with effort, but Jeremy was looking at his hand. Jean belatedly realized he was still holding his neck, and now he felt the stinging bite of his fingernails where they'd broken through skin. Jean slowly relaxed his grip and let his hand fall limp to the island, and only then did Jeremy look up at him again.

"Talk to me," Jeremy said.

"I don't know what you want me to say."

"Tell me about Grayson."

"Raven backliner, number twelve," Jean said. "Most recently partnered with Jasmine. Six foot three, two hundred and forty pounds, right-handed, stick size five, second shift, fifth-year as of this upcoming fall semester." *Tastes like whey*

178

protein and oat milk. Likes to bite. Made me kneel and— "Do not ask me to talk to him."

"Okay," Jeremy said, so readily Jean could only stare at him. "If Lucas asks, I'll tell him it's off the table. Grayson can take his issues up with a therapist."

"Like Wayne did." Jean considered that. "Maybe he will also kill himself."

"That isn't a joke," Jeremy said, with unexpected ferocity.

Cat winced but kept her eyes on Jean. "Babe, you really might want to consider some therapy of your own."

"I don't need—"

Jean had heard the sink cut on, but the sudden press of something warm and wet against his injured neck had him lashing out instinctively. He caught Laila high across her face, knocking her head back and sending her stumbling away from him. Cat was past him in a heartbeat to steady her. Jean took advantage of their distraction to put space between them, scrubbing at his skin as rough as he could to smear away the damp heat.

Cat muttered in agitated Spanish as she took the paper towel from Laila's fingers. Jean saw the too-familiar red of fresh blood before Cat put the towel to Laila's nose. Jean folded his arms tight across his chest to watch and wait for the inevitable retaliation.

When Cat was finally satisfied that the bleeding had stopped, she shoved Jeremy out of her way and put a finger in Jean's face. "Don't you ever hit her again," she said without an ounce of her usual good humor. "Do you understand?"

"I can't promise I won't," Jean said.

Cat waited a beat, then demanded, "Aren't you even going to apologize?"

Surely she was joking, but Jean stared down into her upturned face and saw nothing but muted frustration. There was no violence in her despite the tension in her shoulders and how quickly she'd come for him. Jean meant to mock her for being weak-willed, but his, "Implying that words would somehow be enough to settle this?" came out more curious than anything else. "Blood is only satisfied by blood; words do not qualify as contrition."

"Are you serious?" Cat demanded, but maybe she already knew the answer, because she bulled on with, "I'm mad as hell, yeah, but even I know you didn't mean to do it. Slapping you wouldn't make any of us feel better, so forget that right now."

"I don't understand."

"You are not okay," Cat said. "You see that, right?"

Jean looked past her to Laila. She at least should be ready to exact retribution, but she kept her distance. The look on her face was sharp and prying. Jean wasn't sure what to make of it, but he offered an obedient, "I'm sorry."

"Didn't mean to scare you," she said. She gave him time to come up with rebuttals or excuses, but there was no point lying when all of them had eyes. Laila relaxed a bit when no arguments were forthcoming and said, "You going to explain what that was about?"

"No," Jean said.

"He hit you too," Cat guessed, and pointed at Jean's chest. "Did he do that?"

"I was injured in a scrimmage."

"The hell you were. What did he do to you?"

"I will not talk about him with you."

"You said I could ask about the Ravens," Jeremy reminded him. "We're asking."

"Not Grayson," Jean stressed, and was not above adding a desperate, "Please."

Begging had never saved him from Riko's cruelty, but Riko still liked to hear it. The memory of Riko's hungry smile was so sharp Jean almost felt it against his skin. In front of him Jeremy's expression gentled into something sad and earnest. Jean refused to believe they would so easily give him an out here, but when Jeremy spoke it was only to say, "Not Grayson, then. I'm sorry if we upset you."

Jean waited for the mask to drop, but Jeremy only stepped

180

backwards out of his space. A few moments later Cat went back to work, and Laila returned to the stool at Jeremy's side. She was the one who slid his knife back to him, and Jean let his fingers rest on the blade as he waited for any of this to make sense.

Weakness and vulnerability were unforgivable crimes on the Raven lineup, as they were only as strong as their weakest player. Anyone who faltered or failed had to be corrected. That he could become so undone by a single name was an unforgivable flaw, and they had every right to tear at him until he learned to hide his wounds better. Instead, they quietly went back to what they'd been doing before the phone call.

Finally, Jeremy asked, "Do you want to talk about Wayne?"

Wayne was a neutral topic, at least, and something to drag his thoughts out of shadowed rooms and blood. Jean slowly went through the rest of his peppers as he told them about the ornery striker. Stats were an obvious starting point, though they likely had vague knowledge of his numbers from facing the Ravens in championships. From there it was alarmingly easy to share more subjective memories of the man. He shouldn't, he knew. What happened in the Nest should stay in the Nest. But Jean was not a Raven, and Wayne was dead.

The problem was this: once Jean started with Wayne, it was easy to talk about Sergio and Brayden and Louis. Maybe it was to fill the silence so his new teammates wouldn't ask him for more than he wanted to give, but if he talked about the Ravens he couldn't think about Grayson. The Trojans listened with an unwavering, keen interest that was deeply unsettling, as Jean had learned years ago that he had nothing of value to say. Jean was almost grateful when he ran out of things to dice and slice and finally had a reason to leave them all behind.

He made it to the kitchen doorway before Jeremy's quiet voice stopped him: "You genuinely care about them."

Jean went still but didn't look back. It took Jeremy a moment more to find his voice again, and then all he managed

181

was a hesitant, "Despite every unkind thing they've said about you this spring, you still care about them, don't you?"

"I hate them," Jean said, and left. It was the cold hard truth; it was a blatant lie. How could he possibly make these free-spirited children understand?

He almost went to his bedroom, but the thought of that quiet space with its single bed was so repulsive he turned toward the living room instead. It was cluttered and chaotic, but it felt lived-in. He could sense the others' presence even if they weren't around to bother him, and that was enough to take the edge off the loneliness eating at his heart.

He went straight to the bay window and pulled the blackout curtain open with a hard tug of his hand. He'd wanted light, but it still startled him a bit how bright it was outside. Jean settled on the cushioned seat, content to watch the world outside for a minute, and then finally dug his phone out of his pocket.

Jean tapped through his short list of contacts until he found Renee. His thoughts were too loud, but he didn't bother putting any of them into words. Instead, he typed out the same message he'd sent her more times than he could count last semester when he needed her words to pull him out of his head: "Tell me something."

It only took her a minute to get back to him, and Jean sat there and watched as a flurry of texts came in. She told him about Stephanie's new house, with its corner lot backing up to a wooded park. She'd seen deer in the backyard from time to time but had yet to get a good picture of them. The squirrels and birds were apparently in an all-out war over the feeders in the yard, no matter how many Stephanie and Renee installed to appease them. On and on she went, offering tidbits of her life, and he used them like a lifeline to get away from his thoughts.

When Renee ran out of things to say, she didn't send the same question back to him. She knew he'd messaged her so he wouldn't have to think, so she wouldn't set him back so carelessly. All she sent was, "It's Friday, May 18th. Where are you now?"

She would take either answer, he knew: where were his thoughts, or where was he literally. Jean opted for a bit of truth and sent back, "Wayne Berger killed himself in therapy today."

He looked out the window again, tracking the way the evening sun glinted off windows and cars. He couldn't see bodies from here, but he could hear distant, exciting yelling from where someone was having a party. The blue house two doors down, most likely; they seemed the most popular residence when he and Cat were going back and forth to the grocery store.

Los Angeles was a monster, too big and too loud and too hectic. The Trojans were strange and misguided. There was a cardboard dog in his bedroom that Jeremy treated like a de facto member of the household. Jean didn't understand any of it, but he knew on a bone-deep level that this was better than anything he'd ever had. It was worlds more than he deserved. He feared it as much as he wanted it; the thought that this was his life now was terrifying.

He wondered where Wayne lived and what he'd gone home to. He'd lost his ranking, his master, and his King, but was there no sunlight where he lived, no open sky to consider in dizzying wonder? Was Wayne running from what he had become, or was it the thought of returning to Evermore after this taste of freedom that killed him? Jean didn't know. He'd never know. It didn't matter. It wouldn't bring him back.

"He only had one year left," Jean sent Renee, "and he couldn't do it."

coward washout traitor sellout reject whore
Why should he care if the Ravens fell apart?
-

Ten days later Jeremy was finally released from whatever obligations kept him away, and he showed up at the house with a suitcase of clothes and the sunniest smile he'd worn in weeks. Jean still had two empty drawers in his dresser and over half the closet to spare, so Jeremy moved in with easy efficiency while Jean kept watch. At last Jeremy tucked his empty suitcase into the back corner of the closet and turned a triumphant look on Jean.

"Thanks! I'll try not to get underfoot too much."

"You are my partner," Jean reminded him. "You are supposed to be underfoot."

Jeremy considered that for a moment. "Who was your partner on the Ravens?"

Jean slid his stare away and scowled a little when he spotted Barkbark. Jeremy had picked up the habit of moving the dog into his room on every visit, no matter that Jean always returned it to the living room. He crossed the room and flipped it around so its unblinking stare was pointed at the wall instead. Being annoyed at the nonsensical decoration was easy, and it made Jeremy's question a little easier to answer by proxy.

"After Kevin left, I took his place at Riko's side."

A blessing and a curse: Riko was forced to moderate his violence when Jean's weakened performance meant they were both punished, but he'd embraced the challenge of subtler cruelties. It was a talent once reserved for Kevin, who couldn't be marked up when he always had cameras on him.

Jeremy nodded. "Keeping the perfect Court together, I assume. But there used to be only three of you—excluding that brief stunt with Neil that caused so much fuss around Christmas. Who came before Riko, or is that one harder to answer? You said Ravens got evaluated each semester, yeah?"

Jean turned to face him. "I only had one other."

Not for lack of trying, of course. Despite the friction between him and the rest of the defense line, Jean was perfect Court, a 3 missing his 4. Even Jasmine had angled for a spot at his side, meaning to climb over him to win Riko's approval. But of all the Ravens who tried, only two had any real chance of making it as Jean's permanent partner in the long run, and Jean could only survive one of them.

Zane was supposed to be a temporary solution, except

184

they both had too much to lose if they were reassigned. Zane wanted to be the best and play with the best, and he'd promised to stand between Jean and Grayson no matter what, so long as Jean helped him earn one of Riko's coveted numbers. They'd devoted years to each other, fighting and arguing and pushing each other harder and faster, and Jean had honestly believed Riko would come around and mark Zane for Court before graduation.

He hadn't counted on Riko finding Neil. Once Neil stole the number Zane believed was rightfully his there was no going back. Jean looked to the doorway, half-expecting to see Grayson lounging against the doorframe with that shit-eating grin on his face. The memory of Zane turning his back on them with an impatient, *"At least keep it down. I've got to be on the court in two hours,"* was still devastating enough to make him ill four months later.

"Jean?" Jeremy asked.

Jean realized he hadn't answered the question. He swallowed hard against a roiling stomach and said, "Zane Reacher. Normally freshmen are assigned to fifth years first to help them acclimate to the Nest, but I was so young they feared I would drag them down. Zane was a junior then, so the gap was not quite as noticeable."

"Reacher," Jeremy said with pained recognition. "He's very good. Very violent, too."

"Raven," Jean reminded him as he looked for a second bed. "It is what we were taught."

"Unlearning that is going to be a headache, I imagine," Jeremy said.

"If you would learn to play the sport as it was meant to be played," Jean said, and let the rest of his admonishment hang unspoken. There was no point retreading this argument; Jeremy's smile was wide and unrepentant. In the end it didn't matter that they were fools. They were still the second-best team, on track to be first place this year, and for better or worse Jean had agreed to submit to their ridiculous limitations.

185

"Speaking of playing around," Jeremy said, "shall we see what kind of trouble we can get into?"

It was too much to hope he meant Exy, especially when Jean was still mending, but Jean would have preferred something more interesting than the board game Jeremy settled on. Cat helped him set it up on the coffee table in the living room while Laila brought drinks for everyone from the kitchen. No matter how Jean looked at it, the game seemed pointless. There was nothing in it to work on reflexes or snap judgments; he didn't even have to memorize rules when each player was given a reference card for their turns.

They were halfway through when Jeremy's phone quacked, and Jeremy skimmed his text. "Sounds like Lucas is finally heading home this week," he reported, and nudged Jean with his foot. "Cody wants to know if they can come up for a day first so Lucas can get a good look at you. He's a bit worried about having a Raven on the lineup after seeing how his brother turned out, and Cody threatens to riot if anyone else meets you before they do. What do you think?"

"They are my teammates," Jean said. "I have to meet them."

Laila considered that. "If Lucas is that anxious, we should hang out somewhere neutral and public, somewhere he thinks Jean has to behave."

"Beach?" Cat suggested, surveying the board with serious intent before moving her token a few spaces. "You picked up some swim shorts, yeah?"

"Didn't get that far down the list," Laila said. "One of you can take him shopping tomorrow. I'm still tired from the last trip."

"No," Jean said. "I don't swim."

They looked at him, aghast. Jeremy was the first to find his voice with a disbelieving "Don't or can't?" When Jean only stared mutely back at him, Jeremy tried again. "The distinction matters—Coach Lisinski puts us in the pool at Lyon twice a week at morning practice, water aerobics and laps and such."

Jean's stomach bottomed out. "What?"

Cat nodded enthusiastically. "It's a fantastic workout."

The ghost of Riko's hand on his throat, holding his head still as he poured, was so vivid he expected to hear Riko's voice at his ear. Jean buried his face in the crook of his elbow and forced a cough, needing to know his lungs still worked.

I am Jean Moreau. I am not a Raven. I am not at Evermore.

It wasn't enough. He felt flayed, aching like he only did after Riko put him under the knife. Every inch of him was exposed and raw. His thoughts tipped between Riko and Neil, wet cloth and slick bathroom floors and the bite of rope into his arms as he desperately fought back. The urge to tear his throat open just to open a better path to his lungs was so fierce he had to grab his own ankles to stop himself. The chains creaked; the box rattled. If he didn't get a good breath his chest was going to cave in.

drowning I'm drowning I'm

"Jean?" Jeremy asked. "Hey. You good?"

How could he be? He was a mile out from an Exy court with no gear and three healing ribs. The violence in his memories and fear in his bones had no outlet; he would break under their weight if he couldn't carve it out of him.

"I want to go for a run," he said, thinking *How can I run with water in my lungs?*

Jeremy got to his feet and offered a hand. It felt an eternity before Jean could loosen his death grip enough to reach for him, and Jeremy hauled him to his feet with an ease Jean wasn't expecting. Jeremy went to put his shoes on while Jean detoured to his room for a looser shirt than the one he had on. Cat and Laila were pressed together in the living room doorway when Jean made it back, but he ignored their unblinking stares in favor of toeing into his sneakers and getting his laces tied.

He and Jeremy ran a lap around campus, then a second

that looped down to include the stadiums. The sight of an airplane propped up on the eastern border of Exposition Park startled Jean into slowing down. Jeremy followed his confused stare and started to explain, but Jean wasn't in the mood for conversation yet. He waved Jeremy off and picked up speed again, and Jeremy silently fell in alongside him.

When they made it back to Vermont and Jefferson they finally slowed to stretch out, and Jeremy took advantage of the break to speak.

"If it's going to be a problem, we can talk to Coach," he said.

Jean scrubbed sweat off his face with his sleeve. "It will not be a problem."

"The five miles we just ran say otherwise."

"It will not be a problem," Jean said again. "I will not let it be."

Jeremy studied him with disquieting intensity. "I want to help you, Jean, but you have to actually let me. I'm not a mind reader, you know?" He waited, like he somehow thought that plea would change Jean's mind, and sighed when Jean only stared into the distance in sullen silence. Instead of pushing the matter, he offered, "We don't have to meet at the beach. There are plenty of other places."

"The beach is fine," Jean said.

"Sure," Jeremy said, in a tone that said he was not at all convinced, but he let it drop.

They walked home in silence. Jeremy ceded the first shower to Jean so he could arrange things with Cody. Jean cut the shower on before stripping, but he stood in silence for two minutes as he watched water swirl down the drain.

Most days Jean was in and out as fast as he could go. On bad days at Evermore, when he was beaten half to death and needed the heat on his aching muscles, he could tolerate longer showers by keeping his head out of the spray for as long as possible. It was still always a toss-up if his control would hold, but having the Ravens around helped. There were lines Riko wouldn't cross when he had witnesses. Today Jean had no one, and the longer he stalled the more his thoughts tipped toward what was waiting for him in June.

He dug his fingers into his side over his ribs, looking for a residual ache to center him, and came back with nothing. At last he had no choice but to step into the shower, and he washed up so quickly he still felt dirty afterward. It almost wasn't fast enough, and Jean gave in to weakness long enough to kneel in the tub after he cut the water off. He stayed until his knees ached and went numb, listening to his heart pound a deafening staccato in his ears, and sent his thoughts as far from him as they could go.

CHAPTER ELEVEN
Jean

Jean made it two steps into the kitchen the next morning before his legs stopped working. Jeremy and Laila were at the counter in their swimsuits: Laila in a black one-piece with well-placed cutouts along her waistline and ribs and Jeremy in pale blue shorts that hung dangerously low on his hips. Looking at Laila for too long would be wretchedly inappropriate, all things considered, but staring at Jeremy was dangerous on too many levels to tolerate.

Damn him for looking just as good as a blond as he did a brunette. Jean knew his place; he knew his purpose. He knew that as a Moreau it was his lot in life to endure whatever sadism and degradation the Moriyamas saw fit to heap upon him. What he couldn't stomach was the cruelty behind these nonstop temptations, from Kevin leaning into his space with a conspiratorial whisper, to Renee's lips on his temple, to Jeremy with his easy laugh and easier smile.

"Yes?" Laila asked when he'd been staring a little too long.

He had the distinct feeling she was laughing at him, but Jean cut his losses and left.

At least they covered up for the car ride, the women with shorts and gauzy tops and Jeremy with a baggy USC t-shirt. The three of them were in a grand mood as they got on the road. If they noticed that Jean had nothing to contribute, they did nothing to bully him into speaking. He let their words go in one ear and out the other, content for now just to stare out the window and watch the city go by. It was a cloudless day, almost warm enough to be uncomfortable. Every storefront window they passed threatened to throw the morning sun right back at them, and Jean was belatedly grateful for the sunglasses Laila had forced him to buy.

It took a couple tries to find a lot with space for their car, but at last they parked a block away and could head down to the beach. Jean paused at the first soft crush of sand beneath his shoe, so caught off-guard by memories he couldn't move. Cat and Laila kept moving forward arm-in-arm, with Cat singing the rest of a song they'd been listening to on the radio. Jeremy was closer to Jean, and he immediately noticed when Jean stopped.

"You good?" he asked.

"Marseille was on the coast," Jean said. "The Mediterranean."

"Oh, yeah?" Jeremy asked, looking absurdly pleased by this tidbit. "I've never been to Europe. Dad's been stationed there a couple times, but..." He shrugged and didn't bother to elaborate. "Can you tell me about France?"

"No," Jean said, and the disappointed look that flickered across Jeremy's face sent a jagged prickle through his veins. He should leave it at that; he needed to leave it at that. Instead he said, "I don't want to talk about home. I wouldn't trust my memories, anyway. I came to America when I was fourteen, but five years in Raven time are a lifetime."

It was closer to seven and a half years in his head, but if Jean spelled it out like that, he knew what Jeremy would say. The look on Jeremy's face said discretion hadn't saved him, and Jean stepped forward like he could leave this conversation behind.

Jeremy kept pace. "That's what I don't get about you," he admitted quietly. "This heinous crime was committed against you, against all of you, but you're not angry about it. I mean, you're angry at the little things, but not about what really matters. Coach Moriyama never should have put you through this."

"Everything that happened to me happened for a reason,"

191

Jean said. *I am Jean Moreau. I am perfect Court.* "I have no reason to be angry about what made me into this."

"If you say you deserved it, I'll trip you," Jeremy warned him.

"You wouldn't," Jean returned.

"Maybe not," Jeremy allowed. "But I'll think about it really hard."

They caught up with Laila and Cat at a lifeguard tower that was striped like a rainbow. Jean stared at the tower so he wouldn't have to watch as the three of them peeled off their extra clothes. They'd brought a shopping bag to carry it all in, though Cat dug out a bottle of sunscreen before stuffing everyone's clothes inside. The lotion was cold in Jean's palm and greasy on his skin, with a too-fake fruity scent that had his nose crinkling in distaste as he worked it into his arms and legs.

"Neck," Jeremy advised him, as Cat and Laila did each other's faces and scalps.

Jean sighed and did as he was told. Why Jeremy had to watch him, Jean didn't know; he kept his gaze on Cat's back as a safer focal point. He hadn't realized until today that she had tattoos, but the string back of her bikini put the vibrant flowers along her upper back and spine on full display. Jean wanted to ask why she was allowed to mark herself so thoroughly, but Jeremy beat him to speaking with:

"Missed a couple spots. Need a hand?"

Jean was saved from having to respond when someone called out, "Jeremy!"

Jean offered silent thanks as Jeremy was immediately distracted from him.

Cody was shorter than Jean had expected, but broad-shouldered and stocky as befit a backliner. Red hair was shaved close to their skull, and Jean was startled by how many piercings they'd managed to fit on their ears and face. He had to believe those came out for game nights, because if someone checked Cody hard enough their lips were done for. Jean almost demanded an explanation for such recklessness, but

192

then Lucas moved up alongside Cody and Jean forgot everything he was going to say.

Lucas Johnson looked so much like Grayson that Jean's blood went cold. He wasn't quite as large, and he bore the sun-bleached hair and bronzed skin of a man who spent far too much time outdoors, but everything from his eyes to his jawline to the way he held himself was a perfect match. Jean had had years to learn all of Grayson's tics; he'd had to learn Grayson inside and out so he could keep Zane two steps ahead of him.

Jean wondered what, if anything, Grayson had told him. Jeremy had warned Jean weeks ago that the Trojans were keeping tabs on the rumors surrounding him and the Ravens. Jean had been waiting for them to confront him about which ones were truth and which ones were unfounded slander, but they'd yet to bring them up with any detail. The look on Lucas's face made him think he was out of time.

Jeremy took a step like he was going to meet them halfway, but Laila snagged him by his hair so she could smear lotion on his back. Jeremy went still and waited for the new arrivals to reach them.

"Cody and Lucas," he said, with a glance at Jean. "This is Jean."

"Hell yeah," Cody said. "He's tall."

Cat laughed. "That's what I said. Someone's got to balance you out."

"I did what I could with what I was given," Cody said with an exaggerated shrug. "You've seen my mom; I was screwed from the get-go. Jeremy! The hair, man. Looks good."

"Thanks!" Jeremy said, lighting up.

"Hey, kiddo," Cat said, giving Lucas' hair a tweak. "How're you holding up?"

Lucas dragged his stare away from Jean with obvious effort. "I don't know," he admitted, and then asked point-blank, "How are *you*? You're living with one of them, too."

"I have more teeth than you do, if you haven't noticed,"

Cat said. Her tone was light, and she was smiling, but even Jean heard the rebuke in it. Lucas glared at her, and Jean had to look away from that too-familiar expression. He was dimly aware of Laila watching him, but he refused to return her calm stare. Cat eased up a bit and said, "He's a little rough around the edges, and I assume he'll be worse once we can finally get him on a court, but I like him."

"We'll see," Lucas said, with a furtive look Jean's way.

"Excited to see what you can bring to the line," Cody said to Jean. "Provided you can behave, and all."

"I am only required to behave in public and during games," Jean reminded them.

"And what makes you think we should listen to anything you have to say?" Lucas asked.

"You've seen his stats," Cat reminded him. "We all have."

"Yeah," Lucas said, "but we've also heard how he made starting lineup."

Cody grimaced. "Stow that, Lucas. We talked about this."

"We agreed we were going to take the rumors with a grain of salt," Lucas sent back. "But Grayson is saying it, too. That's not the kind of drama we need on our lineup right now. People are already talking shit about us for stealing Jean halfway through championships and then giving our win to the Foxes for no good reason. We need a spotless year if we're going to redeem ourselves."

"I trust him," Jeremy said. "Isn't that enough?"

"This time it's not," Lucas said, and he at least had the decency to sound apologetic. "Not when you're—" He was smart enough not to finish it, or maybe that was because Cody grabbed his shoulder in a white-knuckled grip.

"When I'm what?" Jeremy invited Lucas. Lucas averted his eyes and said nothing, but Jeremy only tolerated the silence for a few moments. "I asked you a question."

"I'm sorry," Lucas said, stiff with discomfort. "That was out of line."

Jeremy was wearing that tense smile Jean had only seen on him once before. Laila was watching Jeremy; Cat was watching Lucas. Neither of them looked pleased, but neither was going to step in and help either man out. Jean wasn't entirely sure what Lucas had bitten off at the last second, but he didn't need to know that to know what caged argument was happening behind their words.

It wasn't a conversation he wanted to have anytime soon, but it was past the point Jean could ignore it. "I had my number before I joined the lineup because my position was always guaranteed," Jean said. "Your wretched brother spent three years trying and failing to keep up with me. If I had the rest of the day to waste, I would tell you every single place that both he and you fall short on the court to prove my point. He can lie about why it happened all he likes. It doesn't change the facts."

Lucas lifted his chin a little in defiance. "I won't apologize for being worried."

"Your apologies are as worthless as your opinion."

"Call a truce," Cody ordered Lucas. "Right now."

Lucas glared but sullenly said, "Truce, until you screw us... over."

Jean didn't miss that purposeful beat in his response. Maybe the others looked past it, too eager to put this awkward meeting behind them. Cat swept in as soon as Lucas subsided, hooking an arm around Cody's shoulders to steer her fellow backliners toward the water. Laila and Jeremy exchanged a long look but said nothing. At length Laila shook her head and followed them. Jeremy stayed behind to apply more sunblock, but Jean didn't miss the tension in his hands as he worked at the back of his neck.

"I'm sorry," Jeremy said at last. "He's usually less bitter."

"He is a child spitting smoke," Jean said. "It doesn't matter."

"He shouldn't have said it."

"All of you have heard it," Jean said, not quite an

accusation.

Jeremy didn't answer, but he did meet Jean's eyes for a moment. If there had been anything scheming or hungry in his gaze, Jean could have left it at that, but all he saw was regret. Jeremy had heard the rumors about how far Jean would supposedly go for a chance to play but expected nothing from him.

Safety was a dangerous illusion, but Jean still felt the gentle weight of it. He looked out at the ocean to find his center again, hoping the waves and the heat and the impossibly bright sky would burn this ill-advised feeling out of him.

"It wasn't about the lineup," he said without meaning to.

"Normally I would say something about how everyone is free to experiment," Jeremy said, "or some tried and true nonsense about consenting adults doing what they like. But Jean, you're nineteen. If I'm doing the math right, you were sixteen when you joined the line. That's statutory rape any way you look at it. They never should have said yes when you asked."

"I didn't ask."

It was out before he knew it was coming, ragged with an anger that left his throat aching. Jean's hand went up like he could somehow snatch the words back. Jeremy started to grab at him before thinking better of it and carding his fingers through his own hair instead. Jean put space between them immediately, getting out of Jeremy's reach as fast as he could.

"No," he said. "Don't say anything."

"Jean, you—what—"

Jean pointed a warning finger at him. "I did not say it. You did not hear it."

"Why are you protecting them?" Jeremy asked, voice raw with disbelief. His phone started going off with back-to-back chimes. Jean wished he'd get distracted and forget this conversation, but Jeremy didn't even acknowledge the noise. "You're not a Raven anymore; you're not bound to Edgar Allan. Give me one good reason why you'd let them get away

196

with this, and don't you *dare* say you deserved it."

"I did," Jean said, and Jeremy flinched like he'd been hit. "You cannot understand."

"Can you even hear yourself?" Jeremy asked, despairing.

"Leave it," Jean warned him. "It has nothing to do with you. This conversation was inevitable when we all know what they're saying about me; I won't treat you like an idiot by lying about it when too many people are saying otherwise. The circumstances are none of your business. All you need to know are these two facts: I don't need to fuck any of you to be better than your entire lineup, and if any Trojan ever tries to touch me, I will cut his throat on the spot. Do you understand?"

"-emy! Jeremy!" Cody was sprinting back up the beach toward them, waving their phone wildly above their head. They skidded to a stop, looking a bit like they'd seen a ghost, and flicked a sharp look at Jean. "It's Colleen Jenkins. She's gone."

Jean's stomach bottomed out. Jeremy turned on him, anguish and worry too bright on his face, but Jean didn't see him. The only thing that mattered was his phone as he pulled it out of his pocket and punched in a number out of memory.

Jean had never needed to memorize the Ravens' contact information, seeing how they were in his face all day every day, but he'd called Josiah so many times he could never forget his number. He wasn't sure Josiah would answer an unfamiliar caller, but the Ravens' head nurse picked up on the second ring with a curt, "Josiah Smalls."

"Jean Moreau," Jean answered. He half-expected Josiah to hang up on him, but when he got an annoyed grunt in response he asked, "What happened to Colleen?"

"Stepped onto the subway tracks," Josiah said, and if he didn't sound broken up about it, he at least sounded tired. "I assume they have TVs in California? You could've watched the news instead of bothering me for specifics."

"Find Zane," Jean said. "When he hears about Colleen, he'll try to follow."

Josiah hung up without a word, and Jean could only hope the man was dropping him in favor of the more important emergency. Jean fought the urge to call him back, not wanting to distract him if he was going for Zane's file. Jean flipped his phone closed and squeezed it between both hands. Cody and Jeremy were watching him closely, watching for an explanation or an explosion.

"He loved her," Jean said at last. He shouldn't be so cold when the day was so hot; he had frost in his heart and sweat running down his back. "He wasn't allowed, and he knew it, but he did anyway."

If Jean and Zane weren't roommates, Jean doubted he would have ever picked up on it. With Zane trying so hard to catch Riko's eye, getting caught with a steady partner would have been disastrous. Jean's schedule had always been out of alignment with the rest of the Ravens' due to his status as perfect Court, but he'd walked in on them more than once. In exchange for his discretion Colleen checked Grayson with unmitigated violence during scrimmages.

She hadn't been back to their room since January. Zane hadn't been able to face her, not after what he'd done to Jean, not after what Riko made him do to Grayson. Her absence had done more harm than good in the long run, leaving Zane thoroughly unmoored. If she was well and truly gone—

Jean put his phone away before he could throw it and scrubbed at the goosebumps prickling at his arm.

Cody's voice startled him from dark thoughts: "And now you're trying to save him. I was under the impression you and the Ravens hated each other."

"We do," Jean said. "We don't. We are Ravens."

"You are not a Raven," Jeremy said, a quiet but firm reminder. He treated Cody to a long look before asking, "Cameron?"

Cody got a stubborn set to their jaw. "Not gonna ask. Not my problem."

Jeremy nodded, and Cody jogged back to where the others

198

were still kicking wet sand at each other. Jean stared after them, waiting for the pieces to fall into place. "Winter. Cody and Cameron Winter."

"Cousins," Jeremy confirmed, "but willfully estranged. Cody's extended family has some pretty vulgar opinions about their lifestyle that Cody knows not to tolerate."

That tracked; Cameron was a bigoted asshole who had far too much to say at any given time. Jean tucked it aside to mull over later. He didn't want to stay there with his thoughts and their unfinished conversation, so he collected the bag of clothes and set off down the beach. He expected Jeremy to pick up where they'd left off, but news of Colleen's suicide had taken the wind out of his sails.

"I'm sorry about Colleen," Jeremy finally said, so soft Jean could barely hear him over the wind. When Jean didn't respond, Jeremy tried again: "Zane was your partner. Do you want to talk about it?"

If Jean thought about Zane, he'd go mad. "There is nothing I want less. Leave me alone."

He didn't expect Jeremy to respect that, but his captain held his tongue for a solid ten minutes. When he couldn't tolerate the silence anymore, Jeremy started talking about the local area. Jean wanted to tell him he didn't care, but listening to Jeremy was better than listening to his chaotic and conflicted thoughts, so he kept his mouth shut and let Jeremy distract him from his Ravens.

Now and then Jeremy peeled off to charge into the water, needing a break from the harsh midday sun, but he always came back to Jean's side. Jean wasn't sure what was worse: watching his head go underwater for far too long or watching him emerge again with wet shorts plastered to his well-toned thighs.

Twice the rest of the group returned with him to Jean's side so they could touch up their sunblock. Cat batted Jean's hands out of the way so she could help with his neck and temples. She leaned back to inspect her handiwork, offered him a triumphant thumbs-up, and bolted back to the tide with a whoop that left Jean's ears ringing.

At a quarter to five they finally went their separate ways, Cody and Lucas back south to Carlsbad and the remaining four to Laila's car. By the time they got home, Jeremy had gotten a heads-up from one of his nonstop group chats: Zane Reacher had been found unconscious on his bathroom floor. His family was begging for privacy, but the loudest theory was overdose. He was hospitalized but reportedly stable.

"You saved his life," Laila told Jean as she got the front door open for them. "Be proud."

"They're dropping like flies," Cat said, with a distant look on her face. "Chances are good Coach will send a psychiatrist out to see you as soon as he can find one."

"I don't need one," Jean said. "I will refuse."

Cat flicked him a pitying look. "I can think of very few people who need one more. No judgment, seriously. The right therapist can be legit life changing—just look at Jeremy for proof." She jerked a thumb over at Jeremy, who didn't look at all concerned to be snitched on. "I'd say you should ask for her number since we all know she's good, but I don't think any of us can afford her."

Jeremy gave a helpless shrug. "She was Mom's pick. Speak of the devil," he added as his phone made an awful noise. Jean watched the way his expression went tense and distant as he considered the newest message on his phone. Jeremy tapped out a quick response and stuffed his phone into the bag Jean was still carrying. When he realized Jean was watching him, he offered a see-through smile and said, "Nothing to worry about."

Jean turned away, but Laila put a hand in his way and asked, "Do you want to talk?"

"I want to be left alone," Jean said.

"Even by me?" Jeremy asked. When Jean looked at him, Jeremy shrugged and said, "You said I'm supposed to be underfoot. We don't have to talk if you don't want to talk, but I just feel like you shouldn't be alone today."

"After you're dressed," Jean said, and Laila dropped her hand.

Jeremy trailed him down the hall to his bedroom so he could get some clothes out of the closet. It was inevitable Jean would end up by his dresser, but he waited to go through it until Jeremy left for a quick rinse-off shower. Jean opened the top drawer and let his long fingers drift over his destroyed magnets and postcards.

He pulled one of his notebooks out at random and slowly flipped through it, scanning the jet-black insults scribbled across each odd page. He checked the letters as he found them, skimming for names or jersey numbers, but Jeremy returned before Jean could find a letter from Colleen or Wayne. Jean closed his notebook before Jeremy could see what the Ravens had done to the pages.

Jeremy turned Barkbark back around before inviting himself to sit cross-legged in the middle of Jean's bed. He studied Jean but said nothing. Jean surveyed the room with a slow gaze: the pale white and gray sheets on the only bed, the darker gray curtains that helped filter out most of the evening sun, and the closet with trendy clothes in a half-dozen muted colors. Jean looked down at his hands, free of bruises but faintly mottled with small scars from years of violence.

He thought of Wayne's ambition and unrelenting drive and how Colleen moved with unrepentant violence on the court. He thought of three years as Zane's roommate, two years as partners, and one wretched little runaway that broke Zane's threadbare patience at long last. He thought of Zane's unwavering gaze on the back of Colleen's head while she was getting dressed, the way he reached for her hair when her back was turned to him and the way he always pulled back before he could give himself away with a tender touch.

I am a Moreau, he thought. He had his place. He had his purpose. It was his job to submit to the Moriyamas, to be whatever they demanded of him and to take whatever punishments they felt like doling out. He'd been sold into this with no choice and no way out. But what of his hateful, hated Ravens? Surely they'd heard the indoctrination rumors before signing their names on Edgar Allan's contracts, but no gossip could have prepared them for the ugly reality of the Nest. They came for fame and fortune without knowing what it would cost them.

Cat's words haunted him: *"What we don't understand is how a grown-ass man took a bunch of kids and turned them into monsters for sport."*

The master knew what he was doing. This was his sport; this was his legacy. Everything he'd done to them, he'd done for a reason. Everything he'd demanded of them had been demanded with the sole purpose of making them legends. The master knew best.

Did he?

It was sacrilegious even in the privacy of his head, and Jean hunched his shoulders against a blow that never came. He ran a nervous hand over his ribs, but the pain was gone. He'd been out of Evermore for too long to find even a bruise to dig into. In a few weeks he'd be back on a court, and life would start making sense again, but right now he was trapped between who he was and who the Trojans were asking him to be.

He wasn't sure where the words came from. "They didn't deserve this."

"No," Jeremy agreed quietly. "I'm sorry."

Apologies wouldn't bring them back. It wouldn't undo what had been done to them or erase what they'd done to each other. But what else could either of them say? Jean put his notebook away and went to sit beside Jeremy. In the quiet he could hear Jeremy breathing, and it was almost as comforting as the heat of another body this close to his. It thawed the parts of him the sun hadn't reached despite soaking up its glare all day.

Jean closed his eyes and let his thoughts drift far away.

The sound of pots and pans dragged him out of a near-doze sometime later, and Jeremy noticed his distraction.

"She can handle it," he said before Jean could get up. "Stay with me."

Jean didn't mind cooking, but he didn't say that. This was the first time his room truly felt safe and right, and he was content to hold onto it for as long as he could. He closed his eyes again, but now his thoughts were snagged on Jeremy. At length he broke the silence to say, "Two beds would fit in here."

It took Jeremy a moment to figure out how to respond. "Two twins, maybe," he said slowly, "but isn't it nice to have your own space? After having a roommate for so long, I mean, and after—" He didn't finish that train of thought, but he didn't need to. Jean knew from his tone what he was biting off. Jean hated his earlier carelessness, but it was too late to take it back.

That didn't mean he had to acknowledge it. All he said was, "You are my partner and my captain. You don't need to be sleeping on a couch."

Jeremy didn't let him get away with it. "That's not the issue and you know it. I don't want to crowd you."

"You are not them," Jean said. "Kevin would not have sent me here if you were."

Jeremy was quiet for so long Jean finally had to look at him. He wasn't sure what to make of the look on the other man's face. It wasn't wounded, but there was still an undercurrent of pain. Jean didn't know how to interpret it; no Raven had ever looked so gutted. He tipped his head in silent question, but Jeremy only looked away.

Jean searched for anything else to say that would get him what he needed and settled on, "Ravens aren't meant to be alone."

"You are not a Raven," Jeremy said, right on cue.

Jean resisted the urge to shove him off the bed, but just barely. "Until I left Evermore, I never had a room of my own. I

203

shared with Kevin and Riko until my freshman year and Zane every year after that. It is too quiet with just me."

"What about before?" Jeremy asked. "Back home, I mean?"

Jean trailed a thumb over his palm, chasing the fractured memory of a small hand in his. He remembered the weight and warmth of her burrowed against his side; he remembered her wide-eyed and unblinking stare as he read her stories late into the night. He could almost remember the sound of her voice as she begged him for one more chapter, but louder in his thoughts was the crack of his mother's belt against bare skin when she overheard them talking. Jean felt his stomach tip and heart crack, and he slammed Marseille as deep as he could go.

"I don't want to talk about home," he said. "Now or ever."

Jeremy let it slide without argument, and silence fell in the room once more. It wasn't until Cat called down the hall to summon them for dinner that Jeremy finally said, "I'll see what I can do about a bed."

-

The next morning a suited stranger was on their doorstep. Jean let his introduction go in one ear and out the other and refused to take the business card that was offered to him. The man was one of the campus psychiatrists, sent over by the school board to evaluate their newest player in the wake of the Ravens' escalating tragedies. Jean wanted to close the door in his face, but if the coaches had signed off on this, he didn't have the right to turn the man away.

They ended up in the study with the door closed. Someone—Cat, likely—got some music going loud down the hall to help cover their voices and buy them a bit of privacy. Jean should have told her not to bother. Just because he had to meet with this man didn't mean he had to speak to him. He spent the next thirty minutes staring at the doctor in stony silence, patiently outlasting every attempt to bait him into conversation. By the fifteen-minute mark he could sense the other man's impatience, but somehow the doctor lasted the

204

entire session without giving up.

"You had the chance to make this painless," the doctor said as he finally got ready to go. He dropped his business card on the desk in front of Jean. "You've forced my hand with your hostility and unwillingness to cooperate. I'm recommending mandatory counseling twice a week. Figure out which days and time slots will work best around summer practices and let me know by the end of tomorrow. My office location and hours are on my card."

"I won't," Jean said.

"You will, or I will have your coaches make a decision for you."

Jean tore his card into scraps as the doctor started for the door. It earned him an assessing look but no comment. Jean refused to watch him go, but his thoughts teetered in anxious circles as he looked for a way out of this. In no universe could he defy his coaches, but how could he possibly stand meeting with this wretched know-nothing twice a week?

He hadn't sorted out a way out by the time Jeremy stepped into the doorway to check on him, but Jean still said, "I won't do it."

"I can't get you out of it," Jeremy said. "But if you don't like him, we can always find you a different doctor. He can't be the only one on USC's payroll. I'm sure you'll click with one of them. It just might take a bit of trial and error."

"There is nothing I can say to them," Jean said. He couldn't talk about the Moriyamas; he wouldn't talk about what he'd endured. Perhaps he could fill the silence talking about his teammates, but how long would the doctors tolerate that deflection before they got his coaches involved? "None of them will understand."

"Someone will," Jeremy promised.

No one in the world, Jean thought sullenly, and it haunted his thoughts for the rest of the day. It wasn't until his phone hummed with an incoming message later that afternoon that he finally put it together. One moment he was looking down at

Renee's text and the picture she'd sent him of her backyard deer; in the next moment realization left him dizzy with desperate hope. This wasn't a good solution by far, but it was still the best one he could think of.

Jean tapped out a quick message to Renee: "Do you have Dobson's number?" He'd deleted it from his phone weeks ago, sure he'd never have to use it.

Renee didn't ask why but forwarded him Dobson's contact card to save to his phone. Jean wavered between her cell and office numbers before deciding he really didn't want to hear her voice for this conversation. Text was a safer medium to start with, but a half-dozen tries later he still didn't know what to say. He cast his phone aside in frustrated defeat and didn't try again until dinner was in the oven that night.

"USC ordered me to find a counselor," was the best he finally came up with, and he sent it before he could second-guess himself yet again. It wasn't until a few minutes later that he realized he didn't sign it. Maybe Wymack had given her his number when he programmed hers into his, because Dobson came back with an unhesitating,

"Hello, Jean! I would be happy to make an appointment with you."

He couldn't say the same, but she was his only option. If Kevin had told the Foxes about Evermore and the Moriyamas, then it was safe to assume he'd extended his indiscretion to his shrink. Jean couldn't imagine telling her such things—or anything, really—but she had the necessary groundwork to understand his dishonesty and reticence. It was more than he would get from anyone else.

"It was not my choice," he sent back in warning. "I do not need counseling."

"We will make the best of it," she promised. "Thank you for trusting me with your time."

He didn't trust her at all, but there was no point spelling it out. Hashing out a schedule took only a little bit of work, as she had her appointment book with her at home and Jeremy

206

could provide the start and end times for the Trojans' summer practices. The only trick was remembering the time zone difference.

Jean had to go back to Jeremy halfway through the conversation for Coach Rhemann's contact information, since Dobson offered to reach out to him on Jean's behalf and square things away, but at last he had days and times locked in. Jean didn't feel any better about the ordeal, but at least he wouldn't have to see that annoying man from earlier ever again.

Lesser evils, he thought tiredly, and he turned his phone off for the rest of the evening.

CHAPTER TWELVE
Jeremy

June felt like a bated breath. After two suicides and one near miss, the Ravens' parents and school board put the rest of the lineup on suicide watch. What they were dealing with was no one else's business, but of course the press made nuisances of themselves as they tried to track the Ravens' downfall. At last guess at least sixteen of the remaining Ravens had been committed to full-time inpatient care, and Lucas confirmed Grayson was one of them.

The conversation finally shifted away from the Foxes and Trojans back to the Ravens' spiraling issues. The chances of the Ravens recovering in time for summer practices were looking slim, but that was such a heartless topic to linger over Jeremy felt ill. Edgar Allan's Exy staff was also under investigation, but no one could locate Tetsuji Moriyama for a comment. The last time anyone remembered seeing him was at the press conference following Riko's death. Rumor had it he'd returned to Japan, but where he'd gone from there was anyone's guess.

For the first time ever, someone managed to get a microphone in Ichirou Moriyama's face. Jeremy had almost forgotten Riko was survived by an older brother. There'd been a short piece about him back when Kengo Moriyama died, but Ichirou was generally good about staying as far away from the press and public eye as possible. Jeremy studied his young face as he regarded the press with calm contempt. He was jarringly handsome and perfectly dressed in a suit that screamed obscene wealth. Seemed business was good despite the recent tragic loss of the company's CEO.

Movement in the corner of his eye warned him Jean had entered the room at some point. He stared at the TV now like he'd seen a ghost, and Jeremy wondered if it was easier for him to see Riko in Ichirou's features than Jeremy could.

Jeremy meant to say something, but he was trying to hear. Ichirou himself didn't address any of the questions thrown his way; the woman at his side handled everything on his behalf. No matter how many ways it was approached, the answer was the same: Tetsuji's current whereabouts were not Ichirou's business or concern. Ichirou had no insights that could assist the ongoing investigations and no interest in helping. All he wanted to do was run his company and focus on his recent engagement. Jean gave a hollow laugh at that last bit and left the room.

Kevin hadn't been a Raven in over a year, but Jeremy still checked in with him to see how he was holding up as his former team fell apart. Kevin was less interested in their problems than he was his own: the Ravens' fans had been making his life a living hell so far this summer. Now that they were fretting over the Ravens' issues he could finally get to work in peace.

His single-mindedness was familiar enough to be reassuring, but Jeremy wondered if he ought to push for a more honest answer. There had to be more to it if Kevin was still refusing all requests for an interview. Kevin knew how much influence and power he held, but he didn't have the stomach or the strength to put on his public-friendly face right now. Jeremy ached for him, but there was only so much he could do from the other side of the country. In the end he decided to trust Kevin to the Foxes' care.

It was a necessary sacrifice, because Jean required significantly more of his attention. Jean wasn't the liveliest of personalities on a good day, but he was noticeably more withdrawn in the weeks following Colleen's death. Jeremy was glad the coaches had forced him into therapy, even if Jean had picked a long-distance psychiatrist, but there was no quick fix for what Jean was dealing with.

Jeremy wondered if he'd ever really understand Jean's relationship with the Ravens, but every time he thought of the fallen team he felt ill to his stomach. It was too much to work through, with too many missing pieces still.

Jeremy, Cat, and Laila did what they could to keep Jean out of his head, but their grip felt slippery at best. The most present Jean felt was when they were able to haul out Jillian's old queen bed and replace it with two twins. Jean was so satisfied by the new setup he even tolerated another shopping trip to replace his bedding without hesitation or complaint.

Jeremy was less sure of the arrangement, since he wasn't used to sharing a room for more than a quick hookup, but the bed was a step up from the couch and Jean was eerily quiet at rest. Silent, but not restful. It wasn't until Jeremy moved into his room that he realized how often Jean jerked awake from nightmares. The first time it happened he slurred a sleepy query that Jean immediately dismissed. After that Jeremy resigned himself to simply watching as Jean balled up in bed and relearned how to breathe.

All in all, Jeremy was desperate for summer practices to start and distract them all. The Trojans' first day back was June 25th, so by Sunday the 17th most of the staff were back in town to get their files sorted. On Monday the 18th Jeremy and Jean were summoned to the stadium. Davis was out of town on a last-minute trip, but Coach Lisinski and Nurse Binh Nguyen were on hand to do Jean's follow-up appointment.

Jeremy left the three to each other and went to check Jean's locker. It was packed full of gear in red and gold, so he waited on the bench across from it for Jean to catch up with him.

When Jean did, there was a purpose in his step Jeremy had never seen in him, and Jeremy knew the words before Jean had to say them: "I'm cleared for practice, albeit with a no-touch jersey for the first week."

"That's great," Jeremy said, buoyed by Jean's rare good

mood. "Have a look!"

Jean followed the tip of his hand toward the locker, and he immediately went to inspect his gear. For a man who claimed he didn't enjoy Exy, he had no disgust or weariness on his face as he held his new jersey up to the light. He traced his new number with the tips of two fingers and put his hand to the three on his face.

"Atrocious colors," Jean said. "Whoever chose them was a fool."

"They'll look good on you now that we've finally gotten you a bit of sun," Jeremy said. "Want to try them on? I could see if Coach Lisinski has her equipment keys on her, if you want to take your racquets for a test run." The look Jean sent him was answer enough, and Jeremy hopped off the bench with a laugh. He found Lisinski in her office with Jean's file open on the desk in front of her. "Hey, Coach. Mind if I take Jean down to the court?"

"I'm only going to be here for an hour or two," she warned him as she scooped her keys up and gently tossed them to him. "Keep an eye on him."

"Yes, Coach."

He stopped by the equipment room on the way back. Three buckets of balls were sitting on shelves just inside the door, and he moved one out into the hallway to collect later. There were separate stick racks for each line, with stickers labeling the rows by player name and number. He took one of his and one of Jean's, whistling a little at the weight of Jean's racquet. Jeremy had tried heavies at the end of his senior year of high school and into his freshman year of college, but he'd gone back to lighter sticks as soon as he could get Coach White to sign off on it. It put him at a disadvantage during stick checks, as most backliners he went up against used heavies, but he'd sacrifice that in favor of more control on his passes.

"Good news," he said, turning into the locker room with the sticks held high.

Whatever he'd meant to follow up with was immediately forgotten, as Jean was sitting shirtless on the bench. A few months of injured reserve had inevitably taken some of the definition out of him, but Jean was all coiled strength and long limbs. He stood at Jeremy's entrance, one hand out in silent demand for his racquet. Jeremy had a moment to notice the silver cross necklace he wore before the scars littering Jean's skin put everything else out of mind.

To say there were too many was an offensive understatement. It was only on the second look that the niggling alarm at the back of his thoughts sharpened into focus: almost all of Jean's scars were on the untanned stretches of him, placed where his baggy jersey would always hide them from curious eyes. Most were overlapping lines of varying thickness, but here and there were clusters of small burns no bigger than a match head.

These were not injuries from scrimmages or childhood accidents; they were far too numerous and precise. Every one of these was intentional.

How Jeremy found his voice, he didn't know. All he got out was a weak, "Jean?"

"It is a problem for the nurses, not you," Jean said dismissively. He was too distracted by his racquet to care about what was showing on his body.

Jeremy tried to watch the way his fingers looked as they hooked through the laces of his racquet head or appreciate the cool approval in Jean's hooded stare as he tested the weight of his stick, but how could any of that matter when someone had carved literal whorls over Jean's heart?

A hand on his chin startled him into looking up. When he met Jean's eyes, Jean only said, "Focus on what's important."

"I am," Jeremy said. Jean opened his mouth, closed it again, and let go of Jeremy without a word. Jeremy snagged his arm when he started to turn away. "Who did this to you?"

Jean said nothing, seemingly content to stare at him in steady silence. Maybe he saw the stubborn set to Jeremy's face,

212

because at long last he said: "My father."

It felt like getting kicked. Jeremy dropped Jean's arm with a startled, "Oh." It was a pathetic response for such an awful confession, but Jeremy struggled to come up with something better. His family had its problems—all families did, he supposed—but never in his life had his mother raised a hand at her rowdy children. He couldn't fathom being struck by a parent; how could he possibly wrap his mind around the malice behind something like this?

"Do not let it bother you," Jean said, setting his racquet aside so he could finish getting dressed. "It will not affect my performance on the court."

"That's not the issue. Your parents are supposed to love and protect you, not—" Jeremy gestured helplessly toward Jean. "I'm sorry. I can't even imagine what that was like for you."

"Imagine getting changed so we can practice," Jean said.

Jeremy weighed all the things he could say, all the questions he knew Jean would never answer, and sighed as he went in search of his own locker. Jean caught up with him when he was halfway done. Jeremy grabbed the balls as they passed the equipment room again, and they went down to the court together.

Jeremy unlocked the door but motioned Jean on ahead of him. He half-expected Jean to head to center court where he could get a look at the full thing, but the man unerringly went for his starting spot on the first-fourth line. Once there he did a slow turn in place, studying the freshly redone floors before tipping his head back to look up at the scoreboard hanging far overhead.

Jeremy secured the door and went to stand with him. The bucket he set at his feet long enough to tug his gloves on, and he grinned up at Jean. "What do you think of her?"

"Tacky," Jean said, gazing out at the stands through the walls as he worked on his own gloves. "Smaller than expected, considering your school's rank."

"We only had so much space to work with around here," Jeremy said with a helpless shrug. "It's not about size, anyway."

"Defensive," Jean said, tugging his glove straps with his teeth.

Jeremy straightened in indignation. "I don't have anything to be defensive about." Jean lost his grip and bit his lip, and Jeremy hurried on before either of them could think too much about that double entendre. "Let's start with a couple laps and work our way up from there. You have to let me know if you feel anything pull, okay? I told Coach Lisinski I'd watch out for you." He waited a beat, was unsurprised by the silence, and said, "Say 'yes, Jeremy'."

He had the distinct impression Jean wanted to roll his eyes. "Yes, Jeremy."

Jeremy forgot everything else he could have said in favor of staring. It was the first time he'd heard Jean say his name. Hearing it in Jean's accent put a wicked flutter in Jeremy's stomach. He stared a moment too long, and Jean quirked an eyebrow at him in silent question.

"Nothing," Jeremy said, and leaned over to set his helmet beside the balls. He changed his mind just a moment later. "Jean, if I—" he started, but faltered until Jean turned toward him. "If I ever make you uncomfortable or make you feel unsafe, will you promise to tell me? If you don't trust me enough to tell me what's wrong and why, at least trust me enough to tell me that something *is* wrong. I can't fix things if I don't know there's a problem. As your captain and your partner, don't I at least deserve the chance to not be a villain in your story?"

Jean favored him with a pitying look. "You are the captain of the sunshine court. In no universe could you be anyone's villain."

That unhesitating trust warmed him all the way through, but all Jeremy said was, "Technically it's the Gold Court."

"Do not act like you don't enjoy the moniker."

214

"I do," Jeremy admitted with a smile. "Ready?"

He kept an easy pace on account of it being Jean's first day on the court in three months. They alternated workouts and warmup drills, 1-2's and half-steps and corner shots. There were two versions of nearly every drill: one static and one that involved checking the player while they were trying to make their shots, but since Jean was no-contact for at least a little longer Jeremy neatly excised the second half. He thought the restrictions would irritate Jean, but Jean followed his lead without hesitation or complaint.

He noticed when Lisinski sat on the bench to watch them, but since she wasn't at the door to call them off, he pushed his luck and kept Jean moving. Finally she got up and rapped on the court wall, and Jeremy set to work collecting the scattered balls. Jean pulled his helmet and gloves off before helping Jeremy tidy up. Between the two of them, it was easy work, and Jean trailed him off the court.

Since Lisinski had stuck around, Jeremy led Jean over to her. She gave Jean a once-over before nodding approval. "Form looks good. How do you feel?"

"Unforgivably rusty, Coach," Jean answered.

"You'll be back up to speed in no time," Lisinski promised him. "You two have a few minutes to stop by Lyon with me? I want to check your baseline in case I need to adjust your routine." Jean looked to Jeremy, who nodded easy agreement, and Lisinski motioned for them to precede her back to the locker room. "All right, then. Let's get you in something easier to move in and I'll give you a ride over there."

They put away the balls and racquets first so Lisinski could take her keys back, then peeled off their uniforms and dropped them in the bins to be collected and washed. The shower room was too large for just the two of them, and they washed up facing opposite walls. Jean was in and out before Jeremy had even finished scrubbing down his body, and Jeremy sent a bemused look toward the door. He'd noticed since moving in that Jean took impossibly fast showers, but he'd assumed the sweat of practice would take a little longer to wash clean. He guessed the haste had to do with the Ravens' airtight schedule, and he sighed a little as he picked up the pace.

Lyon was a short walk but a shorter ride, and Jeremy trailed the two as Lisinski put Jean on different machines. He went where she pointed and lifted whatever she asked, testing both the strain it put on his healed body and the consequences of three months sidelined. Jean wasn't crass enough to complain about his performance to a coach, but Jeremy saw the muted frustration in his stare as he had to face his new limitations. Maybe Lisinski sensed it, too, because her comments leaned more toward optimistic than her usual brisk assessments.

All in all, it was a mixed success until Lisinski took them to the aquatics center. She was chatting away about the water aerobics program and its benefits with her back to them, so she missed the way Jean went still when he realized where he was.

Jeremy almost put a hand on his shoulder, decided at the last second he didn't want to get decked, and settled for a quiet, "Hey. You good?"

"Good," Jean said, toneless and unconvincing, and he moved to catch up with Lisinski where she'd stopped to wait for them. She half-turned their way as they stopped near her, but it didn't take her long to realize Jean wasn't listening to her anymore. He didn't even react when she trailed off to consider him; he was staring at the pool like he thought it'd bite him if he looked away.

"Am I boring you, Moreau?" she asked.

"No, Coach," Jean said.

Jeremy idly wondered if he was crossing a line. "I don't think Jean can swim."

Lisinski arched a brow at Jean. "A little old to not know."

"No, I—I can swim, Coach." Jean started to reach for his neck but caught himself halfway there and grabbed his necklace instead. His mouth was pulled to a bloodless line as he watched sunlight dance off the water, and he gave the silver chain an agitated tug before saying, "It has been many years, but I should remember."

Lisinski studied him for an endless minute, then caught his shoulder and gave him a hard push toward the edge of the pool. He was too far from the edge for it to be a real threat, but Jean reacted immediately. How he got out of her grip and to the nearest wall so fast, Jeremy would never know, but Jean caught at it for balance when his legs threatened to give out on him and closed his eyes.

"Sorry," he managed, thready and faint. "Sorry, I'm—"

If he had anything else to say, he lost it when he locked his own hand white-knuckled around his throat. Jeremy dove for him and grabbed his wrist. Jean's heartbeat was like a hummingbird's against his fingertips, and Jean shuddered so hard Jeremy felt it to his elbow.

"Jean, stop," he tried. "Jean, you have to let go."

Jean's fingernails left bloody lines behind when Jeremy finally managed to drag his hand loose. Jean wrenched his hand out of Jeremy's in favor of digging the heel of his palm into his temple. Every breath he managed sounded like it was ripping his lungs in half, too fast and too sharp and too short to help him. He had yet to open his eyes, but he turned his face away from Jeremy like he could feel the prying weight of Jeremy's stare.

Lisinski put a hand to his shoulder, and Jean let her shove him to his knees. He planted his hands against the ground and bowed his head as he gasped. Jeremy sat cross-legged beside him while Lisinski towered over them both. Jeremy wasn't sure what to do, so he held tight to Jean's wrist and just murmured, "You're okay, you're okay," until Jean found his way back to them. Finally Jean sat back on his heels and stared defeated at the floor in front of him. His heartbeat was still faster than Jeremy would've liked, but Jeremy slowly let go of him.

Lisinski crouched in front of them. "I'll take an
217

explanation now."

"I'm sorry, Coach."

"Don't apologize to me," Lisinski said, incensed, and Jean subsided. "I've met people who can't swim, and I've met people who were afraid to try, but I've never in my life seen someone react like that. Tell me what that was about."

Jeremy expected a story about childhood trauma. Jean had just told him the other week that Marseille was on the coast. Surely there was a story there about a reckless child going too far into the water and almost drowning, or a local tragedy that had fueled nightmares for years. He was ticking through every possible option when Jean answered, and the hideous truth was not one Jeremy would have ever considered:

"Water was used as a correctional tool at Evermore, for performance and attitude," Jean said, sounding worn to the bone. "I have some lingering issues, but I will work through them, Coach. I promise I will not fall behind."

"Quiet," Lisinski warned him, and Jean obediently fell silent. Lisinski drummed her fingers on her knees as she considered him. At long last she shook her head and said, "I will find something else for you to do while we're in the water. Official story if the Trojans ask is you can't swim."

"Coach, I can do it. I will not fail."

"I said no," she said, and Jean had no choice but to subside. "James said you found a doctor, yes?" When Jean gave a stiff nod, she continued, "Then you are going to talk to him or her about this, understand? You can revisit this with me after you've made some actual progress and not before."

She looked between them, so Jeremy added a quick "Yes, Coach," to Jean's more subdued response.

"That's about it for today," she said, getting to her feet. "I can give you a ride home."

Jeremy glanced over at Jean. "I'd rather walk, I think. Some fresh air will do us good." When Jean murmured quiet agreement, Jeremy looked up at Lisinski and said, "Thank you, though, Coach. And thanks for letting us take a crack at the court today."

Lisinski sent Jeremy a hard look that he interpreted as *Keep an eye on him*. When Jeremy nodded understanding, Lisinski returned it and said, "I will see you two on Monday."

She turned and left them there. Jeremy waited until she left before scooting across the ground and leaning against the wall at Jean's side. Maybe Jean sensed an interrogation was coming, because he loosely hugged his knees to his chest and stared balefully in the opposite direction. Jeremy considered taking pity on him for only one second, and then he carefully leaned to one side to press his shoulder into Jean's. Jean was still trembling, though in faint and scattered bursts.

"You were going to go through with it, weren't you?" Jeremy asked. "You were really going to get in the pool with us next week knowing what it would do to you."

"My issues are mine alone," Jean said. "I will not ask for accommodations and hold back the team. I will figure something out."

"That's not fair," Jeremy said, and when Jean opened his mouth to argue, added, "to you or us. For someone who seems so sure of what he deserves, you don't seem to give any thought to what anyone else does. You're forcing us to hurt you without giving us any say in the matter."

"I am horrifically behind as it is," Jean said, and the self-loathing bleeding into his voice was painful to hear. "You do not know how much is riding on this. I cannot afford handicaps and special treatment, and you should not waste your time coddling me. You are my captain and my partner. Do you know what that means? Your success is my success; your failure is my failure. This is the covenant which every pair operates under."

"Coddling," Jeremy echoed, and it was a wonder he didn't choke on it. "They really hurt you. You are not okay in ways I can't even imagine. Can you see that?"

"I can still play."

"I don't care," Jeremy shot back, and the confusion that

flickered across Jean's face hurt to see. He gave a frustrated jerk of his hand and said, "That's not—I *do* care. I want you to play with us, and I want you to have fun again. I want to see what you can do on the court and what you bring to our defense line. I want us to finally win this year after coming so close and failing too many times. But it's just a game, Jean. Your safety and happiness will always be more important than our season."

"You are naïve."

"Maybe you'll define success by how we do this season, but I'm not obligated to do the same. You are going to be my success story: Jean Moreau the person, not Jean Moreau of the perfect Court. You take care of one, and I'll take care of the other."

"That is not how it works."

"Is there a rule against it?"

"There is no merit to it. This is all I am."

Jeremy ignored that and asked again, "Is there a rule against it?"

Jean opened his mouth, closed it, and gave an impatient gesture. "Technically, no, but—"

"Good," Jeremy said, lifting his chin in defiance. He knew what the answer was going to be, but he still had to try: "Do you want to talk about it?"

"There is nothing to talk about."

"You sure about that?"

"Stop asking," Jean said. "You only think you want these answers."

And that—that wasn't much, but Jeremy still felt a sick trickle of hope. Jean knew his secrets were horrible and cruel; he knew no one outside of the Ravens would ever be able to justify them. That meant some part of Jean understood that what had happened to him was a monstrous crime even as he deflected and brushed it all aside as necessary and deserved. Maybe he couldn't face that truth yet, and until he could he'd never really heal, but the seed was planted. Jean was just

220

smothering it with everything he had so he could survive.

What happens when he loses his grip? Jeremy wondered. When Jean finally had to accept that the inhumanity inflicted on him for years had been for nothing, would he rage against the unfairness or shatter under a weight carried far too long?

-

For reasons Jeremy couldn't really understand, he didn't tell Laila and Cat about what happened at Lyon on Monday. It made him a little anxious, keeping a secret from them, but Jean proved to be a good distraction from that guilt. Having access to the court again after three months away settled Jean's nerves in a way nothing else had. He seemed more aware of himself and where he was than he had since Wayne died. Jeremy might've called it wishful thinking, but Laila and Cat commented on his improved mood as well.

Laila was optimistic enough about his rebound she even subjected herself to another shopping trip with him to fill out more of his wardrobe on Friday. Jeremy and Cat were uninvited before they could even offer to go along, so Jeremy spent the afternoon tracking down the rest of his inner circle. Jean would get a chance to meet all of the Trojans on Monday, but throwing twenty-odd new faces at him at once didn't seem an ideal route to take. If Jeremy could at least get his friends together for a preemptive meetup and show them Jean was not a threat, it'd be a good start.

He had a long-established group chat for the eight of them, but since Laila was busy with Jean, Jeremy didn't want to blow up her phone. He scrolled to the captains' chat that included only himself, Cody, and Xavier. Xavier could speak for Min, and Cody should still have Pat and Ananya close by, so Jeremy could get word out to the whole group through just the two of them. He went back and forth with them as Cat whipped up two different kinds of muffins.

Jeremy fired off a quick selfie to show off his hair before asking Cat, "Restaurant or here?"

"Nine might be a tight squeeze," she said. "Maybe we can

221

go to that Hawaiian place on the far side of campus? Easy walk from where they'll have to leave their cars, anyway, and it should have something even Jean will agree to eat."

Jeremy only got the message half-typed when a text from Laila derailed him. Cat couldn't check her phone, since she had a muffin pan in one hand and a spatula in the other, so Jeremy grimaced and passed Laila's news along: "Jean's been made. Lot of rude questions about Wayne and Colleen, sounds like, so they're heading home early."

"Great," Cat said wearily. "And he was finally cheering up, too." She tipped her head back to stare at the ceiling, considering her options. "Guess we ought to host them here, then. I'm not sure Jean will want to go out again after dealing with nosey strangers. Soon as I figure out what I'm feeding us I'll head out to the store."

Jeremy erased his original message and started over. It only took a few more texts to nail down a meeting time and get some dinner suggestions, and then there was nothing to do but taste test Cat's muffins and get the dishes going.

They were sprawled together in the living room when they heard Laila's car pull up, and Cat got up immediately to get the door. Jeremy waited for their arrival in the hall. Jean's expression was unreadable as he slipped past, but Jeremy didn't miss the way Laila watched him go. He took Jean's bags from her so she could stay behind with Cat, and he turned away as Cat kissed the tension out of her.

Jean upended his bags onto his bed and set to work tearing stickers and snapping tags off his new clothes. Jeremy was slower at his share so he could inspect them as he went, and he was grateful for Laila's sacrifice today. She had a good eye for style and could work within the narrow confines of what few colors Jean tolerated. This shirt was a new shade for him, a deep blue that reminded Jeremy of the ocean at dusk.

Jean caught hold of the shirt sleeve and tilted it so he could see the front. He'd noticed Jeremy staring and was looking for a problem spot, Jeremy guessed. Jeremy couldn't

222

say he was imagining what Jean would look like in it, with the scoop neck dipping down below the hollow of his throat, so he just said, "It's a good color."

Jean let it slide without comment and went back to his own pile. He finished first and carted the lot to his laundry basket. He lingered there a few moments before turning a speculative look on the small pile at Jeremy's side. Jeremy quirked a brow at him in silent question, but Jean only sighed and went to his dresser. Jeremy didn't have long to wonder, because Jean tugged open the top drawer and began unloading it. Jeremy expected to see socks and underwear, but Jean came back with a half-dozen spiral notebooks.

"You've had a desk this whole time," Jeremy reminded him, amused.

Jean didn't deign to respond but carried the stack out of the room toward the study. Jeremy finished up the clothes he was working on, chucked them into Jean's hamper, and watched with renewed interest as Jean came back. This time he gathered handfuls of what looked like magnets, and the need to rifle through them for a sneak peek at Jean's interests had Jeremy rocking on the balls of his feet.

"We can make room on the fridge," he said.

"They do not stick anymore," Jean said.

Well-worn and sentimental, Jeremy assumed, and he followed Jean down the hall to the study. Maybe Jean sensed his wide-eyed curiosity, because he dumped all of them into the desk's single drawer and slid it closed with a firm hand. Jeremy obediently sat at Cat's desk instead to watch. It only took Jean one more trip. Postcards were dropped in the drawer alongside the magnets, whereas a laptop and a photograph were set on the desk's surface. Since he set the photo face-up, Jeremy invited himself to come look.

He was more startled than he should be that it was of a girl. Her hair was distinctive enough to be familiar, bright white with pastel tips, but he struggled to place her. He'd seen her before, but—

"Goalkeeper," he said when it finally clicked. "Palmetto State Foxes."

"Renee Walker," Jean agreed, and did not elaborate.

"She's cute," Jeremy said. It came out convincing enough, considering Jeremy had no strong opinion either way.

He was immediately betrayed by Cat, who wandered into the study at the tail-end of the conversation and said, "As if you can tell a girl apart from a cow on a good day. Let me see, I'm a far better judge." She made a beeline for Jean's desk and plucked up Renee's picture. "Oh, for once you're right."

Jean stared at Cat like he didn't understand her words before turning a curious look on Jeremy. "You like men."

It wasn't quite a question, but it wasn't said with any real certainty, either. The best answer was a simple *yes*, but Jeremy hesitated. He'd noticed the lingering looks Jean gave Cat and Laila, and he hadn't missed the way Jean's gaze tracked him when he readied for bed. Since Jean was quick to look away when he was caught, Jeremy had promised himself he wouldn't ask. This was too good an opening to pass up, though, so he finally said, "More exclusively than you do, I think. Does that bother you?"

Jean was quiet so long Jeremy thought he was refusing to answer. Then: "Lucas."

Jeremy stared at him, bewildered, and Jean gave an impatient flick of his fingers as he elaborated. "He said he didn't trust your judgment when it came to me. His brother told him I'm a whore, and he knows you like men. He insulted your integrity by implying you signed me for such a reason."

"He insulted both of us with that one," Jeremy said. "I trust him to come around sooner or later."

Jean made a rude noise and motioned to Cat. She returned Renee's picture with a cheery, "Not a bad catch, Jean."

"She is not my catch." Jean set her picture upside-down on his desk.

Cat pushed her toes into the side of Jeremy's foot and asked, "Friend who happens to be a girl?" with exaggerated

224

innocence.

"Perhaps," Jean said.

He sounded almost melancholic, and Jeremy's thoughts snagged on that instead of the triumphant smile that tugged at the corner of Cat's mouth. He expected Jean to leave it at that, but after a minute of gazing down at the back of the photograph Jean added, "She is the one who took me from Edgar Allan when I was injured."

"Took," Jeremy echoed.

"Transferring was not my choice," Jean said. "Ravens do not leave Evermore."

It was an overdue confession that chilled Jeremy's blood in his veins. "After everything they did to you, you would have stayed?" he asked, but of course Jean would have. Between Jean claiming he deserved what had been done to him and the Ravens falling apart without their Nest, it was a wretched and undeniable truth. "Even after they broke your ribs?"

Right on cue: "Injuries happen in scrimmages."

Laila entered the room in time to hear that, and she pointed her boba tea at him. "Every time you say that you take a year off my life. I'd really like to live to ninety, so please knock it off."

"I do not believe you when you are drinking such filth," Jean said, with a disapproving look toward her drink. Laila stared him down as she sucked a long gulp through the straw, and Jean turned to Jeremy. "Take me to the court."

"Patience, babe. Practices start Monday," Cat reminded him. "You wanna help me brainstorm tomorrow's dinner? I'm thinking pernil asado, but if we go that route, I need something tasty for Ananya to eat instead. Vegetarian," she said, and put the back of her hand to her forehead as if feeling faint. "I tried it once, but I only lasted three weeks. How she's made it this long I do not know, but good on her."

Jean thought a few moments, but it wasn't about food: "Ananya Deshmukh."

"One and the same. Did we even tell you who all will be

here?" Cat asked. "You'll finally be meeting the floozy line."

Jeremy looked to the sky for patience. "You know Coach hates that nickname."

"Says the man who named our group chat the floozies the second I suggested it," Cat said with a careless shrug.

Jean frowned. "I do not know that word."

"Oh, sorry. Sometimes I forget English is your second language," Cat said.

"It is my third," Jean said.

They all turned to stare at him, but Jean only looked away. When Cat got tired of waiting for him to elaborate on his own, she asked, "What was the second?" but Jean feigned not to hear. She gave him a few seconds more to come around before dropping it for another day. "A floozy is uhh—" she looked to Laila for help before saying, "—a tramp? A whore? Jesus, I had it until I had to define it. Don't take it at face value, okay? It was just in response to some drama my freshman year."

Cat counted them off on her fingers. "First up you've got Xavier and Min. Xavier's our vice-captain, and Min should be replacing Jillian as starting dealer in second-half. They're adorable in the worst way. You'll understand as soon as you see them. I can't wait for them to get married. It's going to be so wonderfully tacky."

"You remember Cody from Venice Beach?" Jeremy asked. "They'll be here too, along with Ananya and Pat."

"Bold of Pat to show up when I'm going to kick the shit out of him," Cat said, with more exasperation than genuine frustration. When Jean flicked her a sidelong look, Cat threw her hands up and explained. "Pat and Ananya have wanted to fuck Cody's brains out for almost a year now. I really thought Cody moving in with them this summer was going to finally get that ball moving, but *apparently not*. It's getting kind of pitiful."

"Pat and Ananya have been engaged almost as long as Cody has known them," Laila pointed out as she fit herself against Cat's side. "You can't blame Cody for being scared of where they might belong in something like that."

"Watching them pine over each other is so boring," Cat complained. "At some point one of them has got to make a real move."

Laila tweaked her hair. "Not everyone is as recklessly brave as you."

"I was terrified," Cat said with a shrug. She wagged her finger as she quoted someone else's words to her: "If you don't want something enough to fight for it, you don't deserve to have it." She hooked her arm around Laila's shoulders and pecked her cheek. "You were worth the risk. Then and always."

"Gay," Laila said, but she was wearing that radiant smile only Cat could draw from her.

Cat sneaked another kiss, and Laila turned into it. Cat hummed contented approval against Laila's painted lips before saying, "Changed my mind. You should definitely take Jean to the court, Jeremy. Don't come back until dinnertime."

Jeremy laughed and started for the door. "Leaving immediately."

CHAPTER THIRTEEN
Jean

Saturday morning dragged on eternal. Cat had started prepping tonight's dinner the night before, which meant there wasn't much for Jean to do in the kitchen today to help. Outside of some basic straightening up, there was nothing to do around the house. He managed to con Jeremy into a long run, failed to convince him to go to the stadium again, and retreated to the study after a quick shower to watch games on his laptop and text Renee. He hadn't realized how much time he lost until Jeremy came looking for him with lunch.

"Oh," Jeremy said as he stopped beside Jean.

Jean noticed the flick of his gaze over Jean's face and down to his shirt: the deep blue top Jeremy had seemed so taken with yesterday. It wasn't the first time Jeremy had studied him, but until this point Jean had assumed it was curiosity. Yesterday's conversation cast a different light on his distraction, but if Riko put a knife to Jean's throat right now Jean couldn't explain why he was testing that line between them. He wasn't allowed to look; it shouldn't matter where Jeremy stood.

Threat assessment, he told himself, and it was almost the truth. He needed to see the easy way Jeremy ceded Jean's space to him. Jean couldn't remember the last time someone allowed him any boundaries, and the feeling was as novel as it was addicting.

"Yes?" Jean asked.

"Nothing," Jeremy said, too quickly, and offered Jean's plate. "Hungry?"

He beat a hasty retreat as soon as Jean took it from him,

and Jean turned back to his match with a satisfaction he refused to dwell on.

Jeremy left him in peace for the rest of the afternoon, but by half-past five the Trojans' first guests were arriving. Jean closed his laptop and pushed it aside when he heard the doorbell ring. He was content to wait in the doorway to the study while Cat got the door, and she greeted the trio with such deafening enthusiasm he was grateful for the distance between them.

Since Cody was one of them, Jean assumed the other two were Patrick Toppings and Ananya. Ananya managed to slip past Cat first, only to be swept into a tight hug by Jeremy as soon as she reached the living room doorway. She laughed as he gave her a quick spin around, and Jeremy threw a wide grin down the hall toward Jean.

"Jean, this is Ananya," he said. "She's starting line with me in second half."

Ananya moved to shake Jean's hand. "Nice to meet you at last. How are you finding Los Angeles?"

"It's unnecessarily crowded and hectic," Jean said.

"Especially after Charleston," she guessed, and looked back to see if her teammates—lovers?—would be joining her for this meet-and-greet.

Cat had trapped them at the front door and was going a mile a minute about a new game she'd picked up earlier this week. Laila had a hand on her arm and was trying to guide her down the hallway so their guests could at least sit down somewhere, but none of the backliners seemed in a hurry to move. From the sound of things, Cody had gotten into the same game, and they kept up with Cat with eager enthusiasm. Jean was less interested in what they were saying and more in the way Pat watched Cody with unabashed fondness.

"Darling," Ananya called, and both Cody and Pat looked her way. Cat's grin was taunting and unrepentant, and Cody gave her a discreet kick in the ankle as they hurriedly dropped their gaze. "Maybe you can argue best-in-slot after you've met your newest teammate?"

Pat didn't have to touch Cody to get around them, but he did, catching Cody's shoulders to half-turn them and nudge them to one side. As soon as Pat's back was to them, Cat gave Cody's shoulder a quick poke. Cody batted her away with a weak scowl. Then Pat was between Jean and the pair at the door, and Jean obediently turned his attention to the broad-shouldered brunette. Idly Jean wondered what USC had against recruiting tall players; Pat was barely taller than Jeremy was.

"'Lo there," Pat said as he gave Jean's hand a firm shake. "Jean, then? Pat or Patty will do. I promise not to take it personally if you kick me out of my starting spot. I mean, I'll have to take it personally, but I'll understand. Not a lot I can do when up against the perfect Court."

"It wouldn't be you," Jean said. "Anderson is your least consistent starter. The only thing working in his favor between the two of us is the violence in my playing style. If your coaches cannot trust me on the line, he wins the spot by default."

"*Our* coaches," Jeremy muttered under his breath.

"The famous Raven charm," Ananya said with a faint smile. "Do I want to know what your opinion of me is, or does our potential friendship hinge on tact?"

"You should be using a heavy," Jean said. The confusion that flickered across her expression was frustrating to see; surely she'd already figured it out? "You play like you're standing on an edge, all precision and coiled power and no will to use it. If you won't betray the Trojans' image or transfer to a more aggressive team, you should at least shore yourself up where you can."

"I've tried heavies," Ananya said. "I don't like the way they feel."

"Get over it," Jean told her.

The sound of the doorbell kept Ananya from having to argue her case further. Cat had finally dragged Cody closer to the living room, but now she wheeled around and made for the door. Their final two guests were the Trojans' starting dealers. Jean had a half-second to be disappointed by their heights— Min Cai was a half-head shorter than Cat, and Xavier Morgan couldn't be any taller than Laila—before he was distracted by the rest of the picture. They'd arrived holding hands and dressed in matching cream-and-teal outfits. Even their gold-rimmed sunglasses and teal sneakers were identical.

"Disgusting," Cat said, with only affection in her voice. "Seriously. When you two finally start popping out babies to dress up I will cry buckets for them."

"Missed you too," Xavier said. "Where's my hug?"

"Is it safe to hug you?" Cat asked, already latching on. "Doesn't hurt?"

"I'm good," Xavier promised.

Jean glanced over at Jeremy. "Is there a team rule against signing anyone over six feet?"

Jeremy only laughed, but Pat answered: "We've got a couple beanstalks on the line. Derek's what, six-three?"

"Six-two on his file," Jeremy said. "Don't believe his lies."

"I knew it," Pat said, triumphant. To Jean he added, "That's Thompson, not Allen. And Shane's got at least two inches on him, if not three. I swear he's wearing inserts, but I can never get my hands on his shoes to check."

"Sebastian and Travis," Jeremy added. "Maybe Jesus. I heard we've got at least two tall freshmen coming in, but of course I haven't met them yet."

Eight out of twenty-nine was tragic, especially when at least one of them was a goalkeeper, but it was too late to do anything about that. Jean let it slide with a disgruntled huff.

Pat wound an arm around Ananya's shoulder as they went down the hall toward the last arrivals. Within seconds there were three different conversations going in the hallway, with Cat's laughter occasionally breaking through the chaos. At Jean's side Jeremy was smiling, wide and energized.

231

When he noticed Jean's gaze on him, he admitted, "I missed having everyone in one place. If it gets to be a bit much, though—"

"I am used to being crowded," Jean reminded him. "We were always together. This feels… normal."

It did and didn't; he'd seen the Ravens laughing and jeering together, but they'd never acted like this. Jean studied the Trojans' faces, looking for the right word to name the mood, and the best he came up with was *joyous*. It wasn't the synchrony he'd seen with the Foxes before leaving South Carolina, but it was buoyant and pervasive.

Jeremy turned that toothy grin on Jean. "Come on, then."

Jean wasn't sure nine bodies would fit in the crowded living room, but somehow they pulled it off. Cat took the floor in front of Laila's papasan chair, whereas Min practically straddled Xavier on one of the couch cushions. Ananya and Cody had the other two cushions, with Pat on the floor in front of them. Jeremy and Jean sat across from the couch on the floor.

The Trojans tried drawing Jean into the conversation more than once, but he bullied his way out of it until they finally picked up on his disinterest. He was content to study his new teammates from the sidelines, tracking the way they interacted with each other and the hints of personalities he'd be dealing with for the next two years.

Xavier and Min managed to finish each other's sentences a half-dozen times, which Cat reacted to very dramatically every time. Ananya spent the evening pressing Cody further into the corner of the couch, so slowly and smoothly Jean never actually saw her move. Pat kept one hand on Ananya's ankle and another on Cody's, and whenever he wasn't speaking, he was tracing his thumbs in slow circles against their skin. Each time Jean saw it happen he felt a bit more tension sneak through his calm.

Cat got up to check on dinner, and Jean immediately stood to follow her. She tried to wave him off with a cheery, "You can stay, if you want!" but didn't refuse him when he shook his head. Cat got all the way to the kitchen without saying anything else to him, then hooked an arm around his waist as soon as they were alone. "What's going on, Jean? You're starting to look a little tense. Getting a bit loud in there for you?"

It didn't matter, and it wasn't his business, but Jean had to ask. Watching Pat and Ananya invade Cody's space when Cody wasn't reaching out for them in return was making his skin crawl. Laila had implied it was reciprocated, but—

"Is Cody safe?" he asked.

Cat stared at him in surprise for a moment before her expression softened. Her quiet, "Oh," was all the warning Jean needed that Jeremy had told her the truth behind the rumors surrounding his freshman year. He almost pulled out of her grip, but Cat tightened her arm around him. She pressed a light kiss to his shoulder and said, "Pat and Ananya are Jeremy's friends first, but Cody's always been mine. You can trust me when I say Cody's interested—if they weren't, I wouldn't be heartless enough to tease them about it.

"Like Laila said, it's just fear," Cat promised. "Cody doesn't want to be a third wheel and is terrified of committing and then getting left behind if they change their minds. That's why they're at a stalemate, see? Pat and Ananya are trying to convince Cody it's forever. It's just taking more time than I thought it would for them to figure it all out. I don't know if you've noticed, but I am not the most patient person in the world, and I'm a sucker for happy endings."

Jean trusted her because he needed to, and when he nodded Cat finally let him step away from her. She snagged his wrist for just a moment and waited for him to look her way before saying, "Thank you for worrying about them. You're a good man, Jean Moreau."

"A ridiculous sentiment," he said.

"I mean it," she insisted, then freed him so he could find dishes for the group.

233

He had to scrounge together plates from three different sets to have enough for everyone. Finding enough glasses was the harder task, but Cat and Cody were drinking beer and could stick with cans. Before dealing with the headache the silverware was bound to be, Jean took his own glass to the sink for water.

Why Cat waited until he was drinking to drop the next bomb on him, he would never know, but in no universe was it not a thousand percent intentional: "Speaking of happy endings, has Laila bought you a sex toy yet?"

Half of his water ended up in his lungs; the rest went down the drain when his glass slipped from his fingers and shattered in the sink. Jean thumped a fist against his chest, coughing and wheezing, as Cat propped herself against the counter at his side. He didn't have to look at her to feel the smugness radiating off her in waves.

"What the *fuck*," was all he could gasp out before he started coughing again.

"Something-something about learning to be comfortable with intimacy in a safe and controlled environment," Cat said. "It sounded nice and logical when she said it, but I was really distracted thinking about what I wanted her to buy me if she went shopping and I didn't retain it verbatim. Not yet? Huh. I guess it'd be a little harder now that Jeremy's in your room, though they do make ones with remo—oh hey Jeremy, what's up?"

"We heard glass breaking," Jeremy said from across the room. "Are you guys all right?"

"Yeah, of course." Cat waved him off and gave Jean a solid whack on the back. "I made Jean try my ghost pepper sauce, is all. I knew the French were dramatic children but *damn*, this guy takes the cake. My theory that the Ravens think salt and pepper are exotic spices is starting to hold water."

"Not everyone enjoys dying," Jeremy said. "That stuff is awful."

"Shush, white boy," Cat said. "Wait, I take it back. Tell

the others they can come grab their food and *then* be quiet."
She waited until Jeremy left before giving Jean a last pop in
the square of his back. "Anyway, if she goes through with it
and brings you one, attempt to act surprised."

Jean shrugged her off. "Don't you dare."

"And stop blushing before everyone else gets in here,"
Cat added.

"I'm *not*."

"You totally are," Cat said with glee. "It's cute.
Sometimes I forget you're just a kid."

"I will check you so hard at practice you will feel it for a
month," Jean warned her.

"Not for another week," Cat reminded him. "No-touch
jersey. All right!" she yelled, launching off the counter as the
Trojans caught up to them at last. "Who's ready for some
food?"

Jean took his time picking glass out of the sink and very
carefully not thinking about Cat's crass joke. It was a joke; it
had to be a joke. He wasn't going to think about it. He was
going to count glass shards as he set them in his left palm.
Seven, eight, nine. He saw a bit of blood on his fingertips
where he cut himself, but he couldn't feel the sting yet, so it
didn't matter.

"A paper towel would be safer," Jeremy said at his side,
and it was all Jean could do to not clench his hand shut in
surprise. Jeremy shooed him off to one side and used a wad of
damp paper towel to scoop up most of what was left. He
showed the sparkling paper to Jean in triumph before setting
off for the trash can, and Jean ran out of reasons to avoid the
rest of the Trojans. He followed Jeremy across the room,
upended his hand into the trash, and went back to wash his
hands as carefully as he could.

Luckily the Trojans had brought their noise with them,
and their conversations filled the space with enthusiastic cheer.
Jean took what Cat served him, scowled at her unrepentant
smirk, and found a place to stand and eat where he could watch

everyone. Cody ended up alongside him at some point to gossip about the missing members of the defense line. Eventually the conversation drifted to the Ravens' and Trojans' most recent matchup, and inevitably they bickered about playstyles versus penalties.

"Did it make you happy?" Cody finally asked. "Knowing you were pissing off your opponents, I mean. Getting under their skin and riling them up?"

"Of course," Jean said.

"Me too," Cody agreed, and Jean just looked at them. "Imagine you're doing everything you can to make me lose my cool. Tripping, shoving, ugly checks when the referees aren't looking, insulting me and my mom and everything under the sun, and I'm just doing this back at you the whole time." They pointed up at their face and gave a bright smile. "Which one of us do you think is gonna snap first?"

"You have permission to use my favorite line if someone tries getting to you," Cat said as she settled in at Jean's other side. She flashed two thumbs up and intoned, "Have a winning day!" She couldn't hold her wide-eyed innocent look for long before dissolving into laughter, and she nudged Jean. "If you use it at the right moment, it has an eighty-percent success rate of starting a fight. Then you just take a couple hits, boom bam bang, and you get to score on the penalty."

"I assumed the Trojans were idiots," Jean said. "Now I think you are all insane."

"It's a step up," Cody said. "I'll take it."

The Trojans stayed for almost another hour before finally heading out as a large group. They'd come in two cars that they'd parked on campus, so Cat and Laila walked them out while Jean got to work tidying up the kitchen. Jeremy joined him, wiping down counters and the island while Jean handled the dishes. Cat and Laila offered to take over halfway through, but ended up eating candy at the island when Jeremy waved them off.

"What do you think?" Jeremy asked Jean.

236

Jean gave it due consideration. "They'll do."

"Your enthusiasm knows no bounds," Laila said dryly.

"We'll make a Trojan of him yet," Cat agreed.

-

Summer practices would be split between the stadium and fitness center, but the Trojans would always start at the court so they could change out and park on-site. The first day started with a boisterous meeting as teammates reconnected after almost two months apart. The team's seven freshmen tried to play it cool and make a good first impression, but Jean caught more than one of them staring around the expansive locker rooms in awe and disbelief.

The coaches allowed them a few minutes to get the excitement out of their system before sitting everyone down for introductions. When it was Jean's turn to speak, he offered up the absolute bare minimum:

"Jean Moreau, defense."

"*The* Jean Moreau," he heard Lucas mutter from a few spots down.

Coach Rhemann didn't seem to hear, too busy watching Jean. "That's it?"

Everyone who'd gone before him had added irrelevant factoids: home states, majors, and, in more than a few cases, what they liked to do in their free time. It had been exhausting to listen to, and Jean would be damned if he followed suit. Speaking to a coach demanded a bit of tact, though, so Jean only said, "It is all I am, Coach."

He half-expected Rhemann to push the matter, but the man only nodded and moved to the next in line. At long last they were finally done, and all four coaches said their bit. Paperwork followed, and Jean idly wondered why the Trojans had to sign their own waivers. The Ravens' coaches had handled all of the behind-the-scenes work. This was tedious and a waste of his time when he could be practicing.

At long last they were dismissed to their lockers to change into their workout uniforms. Each line had been given a different row for their lockers, but the players weren't in numerical order. Jean considered it against the team's introductions before deciding they were arranged by grade. Shawn Anderson, Pat, and Cody had the first three spots as fifth-year seniors. Jean was the only actual senior on the line, and then came the three juniors. Cat had the locker next to his, and she was chatting away with Haoyu Liu as she redid her ponytail.

"Xavier!" one of the younger defensemen—Travis?— called out, and Jean looked to see the vice-captain standing shirtless at Shawn's locker. Travis almost knocked Jean over in his hurry to get by, but Jean didn't notice. He was distracted by the pair of horizontal scars on Xavier's chest. "Heck yeah, man! How are you feeling? Are you okay to be back?"

"Never been better," Xavier said with a wide smile. "I've been walking since the day after I was discharged. Started light weights around week five. I should be good to go for full contact, but Coach L's going to put me on no-touch until closer to the semester just in case. I'm just now getting started on heavier weights and a proper routine, but that means I can keep an eye on our new kids while the rest of you leave us in the dust."

"Awesome," Travis enthused. "Congrats!"

Jean glanced at Cat to see if she knew what was going on. She caught his eye and said, "Xavier had surgery scheduled for right after finals. We got the good news in our floozy chat before you moved out here, so you missed all the excitement on that front. Speaking of—*what the fuck*," Cat said, so loud the locker room was temporarily startled to silence.

Jean stared at her, but she was no longer looking at his face. He'd just peeled his shirt off, and Cat was staring at the scars that cross-hatched and curved over his skin. Jean wasn't altogether surprised that Xavier hurried over to check on them. He was less surprised when Jeremy popped up at the end of the row with worry stamped on his face a few moments later.

"Hey, uh," Cody said, staring at Jean's bared skin. "You,

238

uh. You good?"

"Why wouldn't I be?" Jean tugged his white workout shirt off its shelf. Cat grabbed his elbow like she could stop him from getting dressed, but Jean yanked free with little effort. She didn't try again, but neither did she lift her eyes from his chest even after he'd tugged his clean shirt on. "You will get used to them soon enough, and they do not interfere with my ability to play."

"Get used to them," Cat echoed, sharp with disbelief. "Jeremy said they were bad, but—"

"I am not the only one here with scars," Jean said, motioning toward Xavier.

Xavier arched a brow at him. "Mine are surgical, and yours most definitely are not." He put up a hand when Cat opened her mouth, waited a beat to make sure she understood, and held Jean's gaze. "I only have one question for you: do you want to talk about it?"

"There is nothing to talk about," Jean said.

Xavier weighed that in silence for a minute before saying, "Okay then." He flicked a hard look past Jean when Cat made a disbelieving noise. "It's not our business until you invite us to it. Just keep in mind that that door is always open. Cody?"

"I'll keep an eye on things," Cody agreed.

Xavier left to get dressed. His words sat like a stone on the defense line, and Jean couldn't shake his teammates' prickling scrutiny as he finished changing out. Cat's mouth was pulled in a bloodless line when she finally turned away and focused on getting herself ready. The other rows had gone back to chatting, as they'd been around corners and out of sight, but the Trojans' defensemen got dressed in tense silence. Jean didn't mind; tension was something he was used to, and silence was better than intrusive questions.

Lisinski came to hurry them along when she thought they were taking too long, and the Trojans filed out of the stadium in a long line. They took a slow lap around campus before turning toward the fitness center. Lisinski called them all in close to go over the day's workout before dividing them into groups that would alternate machine order. As Xavier had guessed, he was assigned Jean and the freshmen. Lisinski stopped by their group briefly to stare down Xavier and Jean in turn.

"If anything feels off, you ease up and let me know," she said.

"Yes, Coach," Xavier said. As soon as she was gone the vice-captain slanted a conspiratorial look at Jean. "Nah. We're good, right? I'm beyond ready to get back to it."

When Jean nodded solemn agreement, Xavier waved the freshmen over. Jean didn't miss the way they spent more time staring at him than listening to Xavier, but since every one of them should be familiar with the machines they'd be using today he didn't waste his time redirecting their attention.

It took just over two hours to get through everything, and back to the Gold Court they went. By then it was noon, so they stopped for an hour-long break to scrub dry and eat. Half of the Trojans disappeared to grab something from on or near campus, but Cat and Jean had prepped and packed the week's lunches for the four of them. A couple hours away from him had seemingly restored Cat's good mood, as she broke her frosty silence to chat about some upcoming movie trailers she'd seen.

Eventually everyone was back, and it was time to get dressed for the court. Cat shoveled her armor onto the floor in front of her locker, grumbling the whole while about the Trojans' absent assistants.

"Can't justify having them here over the summer," Cat said. "I know, I know. But they do make the season ten times easier."

"You have four coaches," Jean said. "Why do you need assistants?"

"Waterboys," Cat said. "Well, watergirls. Waterkids?"

"That's not a word," Haoyu said.

"Effective today it is," was Cat's breezy retort. "Anyway, you don't really appreciate what a gift they are until they're

240

not underfoot. You're telling me the Ravens didn't have doting helpers chasing after you with water bottles and clean towels? We have something that you didn't?"

"We did not want outsiders at Evermore."

"Except Neil," Cat said.

"Neil was a special case," Jean allowed.

"Unsurprising the Ravens would try to recruit a gangster's son," Lucas said.

"That news came out a couple months after Neil went to Edgar Allan," Cody reminded him as they painstakingly removed every piercing from their face. "I doubt the Ravens would have taken him on if they'd known, especially when they spent so much time and money playing up a potential showdown between Riko and Kevin. It was a hell of a distraction from their pissing contest."

Lucas had to concede with a grumbled, "I guess."

In no world would Jean correct them, so he focused on gearing up. Xavier was by shortly with a black mesh vest that marked him as hands-off for today's practice. Jean tugged it on over his jersey and glanced over to see Cody studying him with a slight frown. Cody took that look as permission to speak and asked,

"You're not still injured, are you? It's almost July."

"I'm cleared," Jean said. "This is a precaution."

Cody looked unconvinced but didn't push it, and the group finished dressing in silence. Lisinski had rolled their racquet racks down to the inner court while they were changing, and all four coaches were on hand to wrangle the oversized team into shape.

It wasn't quite an even split between offense and defense, as the strikers and dealers made fourteen against the backline's eleven, but it was close enough. Two dealers were set against each other, and Cody took on an extra player. Jeremy was at Jean's side before Rhemann even reached his name. They were all ushered onto the court and divvied up between halves, with two goalkeepers assigned to each side.

They spent hours on drills. Jean knew all of them, though one or two by a different name. Some had been modified, and he wasn't sure if it was the Trojans' doing or the Ravens'. Jeremy looked fascinated every time Jean tried to execute it differently than expected, but all Jean felt was impatience. The no-touch jersey felt like a short leash dragging him down. He wanted to throw Jeremy into a wall just to prove he could; he wanted Jeremy to crash into him so he could tell Lisinski it didn't hurt.

He managed to keep it together until they finally started on short scrimmages, and then instinct interfered with common sense. The first time Jeremy started to get past him Jean stuck a foot around his and sent him stumbling. Jeremy wasn't expecting it, and Jean was able to yank his stick out of his hands with a practiced twist. He stole the ball and flicked it up court, but Jeremy caught his sleeve before he could follow.

"Away," Jeremy warned him. "You have to hook away from me, not toward."

Away was how most players did it, in part for safety and mostly because it was easier to steal a racquet that way. Toward was harder to pull off but worth it, as it forced the other player's wrists to bend in at an unnatural angle. It went without saying that Ravens always defaulted to what would cause the most injuries. Jean grimaced his annoyance but nodded understanding, and then still forgot again six passes later.

Jeremy rubbed his wrists and insisted, "Away."

"Away," Jean agreed.

The third time he did it, Jeremy grabbed his racquet to haul him to a stop. "*Away*, Jean. You're hurting me."

"It has been toward for five years," Jean said, looking past Jeremy at the scrimmage that was still going on without them. "It is not that easy to undo."

Jeremy frowned at him and echoed, "Five? You were only with the Ravens for three."

"I moved into Evermore two years before I enrolled,"

Jean said, and hauled Jeremy to one side. The stray ball that had been coming for them ricocheted off his chest instead of Jeremy's back, and Jean scooped it up on the rebound with a quick snap of his wrist. He hurled it across the court toward Cody one-handed before finally letting go of Jeremy. "I will try harder."

The next time he remembered. The time after that he remembered a half-second too late and saved them both by slamming into Jeremy instead. Jeremy wasn't expecting a check, but he braced against it instinctively and pushed back. They fought each other for a moment with the ball caught between their nets. Their teammates were yelling encouragement and positions for whoever won and passed. Jeremy executed a nimble duck and weave that got him the upper hand, and Jean stole his racquet as soon as he threw the ball.

"Away," he agreed, and heaved Jeremy's racquet as far down the court as he could.

Jeremy laughed as he took off after it, and Jean went to apply pressure where he could.

They played two scrimmages, shuffling the teams for the second go. Jean and Xavier were pulled to be subs this time around so Lisinski could check on them. Xavier reassured her with a breezy familiarity that made Jean's shoulders tighten in warning, but if Lisinski was offended by his casual approach, she gave no sign of it. No Raven would have dared be so bold unless he was desperate to be punished.

Lisinski turned on Jean next. "Does no-contact mean something different where you come from?"

"No, Coach," Jean said. When she continued to stare at him, he dropped his gaze and said, "The only Ravens who were allowed no-contact status were Kevin and the King, when they had upcoming media tours and events. I am unaccustomed to it. I will be better."

"Words are empty," Lisinski said. "Prove it on the court."

She waved them off, so they returned to where the rest of

the subs stood at the court wall.

Xavier considered Jean for a few moments before saying, "Kind of docile for a Raven. We assumed you'd be all rudeness and rage."

"My rage is here," Jean said, with a hand to the court wall. "Ravens know better than to question our coaches. We are nothing without their guidance. The Trojans' informality and disrespect is repulsive."

Xavier shrugged that off. "They're not gods, you know? They trust us to bring our best, and we trust them to help shape us into something even better. We don't have to grovel to show our respect."

Jean glanced past him toward the coaches. White and Jimenez were pacing up and down the wall as they studied their players, clipboards in hands as they made notes. Rhemann was sitting on the bench, arms over his chest as he watched the flow of the game. Jean's gaze had barely settled on him before Rhemann glanced his way and motioned him over. Jean obediently went to stand in front of him, but Rhemann pointed at the bench at his side. A coach who had to get up to strike hit harder than one who could simply take a swing, so Jean sat just within arm's reach.

"Jean Moreau," Rhemann said. "I figure we're overdue for a meeting, hm? I've been kept abreast of your progress from my staff and captain, but I thought it best to keep my distance until things settled down a bit. I assume you've heard the school wants to put a camera in your face."

Jean's jaw worked on refusals he didn't dare voice. "Yes, Coach."

"I've been stalling as long as I can," Rhemann said. "The Ravens' unfortunate collapse worked in your favor on that point, as it was easier to justify your silence when your former teammates were struggling so publicly. However, Edgar Allan has a press conference scheduled for this Wednesday to formally introduce their new coaching team, and their summer practices will start next week barring any additional disasters.

With that will come a renewed interest in your side of the story."

I won't, Jean thought. *I won't, I won't, I can't.* "Yes, Coach."

"Coach Wymack has offered to loan us Kevin for a day," Rhemann said, and Jean stopped breathing. "I don't remember if it was his idea or Kevin's, but he's willing to fly him out here for a joint interview in August. I don't know how well the two of you get on, so I told him I'd have to ask you first. Are you interested?"

"Yes, Coach," he said, quick enough that Rhemann sent him an amused look. "Thank you, Coach."

How they were supposed to get through an interview when they couldn't even talk to each other, Jean didn't know, but that was a problem for another time. Kevin knew Jean wasn't allowed to talk to the press, and he could carry an interview without any help.

"I'll set it up," Rhemann said. "Off with you, then."

Jean got up but only made it a few steps away before Rhemann called after him, "And Moreau—for god's sake, twist *away.*"

Jean swallowed a weary sigh. "Yes, Coach."

CHAPTER FOURTEEN
Jeremy

Before leaving practice on Monday, five Trojans stopped by Jeremy's locker to hand him printed copies of their schedules: the five most likely Trojans to have overlapping classes with Jean. As soon as Jeremy had gotten a list of potential classmates from Coach Rhemann, he'd called all of them one at a time to explain the Ravens' buddy system and why he was allowing Jean to lean on it here. Dropping Kevin's name had been the most helpful tactic; the Trojans didn't know what to make of this scandal-chased backliner of theirs, but Kevin was a years-long Trojan fan and someone worth listening to.

"Thanks, thanks," he said as he collected them in a tidy stack. "Welcome back! Here's to another exciting day tomorrow!"

Jean caught up to him before Cat and Laila did and sat beside Jeremy on the bench. Jeremy lifted his papers to show Jean and said, "Your class registration window will have opened this morning, so that'll give you something to stress over tonight. Turns out seven of us are in business or business-adjacent majors, but two are freshmen and will be too far behind you. Shane will probably be your best bet, since he's also a senior majoring in business. Have you had time to look over the catalogue at all?"

"Yes," Jean said as he accepted the papers. "The degree requirements between our universities are fairly similar."

Jeremy nodded. "If for any reason we can't line some classes up with the others, I'll talk to the teachers about me sitting in. I'm nearly done with my major, so my schedule's sparse this year. Half of what I'm enrolled in is what I need for my degree and the other half is just what sounds interesting so I can hit full-time status. Did you ever give it any thought? Signing up for something fun, I mean."

"The Trojan obsession with fun has not gotten any easier to tolerate," Jean said.

"You could just say 'no'," Jeremy said dryly. "How about this: if I end up sitting in on at least one of your classes, you come along to one of mine in exchange. Fair trade?"

"A reasonable request," Jean agreed.

"More theater classes this year?" Cat asked as she and Laila wandered over.

"Beginner ceramics," Jeremy said with a grin, and mimed shaping a bowl. "Intro to wheelwork, or something like that. Going to fill your living room with so many misshapen cups and pots. Sorry in advance."

Jean eyed him. "For what purpose?"

Jeremy looked to the ceiling for patience. "For *fun*."

Jean sighed as if Jeremy was the one being unreasonable. Cat just laughed and asked, "Dinner?"

It was an easy walk back to their house, though the warm day was uncomfortable after such a long practice. Jeremy couldn't wait for fall to creep in with cooler weather. Cat seemed equally grouchy about it and set herself to brainstorming something light and inoffensive to eat while Laila prodded Jean for his first impression of their teammates. Overall, Jean was satisfied, though he found the team-wide rustiness repulsive and complained yet again about Class I teams having summers off.

"Yes, yes," Laila said tolerantly.

As soon as Cat could get into the kitchen and check the head of lettuce in the fridge, she chucked a pan of chicken in the oven. "Lettuce wraps," she said before Jean could get comfortable at the island for his role in the prep work. "Come on, let's get this schedule sorted out so we can make sure it works."

Jean ended up on the floor of the study so he could spread everything out better, his teammates' printouts and then the catalogue with the semester's classes and schedules. He'd earmarked the appropriate pages, and now he flipped back and forth between them to see if anything lined up. Laila sat in her desk chair to watch while Jeremy sat across from Jean, and Cat stole Jean's desk because it was closer to where he'd gotten settled. She watched over Jeremy's shoulder for a few minutes before saying,

"Scratch paper would probably make this a bit easier, yeah?" She looked toward her desk, then Laila's, but they'd finally cleared away last year's mess. Cat started to get up, likely to scrounge some paper from her bedroom, when she noticed the spiral notebooks taking up space on Jean's desk. "Oh, Jean, you don't mind, right?"

Jean looked up at the sound of his name. As soon as he realized what she was reaching for, he lurched to his feet to stop her, but she wasn't waiting for permission. She plucked up a notebook from the stack and chucked it at him, and Jean only managed to clip it with his fingertips on its way by. It landed open on the floor by Jeremy's knee, and the room went still as stone as the four of them stared down at the bold lettering scratched across the page.

TRAITOR

Laila was the first to find her voice, but all she managed was, "Hello?"

Jean stood frozen, staring down at his notebook with his hand still out in front of him. Jeremy slowly turned the notebook so it'd be right-side up for him, and he flipped the page. The back was scribbled over in black ink, and the odd page opposite it had another angry message: **WHORE**.

Jeremy tried to look up at Jean but couldn't. "Jean, what is this?"

He couldn't stop flipping, but it didn't get any better. Page after page the insults continued, though they started to repeat after a while. The only new bit was a piece of stationery,

248

neatly tucked in between some pages, that was covered in slanted writing. Jeremy started to reach for it, but Jean dropped as quickly as he could to snatch the notebook away from him. Jeremy caught hold of his arm before he could retreat, and Jean met his stare with a baleful glare.

"You want to explain that?" Jeremy asked.

"They're my school notes," Jean said. "I needed them for finals."

"Finals were months ago," Laila pointed out as she got up and went to stand at Cat's side. Cat was flipping through a second notebook, and the livid look on her face suggested it'd been similarly defaced. "You have a good reason for keeping them? For bringing them here, even? You finished finals back in South Carolina. These should have gone in the trash when you packed for the move."

"If you tell me that you can read a single word," Jeremy started.

"Some of them I can read very well," Jean said, wrenching out of Jeremy's grip. He got up and went to take his second notebook away from Cat. It only took him a second to decide he didn't trust them to not go through them again, and then he gathered the rest and turned as if to carry them out of the room. Laila neatly stepped between him and the door with a grim expression.

"Move," Jean warned her.

Laila didn't budge. "Why?"

Jeremy was sure she meant *why did you keep them*, not *why did they do it*, but Jean said, "I left the Raven lineup during championships. They were justifiably angry."

"Justifiably—" Cat was too furious to finish it; Jeremy heard her audibly choke on the rest of her outburst.

"Them losing this spring had nothing to do with you leaving," Jeremy said. "Even if you'd stayed, you couldn't have helped them. You were off the court for twelve weeks with injuries."

"Three fractured ribs," Cat said, as if Jean had somehow

249

forgotten. She and Jean stared each other down, righteous fury on one side and hostile defiance on the other, as she recited Kevin's text message from memory. "Sprained LCL. Twisted ankle. Broken nose. Fuck them. *Fuck* them," she said again when Jean made a quick, dismissive gesture.

"You don't understand," Jean said. "You never will."

"I understand that they beat you within an inch of your life and then rioted when you left," Cat snapped back. "I've been watching and tracking rumors for *months*, and I've lived with you long enough to know how many of them have to be bullshit. They're dragging you through the mud, but you won't even try to defend yourself."

"Cat," Jeremy tried, getting to his feet in case he needed to break them up. "Yelling at him isn't going to fix anything."

Cat ignored him and jabbed a finger at Jean. "How dare they blame you for anything after what they did to you. How dare you grieve them."

It hit like a sucker punch, but Jean's frustrated rejoinder was worse: "They don't know."

It was not at all what he meant to say. Jeremy saw it in the horror that flickered across his face and the hand that came up a half-second too late to cover his mouth. The silence that fell in the room was absolute, until all Jeremy could hear was his heart drumming bruises into his lungs. All of Cat's anger had gone out of her; she could only stare at Jean in stunned disbelief and incomprehension.

Laila moved faster than a snake to catch Jean's wrist. How she held on when Jean flinched at her touch, Jeremy didn't know; he himself took an involuntary step back to give Jean more space.

"What does that mean?" Laila demanded, but Jean wouldn't even look at her.

In another moment he'd draw blood where his fingernails were burrowed into his cheek, and Jeremy had the fleeting idea that Jean wanted to tear his own face off to take back what he'd said. The warning bubbled in his chest, but Jeremy's voice was gone. Maybe Laila saw it too, because her knuckles went bloodless where she was holding onto Jean.

"How could they not know?" she asked.

"No," Jean said, muffled through his hand. "Forget it."

"Jean, please." Cat hooked her fingers over his in a vain attempt to get his hand loose. "Talk to us, okay? Just talk to us."

Jeremy's mind was going a thousand miles a minute, sorting through every aborted and rejected conversation he'd had with Jean these last few weeks. He thought about Jean's grief and his rarer anger. If the Ravens didn't know how badly he'd been hurt, then they couldn't have done this to him. But the Ravens were always at Evermore, so who else could have been responsible? Who else was allowed access to the hive mind? Who else could inflict such violence without any retribution from the coaches?

"Coach Moriyama?" he guessed, but even as he said it, he rejected it. Kevin transferred with a broken hand; Jean transferred with fractured ribs. Why a coach would destroy his star players during championships was unfathomable, especially when he'd gone out of his way to orchestrate a spectacular rematch between Riko and Kevin. But if the Ravens weren't to blame, and the so-called master was innocent, it came down to one person. One improbable, impossible person whom the Foxes hated with an unsubtle and unexplained ferocity.

He wasn't sure what showed on his face, but Jean abruptly yanked out of Laila's grip. She went for him again, but Jean threw his notebooks at her and was out of the room a heartbeat later. Jeremy was a half-second too slow to grab hold of him, so he chased him down the hall instead. Jean tried to slam the bedroom door in his face, but Jeremy shouldered it open. Cat and Laila were kind enough to stop right outside the doorway to watch, but Jeremy crossed the room when Jean did and waited just out of arm's reach.

Jeremy looked him dead in the eyes and demanded,

"Riko?"

Automatic, fierce, false: "He would never hurt me."

"Tell me the truth."

"It is the truth," Jean snapped back.

"I'll call Kevin," Jeremy warned him. "I'll ask him how he broke his hand. I'll ask him who did it. What will he say to me?"

When Jean took too long to answer, Jeremy pulled his phone out. Jean went for it immediately, and Jeremy had to press it into the small of his back to get it out of Jean's reach. Jean shoved him as hard as he could, and Jeremy couldn't keep his balance. He stumbled back a few steps before falling hard to his ass.

For a moment he expected Jean to come after him, but even as he braced for violence, he knew it wouldn't happen. A man who could hand-wave away every cruelty inflicted upon him as well-deserved wasn't someone to fear; Jean was a starving dog on a short chain who'd learned years ago not to bite back. Jean would never hurt him. Jeremy knew it, believed it, with everything he had, so he painstakingly picked himself up and got back in Jean's face.

"You and I both know what Kevin will say," Jeremy said, "but I don't want to hear it from him. I want you to tell me."

"Stop asking me."

"Riko's dead," Jeremy insisted, strident, and it hurt him to his bones to watch the way Jean recoiled. "What are you so afraid of? He can't hurt you anymore." Jean laughed, short and sharp, and Jeremy's heart broke at the sound of it. "Jean, please."

Jean dug trembling fingers into his temples and closed his eyes as he stepped back away from Jeremy. "Call him, then," he said, "because I won't. I *won't*. I am Jean Moreau. I know my place. I am—"

He bit off whatever else he might have said, but the force it took to choke it back had his lips curling in a fierce snarl. Jeremy could only watch in wretched silence as Jean tried to

252

walk himself back from the edge. He cast his phone aside in favor of catching Jean's face in his hands, and the way Jean flinched at his touch was almost his undoing.

"Hey," he said quietly. "Hey. Jean. Look at me."

Jean refused, and Jeremy grasped desperately for anything that could bring Jean back to him. He seized on the only thing he could and threw Jean's words back at him: "You are Jean Moreau. Your place is here with me, with us. I'm your captain. You're my partner. We're supposed to be doing this together, aren't we? Stop leaving me behind. Look at me."

It wouldn't work, but it did. Jean opened his eyes to meet Jeremy's stare. "I told you not to ask me about him."

Jeremy slid his hands up to where Jean was drawing blood at his temples and wound their fingers together. "Then answer me like this, where no one else can hear. If he's the one who hurt you, just give me a squeeze. That's all you need to do. I won't make you say it out loud, I promise."

He felt a tremor in Jean's hands, and for a blinding moment he was sure Jean would lean into the safety of this silent confession. But Jean only sucked in a slow breath and said, "Now I am not safe with you, captain."

Letting go of Jean was the hardest thing Jeremy had ever done. Everything in him railed against this, and for a moment he regretted giving Jean a way out. They were so close to the truth he could taste it, or maybe that was his unsettled stomach threatening to tip over. Jeremy took a careful step back from Jean, then another to get out of arm's reach before he forgot himself.

"Fine," he said quietly, and he went to collect his phone.

Jean moved to stare out the window, arms folded tight over his chest, as Jeremy sat on the edge of his bed. He scrolled through his contacts for Kevin and checked the time before dialing out. It took a few rings, but Kevin answered with an easy "Hello" before it could click over to voicemail.

"I'm sorry," Jeremy said, because he didn't have the strength for small talk or a softer approach right now. "Did

Riko break your hand?"

The silence that followed was profound. Jeremy wanted to make sure the call was still connected, but he was afraid to move his phone away from his ear and miss Kevin's answer.

"That's unexpected," Kevin said at last. "And bold, for you."

"That's not an answer," Jeremy said.

"Answer me first," Kevin invited him. "Did Jean tell you?"

"No," Jeremy said. Was that an implied confirmation? Jeremy flicked a look toward Jean's back and the tense set of his shoulders. "He refuses to talk about what happened at Edgar Allan, so I'm left putting together the pieces from everything he won't say. When he said the Ravens didn't know why he was pulled from the lineup I made the only jump I could. But I don't want you to tell me about Jean; I want him to tell me when he's ready."

"If he's ever ready," Kevin said, and Jeremy didn't think it was the distance that made him so quiet. "Jean was perfect Court, but he was not born into the game, and he was not afforded the same… decency and freedoms Riko and I were allowed. He is not used to having a voice, and he has never had power. I cannot promise he will ever talk to you."

"I will wait as long as it takes," Jeremy said. "Did Riko break your hand?"

"There are maybe a dozen people who know the answer to that question," Kevin told him. "We've decided to withhold most of the details of last year even from our freshmen now that it's mostly resolved. Do you understand?"

Jeremy looked toward Cat and Laila. "It won't leave this room."

Cat mimed zipping her own lips shut and gave her heart a quick cross.

"Then yes," Kevin said. Jeremy had feared it was coming, but hearing it had his stomach bottoming out. He propped his free elbow on his knee so he could bury his face in his hand.

254

Kevin was still talking, and as much as Jeremy needed to hear it, he wished he didn't have to listen: "There was a debate in the ERC that I was the better striker and that I was holding back so as not to outshine Riko. The master pit us against each other to determine the truth."

Hearing *master* from Jean had been hard enough; hearing it from his brilliant, unparalleled friend was a thousand times worse.

"I let him win, but the game was up," Kevin said. "He retaliated."

"Jesus," Jeremy said, because what else could he say? Riko Moriyama had been hailed as the future of Exy his entire life. Jeremy had grown up inundated with interviews of the so-called King and his flawless righthand man. Riko had a sly edge to him that occasionally teetered toward frosty and rude, but he'd never come across as vicious outside of the court.

For months now Riko had been written off as another victim in the news, a shining star who'd detonated under the weight of his own legend. And maybe in many ways he still was, but a martyr could still be a monster when the cameras weren't rolling.

"I'm sorry," he said. "I'm sorry, I didn't—I'm glad they let you go."

"Oh, they didn't mean to," Kevin said, "but they were foolish enough to give me a car my freshman year, and it had just enough fuel in the tank to get to a gas station. A fan paid for my fill when she saw my tattoo. I was on the interstate before they knew I was gone."

Nothing about this was at all funny, but that brazen escape drew a ragged laugh from Jeremy. "Ballsy," he said. "I like it."

"Jeremy," Kevin said, half-away from the phone. Jeremy heard a muffled voice somewhere in the background. "No, Jean is fine. As fine as he can be, anyway. Yes, I know." He sighed a little as he came back on the line. "We're about to head to the court. Is there anything else you needed?"

Jeremy moved his phone away to check the clock. "Did

you change time zones?"

"Night practices with Andrew and Neil," Kevin said.

"Obsessed," Jeremy said, with no heat. "No, I don't think there's anything else right now. Thank you, Kevin. I mean it. Thank you for trusting me with the truth."

"Be careful with it," Kevin said. "Be careful with him."

"I'm trying," Jeremy promised, and Kevin hung up.

Jeremy dropped his phone off to one side and took a minute to try and sort his thoughts into any reasonable order. He was distantly aware of Cat and Laila moving into the room at last. When he looked up, though, he looked to Jean, who still stood ramrod straight with his back to all of them.

A starving dog, he'd thought just a few minutes ago, and Kevin's words only confirmed that unkind assessment. Jeremy thought about Evermore with its suffocating locker rooms, a team that was forced to live and play and take classes together, coaches who handled every interaction with the outside world, and the aggressive brutality that such confinement would inevitably breed. Jeremy knew they'd horrifically hurt Jean his freshman year, but Jean still grieved them. This entire wretched confession started because Cat attacked his love for them.

Jeremy thought about a King who could not afford to be anything but the best, raised by a coach who made his Ravens call him "master". That Riko had broken those closest to him was not a surprise, but the depth of his depravity and cruelty were unforgivable. Every time he blinked Jeremy saw the scars layered over Jean's skin and heard his offhanded *"I have always gotten what I deserved."*

"Jean," he said. "Won't you look at me?"

"No," Jean said. "Go away."

Jeremy looked at his friends. Laila gave Cat's shoulder a gentle push, and they closed the door behind them on the way out. Jeremy waited a minute before crossing the room to stand at Jean's side. Jean continued to stare outside like he'd die if he acknowledged Jeremy's presence. Jeremy looked as well,

256

staring at the daffodils Cat spray painted on the fence and through them as he collected his thoughts. He weighed all the things he could say, all the things he shouldn't, and wondered if it was better to just back down and let Jean pull himself together.

"Look at me," he insisted. When Jean finally turned to face him, Jeremy hooked an arm around his neck to pull him into a fierce hug. "I'm sorry. I'm sorry that he hurt you, I'm sorry that you're still afraid to talk about it, and I'm sorry that you think I'll never understand. I'm sorry that he tricked you into thinking you deserved it. But I'm not sorry he's gone. I can't be."

After a minute he felt fingers tangle in the front of his shirt. He expected to get shoved away, but maybe Jean was looking for strength, because after a tense minute of silence Jean finally admitted, "Neither am I."

He said it like he thought they'd be overheard, but that he said it at all gave Jeremy hope. Jeremy held on for a while longer before slowly relaxing his grip. "What do you need from us?"

"To pretend you don't know," Jean said.

"Are you protecting him or you?" Jeremy asked.

"Yes," was the unhesitating response. "The consequences would be catastrophic."

Jeremy gave it serious consideration as he stepped back out of Jean's space. Kevin had already sworn him to silence regarding his hand, so keeping Jean's secrets would only be an extra step from there. It galled him to think he had to swallow this, not for Jean's sake but because every time he saw Riko honored in the news as a tragic hero he'd want to riot, but it wasn't his place to interfere with Jean's trauma or his healing.

"Okay," Jeremy said at last, hoping he wouldn't regret this. "We'll pretend, but *you* know we know, so if you're ever ready to talk about it or anything else, remember us. We're your friends, and we just want what's best for you."

"Yes," Jean said, and then, "I'm going to stay here a little longer."

Jeremy heard the dismissal in it, but he waited for Jean to let go of his shirt before leaving the room. He closed the door behind himself as quietly as he could and went looking for Cat and Laila. They were tangled together on the couch with twin grim expressions. Jeremy took the open cushion and leaned into Laila for support.

"He did, didn't he?" Laila asked.

"Jean and Kevin both," Jeremy said. Cat swore, low and vicious, and Jeremy waited for her to catch her breath before continuing. "But Jean's still terrified, even with Riko permanently out of the picture. I don't know if he's hiding from Coach Moriyama, if Edgar Allan was involved in the cover-up, or what, but it's important to him that we don't accuse Riko of anything."

"You can't be okay with that," Cat said. "It's not fair."

"It's not just Jean," Jeremy reminded her. "Even Kevin is afraid of coming clean. It's not our call, Cat. If seeking justice jeopardizes their trust and safety, it isn't worth it."

They exchanged a long look before Laila nudged Cat with her shoulder. Cat scowled at the far wall but grudgingly said, "I don't like it, but I'll keep my mouth shut if you think that's for the best."

"I don't like it either," Jeremy admitted, "but it's what he needs from us."

Laila hummed quietly for a bit before saying, "It would explain a lot, wouldn't it? Everything from the Foxes' feud with Riko and the Ravens last year to why Edgar Allan let both Kevin and Jean walk away uncontested during championships. They were buying silence and protecting their precious King.

"I don't forgive the Ravens," she added. "Not after what happened his freshman year, and not after the nastiness they heaped upon him this spring. I refuse to think they had no idea what happened. But until he's willing to share the whole picture, I'll try not to dig too deep into that wound. But you," she pointed at Jeremy, "convince him to get rid of those

258

notebooks. He doesn't need to hold onto that kind of poison."

"I'll try," Jeremy said.

Cat kicked her legs a bit as she stared up at the ceiling. Jeremy couldn't guess at her thoughts, but her expression said they were unpleasant. At last, she clapped her hands together so hard he was sure her palms went numb, and she launched off the couch.

"I'm going to check on the chicken," she said.

Jeremy stood as well, but he headed for the study to consider the work Jean had abandoned. Going back to this with tonight's conversation ricocheting around his skull felt exceedingly unfair, but he checked Cat's drawer for a pen before collecting one of Jean's scattered notebooks. This time he didn't open it but set it face-down on the carpet so he could use the flimsy cardboard backing as scratch paper. Bit by bit he worked his way down the list, skimming lists of tedious class titles and comparing what their teammates had to what Jean needed to take.

Like Jeremy had hoped, Shane overlapped with Jean in two classes, and Cody was enrolled in one Jean could take as an alternate. That left one unaccounted for, and it sounded dreadfully boring, but Jeremy wrote the class number and time on his hand so he could contact the professor for permission to audit it. He'd just set the pen aside when Jean appeared in the doorway.

Jeremy greeted him with a bright smile he didn't feel and patted the ground beside him. "I think we've got something here."

Jean sat and listened as Jeremy walked him through the arrangement. Jean would end up with five classes this semester, one more than the athletes' recommended four, but since one of those would be the ceramics class, Jeremy figured it wouldn't add anything tremendously stressful to Jean's workload.

"Thank you," Jean said.

"What else are friends for?" Jeremy said, as a little of the chill in his veins thawed. "Here, if you can get your laptop down, I'll show you how to navigate the portal."

Jean stretched for it and set it down where they both could see. The link for the site he needed was printed in the front of his catalogue, and Jean had an email with his login information. Getting classes added to his schedule was easy work, and he'd just locked in the last one when Cat arrived. She crossed the room and leaned over, catching Jean's head in her hands so she could plant a kiss to the top of his head.

"Dinner's ready," she said. "Let's stuff our faces and watch something loud so none of us have to think again tonight. Sound good?"

Dinner was easy to put together, and sorting out a movie only took a little longer. Jeremy had seen it a half-dozen times before, and he liked it, but it was hard to focus on the movie when Jean was two cushions down. It took Jean half the movie to stop pushing his food around his plate, and Jeremy wondered if he ought to go with Jean when he finished and inevitably ducked out. But he waited and waited, and still Jean didn't get up.

Jeremy sneaked a glance over at him. Jean seemed to be looking toward the bay window more than the TV, but his plate was empty, and he was still there. It was the first time in six weeks he hadn't abandoned them the moment he could, and Jeremy quickly returned his attention to the movie before Jean realized he was being watched.

Maybe Jean needed the company to distract him from his thoughts, or maybe this was his thanks to them for agreeing not to pry further. Jeremy wasn't sure, but it still felt like a much-needed victory when everything else was unraveling around them.

CHAPTER FIFTEEN
Jean

Derek had just hit the ground when one of the coaches pounded on the wall in warning. Jean assumed it was Coach White again, furious over how often Jean was tripping up his strikers. The outrage was a waste of everyone's time, Jean knew. Their opponents this fall would not play a clean game; it was not his fault that the Trojans were so unprepared for underhandedness during intrateam scrimmages. He huffed a little in aggravation as he stepped away from Derek. Across the court, Derrick caught the ball and held it to stop play, and Jean belatedly realized it wasn't White trying to enter the court.

Rhemann shooed Jesus on ahead of him and put an arm up. "Moreau, with me."

"Thank God," Derek said as he got to his feet.

"Coward," Jean shot back as he started for the door.

Rhemann closed it as soon as Jean was in the inner court, and Jean fixed his eyes on the team bench as he awaited a dressing down. The subs and other coaches were close enough to hear every word Rhemann said, but shame was a critical part of the correction process. Instead of ranting, though, Rhemann set off. It took Jean a moment to decide he was meant to follow, and his shoulders tightened as he realized they were heading back to the locker room. Privacy for a lecture meant more than words were needed to get the message across.

Rhemann brought him all the way to the defense line's huddle room, where the TV was already turned on and set to a news station. Rhemann took a chair near the front and turned his full attention on the screen. Jean looked from him to the

TV and back again in confusion, but he had not been asked to speak so he said nothing.

"Sit," Rhemann finally said, so Jean took a chair near the back.

It took him too long to understand; it wasn't until Louis Andritch stepped up to the microphone that Jean remembered Edgar Allan's press conference was today. His blood was static in his ears, making it hard to focus on anything the campus president was saying, and he had to fold his arms over his chest to keep his heart from shattering his ribs.

"Without further ado, this year's head coach for the Edgar Allan Ravens: Federico Rossi." Andritch held an arm out to one side to welcome the man to the stage, and the sheer number of camera flashes should have blinded both men as Rossi came up for a handshake and joint picture. Andritch leaned in to say something in Rossi's ear that no microphone could catch, and Rossi gave a stoic nod as he was left to fend for himself at the podium.

Jean was out of his chair before he realized he was moving; Rhemann's "Moreau" caught him when he was halfway to the door. Jean knotted a hand in his jersey and willed air back into too-tight lungs as he obediently turned back toward Rhemann.

"I thought you would want to see it," Rhemann said. "This is a step in the right direction for everyone. No offense to Coach Moriyama; he's a brilliant man and half the reason we even have this sport. But I personally don't think he had the right temperament or approach to be a coach. He should have stuck to the ERC in an advisory position."

Past him Rossi was giving a speech about Edgar Allan's historic records and the undeniable tragedies set into motion by the loss of two of their brightest players in spring. Jean fought not to hear him. It didn't matter what Rossi said or thought. He was not the Ravens' coach. He would never be their coach. The Ravens belonged to the master. Evermore belonged to the master.

"All right," Rhemann said, although Jean hadn't said anything. "If you'd rather not watch this, go on back to inner court."

Jean was out the door as soon as he could say "Yes, Coach," but he booked it to the bathroom when he thought he might throw up. All he managed was a rush of bile that left his mouth and nose burning, and Jean braced his gloves against the back wall of the stall as he gasped for breath. He'd known the master was out of the game; he'd known Edgar Allan would need to replace him. But knowing it was coming and having to see it happen were two entirely different monsters, and Jean clenched his teeth against a second rush of nausea.

No master, no perfect Court, no Nest.

Jean slammed his hands against the wall hard enough to feel it in his elbows and flushed the toilet on his way out at the stall. He rinsed and spit at the sink in a vain attempt to get the burn out of his throat before finally heading down to the inner court again.

"Back so soon?" Coach Jimenez asked. "Unexpected."

"I am not a Raven," Jean said. It was no easier to say aloud than it was to hear it in his thoughts. "What happens at Edgar Allan now is not my concern, Coach."

"Sure," Jimenez said, in a tone that said he wasn't convinced. "Keep limber and I'll get you on again in about fifteen minutes or so."

It was a long time to be doing nothing; the easy stretches and inner court drills required no thought whatsoever after too many years of them. Jean watched the court to keep his thoughts from wandering, but here and there they fractured. How many coaches would the Ravens have? Had they brought back any Raven graduates to help, or were they going for a clean slate approach? Did the medical staff stay? Were the Ravens ready to go back, or were they being released from counseling early so as not to delay the season?

That final thought was the snapping point of his patience, perfectly timed with Jimenez sending him onto the court. For a moment Jean thought he would successfully get out of his head, but to everyone's misfortune he was being sent on for Lucas. The backliner made sure to hit him shoulder to shoulder as Jean stepped through the door first, and his quiet but heated "Whore" was the last straw. Jean caught him around his throat guard in one easy move and threw him down on the court floor.

Jimenez had followed him to the door so he could call Lucas off, and now he hauled Jean back with a tight grip on his arm. "That's enough, Moreau!"

Lucas started to get up, eyes flashing with rage. Jean didn't have to yank out of Jimenez's grip to reach him; his legs were long enough he could kick Lucas in his chest armor and knock him back down. Jimenez bodied him off the court a heartbeat before the rest of the Trojans on-court could catch up to them, and Jean shoved through the gaping subs waiting in the inner court.

It took all of two seconds for White and Lisinski to catch up to him. Being trapped between three coaches and a bench was the worst thing Jean could think of until Jimenez shoved Lucas into the scant space at Jean's side.

"You want to explain yourself?" Jimenez demanded, looking between his backliners.

"Your fourth line has a smart mouth, Coach," Jean said. "I was hoping he would bite his tongue off in the fall and save us both some grief in the long run."

"Fuck you," Lucas said. "Fourth line nothing."

"You are lucky to be on a line at all," Jean shot back. "That they afforded you two games last season speaks volumes of their disdain for your opponents. I would have stopped after your performance in the first."

White realized this wasn't going to be a quick or clean resolution and sent the subs on a run around the inner court to get them more space.

"Enough," Lisinski said, flicking a sharp look between them. "Accusations and insults aren't going to fix anything. Tell us what the problem is so we can find a way forward,

264

because we are not going to spend the year with this kind of disunity. You," she stabbed a finger at Jean, "explain what started this today."

"I will not be insulted by a know-nothing child, Coach," Jean said.

"Are you going to fight everyone who insults you?" Lisinski asked.

"Raven," White reminded her.

Jimenez cut in like he could somehow smother that easy explanation before Jean heard it. "That's not a good excuse. You're going to be dealing with a lot of aggressive attitudes on the court this fall. If you let them all get to you, that's a problem for all of us. You agreed to play by our standards when you transferred here. If you can't even watch your temper when playing your own team, how can we trust you on the court this fall?"

He didn't wait for a response but rounded on Lucas. "And you," he said, stabbing a finger at Lucas's face, "know better than to start fights here. How many times are we going to have this conversation before you start taking it to heart? I know this isn't the first time you two have gone at each other. You think Winter hasn't already warned me there was going to be a problem here?"

"Cody's a snitch," Lucas said.

"They are trying to look out for the entire defense line, which includes both of you," Jimenez said. "What's going on with you?"

"I think signing him was a mistake," Lucas said flatly. His opinion was no surprise to Jean, but that he'd say it so boldly to his coaches was unfathomable. Jean put a little more space between them in case someone started swinging, but there was only so far he could go. Lucas noticed the movement and sent him a heated look. "Kevin tricked us into signing him so we could sabotage the Ravens for him and made us into villains in the process. We're complicit in everything that happened during championships. We're not the good guys or the good

265

sports anymore, we're underhanded schemers. I didn't sign up to be a part of that!"

Jean curled his lip at Lucas in disgust. "Those are Grayson's words. I know his voice."

"Tell me he's wrong," Lucas accused him.

"The only thing that wretched beast does right is Exy."

"Don't you dare talk about my brother that way."

"He's not your brother," Jean shot back. "He is a Raven. He stopped being yours the day he signed with Edgar Allan. You are lucky to have lost him."

It took all three coaches to break them apart when Lucas lunged for him. Jean tongued the corner of his mouth and tasted a bit of blood; his jaw was numb for the moment but likely would flare hot before long. White's hands on him were tense, like he expected violence, but in no universe would Jean ever touch a coach. He kept his gloved hands at his side and waited for Lucas to stop struggling.

"I'm not going to take your word over his," Lucas said when the coaches finally got him to back off.

"Then take his word," Jean said, and Lucas sent him a suspicious look past Lisinski's shoulder. Jean wished he had the common sense to shut up, but the challenge was already crawling out of him, icy with a bottomless rage. "Ask him why he's so sure the rumors are true. Ask him what his part in it was. If you're going to believe him just because he's blood, then at least make him tell you the truth."

"What's that supposed to mean?" Lucas demanded.

"And keep Kevin's name out of your ignorant mouth," Jean continued. "My transfer had nothing to do with championships. You think I would have come here if I had any real choice in the matter? *Here*?"

"Thanks," White said dryly. "Do you have to say it like that?"

"Beside the point," Lisinski said, exasperated. To Lucas she said, "It's the truth, Lucas. We couldn't have signed Jean if Edgar Allan wasn't willing to negotiate his scholarship with us.

We confirmed his status with both President Andritch and Coach Moriyama before we faxed the paperwork to South Carolina. Jean was removed from the Raven lineup in March due to egregious injuries."

Jean didn't recognize that word, but since Lucas was already running his mouth, he didn't get a chance to ask.

"That's not reassuring," Lucas said, leaning past Lisinski to see Jean. "Everyone knows you sprained your LCL in scrimmages. If they cut you over something that small, it means they were just looking for an excuse to throw you in the trash. I'm right," he insisted when Jimenez gave him a shake. "Why else would they only ever parade two of the perfect Court around? They knew Jean was a mistake and were too afraid to cop to it."

"Permission to break his face, Coach?" Jean asked.

"Denied," White said.

"It wasn't just his LCL," Jimenez said. He glanced at Jean at that, hesitating. It took Jean a moment to realize the coach was testing his resistance to this conversation. Jean slid his gaze away, leaving it to Jimenez to decide how much he wanted to disclose. When he didn't protest, the defense coach turned on Lucas and said, "You did notice the no-touch jersey, I assume? The Ravens kicked his ribs in."

That startled Lucas into a moment of silence, and Jean thought it telling that his first hesitant response was, "Did Grayson...?"

As angry as he was, Jean couldn't lie. "Not this."

Lucas subsided for a moment, and Jimenez risked letting go of him at last. Lucas betrayed that trust a scant second later when he asked, "What'd you do? What?" he asked at the molten look Lisinski sent him. "If you can break ribs through someone's chest armor you must really want to hurt him. I don't think I'm out of line asking why they did it."

Why? Jean thought, and for one wretched, ridiculous moment all he could hear was Jeremy's voice in his head: *"I'm sorry that he tricked you into thinking you deserved it."* Jean made a cutting gesture with his hand like he could dislodge such a useless sentiment. Jean was a Moreau. He belonged to the Moriyamas now and always. His job was to be whatever they needed him to be. For Ichirou that was a reliable source of income; for Riko it had been an outlet for the cruelty and violence eating through Riko's heart. Maybe 'deserve' wasn't the best term, but it wasn't wrong.

"Accidents happen in scrimmages," Jean said.

"Piss on that," Lucas said.

"Enough," Jimenez said, losing his patience with both of them. He turned on Jean first, expression stern. "I know this isn't ideal for you, but it's a done deal. We're willing to make a home for you here, but you have to meet us halfway. Keep that temper of yours in check and start acting like a Trojan if you want to see any time on the court this fall. Understood?" He waited for Jean's tense nod before turning an equally frustrated look on Lucas.

"And you," he said, and Lucas had to look away. "You know better, so be better. Forget everything you saw on the news and anything your brother's told you; it's obvious there's a lot more to the story than any of us know yet, so stop jumping to conclusions and wipe the slate clean. You worry about your performance on the court and your academic year. Let us worry about our team's reputation. Yes?"

"Yes, Coach," Lucas said, with a stiffness Jean didn't believe.

"The next time I see you two fighting, you'll both be benched until October. Now run it off. I'll tell you when you can stop."

The backliners peeled off their gloves and helmets before starting off around the inner court at a slow jog. Jean started first, so Lucas waited a few seconds before following a safe distance behind. Jean counted steps then heartbeats to try and stay out of his head. He ended up mentally listing and reviewing drills when that wasn't enough to distract him. He'd finally found a comfortable place of not-existing when Lucas drew even with him.

"Tell me why you hate him."

Jean flicked him a cool look. "There are not enough hours in the day."

Lucas scowled out at the empty stands. It took him half a lap before he replied, and Jean didn't miss the way the coaches watched them like a hawk as they passed side by side. When they turned the corner and put a safe distance between them and the benches, Lucas finally figured out what he wanted to say.

"I don't know him anymore," he admitted. It annoyed him to say it, judging by the look that pulled hard at his face, but Lucas looked away when he felt Jean's eyes on him. "He fell off the face of the planet for four years. We figured out his first day back he wouldn't have even come home if his coaches hadn't made him. He didn't apologize for ghosting us, didn't ask what we'd been up to in his absence, didn't even ask me how things were going with the Trojans. I couldn't even get him to look at me until I asked him about you.

"I don't know what it was like to be a Raven or how he felt learning from Coach Moriyama himself. I don't know if he had friends or girlfriends. I don't know what kind of music he likes anymore." Lucas paused as they passed the coaches' bench before saying, "I don't even know his fucking major. Do you get it? The only thing I know about my own brother, my only brother, is that he hates you. He hates me for being on the team that stole you."

"So you hate me in solidarity," Jean concluded. "Perhaps you should have been a Raven, except you never would have qualified with those stats."

"Get fucked."

"Business."

"What?"

Jean said it loud and slow: "All Ravens are required to major in business."

It earned him a lap of peace before Lucas said again, "Tell

269

me why you hate him."

"You might not know him, but I do," Jean said.

"That's not an answer," Lucas said, but Jean had nothing more to say on the matter. Lucas tried to outlast him before asking, "Did you fuck my brother?"

Teeth, Jean thought. Fingers in his hair; a bruising grip on his chin. For a moment he felt the sticky heat of breath on his face, and he scrubbed the memory away as hard as he could. Reaching for his neck was instinctive, but his fingernails hit his neck guard first. He ran his tongue along the backs of his teeth, trying to erase the taste of Grayson's skin, and bit the inside of his cheek to bleeding.

"I asked you a question," Lucas said.

"I'm ignoring you," Jean said, as if that wasn't obvious.

"You want me to take his word," Lucas reminded him. "If I'm supposed to be weighing his words, give me something to weigh them against. I already know—think I know—the answer based on what you said in front of the coaches, but I need you to say it."

"I do not care what you need," Jean said, peeling his neck guard off. His fingers found the spot where Grayson liked to bite and dug in with his fingernails. He wanted to claw this memory out of him, but the best he could do was draw blood.

They rounded the corner to find Jeremy off the court and in their path, and they both slowed to a halt in front of him. Jeremy didn't look at Lucas but moved to Jean immediately and caught hold of his wrist. Jean realized with a start that this was what had pulled Jeremy out of the scrimmage. Thinking Jeremy had been paying more attention to him than to practice was unsettling.

Jeremy gave his hand a careful tug. When Jean held fast, Jeremy looked over at Lucas and said, "See if Coach will put you back in."

Lucas took a half-step back, then another, and finally turned to go. Jean never wanted to talk to him again, but he couldn't stop himself from asking: "Is he home?"

Lucas could have ignored him, but the other man came to an abrupt stop. Jean used his free hand to push Jeremy's shoulder, and Jeremy obediently turned so Jean could see past him. Lucas was quiet for a minute as if debating whether he wanted to respond, then finally said, "He was released yesterday, and he has a flight back to West Virginia on Saturday. He didn't even call me to say he was out. I had to find out from Mom."

He didn't wait for a response before setting off again. Jeremy turned a worried look on Jean and gave his hand another tug. This time Jean loosened his grip and let Jeremy pull his hand free. Jeremy touched his chin, trying to get him to turn his head so he could see the damage better, but Jean snapped his neck guard back into place. It stung, and he'd feel it all practice, but it was too sharp to be teeth and that was fine by him.

"Talk to me," Jeremy said, almost too quiet for Jean to hear him.

There were only so many ways to argue with Jeremy, so Jean went the route most likely to buy him some peace: "Not today."

Jean had no intentions of ever explaining, but the lack of an outright 'no' gave Jeremy enough false hope to let it go for now. He sighed defeat as he backed out of Jean's space. "Another day, maybe."

The rest of the day's practice felt endless. When they finally let him onto the court again, Jean put every ounce of his concentration into what he was doing and how he was playing. When he was pulled to give someone else time, there wasn't enough action on the sidelines to keep his thoughts from wandering. He thought about Grayson and Federico Rossi and Evermore and Riko, and he ran the stadium steps to try and burn his thoughts away.

At long last it was time to go. The coaches split the lines between huddle rooms to review the day's progress before freeing them to the showers. Jean was clean and gone again

271

before half of the men had finished soaping up, and he waited on the strikers' row for Jeremy to catch up with him.

The end of practice was lazily chaotic as Trojans drifted around in search of their clothes and keys. They were worn out and ready to be on their way but still half-caught in cheery conversations with one another. Jean closed his eyes and let the noise drive his thoughts far away. The bench shifted now and then as strikers sat to tie their shoes, but Jean waited until he heard Jeremy's voice before opening his eyes again.

As usual, they were two of the last to leave, since Cat and Laila couldn't take quick showers if their lives depended on it. The considering looks the women treated Jean to as they headed over made Jean wonder what Jeremy had said to them, but he was used to that lack of filter by now. He didn't hold it against them; the Ravens hadn't been particularly good at keeping secrets either, seeing as they were permanently entrenched in each other's lives.

"Shall we?" Laila asked.

The walk home was quiet, and not quite the comfortable kind. Cat was the first in the door, but she snagged Jean's sleeve on his way by to stop him. "Hey," she said, not to him but the others. "Can you two get takeout tonight? Is that okay?"

"Of course," Laila said.

Cat gave her a quick kiss in gratitude and motioned to Jean. "Wait here."

Laila and Jeremy exchanged curious looks as Cat headed to her room. Jean heard the rattle of her closet door opening and closing. She was back a minute later, wearing a jacket he only saw on her when she was about to take her motorcycle out. Her gloves were tucked inside the helmet dangling from her fingers, and she caught him by his shoulder to propel him out the door ahead of her. Jean wasn't sure why she wanted him to see her off, but he watched as she walked her bike to the foot of the driveway.

"Let's go," she said.

Jean looked from her to the bike and back again. It had two seats, but there was no way that slim thing was meant to carry two bodies. "Absolutely not."

She tugged on her helmet and gloves, took the front seat, and turned an expectant look on him. "Chickenshit."

"Refusal is not unreasonable," Jean said. "I just got cleared to practice again."

"I'm not going to crash us." Cat gave the seat behind her an impatient pat. "Haven't totaled a bike since I was sixteen."

"That's not reassuring."

There were a million reasons this was a terrible idea, but Jean finally climbed on behind her. She tugged his arms around her waist, said, "Don't fight me, yeah?" and took off down the road before he had a chance to change his mind.

Jean experienced an immediate and profound sense of regret. The absence of seatbelts and a solid frame to protect them was alarming, and the cars Cat slipped between looked monstrously large from this fragile vantage point. Jean seriously considered climbing off the next time she hit a red light, but he hadn't quite worked up to it before she pulled into a dealership and parked at the curb.

"This is my uncle's place," she said with no little pride, and she sailed through the front door ahead of him. "He's off today or I'd introduce you, but I'll bring you back another time for a proper meet-and-greet. Tomás!"

She was off like a shot, rattling away a mile a minute in Spanish to one of the salesmen. Jean followed her around because he wasn't sure what else he was supposed to do, and eventually the pair led him over to a section with apparel. Cat snagged two jackets off the shelf, held them up against him in turn, and snapped the tag off one. The tag was turned over to Tomás for safekeeping, and Cat darted away to find a helmet and gloves. Ten minutes later they were out the door again, and Cat pushed the helmet into Jean's hands.

"Onward!"

Having a bit of gear made Jean feel only marginally safer.

273

He had the fleeting hope that Cat would take them back to the house, but of course she was just getting started. Jean was idly sure she was picking the busiest streets on purpose. The third time a car changed lanes right in front of them like they weren't even there, Jean decided it was best to just close his eyes until the crash finally came. He didn't open them again until Cat whooped triumph ahead of him, and Jean looked up as they took one last turn to merge onto the Pacific Coast Highway.

The ocean came up on their left, so close and so vast Jean wasn't sure how the cars weren't sliding off the road into it. On his right, buildings and storefronts gave way to rocky hills covered with scattered tufts of underbrush. Maybe it was the tint in his visor, but the cloudless sky looked deep enough to get lost in. The further north they went, the less traffic they had to contend with, and Jean could worry less about getting mutilated in a crash and more about the world unfurling all around him.

Oh, he thought. *It's so big.*

It was such an inane observation he bit his own tongue in annoyance, but that nagging sense of wonder remained. On its heels was the dizzying realization he'd seen more of Los Angeles than he had of any other place he'd lived in his life. Back in Marseille he'd been homeschooled so his parents could keep an eye on him, and his youth Exy team had been only ten minutes up the road. The Ravens had traveled all over the northeast for games, but they'd been in and out of buses and planes and stadiums without any time to look around. Kevin's postcards had been Jean's only real glimpse of the greater world outside of Evermore.

He and Cat stopped for dinner at a café on the beach where the outdoor tables were covered with thatch umbrellas and half of the patrons were sipping cocktails from carved fruits. The wait for outdoor seating was estimated to be close to half an hour, but Cat swore it was worth it as she put her name on the list.

If it wasn't for the evening hour and the breeze coming in off the ocean, their jackets would have made the heat unbearable. Jean carried their helmets and gloves as they wandered the beach so Cat could dig up cracked sand dollars and seashells. She finally found one that was intact, and she ran down to the tide to rinse it off with childish glee. Jean obediently inspected it when she brought it back, and she tucked it into his breast pocket with a cheerful "For you!"

At last, they were called back to take their table. Almost everything on the menu would get a fierce side eye from the Ravens' nurses, but Jean managed to find an inoffensive salad before he gave up hope entirely. Cat ordered the fish and chips and offered him a bite as soon as it was delivered. Jean waved her off, and Cat let it go with an exaggerated shrug. She hummed as she ate, as she tended to do when she was happy, and Jean watched her as she stared out at the ocean. Now that they were settled, he expected an interrogation or a reason for this unscheduled trip out.

When she failed to explain herself, Jean finally asked, "Why are we here?"

"I love it here," Cat said, licking grease from her fingers before remembering she had a napkin. Before Jean had to press her again, she turned a more serious look on him. "I don't know. I just felt like some fresh air would do you good. There's nothing like a ride to get you out of your head and into the moment, you know?"

Jean considered that for a minute. "Thank you."

"Not as terrible as you thought it'd be, right?" Cat asked. "I could teach you on the weekends if you want. We have an old bike at the house we used to practice on, but it's just collecting dust now that all us kids have our own rides. They wouldn't mind if I borrowed it for a bit, I'm sure. I could probably even talk Vivi into riding it down here for us."

Jean wasn't sure how to respond to that, so he asked, "How many are you?"

It startled some of the earnestness out of her, and she

275

stared at him in contemplative silence for a bit. "I think that's the first personal question you've asked me," she said, and answered before he could reconsider. "Seven of us in total. I don't really know the oldest two, though. They're from Dad's first marriage and they've got like ten years on me, so they left home when I was still little.

"Laila's an only child," she continued, though she'd told him that before. "Jeremy has—three. One sister, two brothers. The older brother's an absolute tool, but there's bound to be a jerk or two once you pass four kids." Jean idly wondered what she'd changed at the last minute and why, but he watched her nervously push her fries around her plate and decided not to ask. Cat pressed on a moment later with, "What about you? Was I right about it being just you?"

It would be easy to let her believe it and save him any uncomfortable follow-up questions, but Jean attempted a bit of honesty. "One sister, four years younger. I haven't spoken to her since I left home," he said when Cat turned on him with renewed energy and interest. "Ravens are not allowed to have families."

"So I heard," Cat said, and he guessed she meant Lucas. "But you're not a Raven anymore, right? You should try and reconnect."

The thought that maybe he could was at once baffling and nonsensical. She'd been ten when he left home, just ten when he'd stopped protecting her from their mother's temper and father's violent business. Did she know he hadn't gone by choice? Did she blame him or forgive him? Jean wasn't sure he wanted to know what time had done to her. So long as she existed as fractured memories, she was safe and small and sheltered.

"Maybe," he said, because he had the feeling Cat would argue with an outright rejection.

Like Jeremy, she was easily wooed by that false sense of progress, and she ate the rest of her dinner in satisfied silence. As soon as she settled the check they headed back to the bike.

They made one last stop up the road at Point Dume, a bluff that overlooked sandy trails and a rocky coastline. Cat spread her arms as she leaned into the gusting wind. Jean gazed out at the endless horizon, feeling small and infinite from one moment to the next.

He tapped his gloved fingers together. *A cool evening breeze. Rainbows. Open roads.*

CHAPTER SIXTEEN
Jean

Since neither Jean nor Lucas wanted to be benched for the next four months, they decided by unspoken agreement to simply ignore each other the next day. Seeing how Jean was still in Xavier's group at the gym and they played the same position on the court, it was fairly easy to pull off without dragging the rest of the team down. Lucas kept his smart mouth shut, Jean passed to him when it was the best play during scrimmages, and they changed out with at least two bodies between them in the locker room.

For better or worse, the stalemate meant the coaches could narrow their focus down to Jean: rather, their issues with how he was playing on their court. On Thursday afternoon Coach Rhemann joined his team on the court for scrimmages. He wore a helmet for protection but no other gear, and he paced the walls as he watched Jean like a hawk. Every time Jean did something Rhemann didn't agree with—brutal hooks, back-to-back trips, and more contact than a no-touch jersey should allow, he gave a short blast on a silver whistle. He didn't bother to stop the play, trusting Jean to interpret the noise as a need for correction.

At first it was simply annoying, but as the afternoon wore on the strikers found the constant warnings more and more amusing and Jean found it steadily less so. The cheerful "Oops!" and "You can do it!" remarks from his teammates did nothing at all to improve his mood. He was forced to second-guess every check he made, but every time he hesitated to think through what he was doing he risked falling behind and losing control of the play. It was easy to default to muscle memory, which inevitably brought another scolding tweet from Rhemann's whistle.

Jeremy was smart enough to not make such comments, but he had the misfortune of being Jean's fourth mark of the day. Jeremy's startled "Ouch" was not the gleeful taunts Jean had suffered all afternoon, but enough was enough. Jean hooked his shoulder and racquet around Jeremy's arm to throw him flat on his back. Jeremy grunted as he hit the floor hard, and the scrimmage ground to a halt as the Trojans reacted to the echoing thud. Jean knelt beside Jeremy to wait and laid his racquet on the ground in front of him.

Jeremy pushed himself up on his arms as Rhemann headed their way. Jean felt his searching look but didn't bother to return it, instead fixing a calm stare on a safe point across the court. Rhemann crouched on the other side of Jean's racquet and looked at Jeremy first.

"Good?" he asked. When Jeremy nodded an easy okay, the head coach turned a pensive look on Jean. "Kind of going the opposite direction than intended."

"I'm sorry, Coach," Jean said.

"Are you actually sorry, or are you saying it because you think I want to hear it?"

"I do not like failing, Coach."

"It's going to take time," Rhemann said, and tapped the whistle hanging from his neck. "This is not an attempt to shame you; it is a means of helping you. I don't think you can see all the places we are out of alignment with each other. Now that we both have a better idea of how much there is to work on, we can take it one infraction at a time. Too much to fix in one fell swoop, it seems. Are you good to keep going, or do you need a break to clear your head?"

"I will play as long as you let me, Coach."

"Then off your knees and let's get to it," Rhemann said as he stood.

Jean collected his racquet on the way up and held it out in offering. Rhemann accepted it and turned it over in his hands as Jeremy picked himself up. Jean waited patiently, but all Rhemann did was treat it to a serious inspection. He tugged the netting to test the tension and squeezed the head in search of cracks before arching a brow at Jean.

"I'm missing something," he said. "What am I doing with this?"

He wasn't the first coach who enjoyed making his players ask for it, but Jean wouldn't have expected that sadistic streak in someone so widely revered in the NCAA. It was more comforting than upsetting to get a glimpse behind that mask; better to get the guesswork out of the way now since he had another two years under Rhemann's tutelage.

Jean kept his gaze pointed elsewhere and obediently answered, "Contrition, Coach."

Rhemann said nothing, savoring the wait, but then Jeremy clued in with an incredulous, "Jesus, Jean." He snatched Jean's racquet out of Rhemann's hands with a boldness that had Jean taking two quick steps away from him. Jeremy put his free hand out toward Jean, careful not to touch him, and stressed, "He is not going to hit you. Okay? We don't do that here. You said you'd try to do better and that's enough for us."

Rhemann's stare was so heavy Jean could hardly breathe beneath its weight, but he risked a cool glance at Jeremy. "Yet again you think words are sufficient when they obviously are not. I signed a contract agreeing to abide by your standards and I've promised all week to behave, but I have continually betrayed that trust and refused to improve. I am making the same mistakes today I was making on Monday."

"Do not tell me your coaches used to hit you with your racquet," Rhemann said. It was a dangerous line to tread, but Jean took that 'do not' literally and kept his mouth shut. Rhemann tolerated the silence for only a few seconds before demanding, "Look at me right now. I asked you a question."

It hadn't been a question, but Jean knew better than to correct him. He forced himself to meet Rhemann's stare and kept his tone as neutral as possible. "They did whatever was

280

necessary to ensure we performed at our best, Coach."

"Whatever was—" Rhemann bit off the rest of his sentence and half-turned away from them to tap an agitated beat on his whistle.

Jean had never seen a coach fidget before, and he wasn't sure how to react to this hint of weakness. He glanced at Jeremy again, whose grim expression was no help at all, and looked back at Rhemann before the coach realized he'd gotten distracted. It was almost a full minute before Rhemann calmed down enough to go still, and he motioned to Jeremy. Jeremy wordlessly held Jean's racquet out in offering, and Jean slowly took it from him.

"Let's run it again," Rhemann said, and he walked away.

Jean waited until he was out of earshot. "I don't understand."

"Trust us," Jeremy said tiredly. "Neither do we."

Jean had the feeling they were talking about two different problems, but he didn't have the energy to ask. Rather than send the two teams to foul spots for Jean's unsportsmanlike behavior, Rhemann reset the entire game and sent them all back to their starting spots. Jean endured more than a few searching looks as he headed across the court to his line. He wasn't sure if anyone had overheard them or if there'd been just enough space between them to muffle the conversation. Whichever it was, no one was reckless enough to ask when it was a half-hour before the edge left Rhemann's voice.

Now that Rhemann was going to pick one problem area to focus on at a time, the whistles were fewer and further between. Today's issue was Jean's habit of slipping a foot between Jeremy's every time they paused to watch their teammates. It was an effortless way to trip him up and an easy way to get an opponent off the court with injuries, and one of the first stances Ravens were taught. Breaking that habit took a conscious effort, but if this was the only thing Jean had to change today, he could spare the energy to correct it without sacrificing the rest of his game.

At long last practice was over. Rhemann called Jean over while the rest of the Trojans went ahead to the showers. Lisinski was nowhere to be seen, but Jimenez and White were comparing notes as they followed their players toward the locker room. Rhemann sat on the home bench and waited for Jean to catch up with him. Jean sat only when Rhemann motioned for him to do so.

It only took Rhemann a minute to sort out his thoughts, and he studied Jean with a distant look. "Just so you know, we asked Edgar Allan to send along your full medical records back in April. They agreed and even gave us a tracking number for it, but somehow the package never actually made it to us. Something tells me that wasn't an accident. What do you think?"

"I am unfamiliar with the mail system here, Coach," Jean said.

"Did one of your coaches break your ribs?"

"I was injured in a scrimmage, Coach."

"Funny that you're still calling it that when Kevin told Jeremy it was hazing," Rhemann said, and Jean wished a thousand painful deaths on the Court's Queen. Rhemann let that sink in before saying, "I'm going to ask you one more time, and I trust you'll be more honest with me. Was it your coaches who broke your ribs this spring?"

"No, Coach," Jean said.

Rhemann continued to study him, as if weighing the truth in that response. "You should know that Jackie called Edgar Allan to ask them about their training program. She made sure to ask for examples of effective disciplinary action. Turns out there isn't a single pool on Edgar Allan's campus. Do you want to explain that?"

For a blinding moment Jean could taste wet cloth. His control teetered, but Jean clenched his fingers harder together and said, "No, Coach."

"Here's the deal," Rhemann said. "I don't want to push you for more than you're willing to give me, but sooner or

282

later I'm going to have to ask some really unpleasant questions. It's my hope we can come to some sort of understanding before we hit that point, because I need you to understand I wouldn't pry if I didn't feel I had to. You're one of my kids now. I'm trying to do right by you, but that requires a bit of give and take from both of us. Do you understand?"

Jean didn't, but he obediently said, "Yes, Coach."

"Go on, then. I've kept you too long as it is. Good work today."

Despite being the last to the showers, Jean was still the first finished by a slim margin. He dried and dressed as quickly as he could and made it over to the strikers' row as the first of his teammates came drifting through the locker room. Jeremy was always a half-dozen bodies behind Jean, on account of chatting with too many people when he was supposed to be washing up, but Jean was content to wait and review the day's mistakes.

Lucas made it to Jean before Jeremy did, and the tight look on his face did nothing to improve Jean's mood. Jean didn't miss the way Nabil went still in case he needed to intervene; judging by the impatient look Lucas flicked him he noticed it as well. Whether or not he noticed the speculative looks Derek and Derrick sent his back was another story, but Jean kept his gaze on Lucas's face and waited for the point of this unwanted visit.

"I need to talk to you. Without…" Lucas gestured to indicate their nosey teammates. "Can you stay a few minutes late today?"

His first thought was to refuse, but Jean studied the tense pull of his mouth and hunched line of his shoulders. This wasn't anger, but anxious anticipation. Jean would have preferred the anger, but he'd set himself up by daring Lucas to demand answers from Grayson. Jean looked down at the phone in Lucas's white-knuckled grip and felt preemptively wearied by the conversation that awaited him.

"Hey, Lucas," Jeremy said, cheery and loud as he sailed

onto the row and made for his locker. "Nice work out there today."

Jean was distantly aware Lucas had asked him a question, but his train of thought derailed somewhere in the damp line of Jeremy's freckled shoulder blades. Jeremy's roots were starting to come in, and it was more obvious now that his hair was plastered to his skull from the shower. Jean watched a rivulet of water streak down his spine toward the towel wound around Jeremy's hips, and then the disgusted grunt Lucas made reminded Jean he had more important things to worry about. He forcibly returned his attention to his loathsome teammate as Jeremy set to work scrubbing his hands through his hair.

"Well?" Lucas demanded.

"Yes," Jean said, though the contempt on Lucas's face made him want to refuse out of spite. "I'll wait."

Lucas stormed off, the strikers went back to what they were doing, and Jeremy sent a curious look over at Jean. "Everything okay?"

"It remains to be seen," Jean said.

Most of the team and two of the coaches were gone before Lucas came looking for him again. He looked more uptight now than he had ten minutes ago, and Jean recalculated their odds of coming out of this conversation unscathed at an exhausting zero. He got up when Lucas didn't approach and put a hand on Jeremy's shoulder when Jeremy moved to follow. Lucas jammed his hands in his pockets and flicked Jeremy a wary look.

"Just Jean," he said. "Give me a few minutes."

"Yeah?" Jeremy asked Jean.

"Five minutes," Jean promised, and started toward Lucas.

He expected Lucas to take them to the other end of the locker room, or maybe to one of the huddle rooms, but Lucas went for the door and down the tunnel to the exit. Lucas cut between Rhemann's and Lisinski's cars to reach the outer gate, and while Jean followed him over there without hesitation he refused to step through. Lucas himself seemed content to stop in the opening, one hand on the gate and the other on the fence as he stared out at the few cars still scattered around the lot.

"I talked to Grayson," Lucas said. "Tried to, anyway. He still didn't want to talk to me."

"An unexpected bit of discretion," Jean said, "but not my problem."

"He didn't want to talk to *me*," Lucas said again, with emphasis.

Jean stared at him, hearing the words but refusing to read into them. Denial could only save him so long, and he followed Lucas's gaze to the car parked adjacent to the fence. He knew what was coming when the driver's door opened, but there was nothing he could do but stand frozen as Grayson got out and started his way.

Freedom had not soothed any of the fire in him; months apart had not tamed any of the rage. Jean was looking at a man who desperately wanted to hurt him and who intimately knew where his scars were. Jean couldn't feel the asphalt beneath his shoes or the warm wind tugging at his hair. There was ice where his marrow should be and a clammy sickness crawling through his chest like a worm.

Metal rattled as Lucas closed the gate again. Jean could have told him no door could keep Grayson out, but he was suffocating on memory and couldn't find his voice. Grayson slowed to a stop on the other side, but it wasn't obedience or restraint. He was simply relishing the effect his presence had on Jean, judging by the look on his face. Jean tried to remember what he'd looked like in January, bruised and bloodied and bettered, but it did nothing to steel his nerves.

"You said you just wanted to talk," Lucas reminded Grayson. "You can talk to him from out there."

Grayson hooked his fingers in the fence. "You owe me a number, Johnny."

Zane's nickname on Grayson's lips had Jean swallowing hard against a rush of bile. "Fuck you. Zane won that contest, not you."

"He's not here to claim it," Grayson said. "I am. I'm back in the Nest in two days, and you're going to make sure they give me the respect I'm owed."

"I won't lie for you."

"You're going to tell everyone I was promised to the perfect Court, or I'm going to come in there, peel the skin off your face, and fuck your bloody skull. Do you understand? I know where you play. I know where you live. Who is going to protect you now?"

"Jesus, Grayson—" Lucas started, but Grayson was already moving.

He threw his considerable weight against the gate, and Lucas wasn't ready to hold him off. Lucas yelped a bit as he was knocked back, but Jean wasn't sticking around to help him. He ran for the stadium door knowing he wasn't going to be fast enough. His fingers grazed the keypad before a hand caught his shoulder to spin him around.

The first fist caught him in his mouth, sending him back into the stadium wall, and Jean fought back like a caged beast. Grayson got a hand past Jean's guard and caught his face to slam his head into the hard wall. The world spun in a sickening blur, then narrowed to a too-bright focus when Grayson bit down hard on the juncture of his neck and shoulder. The cry it ripped out of Jean was more animal than human, and Jean went for Grayson's face and throat with frantic fingers.

Lucas came out of nowhere, grabbing his brother's arm to pull at him. "Stop it," he tried, desperate. "Grayson, stop!"

Grayson let go of Jean long enough to whale on his brother. Three hits were enough to knock Lucas clean off his feet, and Grayson was back before Jean made it more than two steps away from the wall. Grayson caught Jean's face in both hands and carved vicious lines down his cheeks with his thumbs as he bodily pinned him to the wall once more.

Jean grabbed his wrists before Grayson could claw his eyes out and headbutted Grayson as hard as he could. Jean was

286

pulled with him when Grayson stumbled back a step, but Grayson recovered before he could pry his hands free. Grayson dug his nails in as he shoved Jean back again. Jean kicked his ankle as hard as he could with them pressed this close together, and Grayson responded by knocking his head back into the wall so hard Jean's teeth ached.

"Give me my fucking number," Grayson said.

"It isn't yours," Jean managed. "*Fuck* you."

It was the wrong answer. Grayson bit down on Jean's left wrist with shattering intent. Jean tried wrenching his hand free, and Grayson's thumbnail sliced through the soft skin at the corner of his eye when Jean's grip slipped.

The stadium door swung open only to jolt to a stop when it hit Lucas's crumpled body, and Grayson immediately retreated out of Jean's space. Jean hunched over to grab his knees before he fell face-first onto the asphalt. Someone was yelling now, and he knew he recognized her voice, but his ears were ringing too loudly for him to make sense of the words. He couldn't look to see who'd inadvertently saved him; he couldn't take his eyes off the blood sluggishly running down his hand to his fingers.

Jean reached for his throat with his uninjured hand, and the feel of broken, wet skin beneath his fingers almost took him off his feet. He sucked in a deep breath, needing to know he wasn't suffocating against a pillow, but his lungs were so tight his chest was burning.

Hands grabbed at his shoulders, and Jean reacted instinctively. His attacker wasn't expecting such force, and he managed to throw Lisinski against her car before he realized who he'd hit. The white-hot panic of striking a coach erased everything else, and Jean retreated from her as fast as he could go. The first hit of the stadium wall against his shoulder blades startled ten years off his life, and Jean dropped his gaze immediately.

"Sorry," he managed. "I'm sorry, Coach, I didn't—"

"Enough," she warned him, and Jean bit off the rest of his

apologies. Tires squealed as Grayson peeled out of the parking lot. Lisinski sent a furious look after his car, but with Lucas sitting groaning at her feet and Jean barely standing she had to let him go. She had her phone out a second later as she knelt to check Lucas's eyes. "James, we need you out here right now," she said, and she flipped her phone closed without explaining.

Rhemann was out of the stadium in record time, and he didn't come alone. He went for Lucas first, since Lucas and Lisinski were in his direct line of sight, but Jeremy was right on his heels and he made a beeline for Jean. Alarm looked wrong on a face born for smiling, and Jean looked away before Jeremy's panic could send him over the edge. Jeremy reached for him, but Jean pushed off the wall and shoved Jeremy out of his way.

He could finally reach the stadium door unimpeded, but no one had given him the code for this keypad. Unsteady fingers put in the Raven digits over and over and over. He knew it was wrong. He didn't know why it wouldn't work. He couldn't stop trying.

"Jean, I've got it," Jeremy said as he pulled Jean's hand away from the buttons.

Jean watched in numb silence as Jeremy put in the right code. Jean only pulled the door open enough to squeeze through, and he went for the locker room as fast as he could without running. He nearly mowed down two straggling Trojans as he shoved through the second door, but he tuned out their annoyed cries and kept moving. He thought he heard Cat's voice, but Cat could wait. She had to wait. Jean had about thirty seconds to get Grayson's touch off him before he was violently ill.

The showers were empty when Jean burst in, and he slowed only to kick his shoes off. He went for the nearest shower head and wrenched the knob as hard as he could. The first hit of water against his face almost broke him in half, and Jean buried his face in the crook of his elbow as he fought to breathe. *Teeth*, he thought, and *drowning*, and *I know where*

288

you live.

Jean scrubbed desperately at his neck with his free hand, trying to wash away the spit and blood as quickly as he could. He had worked through Riko's violence for years; he'd survived Grayson at his worst. He just needed a moment to lock this away. One moment, or two, or ten, to forget the weight of Grayson's hands on his face and teeth on his skin. But the arm that was shielding his face from the water was also making it hard to breathe, and Jean teetered between the Trojans' showers and his shadowy room in Evermore.

"Jean." Jeremy again, somewhere off to his right. Jean was out of time. "Look at me."

I am Jean Moreau. I belong to the Moriyamas. I will endure. I will endure. I will endure.

Piece by piece he locked himself down again, pushing his fear and heartache so deep he felt numb. The tension eased out of his shoulders, and Jean cracked open his eyes to find the shower knob. A quick twist cut the shower off, and Jean raked both hands across his face to swipe away as much water as he could. Only then did he turn to face Jeremy, who was standing so close he had damp patches on his shirt and shorts from the spray. Jean felt settled, or as settled as he could be when he'd forcibly disconnected himself from this moment, but Jeremy still looked haunted.

"I will need to change before we leave," Jean said. "Give me a moment."

Jeremy moved in his path when Jean started for the door. "Jean, stop."

"Let me by," Jean said. "I'm cold."

"Please talk to me."

"I have nothing to say to you."

"He hurt you," Jeremy insisted, and Jean was fleetingly grateful that Jeremy refrained from saying Grayson's name. Jean made a dismissive gesture and tried to push past, but Jeremy doggedly stepped in front of him again. "You are very obviously not okay, so please stop pretending like we can just

289

ignore what's happening to you."

"Stop looking if it is going to bother you," Jean said. He wasn't sure if that was disapproval or hurt tugging at the corner of Jeremy's mouth, and Jean forced himself to try and put it into better words. "The Ravens knew it was not their business, and they knew better than to dwell on it. It would be better for all of us if you would do the same."

Jeremy's response was low but unhesitating: "I will not look away."

"I do not want you to look."

It frightened him how much it sounded like a lie, but he didn't have time to dwell on it before the door opened to admit Rhemann. The head coach had his mouth open, but he hesitated when he took in Jean's drowned rat appearance. After a beat he motioned for them to follow, but he caught Jeremy's eye as he turned away and said, "Get him a towel. We'll be in medical."

They had to pass the remaining Trojans on the way: Cat and Laila, of course, and then Travis and Haoyu. Jean assumed the latter two were the ones he'd nearly barreled over earlier; they were Lucas's roommates in the summer dorm and were stuck here waiting for a resolution the same way the girls were. A sharp gesture from Rhemann warned the group to silence as he went by, and Jean kept his stare on Rhemann's back as he followed.

Lucas and Lisinski were in the first office, so Rhemann waved Jean into the second. Jeremy must have run, because he caught up with them before Rhemann had the door more than halfway closed. Jeremy passed a towel over but held onto the knob, and Rhemann knew what that tense look on his face meant. He looked over to Jean and said,

"Your call. In or out?"

Jean answered with an immediate, "Out."

Jeremy had no choice but to retreat, and Rhemann closed the door. Jean took the towel that was offered and sat where Rhemann pointed. Jean hadn't even realized there was a clock in here, but now he could hear its secondhand ticking. Maybe it was a watch. He hadn't owned one in years, but he checked his wrists anyway. All he found were the jagged lines of Grayson's teeth. He wound the towel around his arm so he wouldn't have to see it.

Rhemann worked his way around the room, opening and closing drawers in search of the bandages and antiseptics he would need. Jean tried to take them from him, but Rhemann's stony stare had him dropping his hand and sitting silent. Rhemann dragged a stool over and set to work, starting with Jean's wrist. After he was done cleaning and wrapping it, he had Jean test his range of movement. It ached, but Jean could rotate his hand and flex his fingers, and that was enough to settle some of the lingering ice in Jean's chest.

"Talk to me," Rhemann said as he dabbed at Jean's face.

"I do not know what you want me to say, Coach."

"Are you all right?"

"Yes, Coach," Jean said. "I can still play."

"That isn't what I asked you."

He gave Jean a minute to come up with something better, and the silence was worse than his questions. Jean jiggled his leg to shake his thoughts out of alignment, knowing he was giving himself away with that restlessness but unable to stop. He finally had to cover his bandages with his free hand so he could stop staring at them.

"Coach, please tell me what to say. I promise I will make it right."

"I don't want you to make it right," Rhemann said, sitting back a bit to stare at him. "I want to know that you're okay."

That was easy enough. "I'm okay, Coach."

Maybe not so easy, because Rhemann looked stuck somewhere between incredulity and pity. Jean forced himself to stillness. That best attempt at a serene front was all that saved him when Rhemann shook his head and set to work on Jean's throat.

Jean looked to the far wall, where one of the nurses had

hung up a framed black & white photograph of a lone boat in a harbor, and put himself as far away from here as he could. He thought of riding up the coast with Cat. He thought about the wall of photographs at the Foxhole Court. He thought of postcards and magnets destroyed by furious teammates, and Jean's control gave a threatening creak. He swallowed hard against a rush of nausea.

Maybe Rhemann heard him choke, because he tried again with a quiet but firm, "Jean."

"I will call Dr. Dobson." It was enough to give Rhemann pause, and Jean leaned into the lie with everything he had. "I will call her as soon as I am home, Coach."

There was a knock at the door. Rhemann finished taping bandages into place before rolling his stool across the room to open it. Lisinski was in the doorway with Lucas at her side. Jean took one look at him and knew his nose was broken; Grayson hadn't pulled any of the hits he'd aimed at his brother. Jean wanted to be satisfied that Lucas had paid for his part in this wretched reunion, but all he felt was tired and cold. Rhemann scooted out of the way so they could come in and close the door again.

Jean tuned out Rhemann's concerned questions and Lisinski's assessment of Lucas's injuries. When Rhemann was sure Lucas wasn't going to keel over any time soon, he said, "Start from the top."

Lucas's story came out as a halting mess, torn through with self-censorship and regret. He'd failed to get a good explanation from Jean yesterday as to what started the antagonism between Jean and his brother, so he'd done as Jean dared him and demanded the truth from Grayson. Grayson refused to engage in the conversation, only to turn around and message Lucas at lunch today for information about the timing of the Trojans' practices. He had nothing to say to Lucas, but he would speak to Jean, if Lucas could get him time alone.

"It's only the second thing he's said to me this summer." Lucas stared down at his shoes, the very picture of misery. "He walked away from me four years ago and forgot I existed, and both times he's bothered to talk to me since coming home it's been about Jean. He leaves for West Virginia this weekend. It was my last chance to see him before he went, and I didn't—I didn't know how to refuse him. I'm sorry. I fucked up."

Rhemann looked over at Jean. Jean wasn't sure if he was waiting for Jean's version of events or Jean's righteous fury. Jean kept his stare on Lucas's face and said, "The next time he leaves, let him go and change the locks behind him."

"He's my brother," Lucas said, but his protest was weak.

"I already told you," Jean said, voice flat. "He stopped being your brother the day he went to the Nest."

Lucas made a face at the floor but didn't argue immediately. "He hurt you. At Edgar Allan, I mean," he said when Jean reflexively tightened his grip on his bandaged wrist. Jean didn't answer, but Lucas wasn't waiting for confirmation when they both knew what the answer was. "I heard what he said to you."

"I will not talk about this with you."

"Did he—"

Jean refused to hear the rest of that question. "I will not talk about this with you," he said again, louder. This time Lucas took the hint, and Jean dug his nails into his bandage until the pain took the fierce edge out of his voice. When he trusted himself not to disrespect his coach with his tone, he turned a calm stare on Rhemann and asked, "Coach, may I go?"

"Are you really good to leave it like this?" Rhemann asked. "We have security cameras. We can call the police."

Jean's stomach bottomed out. "No, Coach."

"Jean." That muted protest was from Lucas, of all people, but Jean refused to look at him.

"I'll send Jeremy away first," Rhemann said, like that somehow would win Jean over.

"Ravens do not—" Jean started. At the look on Rhemann's face he changed tracks and said, "I cannot talk to the police, Coach."

Rhemann gave him a minute to change his mind, then gave up with a shake of his head. "I am trusting you to make the call that's best for you, but I will not allow him to trespass on our stadium again. I'm going to contact campus security with his picture," he said, with a glance at Lucas, "and inform them he is not welcome on the property. Lucas, if you hear another antagonistic word from him tonight, I would appreciate a heads-up. Thank you," he added when Lucas gave a jerky nod. "Jackie can give you a ride back to the dorm."

"I've got Haoyu and Travis," Lucas said, still sounding defeated. "I'll be fine."

"You?" Rhemann asked Jean, then made up his mind before Jean could answer. "You're with Laila. I'll give the four of you a lift."

Rhemann got up from the stool. Lisinski didn't look pleased by any of this but left the office first. Lucas didn't move, even when Rhemann stepped past him. Jean got a glimpse of Jeremy hovering in the hall like an anxious mother hen, but then Lucas reached for the doorknob. Lucas tipped his head toward Rhemann but kept his eyes on Jean as he asked, "Two minutes. Please?"

Jean looked at Rhemann, but Rhemann was watching him, and the look on his face was almost his undoing. This was the belligerent stare of a man who'd haul Lucas out of there by force if Jean indicated he didn't want to be alone with him. Jean tried to tell himself he was reading too much into it, but discomfort and safety were warring knots of poison eating through his heart. He forced himself to look away from his coach before he could be taken in by such a farce and answered a stilted, "One minute."

Lucas pushed the door closed immediately, only to waste twenty seconds just staring at it instead of facing Jean.

At twenty-one, the best he managed was, "I'm sorry."

"Your apologies are as useful as perfume on a frog," Jean said. When Lucas looked like he would protest, Jean cut him

294

off with a short jerk of his hand and said, "I do not care what you thought you'd get out of this experiment or what you think you learned. The entire reason I pointed you at Grayson was so I would not have to have this conversation with you. The only thing that matters is whether you are willing to play with me on the court."

"He bit you," Lucas said.

"I was there," Jean said icily.

"I've seen you looking at Jeremy. I've heard the rumors. I'm sure you're gay." Lucas fixed him with a stubborn look that was completely undermined by the nervous edge in his voice. "Is this like—is this a bad breakup thing?"

For a moment Jean was tempted to lie, if only to bring a swift end to this conversation. He was equally tempted to tell the truth just to twist the knife deeper. Miserable evasion was the only middle ground, and Jean fought hard against his roiling stomach. "Do not dare offload the burden of your brother's psychosis onto me. You will not assuage your guilt by assuming I wanted any part of it."

"I'm not—Jesus, I just—" Lucas couldn't seem to figure out where he wanted to go with this, but Jean didn't have all day to wait on him. He got off the bed and started for the door, and Lucas almost wasn't fast enough to stop him.

As soon as Jean's hand touched the knob Lucas put a hand and foot against the door to keep it closed, and the expression he turned on Jean was grim. Jean was fairly sure he could get Lucas out of his way if push came to shove, but he curled his lip at Lucas in scorn and gave him a last chance to get his head together.

At last Lucas said, "I'm sorry."

"I don't want your fucking—"

"I'm sorry I said it," Lucas clarified as he eased off the door. "It wasn't right. I saw your face when he got out of the car, so I know I shouldn't have even—" He gestured, helpless and miserable, as words failed him again. "The Grayson I grew up with was nothing like this. I can't make sense of what he's become."

"That is your problem, not mine." Despite that easy dismissal, Jean couldn't turn the knob. He stared at his hand, willing it to move, but dread overrode common sense and he had to know. "He said he knows where I live. Did you tell him?"

Lucas gave a short shake of his head. "I told him where the summer dorms are in case he wanted to come up and see me before he left. He doesn't know you're off campus."

It did little to quell the prickling bite in his heart, but it would have to do. Jean tugged the door open to find the coaches and Jeremy waiting just a few feet down the hall. Jean looked only at Jeremy and said, "I have to change before we leave."

"Sure," Jeremy agreed, with a fleeting, empty smile.

Jean trusted the coaches to call him back should they need anything else and set off for his locker. He passed Cat and Laila first, then Haoyu and Travis again, and made it to his locker without further interruption. That was only half the problem, as he'd already changed into his own clothes before following Lucas outside. He had no choice but to peel off his soaked outfit and put on tomorrow's workout wear. The wet clothes were bundled up in his discarded shirt for the ride home, and he found everyone waiting for him at the exit when he was through.

Haoyu, Travis, and Lucas set off across the parking lot toward campus, and Rhemann got the other four Trojans into his station wagon. The trip home by car was short enough to be disorienting, and Rhemann let them out at the end of the driveway. He rolled his window down as they stepped away and said, "Let us know if you need anything, all right?"

"Yes, Coach," Laila said, and ushered Jean up the stairs ahead of her.

Jean got the door unlocked and went inside, but he stood off to one side until the other three were in. As soon as the door was closed, Jean put the deadbolt and chain into place.

Every passing second made Lucas's reassurances less comforting, and Jean gave the chain a nervous tug. If Grayson found him, would this be enough? Doors had never stopped him before. Granted, the last one had been left open for him. Memories put a feverish heat in Jean's chest, and he gave the chain another hard yank.

"I have something for that," Laila said. "Wait here."

Jean listened to her rummage around in her room for a few minutes. She came back with a squat pole. One end had a flat rubber base, and the other had a shallow hook. She motioned him out of the way and pushed it into place under the knob. One last kick at the bottom got it as tight as it could go, and Laila gave a satisfied nod.

"My mother bought it for me when I first moved out of the house," she said. "It has never failed me, and people have tried more than once. Okay?"

It wasn't, but it would have to be. "Yes."

"Can we talk?" Jeremy asked.

"I have to change and call Dobson," Jean said, and Jeremy reluctantly got out of his way.

Jean went straight to his bedroom and chucked his wet clothes into his laundry basket. He traded his workout outfit for more casual clothes and sat cross-legged in the middle of his bed to stare down at his bandages. He didn't want to see the bites, but after a moment he reached up and peeled the tape and gauze free. His hand was bruising in a ring around it from the force of Grayson's teeth, and Jean felt his stomach lurch in response.

For one fleeting, foolish moment he considered calling Dobson after all. She'd been Andrew's therapist when Riko sent Drake after him. What had she told him afterward, and had it made any difference? Was false comfort better than no comfort at all? Jean turned his phone over and over in his hands, warring with himself.

In the end revulsion won. There was no way he would expose himself like this to her. Just thinking of putting it into

297

words made him dizzy. He moved to throw his phone out of reach when it hummed in his hand, and in his surprise he almost dropped it.

The area code was familiar, but the number was not. Jean only had a dozen-odd contacts saved in his phone, and half shared the same South Carolina prefix. Jean's first angry thought was Rhemann had called Dobson, not trusting Jean to follow through on his promise to get help, but Jean had her information saved and this message came up with no name attached. Jean drummed his fingernails on the keys for a few agitated seconds before opening the text.

The message was in French: "Where are you?"

Not Kevin's number, which left only one suspect. Jean still sent back a "Who" to be sure.

"Neil," was the quick response, and then, "I am in Los Angeles. We have to talk."

Jean looked at the clock on his phone, and dread was a heavy weight settling in Jean's bones. He knew the Foxes had already started summer practices, and he knew how long the flight here from South Carolina was. If Neil had skipped out on practice to make this trip, he was not coming with good news. Jean pinched the bridge of his nose and decided he absolutely hated twenty-four-hour days. Surely there was a limit to how many things could go wrong in a single day.

He sent his address back in response. Then, since he didn't feel like getting up yet, messaged Jeremy a simple "Visitor."

He assumed Jeremy checked out front before he came to the bedroom, because he was wearing a small frown when he pushed the door open. "I don't see anyone."

"Neil Josten is in town," Jean said, checking Neil's response. "He is on the way from the airport in a rental car."

"Do you want to see him?" Jeremy asked as he sat at the foot of Jean's bed. "I have no problems telling him he has to wait until tomorrow. We can put him in a hotel for the night or something."

"He would not come see me if he had any choice in the matter," Jean said. "I have to meet with him."

Whether or not Jean would survive the meeting was another story, but there was no reason to get into that with Jeremy.

CHAPTER SEVENTEEN
Jean

Jean was sitting on the ledge of the bay window when a car pulled up outside. Neil had sent him the make and color of his rental, but Jean still tensed a little at the sight of it. He waited until he saw Neil get out on the driver's side before nodding an okay to Jeremy, and his captain went ahead to undo the locks at the front door. Jean caught up to him as he was setting the bar to one side, and Jeremy opened the door right as Neil knocked.

"Hello, Neil." Jeremy turned sideways so Neil could fit past him through the doorway, but Neil only stepped backwards off the welcome mat. "An unexpected pleasure."

"Unexpected," Neil agreed as he looked past him. Neil stared at Jean for so long Jean wondered if he was supposed to speak first, but then Neil gestured toward his face and said in French, "I thought this was the team of pacifists. What happened to you?"

"You could have picked a better day to come," Jean said.

"It was not my call." Neil offered a slight shrug that Jean wasn't foolish enough to interpret as an apology. "Shoes?"

Jean toed into them without argument. When Jeremy realized he was leaving, he put a hand in front of Jean's chest and stilled him long enough to ask, "Are you sure about this? I would rather you stayed where I can keep an eye on you."

Jean had never been less sure of anything. "Lock the door behind us."

Jeremy didn't look happy about this, but he dropped his hand and let Jean out. Neil started down the stairs until he realized Jean wasn't following, and then he watched Jean

300

while Jean waited for Jeremy to close the door behind him. He heard the click of the deadbolt sliding home, a distant scratch that might have been the chain, and finally a dull thump that was the security bar going back into place. Satisfied they would be safe in his absence, Jean turned and started after Neil.

There were creased papers in the passenger seat held together by staples. Jean skimmed them before tugging his seatbelt into place, but they were just printouts of directions: LAX to the Gold Court, and the Gold Court to an address he didn't recognize. Jean passed them over to Neil's waiting hand, and Neil took a few moments to study them before tucking them between his thighs and turning the key in the ignition.

"Someone bit you," Neil said.

Jean reached for his neck before realizing Neil meant his uncovered wrist. The heavy look Neil sent him said he hadn't missed that gesture. Jean refused to look at him but said, "It is not your problem."

"It's going to be a problem today," Neil argued as he pulled away from the curb and got them on the road. "We have a few meetings to get through, the first of which is with my uncle. Even if he doesn't ask, the next group will. I need to know how to explain it when people start prying."

Neil could be lying to sate his curiosity, but Jean couldn't risk it. "Grayson Johnson came to see me after practice."

"I know that name," Neil said, but it took him a moment to place it. "Raven backliner. He came all this way just to pick a fight?"

"He wants me to declare him perfect Court," Jean said. "I'm to let slip that a number was promised to him after championships. He thinks it will earn him captaincy this year and solidify his future value."

"Is it the truth?"

Jean laughed. It sounded hollow even to his ears, and he pressed trembling fingers to his lips. "It was Zane's by right, even when you fucked things over so spectacularly by getting found." That wasn't a conversation he wanted to have anytime soon, especially not on the tail end of Grayson's unexpected visit. Jean swallowed hard against his roiling stomach. "Zane shattered when left to his own devices this summer, so Grayson assumes he is next in line by default. I am the only one left who can vouch for him, but I won't do it. I refuse."

"He sounds unhinged," Neil said. "What kind of person bites people in a fight?"

"Drake was not a biter, then."

It was without a doubt the worst thing Jean could have said right then, but he'd spent the wait for Neil staring at Dobson's contact information so he wouldn't have to talk to Jeremy. The thought of her was still rattling around his head, her and Andrew and Drake and Riko. Jean heard the creak of the steering wheel beneath Neil's fingers. For a moment it sounded like bedsprings. He thought about a door left unlocked on purpose and Zane turning his back on them as Grayson shoved Jean down on his own bed. He dug his fingernails into his lower lip and prayed for the courage to just rip his mouth off before he could misspeak further.

"Out of everyone and anyone you could have compared him to," Neil said, quieter than Jean had ever heard him, "you chose Drake."

Jean pressed his injured arm to his stomach, as much to hide the bruised marks as to try and squeeze away that hollow ache in his gut. "It doesn't matter. He will be out of the city this weekend and back at Edgar Allan."

"You wouldn't be barricading your door if he wasn't still a problem."

"He believes I live on campus. That's just—precaution," Jean finished, even as his mind supplied *fear, panic, horror*. He swallowed hard against a rush of nausea. If he stayed on this line of thinking he would lose his mind, so he willed Neil to have an ounce of humanity and said, "Stay out of my business and tell me why you came."

Neil drummed a restless beat on the steering wheel for a few moments, then allowed the change in topic without argument. He gestured to the side of his head as he said, "Word is someone at the FBI finally asked why and when I did this to my appearance if I did not want to be found, and they tracked it back to my stay at Evermore. People are starting to ask questions, and we're supposed to get ahead of it to clear things up."

"We cannot," Jean said as Neil turned into a parking garage.

Neil didn't answer until he'd gotten a ticket from the turnstile. Only when his window was closed again did he say, "We cannot name *him.*"

He left it at that, waiting for Jean to piece it together. Jean stared at him as Neil sought a parking spot, ticking through every possible connotation. When it clicked into place, he felt his stomach bottom out. If they couldn't point the finger at Riko, and Neil's entire defense hinged on his fear of getting caught, there was only one person left who could take the fall.

"They're burning my family," he said.

It wasn't a question, but Neil said, "Yes." He found a space and killed the engine, but instead of getting out he said "Jean," with an urgency that forced Jean to look at him. "I'm sorry."

I am Jean Moreau. I belong to the Moriyamas.

"I am a Moreau," Jean said. "I know my place. I will play my role."

Neil looked like he wanted to say more, but he got out of the car without comment. Jean fell in alongside him as they left the garage and started down the sidewalk. Neil started for a corner store before spotting an ATM, and he withdrew cash that he promptly stuffed in his back pocket.

Jean didn't ask, but Neil explained, "My uncle and I flew into the city on our own passports. Because of my father's open case, that should have set off a few alerts with the local FBI office. Now we just need to create a trail so we can force a confrontation."

It didn't need a response from him, so Jean only made a

half-hearted gesture and followed Neil to a Thai restaurant on a rundown corner. Neil waved aside the hostess in favor of looking around. The place was packed, but Neil only needed a few moments to find the rest of their party. When he set off, Jean followed him. The man they approached looked nothing like Neil, but Neil slid into the corner booth opposite him and motioned for Jean to join him.

Neil passed him a menu as soon as he was seated, but Jean pushed it back his way. "No."

"You might as well eat something," the man across from him said. "You have a very long evening ahead of you, and I doubt your next hosts will be good enough to feed you." Stuart Hatford leaned back against the back of his booth to consider Jean. There was no kindness in him, and barely any interest, but he managed to sound vaguely polite as he said, "Jean-Yves Moreau. A pleasure, I'm sure."

That got Neil's attention, and he looked from his uncle to Jean even as Jean said, "Do not call me that."

The waitress came over before Stuart could respond. Jean tried to send her away, but Neil ordered two portions of something Jean didn't recognize. As soon as she was gone, Neil asked, "Jean-Yves?"

"Don't. I am not allowed to use that name," Jean warned him.

"Says who?" Stuart asked. "The dead kid? Your legal name is more important now than ever before, so get used to hearing it." He didn't wait for Jean to respond but looked at Neil and wagged a hand at his own face. "You drag him here kicking and screaming, or is this an unrelated problem?"

Neil shrugged. "Do you have anyone who can take on local work?"

"Depends on what you can afford. Timing's bad enough to drive the price up."

"The timing can't be helped, so I don't care what the price is. He didn't confiscate anything from me," Neil reminded him. "I didn't bring it with me, but you know I'm good for it. Just

304

find me a way to get it to you." The waitress came around again with orange-hued drinks for Neil and Jean, and Neil offered her a disarming smile that would never sit quite right on his face. "Do you have a pen I could borrow? Thank you, I'll give it back to you as soon as I can."

Neil scribbled on the back of a napkin for a bit and pushed the mess his uncle's way. Stuart considered it for a few minutes before passing it over his shoulder to a woman in the neighboring booth. She got up and left without comment.

They didn't speak again until the waitress was back with their dishes. Neil returned the pen and a bank card to close out their table. Jean eyed his noodles while Neil signed and returned the check. He hadn't seen nutrition information on the menu, but he'd cooked alongside Cat long enough to guess this dish would violate almost every rule in the Ravens' tiny book of acceptable nutrition. He pushed it away in silent refusal and ignored the glance Neil sent him for that.

Luckily—or not—there were bigger things to worry about, because once they'd effectively freed their waitress from checking on them, they had privacy to speak. Stuart leaned back in his seat and said to Jean,

"The entire operation is getting wiped. Tell me now if you are going to resist."

Jean didn't have the right to refuse when these orders came from the top, but he'd survived far too much to hold his tongue now. Nothing Stuart could do to him for his impertinence would be worse than not even trying to save her.

"If that is what is needed of me, I will not fight it," Jean said, "but what does this plan mean for my sister?"

Stuart considered him in silence for what felt like an eternity. Jean counted the seconds to keep himself from thinking too deeply, but he was at thirty-six before Stuart finally asked, "Did you think you were special?"

Jean braced for the inevitable violent retribution, but what Stuart said next was worse than anything Riko had ever done to him: "She was sold off only two years after you were. One

305

of your mother's contacts, if I remember correctly, an arms dealer down in Algiers." He glanced over his shoulder for confirmation and got a nod from one of the men sitting there. "I have the name around here somewhere, but I expect it means more to me than you."

Jean didn't want to say it, but he had to know. The words crawled out of him, tearing his throat on their way: "She's dead, isn't she?"

"A mild term for it."

He was so far from this moment and his body, but the urge to throw up was visceral enough he felt all his hair standing on end. He stared down at the table and through it while his heart knocked holes in his ribcage. He needed to answer, but where had his voice gone? There weren't any words left in him; that growing ache in his chest was the start of a ragged and violent scream.

The sudden weight of another foot pressing against his startled him back to his senses, and Neil's quiet, "Jean," gave him a line to follow home. Jean swallowed hard against everything he knew better than to say and managed a quiet,

"I will burn the house down."

"I had no doubt," Stuart said. "Here's what we're starting from."

He rattled off the bare bones of a story for them to make their own. Neil had apparently resisted giving up any European contacts to the FBI when they'd last brought him in for an interrogation. He'd meant to protect his uncle's interests, but now they could reframe it as an attempt to protect Jean.

The setup was simple: the Butcher and his young son had come to France on a few trips, looking for more European alliances than what Mary could offer, and the boys had bonded over their shared love of a growing sport. Neil filled in the finer details with an ease that would have been impressive to listen to any other day, and Stuart quizzed them both to make sure their answers were complementary without being suspiciously identical.

306

Jean focused everything he had on the exercise, grasping desperately for anything that would hold him together for a little longer, but then there was nothing more to be said. Stuart got up and left, trusting the FBI to let him leave the city uncontested in favor of the more vulnerable marks he was leaving behind. The two booths to either side of theirs cleared out as well, with Stuart's crew falling in line behind him. The silence that fell at the table in his absence was too deep, and Jean's thoughts spun out of control to fill the space like a violent storm.

He didn't remember digging his phone out or deciding to dial, but the call was picked up on the second ring with a short, "Wymack."

"Why did you take him in?" Jean asked, and belatedly added, "Kevin."

"He needed us," Wymack said.

"It is not that simple," Jean said, thinking *They sold us both to monsters and slammed the door on our screams. Why? Why? Why?* "You didn't even know he was your son."

"I didn't need to know," Wymack said.

Jean laughed and heard his voice crack. "You really believe that?"

"I believe we all have the choice to be better than the hands that shaped us. If I have the chance to do right by someone else, then why wouldn't I take it?" Wymack gave him a minute to consider that, then said, "Talk to me. What's going on?"

She was a child. She was my baby sister, and I should have protected her, but I—

I was just a child, too.

It felt like one of Riko's knives was carving a line between Jean's ribs. His lungs were too sharp and too tight; his heart was punctured and torn. Jean pressed a hand to his sternum, checking for blood, but the wet heat he felt was a soft splash against one of his knuckles. His face itched as a second tear slipped free. This one glanced his thumb as it dripped from his chin, and Jean raised trembling fingers to his cheek.

Neil gently took his phone away and checked the caller ID. "I have him, Coach," he promised, before hanging up and setting the phone on the table between them.

"Don't," Jean said. He didn't know if he was talking to Neil: *don't look, don't speak*; or if he meant it for himself: *don't lose control*. "Don't, don't."

"I didn't know you had a sister," Neil said, so quietly Jean almost missed it around his breaking heart.

"Elodie," Jean said, and just hearing her name aloud almost snapped him in half. He clenched his hand into a fist so he wouldn't tear his own face off and bit his knuckles until they bled. It wasn't enough to stop his words. Each one was one of Riko's matches, burning him anew: "She was only ten when I left home. Ten! Why didn't they love her enough to keep her safe? Why didn't they—" *love me?*

Jean lurched out of the booth. Neil caught hold of his wrist and stared up at him with an unreadable look on his face.

"Jean," Neil said, quiet but firm. "We have to deal with this today, but we might not have to deal with it right now. What do you need?"

A hundred things he couldn't have, a thousand things he'd long since lost. The only thing left to ask for was something he barely understood: "I want to go home."

"Okay. Okay. Let's—" Neil was distracted by something in the distance and swore viciously in a language Jean didn't recognize. Jean followed his stare to see two men in suits at the entrance. They had their badges out as they talked to the hostess. Neil let go of Jean and gave his hip a light push. "I can see the kitchen. There should be a door out to where the dumpsters are. We can make it back to the garage from there."

"No," Jean said, pressing the heels of his palms to his eyes. He took his shattered heart and pushed it deep. It was too much to bury; his stomach lurched and roiled and threatened to empty all over the table. Jean swallowed it back with a force borne of desperation and imagined wrapping chains over the

308

lot of it. There would be time to break later, maybe. For now, the only way out was through.

I am Jean Moreau. I know my place. I will endure.

Neil moved to let Jean back in the booth, and they waited for the government's dogs to catch up to them. It didn't take long, and the two agents turned cool stares on Neil as they helped themselves to Stuart's vacated bench.

"Neil Josten," one said as they both presented their badges. "We'd like a word with you."

"Tedious," Neil said. "I'm trying to eat."

The agent chucked a couple to-go boxes across the table, nearly knocking Neil's drink over as he did so. "I wasn't asking. Let's go."

Neil sighed but started packing up his meal. When Jean made no move to do the same, the man closer to him made an imperious gesture and said, "That goes for you too. We've got some questions."

"He has nothing to do with this," Neil said.

"You sure about that?" the agent said.

Jean would've been fine throwing his meal in the trash, but scraping it into a Styrofoam box let him stall here a little longer. Neil waited until he was done before deciding he wanted to finish his drink. Neither agent was impressed with their absolute lack of urgency, but finally the two ran out of excuses to stay. They were escorted out of the restaurant with one agent in front and the other at the rear.

A black SUV with tinted windows and government plates was parked at the curb out front. Neil, being the person he was, pointed at the fire hydrant adjacent to its front bumper and said, "That's illegal, just so you know."

"Shut up and get in the car."

The ride to the local office passed in dead silence. Neil seemed completely at ease, even when they went through the multistep process of getting through security, but Jean watched as Neil cased every exit and guard on his way. Jean, in turn, looked at nothing and no one save Neil. The FBI would likely write it off as nerves, but they'd be mistaken to think he was afraid of them. He couldn't fear a government who was so easily infiltrated and manipulated; he could only fear his own potential missteps and the bloody consequences if he failed his master here.

When they finally made it to the elevators, Neil asked in French, "Chances of them understanding French?"

"None. They're American," Jean said.

"Hey," Neil protested.

"You barely count. Don't waste your time feigning offense."

"Knock it off," the agent nearer Neil said. "English only or we'll separate you until we can get some interpreters onsite."

They were brought to a conference room. Boxes were stacked on one end of the table, a few closed files rested in the middle, and a video camera was already set up on a tripod to record today's discussion. A rolling stand beside the camera had a monitor on it, and they were being broadcast a video of another suited figure hunched over his desk. At the sound of the door closing and chairs scraping across the floor, the man looked up and scowled.

Neil greeted him with no warmth whatsoever: "Agent Browning. Kind of thought I'd never have to see you again."

"Don't start with me," Browning said. "Want to explain to me what you're doing in Los Angeles?"

Neil flipped his takeout box open and started eating. "I'm allowed to visit people."

"People," Browning agreed. Before Jean could decide if that classified him as a non-person, Browning spelled it out for him: "But Stuart Hatford is not just anyone, and last we checked he had no contacts in Los Angeles that would bring you both so far from home. Except perhaps he does," he said, turning a heavy stare on Jean.

One of the agents who'd brought them here flipped open a file and tossed it down into the middle of the table. Jean looked instinctively, and the photograph stapled to the top knocked the wind out of him. He recognized that back deck from his childhood home. His father was standing in the middle, waving expansively as he ranted to an unfamiliar man. His mother straddled a wooden chair off to one side, a bottle of wine in one hand and a stack of papers in the other.

These people were unimportant. All that mattered were the two kids sitting in the backyard: Jean at nine or ten, with a tiny Elodie buried against his side. He remembered that dress of hers, with its little yellow ducks. He'd clumsily patched up the hem a half-dozen times when she tore it on the blackberry bushes taking over their backyard.

The chains creaked; Jean could barely breathe. Under the table he dug his fingernails into the bite on his wrist. *Endure. Endure. Endure.*

"Where did you get this?" he asked in a voice that didn't sound like his.

"Interpol faxed it over from their records just a few minutes ago," the agent said. "Where did you get *this*?"

By the gesture he made, he meant the scratches on Jean's face, but Jean said, "I take after my mother."

"Jean's French," Neil said. "He brings out violence in people every time he opens his mouth. Even the Trojans are human enough to have a breaking point."

"You're one to accuse others of intolerable attitudes," Browning said, and Neil only shrugged indifference. Jean didn't waste his time being offended by Neil's half-assed insult, because the agents let the matter drop and moved on. "Time for one of you to start talking. Let's take it from the top and—for once—without any of your usual bullshit."

Neil looked to Jean, but Jean couldn't drag his eyes off the photograph to respond. At last Neil pushed his dinner aside with a weary sigh and said, "Fine. What do you want to know?"

Neil's spin on things was wretchedly straightforward. He and Jean had seen each other for the first time in years at the

311

fall banquet. If the FBI wanted to ask around, they'd find witnesses to confirm the two had gone at each other in French. They'd realized who the other was and, afraid of getting caught out, had desperately tried to hash out where they stood with one another and whether their friendship was still strong enough to keep them safe. They'd inadvertently outed themselves to Kevin, who panicked and had to leave the banquet to deal with their frightening secrets.

Neil agreed to visit Evermore over Christmas more to reconnect with Jean than out of any real interest in the Ravens. Framed this way, it was easy to excuse Neil's antagonistic opinion of the rest of the team and their captain. His reckless change in looks was inevitably blamed on Jean and their desire to play on the perfect Court together after graduation. Neil was afraid of being found out if he stepped onto a brighter stage, so Jean tried to prove that no one would remember or recognize him so many years later. An idiotic gamble in retrospect, but how could they have known how terribly it would backfire?

Once the FBI was done trying to poke holes in that story, the conversation turned toward Jean's family. Here they were infinitely more interested in what Jean had to say, but he only had so many answers for them. He'd spent most of his childhood on the court, not watching his father's meetings. He knew vague details of what businesses his father invested in but nothing at all about his partners.

His saving grace was that Hervé Moreau was not even half the man Nathan Wesninski was. Tracking his interests and dealings would be easier and didn't require Jean's insights to piece it together. What the FBI seemed most concerned with was simply determining how the two families were tied together and whether Jean was going to be a problem for them. They couldn't afford hiccups when Nathan's case was already a nightmare and a half to work on. Jean had to believe Stuart's assurances that the evidence linking the Moreau and Wesninski families was set in place, and he held his ground against the agents' prying questions.

Eventually Neil let them circle back to Stuart's visit in the city, and he pressed a shoe against the side of Jean's foot as he offered the best—worst—excuse he could. Neil had supposedly asked Stuart months ago to locate Jean's sister. Stuart finally found where her trail ended, and he'd brought them both to the city so he could deliver the bad news in person. Here Neil injected a bit of venom into his story, that the agents had further ruined an already horrible day by forcing them into this interrogation, and one of them had the good grace to look guilty.

After four exhausting hours of arguing, including some long breaks to check in with Interpol, the agents finally decided Jean was the luckiest break they'd had in weeks. Jean himself was deemed a nonthreat thanks to his ignorance and clean history. Now they could set to work dismantling Hervé's ring and drive another nail in Nathan's coffin.

Jean weathered their smug satisfaction with fracturing control. He was two smart remarks from breaking when he and Neil were finally escorted out of the building and stuffed back into the car.

Ten minutes later, they were kicked out in front of the restaurant they'd been abducted from. Jean watched the SUV disappear into evening traffic, but Neil tipped his head back to stare at the sky. Jean couldn't remember where the garage was from here, so he waited in silence for Neil to come back to him.

"I'm sorry," Neil said at last. "It shouldn't have fallen on you."

"I am a Moreau," Jean said. "My family exists to serve."

"Shit existence," Neil said, as if he was somehow better off. He set off down the sidewalk, knowing Jean would fall in alongside him. Jean was half-sure he was getting them lost, because none of this looked familiar, but then he spotted the ATM Neil had used a few hours ago. "Are you going to keep it as-is, then? Jean Moreau?"

"This is all I am, you ignorant child."

"We're the same age," Neil pointed out, and Jean waved

313

that aside as irrelevant. "I just mean… I changed my name because I didn't want to be associated with my family, but they stole yours from you. If you don't want to change it back, that's your choice, but don't choose based on what Riko wanted for you."

"I do not need advice from you," Jean warned him.

"He's dead," Neil reminded him as he turned into the parking garage. "The rules have changed. As long as you deliver what was promised, why would Ichirou care what you call yourself? Exercise a little freedom once in a while. You might like how it feels."

"You'll lose that boldness when he finds out about your goalkeeper."

"I'm sure he knows. Andrew was with me when I came clean with the FBI in Baltimore, and it's obvious to me that at least one person in that office is on the wrong payroll. If someone thought to make a note of him as a person of interest, then of course it would've made it up the chain. I'm not worried," Neil added with a slight shrug. "The more people I hold onto, the less of a threat I am, because I won't want to endanger them by acting out."

"I would believe that from anyone but you," Jean said as they got in the car.

"Who is the safer investment?" Neil challenged him. "A man with a dozen reasons not to slip the leash or a man holding on simply because he was told he couldn't let go?"

Jean ignored him, and Neil let it drop. The drive back to Laila's house passed in tense silence. There was room at the curb for Neil to park in front of Jeremy's car, but he stopped in the middle of the street and put his hazards on. Jean reached for his buckle but went still when Neil caught hold of his sleeve. It took a minute before Neil looked at him. Jean didn't think it was the night that made him look so far away, but Neil's voice was calm when he said,

"Lock your door tonight if it will help, but Grayson will never bother you again."

There were too many thoughts rattling around Jean's exhausted brain for that to make sense at first, and then the memory of Neil's *Do you have anyone who can take on local work?* rang out crystal clear. That he'd boldly taken a hit out on Grayson with Jean sitting right next to him was impossible; that Jean had been too shaken by the impending destruction of his family to realize it was happening was unforgivable.

The only valid response was to refuse. Grayson was due to leave the city this weekend. Whether he would stay gone was a different question, though, and Jean felt his skin crawl as he thought about it. With the Nest closed and Edgar Allan under investigation, the Ravens would surely be sent home for school breaks going forward. Grayson would be in and out of California all year. Was this really the only solution left for Jean, and could he survive if he didn't take it?

"A Wesninski in truth, if not in name," Jean said. "Eager to ingratiate yourself with your new master by protecting his assets?"

"Fuck Ichirou," Neil said, and Jean was not going to sit here and listen to anything that followed that bold remark. He shoved the door open, but Neil grabbed his injured wrist before Jean could get out of the car. Jean gritted his teeth against the pain and glowered at him.

Neil was unmoved by his anger. "Grayson should have just walked away from Riko's tainted legacy and started over. He strung the noose himself when he came all the way here to put his hands on you, and I am not afraid to kick the stool out from under him."

Jean tried to tug free, but Neil's grip was bruising. "Do not pretend this is about me, you miserable wretch."

"Why wouldn't it be?" Neil asked.

"I am just a Moreau," Jean said, flat and fierce. "I am not—"

"So was Elodie," Neil reminded him, and Jean stopped breathing. "Remember that the next time you think you aren't worth saving."

315

Neil let go, and Jean threw himself out of the car. He slammed the door behind him and flew up the steps. Jeremy had the front door open for him, but Jean got him out of the way with a quick hand on his shoulder. Cat and Laila were further down the hall, but they flattened themselves against the wall when they saw his face. Jean wasn't sure where he was going, but he wasn't surprised to find himself standing at his desk a few seconds later. He spread his notebooks out on the desk in front of him but didn't bother to open them.

He thought of France: of blackberries and little ducks and the salty breeze off the Mediterranean, of gun oil and the sting of a wide belt and an eager, immediate yes. He thought of an endless plane ride to hell, a pair of numbered faces, and a monstrous boy saying *Too pretentious a name for a dirty beast like you.*

He thought of Evermore: heavy canes and sharp knives, broken fingers and drowning and fire. He thought of Josiah's steady hands stitching him up just for Riko to kick him down the stairs again, and the sour smell of blood and sweat that couldn't dry in his thick padding. Five volunteers to break him in, Zane's betrayal to destroy him, and a single promise that kept him alive despite it all.

The cracking heat in his chest could have been his ribs snapping or his heart breaking. Jean held onto his control with everything he had left after such a nightmarish day, but he could feel his grip slipping. *Endure*, he warned himself, and on its tail-end came a desperate *How much must I?*

It wasn't his place to ask; it wasn't his place to assume there should be a limit. Whatever they demanded of him, he would give without hesitation or complaint. It was all he was; it was all he ever would be. He wanted to scream until his lungs tore.

"Jean." Jeremy touched the back of his hand gently, like he thought Jean would crumple if he applied any pressure. "Tell us what you need from us."

My name is Jean Moreau. I belong to the Moriyamas.

316

I will always have a master.

In one breath he was wracked with a hatred so fierce he could barely see straight; in the next he was horrified by his own ingratitude. What he had now was better than anything he'd ever been given, and it was certainly more than someone like him deserved. The master and Riko were gone, and Jean was free of the Nest. He had a new team, a new home, and a city he was starting to get familiar with. His hateful parents were a small price to pay to keep what he had, weren't they?

And if Ichirou comes back for more? Jean wondered, but he knew the answer to that. Neil thought making connections made him safer. Jean knew he was only telling Ichirou exactly where to hit him to keep him in line. This wasn't freedom; it was simply a very attractive cage. It should be good enough. It had to be good enough. Jean would never be free of it.

Jean opened one of his notebooks and looked down at the **COWARD** written across the page. Before he could think twice, he caught hold of the page and tore it out. It was easier than he thought it would be, and he crumpled it with a quick clench of his fingers before dropping it on the floor. The next page came out even easier, and Jean managed four on the third pull. He was making a mess, but he couldn't stop. It steadied him, buying him time until he could bury his grief and rage.

Jeremy let him get halfway through the notebook before trying again: "Jean."

"If I asked you to kill me, would you?" Jean asked.

"Don't ever say that," Jeremy said, low and insistent. "Look at me."

"I won't."

"We're your friends. Please let us help you." When Jean refused to answer, Jeremy changed tactics. "You are supposed to be my success story, but you're actively working against me. My failure is your failure, right? Tell me why you're fighting me or let me in."

Jean regretted ever telling Jeremy about Raven pairs. He hadn't realized the so-called captain sunshine would so easily

317

turn it back on him. Every way he looked at it, Jeremy had the right of it: Jean did not know how to ignore the deal struck between them. He didn't have to like or agree with Jeremy's focus; he only had to concede if he wasn't holding up his end of the bargain.

"Damn you," he said, weary with defeat.

At least Jeremy didn't gloat. He seemed content to wait Jean out, secure in his underhanded victory. Jean wanted to be annoyed with him, but his irritation was more a relief than any genuine anger. It gave him thorns to hold off the rest, and he tugged them close for protection. When he could breathe without feeling like each inhale was turning his chest inside-out, he finally turned to face his captain. Jeremy gazed up at him in calm and steady silence.

"This," Jean gestured toward himself, meaning the unstable mood he'd come home with, "is not something I am ready to talk about yet. One day, I promise," he said, because once Nathan's trial started there'd be no hiding the half-truth of his family's bloody affairs from any of them, "but not today."

Jeremy weighed that for a minute before saying. "Okay. So what can we do now?"

"Nothing," Jean said, and knocked his finger against Jeremy's chin when he opened his mouth to protest. "It is not now that is the problem, and it is not then, either. You cannot save me from what came before, and you help neither of us by trying to dig up those graves. Leave Evermore to me and Dobson," he said, and it was a wonder he didn't grimace at her name. "You made me a promise, so I will hold you to that: help me survive what comes next."

"Is that all I can do?"

"It is what only you can do," Jean said. "I trust you."

He was trying so hard to not say *I have no choice* that he was slow to realize he meant it. He didn't understand the Trojans and wasn't sure he ever would, but he believed their earnest devotion was real. *"Their kindness matters,"* Kevin

318

had said just this spring. He hadn't been talking about this, but Jean finally felt the truth in it.

"Will you help me?" he asked.

"Anything you need."

"A blank check is a dangerous thing to offer."

"Try me," Jeremy said. "I can afford it."

There was no good way to answer that, so Jean turned back to his notebooks and stacked them in a haphazard pile. The move just drew his attention back to his injured wrist, and he covered it up with his other hand. Movement in the corner of his eye warned him Cat and Laila had grown tired of watching this unfold from a distance. Laila held out a large bandage, then withdrew it to peel it open when Jean reached for it. He let her press it into place on his arm without argument.

"I need to eat," Jean said, though he had no idea what time it was.

"Oh, good," Cat said, with exaggerated enthusiasm. "I found a new recipe and I need a test subject. Let's go."

Out to the kitchen they went, where Cat stepped on the latch for the trash can so Jean could throw away his school notes. She pointed him to the stools when he moved to help, so he settled in between Jeremy and Laila. Jean saw the clock and considered apologizing for keeping them all up after midnight when they had practice in the morning, but Cat poked her boombox awake before he could decide what to say. Jean started to reach for the bandage on his arm before dropping his hand to his thigh.

"Okay, here's what I've got," Cat said, and Jean let her rambling voice pull him out of his thoughts. When she darted across the kitchen for a missed ingredient halfway through her slicing, Jean tapped out a quiet beat on his leg and counted.

A cool evening breeze. Rainbows. Open roads. Teammates.

But that last wasn't quite right; he'd been on teams since he was seven years old. He could barely remember the children

319

he'd played with in France when the Ravens were an overbearing presence in his memories. He loved the Ravens, he hated them, he wished he'd never met them. The Trojans could not exist in the same category. He could not be grateful for one without summoning unpleasant memories of the other. Jean tapped his thumb against his thigh in thought and tried again.

Friends?

Jean's past was ash and broken bone. The only thing his future held was a deal made on his behalf: a demand he play a game he could barely stand anymore for as long as he could hold a racquet. Jean would drag himself onward because following orders was all he knew to do, but he was so prematurely exhausted and defeated he didn't know how to take that first step. If these three could at least pull him away from the ledge until he found his feet again, that would be enough.

He wouldn't stop to think what would happen at graduation. For now, all that mattered was this moment. He considered the weight of Laila's foot hooked around the leg of his stool, the ridiculous way Cat bobbed and danced as she made an absolute mess of the island, and the heat of Jeremy's shoulder where he sat almost pressed into Jean's side.

Friends, he thought again, and this time it almost felt real.

Acknowledgements

My undying love to my friends Tashie, Hazel, Elise, Anna M, and Jeni M. Thank you for the writing sprints and the enduring patience all ten million times I came back to you with nitpicky and incessant "but what if" cries for help. Thank you for not drop-kicking me off a cliff every time I mixed up Jeremy & Jean's names while drafting and for cleaning a chaotic mess up into something legible. Without your enthusiasm and support I would've escaped into the woods months ago.

Thank you to my sister for once again providing me with cover art. I'd apologize for changing the idea on you so many times, but it was kind of fun being intolerable. These books mean more to me for having your mark on them.

USC TROJANS
Administration

Coaching Staff:
James Rhemann : head coach
Jackie Lisinski : fitness coach
Michael White : offensive line coach
Eduardo Jimenez : defensive line coach

Nurses:
Jeffrey Davis
Ashley Young
Binh Nguyen

Assistants:
Angela "Angie" Lewis
Antonio "Tony" Jones
Roberta "Bobby" Blackwell

Mascot:
Diego Rodriguez

USC TROJANS
Players
(academic year for 2007 fall semester)

Strikers:
Jeremy Knox, #11 : Captain, 5th year senior
Derek Thompson, #15 : 5th year senior
Derrick Allen, #9 : senior
Ananya Deshmukh, #13 : junior
Nabil Mahmoud, #17 : junior
Ashton Cox, #19 : sophomore
Timothy Eitzen, #8 : sophomore
Emma Swift, #6 : freshman
Preston Short, #14 : freshman

Dealers:
Xavier Morgan, #3 : Vice-captain, senior
Min Cai, #1 : junior
Sebastian Moore, #2 : sophomore
Dillon Bailey, #4 : freshman
Charles Roy, #5 : freshman

Backliners:
Cody Winter, #20 : 5th year senior
Patrick Toppings, #36 : 5th year senior
Shawn Anderson, #26 : 5th year senior
Jean Moreau, #29 : senior
Catalina Alvarez, #37 : junior
Haoyu Liu, #33 : junior
Lucas Johnson, #25 : junior
Jesus Rivera, #31 : sophomore
Travis Jordan, #32 : sophomore
Tanner Adams, #21 : freshman
Madeline Hill, #28 : freshman

Goalkeepers:
Laila Dermott, #40 : 5th year senior
Shane Reed, #41 : senior
William Foster, #46 : sophomore
Zachary Price, #42 : freshman

Made in United States
Cleveland, OH
19 December 2024

12310632R00184